SOUL FLYER

Book One | THE DANCING STONES TRILOGY

KARIN RAVEN STEININGER

ISBN: 979-86-43418-65-8

Cover design by Lesley Vamos

To Paul, Zack and Cookie

Antonella and Elizabeth

Sally and Karina.

You know it's real

xxx

"... I would stand,

If the night blackened with a coming storm,

Beneath some rock, listening to notes that are

The ghostly language of the ancient earth..."

William Wordsworth

ONE

The eagle swept over the valley, soaring across the expanse of blue-grey trees and falling sandstone canyons. Her wings, barely moving, were inky black and spread wide.

Warm air spiralled, cut with the sharp scent of eucalypt.

Far below, a creek bed snaked through the forest, hidden by the dense canopy and twists and folds of the land. Pinion feathers dipped and she banked high over the sheer edge of a cliff. Yet rising through the heat, came not the sweet spray of tumbling water, but a dryness; a thin musty staleness reeking of choked spillways and shallow, silted pools.

Abruptly, the sound of a hard crack cut through the stillness.

A girl was marching through the trees, her anger ricocheting off the red sandstone walls. She was young, but strong and lithe as she kicked another stone, sending it flying across the path.

The whistling cry echoed again.

Squinting, fifteen-year-old Ellie stared at the dark shape circling overhead.

The bird's body was dark, almost black. It's wings long and etched clear against the glare of the sky. In a moment it was gone. Ellie scowled, her hazel green eyes hot and defiant in a face framed by abundant red-gold hair.

Ellie's boot connected with another rock and, with a satisfying thwack, it sailed clean over the undergrowth, and landed with a thud. In the sudden quiet, Ellie sighed. The track, narrow and scattered with fallen twigs and branches, meandered on ahead, hugging the course of a creek bed before disappearing into a grove of trees, their trunks ghost-white and stark against the rich red ochre of the cliffs.

Shielding her eyes, Ellie walked on, gazing up into the canopy. The trees were beautiful; they stood tall and straight, their long branches like a sunshade holding back the worst of the daytime heat. Ellie slowly trailed her fingers over pale, bare bark, studying the surrounding forest.

Dropping her backpack, she pulled out a bottle and took a long gulp. The water was warm and tasted of plastic, but at least it soothed her throat, washing away the dusty dryness.

'Don't panic,' she murmured, her voice loud in the quiet of the trees.

Frowning, Ellie tried to recall if she'd accidently taken any turning off the path. She had been in the forest since morning, at first furious, striding as fast as she could, not noticing particularly where she'd been going, but she hadn't made the mistake of leaving the main track, she was sure of it. Not once. Ellie shook her head. It was a straighforward path, clearly marked - a simple, circular walking track cut through the trees. She knew it like the back of her hand.

Dropping the half-empty bottle back in her bag, she looked up.

At once, movement darted overhead. Ellie froze, her eyes scanning the canopy as a hot breeze flicked over her skin. A branch trembled, dropping leaves and twigs, and a soft boom of thunder echoed off the darkening cliffs.

Still, Ellie kept her gaze trained up into the trees. Sometimes in the forest she had a strange sense of being watched, as though every footfall, every move she made was the focus of tight, intense scrutiny. Abruptly, she scowled.

It was useless. Nothing lived here. The forest was as silent as a mausoleum. The autumn rains hadn't come and no rain meant no life. It was a simple, brutal equation.

Heat shimmered, and in the light of the lowering sun, she could see her footprints scuffed through the dust. Ellie hesitated. It *would* make sense to try and retrace her steps back to the start of the track... but that could take hours.

Around her, the light shifted and up through the canopy she could see streaks of cloud racing across the sky. Another crackle echoed, but Ellie didn't notice. Her attention was caught by a young sapling, its trunk gleaming in a shard of sunlight, its branches bare, save for a last handful of desiccated leaves.

On impulse, Ellie poured the rest of her water onto the parched earth. 'I'd do more if I could,' she whispered, running her fingers along the smooth pale wood. In the answering quiet, a flash forked high overhead, followed by a crack of sound. The forest rippled, and a wind, wild and hot, whipped towards her through the canyon.

'No!' Ellie turned to run. The canopy was in turmoil. Branches knocked with a percussive urgency, wrenched together in a rising fury.

Thunder boomed and a giant shuddered, its great limbs groaning with the effort to keep aloft, its massive girth resisting the push and pull of the storm. They came constantly now. Mean, vicious thunderheads carrying bursts of heat and lightning, but never, ever rain.

Ellie dropped to the ground, and a heartbeat later, in a tearing, wrenching defeat, a tree limb crashed to the floor. Ellie threw herself aside, as debris exploded through the forest. She closed her eyes and curled her body into a tight, protective ball.

Mercifully, this storm was quick. The dark clouds raged overhead but almost as soon as it had arrived, the wind began to slacken and the last roll of thunder reverberated off the cliff walls.

A fragment bit into her side, and Ellie shifted, ready to tense at any sign of damage. Carefully, she wriggled her toes and then slowly straightened each of her legs. Shattered bits of twigs and branches slid to the ground and Ellie froze, but - nothing.

Preparing to sit up, Ellie rolled her weight onto her hands but immediately was engulfed by a singular, piercing pain. Red-hot, it shot up through her left palm, and radiated in waves along her fingers. Crying out, Ellie leaned forward, pain drying her mouth and making her heart pound in her chest.

Her hand was broken, she was sure of it.

In the dim light it was hard to assess the damage. The injury was obscured beneath a lumpy mass of grass and twigs. With her free hand she dislodged what she could, but a tangle remained, snagged tightly on her silver rings. Warily Ellie looked closer. A large, ugly thorn lay embedded in her skin. That was all. No broken bones.

Ellie almost fainted with relief.

Gently, she teased it out, leaving bright drops of blood smeared across her palm. She threw the thorn to the ground, and then carefully prised the matted concoction from her rings. Ellie stopped; it was the weirdest thing she had ever seen. A long, conical shape, it was intricately woven and tightly bound with tufts of dried moss sticking out from its side. Frowning, she pulled it clear, and as she did so a spark flashed and an object fell to the ground with a thud.

Ellie stared in shock. Above her, the trees stood quiet and calm after the storm's fury and the afternoon sun was long gone. But from the shadows at her feet, came a dazzling, blue-white light.

It was some sort of stone, and from its centre streamed a persistent, pulsing glow.

'That is very, very strange.' Ellie said out loud, and then she shook her head, acutely aware of the forest and the encroaching darkness.

Maybe the crazy rock could help? But as she considered the idea, the light wavered and abruptly vanished. Ellie stared for a moment then, with a shrug, shoved the strange stone deep into the pocket of her jeans. She reached for her backpack and on impulse, threw in the woven bunch of twigs.

'You can come with me too.' Ellie smiled; glad, suddenly, that she was on her own in the forest; at least here no one could tease her for her habit of talking outloud to inanimate objects. She looked around for the path.

On a sudden hunch, Ellie walked into the almost-dark trees. Leaves draped her face, and a single star flickered above through the canopy. She stopped. 'I don't believe it…' Ellie whispered. Metres away, she could see a set of high, narrow stairs, bolted to the cliff face. They were made of steel and encased in a protective mesh to shield walkers from falling rocks.

Higher up, Ellie could make out the top of the iron rails as they disappeared up over the cliff edge - just visible in the last light of the day.

That doesn't make sense. Ellie shook her head. How could she have got back to the start of circular track, and so soon? She stood staring at the stairs for a long moment, and then with a laugh of disbelief, tightened her bag over her shoulder and headed up out of the forest for home.

TWO

It was dark by the time Ellie made it to the top. Light-headed, she stood for a moment, fighting to catch her breath. A dog barked behind a high wooden fence. Ignoring it, Ellie shook her hair out and set off down the street. Lights flicked on, throwing a pale orange glow across the blackness of the night.

Turning the corner, Ellie slowed to a walk. The road was lined with single-storey houses, complete with small garages and fenced-in yards. Others were older, built of painted weatherboard with carved ornate porches and stained glass windows in the doors. This was an old mountain suburb, with generous yards once filled with proud gardens. Looking away, Ellie trudged past remnants of cold climate conifers that had, in their heyday, scraped the sky, their great green spires heralding the great forests of Europe. But now they sagged brown and haggard, or only stumps remained, the colourful plots gone to dust.

Nearing her house, Ellie stopped. Its wraparound porch framed a row of delicate leadlight windows that once would've been pretty, she supposed, though now the panels were cracked with age and the white weatherboard dull and badly in need of paint. Dumped boxes of the neighbours' rubbish sat strewn across the front lawn.

'Hey Dad, throw it all in now, *now.*'

Ellie could hear her brother yelling out back, as smoke, thick with grit and filth, twisted into the sky.

Shaking her head, Ellie wrenched open the metal gate. In the far corner of the yard her dad was bent over, his head obscured, his sinewy arms shoving in a bundle of discarded junk into a belching, roaring incinerator.

'Come on, Ben, keep it coming.'

Behind in the shadows, Ellie's brother scraped an armful of old newspapers and kitchen waste into a pile. The flames leapt higher, throwing sparks and heat into the night. Keeping her head down low, Ellie crept along the concrete paving stones, angling not to be seen, her eyes squinting against the smoke.

'Hey catch.' A wedge of flattened cardboard hurtled through the air.

'No!' She gasped, ducking low as it landed with a heavy thud onto the grass.

'Hey, where are you sneaking off to, slacker?' Ben grabbed for her shoulder, spilling her backpack to the ground. He was tall and heavily built, a few years older, with curly brown hair and a rough teasing manner.

'Come on, you can help.' Handing her a spade, Ben pushed her towards a pile of splintered toys and forgotten old dolls. Once loved and cherished, they lay with their blue eyes unblinking, useless and unwanted. There was a loud laugh as Ellie's dad, stripped to his shorts, his chest wide and powerful, stepped back and closed the lid with a bang.

'Hey, Ben, where are you? Bring us some more!' He wiped a slick of sweat with the back of his hand.

A roar bellowed from inside the metal tank. Even from across the yard, Ellie could feel its heat prickling the skin on her face. The incinerator was almost full to bursting, with burning, churning refuse. A monster, hungry and illegal in this time of drought and extreme weather, Ellie stared at it appalled, but no one else around here seemed to care - not the neighbours and especially not her family. As her dad always said, 'The rubbish trucks rarely come and someone's gotta do it.'

Through gaps in the smoke, Ellie glimpsed the sky, clear and patterned with high, bright stars. A cloud burst in the distance, bright with lightning, as a wind kicked in; dry and tasting of dust. Ben whistled cheerfully. Queasiness rose in Ellie's stomach.

'I can't help you,' she mumbled. Turning, she hurried to the porch and, pulling open the wire door, escaped into the brightness of the kitchen.

Ellie's mother, Claire stood at the stove decanting a tin of peas into boiling water. A plume of steam spiralled into the heated air. She was a pretty woman, small and fine-boned, with light-brown curly hair and a cautious manner.

'Hi Mum.' Ellie called as she passed, but her mother didn't respond immediately.

Pulling on some heatproof mitts, she opened the oven. 'Where have you been, Ellie? At Rose's?' She asked as she pulled out an earthenware pot, and placed it heavily on the bench.

'Oh, sort of...' mumbled Ellie. The kitchen was simple and plain, with black and white linoleum covering the floor and a wide wooden table in the centre. The walls were a faded yellow and stencilled with blue flowers years ago when her mother still cared about such things.

Ellie poured herself a juice, as a high-pitched shrieking alerted her to the presence of her five-year-old twin siblings. Annie and Tom raced past her legs, their hands flying in every direction as they sought to pinch and slap each other. Blonde-haired Annie pushed her brother and, with a squeal of outrage, he thumped at her hard, knocking askew a framed piece of embroidery.

Ellie tickled her little sister, making her fall to the floor, banging her feet against the chairs.

'Stop that at once!' Claire banged her hand down hard on the bench. 'Can't you see I have hot things on the stove!' She glared at Ellie. 'And you should know better!'

Biting back a retort, Ellie stared down at her feet while the kids pulled faces and giggled.

'Go and wash your hands, you two,' snapped their mother. 'Ellie, you can help me with serving dinner.'

'It's not my fault,' Ellie muttered, arranging dinner plates around the kitchen table. The wire door banged open, allowing the smell of smoke and burning rubber into the kitchen.

Ben headed to the sink. 'What's for dinner, Mum?' He poured water over his blackened hands.

'Please use the bathroom,' she sighed.

Later, with the steaming pot of beef casserole, potatoes, and peas on the table, the family sat down. Ben's hands were scrubbed red, and Ellie's father was dressed in a fresh plaid shirt, his brown hair combed flat. They bowed their heads.

'Heavenly Father,' Brian prayed, his voice hoarse. 'Bless this meal and those who prepared it. Thank you for keeping us safe this day until you return in glory. Claim us soon. In the name of the Lord our Father, amen.'

He paused, his eyes remaining closed. As the silence stretched, Tom pulled a face at Annie and, giggling loudly, she stretched out to kick him, knocking her fork off the table.

'Stop that!' roared their father. 'Can't we have a quiet table just this once!'

The children wilted and Ellie slowly picked up the utensil off the floor. She glanced at her brother, but his eyes remained firmly cast down towards his plate. In the silence that followed, Claire dished up the meal and the family ate quickly without speaking. Except for Ellie; she felt ill.

The windows of the kitchen dripped with moisture. The air was thick with the residue of toxic smoke, mixed with the dinner juices and the damp heat from the bathroom. Pushing the food around, Ellie tried to breathe the air through her mouth. No one else seemed to mind.

'We finished most of that lot.' Brian's gaze settled on Ellie. 'We all must do our part.'

'Yeah,' mumbled Ben, his mouth still full of food. 'We can get to the rest after dinner.'

'Why? It smells so awful,' complained Annie screwing up her nose. Tom kicked her under the table and yelping in pain she struggled to whack him in return. Their father glared.

'Who's for dessert?' interrupted Claire.

'Me, me, me,' cried the twins, twisting in their chairs. As Claire opened the oven door, the sweet smell of apple pie billowed out into the room, adding to the already thick brew.

Ellie's stomach heaved, 'I'll help you with the dishes later, Mum,' she said faintly. 'I'm not feeling very well at all.'

'Oh dear, aren't you? You work too hard.' Her mother's face crinkled with concern, her hand poised to cut into the gooey-hot dessert. 'I'll leave you some pie.'

'Just a minute, young lady.' The twins shrank as their father scraped his chair back and left the kitchen on a heavy tread. Ellie stared after him, as a sudden whip of anxiety lashed through her being. The back door slammed open and her father returned, his face closed and eyes hard. Looming tall against the ceiling, he dropped Ellie's backpack onto the table. It toppled for a moment then fell, strewing leaves and bits of twig over Ellie's half-finished dinner.

'Brian! What are you doing?' cried Claire. 'Get that thing off the table.'

But Brian ignored his wife and, reaching into Ellie's bag, he lifted out the bundle of twisted grass and trailing dried-up creek moss.

Appalled silence gripped the table.

Ellie's mother began to speak.

'Not now, Claire,' growled Brian, his green eyes hot with anger. 'Where did you get this, Ellie?'

She could see the woven concoction clearer now in the bright light of the kitchen. A nest; it was an elongated nest, slightly squashed, and layered with strips of bark, dried fibre, and leaves - all bound together with fine threads of silk.

It is beautiful, Ellie thought, gazing at it with wonder - even though the edges were slightly frayed, damaged perhaps by its brief sojourn in her bag.

Eyes wide, Annie's little outstretched hand reached forward slowly, but it was swiftly smacked back by her mother.

'Answer me, Ellie', her father growled. 'Where did this come from?'

Ellie fought for words, her mouth dry, and guilt seeping out from every pore.

'You disobeyed me, didn't you? Didn't you!' He shouted the last words and banged his hand on the table. The sound slapped the bare walls and Annie began to cry.

'She didn't, Brian.' Claire said firmly to her husband, hugging her youngest daughter. 'It's a study day. Ellie's been at Rose's, doing her homework.' She smiled at Ellie with pride in her warm brown eyes.

'Mum... Dad...' Ellie began, feeling awful, not daring to meet her mother's gaze. 'We used to hang out in the forest all the time...'

Her father glared at her without speaking.

Little Tom, meanwhile, had crept his fingers until they were almost touching the pile of twigs. Claire hissed, recoiling back in horror. 'Take that thing away,' she shuddered. 'It's horrible. Horrible. I won't have it in the house.'

Ellie stared at her in silence. 'Mum,' she said softly at last. 'It's just a nest, it won't hurt anyone.'

Her mother looked at her, lips thin with disappointment. 'You said you were at Rose's.' Claire said, her voice brittle.

Her father looked at her sadly and whispered. 'Oh Ellie, what have you done?'

'Dad, it's just a nest, a tiny little nest, it blew out of the trees in the storm.' Ellie said, relieved that his anger seemed to have disappeared.

His roar of fury hit like a blow. 'You were in the forest? Despite me telling you *again* it is off limits!'

'Why?' Ellie shouted back. 'It's just a bunch of trees and a stupid old dried up creek. What's so bad? You need to get out of the house like you used to.'

'You're a fool with no understanding.' He snapped.

Claire bowed her head in prayer, 'Thank you Lord for leading us,' she murmured, beginning to pray softly.

Ellie gripped her fists in anger. *They are fools*, she thought. *So quick to believe any rubbish the Reverend stupid Matthew spouted.*

'And get rid of this thing,' her father said firmly. 'Now. Tonight. We will not have it in the house.'

Ellie stared at him, choking back a giggle that threatened to burst out of her throat. She wanted to run around screaming, 'You're all mad, it's a nest for God's sake, just a nest.'

Ben, who over the years had soothed Ellie's temper and tried to reason her side with their devoutly religious parents, had been listening quietly. He walked over to her, placing his hand heavily on her shoulder.

'Ellie,' he began, his voice uneasy. 'Listen, it's all different now, if you came to the meetings more, you'd know.'

She didn't look up. 'What are you talking about?' she scowled.

Ben turned her chin to face him. 'Get rid of it, Ellie,' he warned softly, 'it could drive you mad.'

'But not in here,' cut in their mother, hugging Annie and Tom close to her chest.

Ellie stared up at her brother, waiting for him to grin or wink, but he was perfectly serious. With a pointed sigh, she scraped back her chair, not quite believing all this hysteria was over one wonky nest that she'd found tossed about in a bunch of trees.

Head down, Ellie gathered the bundle from the table and a few snapped twigs scattered down. Her mother flinched. Biting back a comment, Ellie gathered all the tiny pieces she could before quietly closing the kitchen door behind her. As she walked down the hallway, Ellie could hear her mother and father's voices in prayer behind her, and a beat later, the sound of her brother's husky voice joining in.

The floorboards creaked as she headed to the small room at the back of the house, her bedroom, her sanctuary, the only part in this whole crazy place that was a tiny bit sane. Kicking the door open, Ellie stood for a moment on the threshold. Bare white walls, a narrow single bed in the corner, and desk loaded with books and potted plants scavenged from the forest and other people's gardens.

Outside, on the front strip near the road, an old tree creaked in the evening wind. Red with smooth, voluptuous limbs, its branches undulated out from its bare trunk. One hung close to the house, its leaves gently hitting the wooden walls. Ellie opened her window and a gust of gritty air swirled into her room, lifting the school papers on her desk.

The back door crashed open and she could hear her brother's heavy boots hurrying down the steps. A moment later, the incinerator lid clanged to the ground. Hugging herself, Ellie stared up into the night as fingers of red-tinged smoke began to drift over the roofs of the houses opposite. Further away, another burst of lightning split the sky.

Ellie watched as the storm disappeared. She turned to hide the strange stone behind the books on her desk, and shoved the wonky nest into the bottom of her clothes cupboard.

THREE

Ellie woke with a jolt, the last frenzied images of a dream vanishing the moment she opened her eyes. Grimacing, she tried to lick her lips, but her tongue felt thick and strange, and her mouth dry. It tasted horrible and she felt awful; her belly was knotted, weighed down by a sick sense of foreboding. Ellie exhaled loudly. She'd slept badly that was all, half in and out of her covers, and the night was so hot that in the end she'd just kicked them off in disgust.

Fumbling in the dark for her bedside clock, Ellie sat up. A glow flashed up into her face: 8.30 a.m. She squeezed her eyes shut; they felt irritated and sore, edged with some kind of grit. It didn't make sense. How could it be 8.30 in the morning? She glanced up; her room looked weird, shrouded in a dark night-time silence and yet, standing tall and solid in the corner, her clothes cupboard appeared oddly visible, laced with a fine red haze seeping in from the window.

Ellie climbed out of bed and, stepping over her clothes on her way to the window, pushed the curtains open and peered out into the street.

A mist hung low, the colour of blood ochre or flaked, rusty iron. It covered the lawn and draped over the houses opposite, reducing the muscular, old gum tree out front into a dim, ghost-grey outline. The sky was a flat, dark red. A disc hung low, ringed by a milky blue halo, it emitted a wavering, feeble light. Ellie yawned, wondering if somehow she was still asleep. Her senses felt dull, muted, like she was caught in some kind of strange, unfathomable dream.

Wrenching the window open, Ellie leant over the sill, trying to see further. She coughed, her throat irritated by a dry persistent scratching, but that was the only sound. In the gritty air, no car engine, no child's shriek disturbed the silent calm. The street, indeed the entire surrounding suburb, sat empty, covered in a strange red mist, devoid of any sign of life.

Ellie's heart thudded. Breathing quickly, she tried to think.

Pulling on a pair of jeans and a t-shirt, she slid to the floor, where she sat for a long moment, gazing dumbly around her room. An eddy of dust spiralled slowly before her gaze.

Oh my God.. Ellie dropped her head in her hands and tried to think. *It had happened.*

Ellie had never actually paid that much attention what they'd said in the meetings, but… it had actually happened. Like they were continually warned. The prophesy; everyone gone, taken full in body to heaven.

And she was left behind.

I could just go back to sleep, Ellie thought, gazing into the gloom, *and hope to never, ever wake up.*

She breathed slowly. Then, out of the silence came a loud, sharp crash, followed by an indignant yell.

'Ellie, get on down here and help your brother clean up this mess!'

Frozen in stunned surprise, Ellie leapt to her feet and dashed down the hallway. Thick clouds of grit churned as Ellie pushed open the kitchen door. The air cleared and she could see her mother on the floor streaking a trail through the dust with a rag.

'Please Ellie,' Claire sighed.

At the backdoor, Annie and Tom were standing with their noses pressed against the glass, staring out at the mess in the yard.

She coughed, feeling oddly embarrassed.

'It's happening as was foretold.' Her father turned, his weatherworn features reflecting a calm, satisfied gaze. 'And the Lord watches over His own.'

Elle didn't reply. She traced a line through the layer of red grit coating the top of the bench. 'What's happening?'

'It's muck, Ellie. Muck, from the centre of the country.' Ellie's mother got up off the floor and rinsed the cloth out at the sink. 'And it's just such a nuisance. It would've blown in on the storms last night, didn't you hear it?'

'Yeah, sort of...' Ellie's voice trailed off. She frowned 'But I thought I was just dreaming.'

The wire door to the porch banged open. 'Hey, can someone give me a hand?' Ben stomped inside, his hair and clothes layered in dust.

'Don't come dragging that in here.' Claire snapped, shooing him outside. 'Get cleaned up under the tap, I won't have it.'

'But there's still crap all over the yard!'

'Don't you use that language!' spluttered Claire, her face heating red with indignation, 'You know I-'

'I'll help,' interrupted Ellie, as she pushed him outside into the dust choked air.

By late morning the yard was clear, though the day remained suffocatingly hot. Inside the house was dark and quiet, the curtains drawn to protect the rooms from the heat and the fine powdery grit. In the living room, seated in his favourite chair, Ellie's father jotted down notes, nodding as he checked lines and graphs on the family computer. Ellie crept past, with her bag slung over her shoulder.

Easing her bike out of the shed, she wheeled it out and onto the street. Adjusting a damp scarf tied around her nose and mouth, Ellie rode low over the handlebars, breathing as shallowly as she could, as rows of suburban houses blurred behind her in the dusty air.

A few turns later and Ellie joined the road that hugged the edge of the cliffs, winding around sharp bends and rocks worn smooth by the once relentless splash of mountain streams. Lifting her feet off the pedals, she freewheeled down the last long hill and into the neighbouring town. The houses here were the grandest in the whole area, each one made of solid stone with high windows and jutting balconies, commanding the best views over the valley.

Heaving against its weight, Ellie pushed open the iron gate of the largest house of all. Dropping her bike, she wiped her face and grimaced at the damp streak of red. Ellie shoved her scarf into the pocket of her jeans and glanced down at the summerhouse tucked away at the bottom of the garden. A fresh crack had appeared in the glass, and half the structure lay obscured by dead clumps of ivy that fell into the silted pond beneath.

Not so long ago, when the weather had been cooler and Ellie had been younger, she'd played with her friend Rose in the garden while their

26

mothers looked on, bright and smiling. Now it was too hot to play and Rose's mother had gone, taken by a lingering disease with a common name.

A shadow moved in one of the upstairs windows as she rapped on the back door; it was the sharp profile of the Reverend Matthew Hopkins. She half waved hello, but he turned away. Ellie dropped her hand; her friend's father never seemed particularly pleased to see her, as he rarely smiled or said hello. She shrugged; at least he hadn't tried to keep them apart.

The sound of feet running on wooden floors interrupted Ellie's thoughts. The door flew open and a riot of feathers, perfume, and silk scarves descended as she was enveloped in a tight, laughing hug.

'Oh my God, hi,' Rose coughed. 'What crazy weather.' Without waiting for a reply, she grabbed Ellie by the hand. 'Come on!' She commanded, pulling her at once into a cool, dark world.

In the panelled hallway, Rose turned and smiled at Ellie; her eyes, a brown so light they were almost golden, shone with delight. 'I'm so glad you're here,' she said. 'I was going completely mad. But look, I've found the most marvellous clothes.'

She twirled around, showing off a short, black-crocheted dress and rainbow tights. Flicking a red and black feather boa dramatically across her shoulders, Rose grinned and shook her long dark hair until it curled all the way down her back.

'Ta dah,' she posed, smiling. 'But let's not go on about me, let's find something for you. *Come on.*'

'Oh my God, where did you find these?'

'In a box hidden in the attic.' Rose giggled, and then stopped as a door creaked open upstairs and a footstep trod heavily on the floor boards. 'Eek, come *on*.'

The two girls ran laughing down the hallway and up a different flight of stairs at the back of the house. Scooting past the library, they burst into Rose's bedroom. It was huge and bright with high ceilings and windows, almost three times the size of Ellie's, but it too was sparsely furnished with bare walls and narrow bed. Tossed in the middle of the floor was a riot of colour and fabrics.

'Here, try this.'

Crocheted in white silk, beaded at the neck and sleeves with tiny iridescent pearls, the dress was so beautiful Ellie could only reach out and stroke the soft fabric.

'My God, where did you find it?'

'I told you, in a box at the back of the attic.' Rose shrugged, nonchalantly, eyeing her reflection in the mirror.

'What were you doing in the attic, are you allowed up there?'

'Oh, I was bored. Enough with the questions!' Rose tossed her head defiantly. 'Dad was crowing about the weather, he was driving me nuts,' she paused and glanced out the window with a frown. 'But the weather *is* getting weirder, don't you think?'

'Yeah,' Ellie agreed, following her gaze. 'I was so freaked out I thought it had actually happened, you know, the End of the World.'

Rose snorted. 'Yeah, me too. I thought Daddy had finally risen to heaven and I was could get some peace, finally.'

They both giggled and at Rose's urging, Ellie took off her top and jeans and slipped the white dress over her head. Lined with soft peach silk, it felt gentle and cool against her skin. Ellie had never worn anything like this before and she looked down, suddenly feeling shy.

'Here try this too.' Rose tossed her a long, pale green scarf. Ellie held it up against her face in the mirror.

'Ooh it matches your eyes.' Rose said, teasing. Ellie's eyes flashed green as she laughed, watching herself in the mirror. And then she sighed. 'It's so beautiful.'

'Well, so are we,' giggled Rose, blowing herself a kiss.

'Yeah…' breathed Ellie, almost afraid to believe it.

Rose grabbed her hand and they stood admiring themselves. Ellie's long, red-gold hair contrasting with her friend's locks of raven black. Striking poses, Rose and Ellie pouted and blew kisses, undulating their bodies until they were giggling so loudly they didn't hear the first sharp rap at the door.

Bending forward, Ellie leant to kiss herself in the glass as a second loud knock thudded on the door. It swung open wide. In the glass, she saw the appalled reflection of Rose's father standing in the doorway, his Adam's apple working in fury as though choked too full of words to speak.

'What do you think you are doing?' Matthew spat out at last.

The red feather boa curled onto the floor. 'Hey Daddy,' Rose began smiling.

He cut her off, his blue eyes bulging with outrage. 'Where did you get those clothes? They're not yours.' His glance cut sharply to Ellie. 'You look like prostitutes,' he snapped, coldly.

Heat flooded her face and Ellie dropped the green scarf to the floor. Beside her Rosie merely laughed as she turned to face her father. 'Don't say that, Daddy, really. That's mean.' She smiled again and stepped closer, sashaying a little towards him.

He averted his eyes. 'Just take the dresses off, Rosalind.' He backed away. 'And now.' Bumping into the back of the wall, the Reverend fled down the hallway.

Rosie turned back to Ellie and, picking up the green scarf, she twirled it around her neck with a cheeky grin.

Ellie glanced down at the clothes heaped over the wooden floor. 'I wonder who they belong to?'

Rose kicked at the pile. 'Who knows,' she sniffed in disdain. 'The attic's full of old junk.'

'Maybe they're his?'

Rose grinned. 'Yeah, he probably wears them in his spare time.'

Ellie's eyes widened and they both collapsed helpless with laughter on the bed.

'Hey.' Rose jumped up. 'Let's get out of here.'

'Where?' spluttered Ellie, 'it's so stinking hot and horrible.'

'Your favourite place,' Rose grinned, glancing out at the red dusty sky.

Ellie hesitated, remembering the fury on her father's face the night before.

'Oh come *on,*' Rose pulled at her hand, 'I won't tell if you won't tell, and besides, what can be so wrong?'

FOUR

Closing the heavy front door behind her, Ellie wrapped her scarf again around her face. The day was still suffocatingly close. Though some of the dust had lifted, particles of grit remained swirling in the air.

At the lookout at the end of the road, the valley stretched out, draped beneath a fine red haze that faded to white over the horizon. A wail floated over the trees as a lone eagle, its wings spread wide beneath the ochre sky, swept overhead and down into the expanse below.

'I think I saw that the other day.' Ellie watched its low soaring flight.

'What?' mumbled Rose.

Ellie pushed her scarf out of her mouth. 'You know, that Wedge-tailed eagle. I thought they'd all gone extinct.'

'Well, whatever, I guess they're back.'

From the clifftop the two friends followed the wooden stairs that led down to the path hewn into the side of the cliff. Rose led the way, she was older than Ellie – sixteen, and she marched down the steps filling the air with comments about what clothes she would buy if only her father wasn't so mean.

Under an outcrop of rock, the steps levelled out. Ellie stopped by a seat and rummaged in her backpack for a water bottle. Rose uncapped a small aluminium thermos and filled a cup with lemon-iced tea.

Ellie laughed in amazement.

'What?' asked Rose, indignantly. 'I had a feeling you were going to come over and so I made us some tea. Is that a crime?'

Descending further into the valley, they emerged at last out onto a dappled shadowy path. Fern Gully had been a favoured picnic area for walkers, and the remnants of wooded tables lay scattered between the trees. Rose was right - the air here was cooler, easier to breathe, as though the seeping dust hadn't the energy to make it this far down.

Ellie walked slowly, her head tilted back and her eyes trained up at the light cascading through the tall, moss speckled forest. Giant tree ferns fanned above, their wide delicate fronds protected from the heat, and hidden within this veiled, shadowed canyon.

A flitter overhead, and a bird with sharp darting movements landed on the branch of a sapling.

'Oh my God,' Ellie breathed. 'Look.'

'Oh right,' Rose sniffed, untying her hair and combing the curls out with her fingers. 'A bird.'

'No, you don't understand, there hasn't been a bird in the forest for months. I don't even remember the last time I saw one.'

'Except for that wedged-tail thing.'

'Yes, but - oh Rose.'

Ignoring her friend's disinterest, Ellie hurried through the trees after the tiny wren. It flew along a snaking path and then, a moment later, it darted around a tall, sloping boulder and disappeared into the dry forest beyond. Disappointed, Ellie slowed to a walk.

Here out in the open, and away from the protective shadows of the cliffs, the air pressed close and hot, speckling her skin with rusty flecks of dust. Sighing, Ellie brushed off her arms when, all at once, a shadow, fast-winged and high, dashed overhead. Whirling, trying to catch a glimpse against the glare of the sky, Ellie gazed up into the canopy. Branches creaked and a breeze dropped a handful of leaves to the forest floor, sending a pattern of sunlight dancing across the trees.

'I love it here...' She whispered out loud. Flinging her arms wide, Ellie twirled around and around, the surrounding forest blurring and shifting, flashing shards of bright and dark into her eyes. *I love it here...* whirling faster and faster, Ellie tilted her face upwards, losing herself in the sensation of light streaking across her vision.

All at once she spun to a stop, her feet skidding on the path. Mortified, Ellie dropped her hands, bracing herself for a peal of teasing laughter from her friend. Around her it seemed the enormous forest held its breath. She could sense it, miles and miles of dense thick bushland - some so tangled and inaccessible that Ellie doubted a soul had set foot in it for hundreds of years.

Wincing, she stole a glance behind, but with one arm flung carelessly over her eyes, Rose lay stretched out across a low picnic bench; she appeared to be fast asleep. Exhaling loudly in relief, Ellie slung her bag over her shoulder and turned to rejoin her friend.

Then all at once, a whisper rasped, tight and close behind her. Followed by a footfall, and a sudden crunch of leaves, as though stepped on, once, twice-

Ellie's heart pounded. Her skin prickled, and her attention contracted to the sensation of being watched by a bright, hard gaze.

Ellie warily raised her hands - in supplication or self-protection she didn't know. In the ensuing silence, the trunks of the surrounding trees - magnificent mountain ash - soared up towards the sky, tall and straight, and unyielding in the eucalyptus-tinged heat.

'Is anyone there?' Ellie whispered.

Leaves swirled around her feet. A flash of movement skittered at the edge of her vision.

'Stop playing around, show yourself!'

A small rock rolled across another at her feet, until teetering it fell to the ground.

Oh please, she begged silently, lowering her hands. *Whatever you are, I can feel you're here, I don't know how, but please stop playing games…*

It was so strange. Ellie didn't know how it happened, but as she stood gazing into the forest her vision seemed to shift; it was like an inkblot test, or a 3D illusion picture coming suddenly into focus. One minute nothing, and then...

A face...

Ellie gasped. Emerging from within the pale bark of a eucalypt, a face appeared in the smooth wood, so close, just a handful of steps away. Its sharp features eyed her intently, and behind it the tree bulged as though the trunk held a baby pushing the limits of its mother's belly.

'I'm dreaming,' Ellie whispered, scarcely daring to breathe.

As she watched, the creature seemed to relax. Blinking, it adjusted its position in an unhurried fashion, and proceeded to slowly unfurl the entire length of its body. Ducking a shoulder through the very fabric of the

34

wood, it stretched forth a long, sinuous leg, and stepped cautiously to the ground. Tall and straight, its wide feet splayed across the earth like roots - and its skin was as pale and smooth, and as speckled with grey, as the towering mountain ash behind.

Ellie gazed for a long moment at the being, the *faery*, for that is what it seemed to be. She had seen pictures in a book - finely etched drawings and watercolours of nature spirits, fae beings, who lived within the cool of rocks, in trees, and deep within rivers. But that had been about magical creatures living in the hills and dales of England and Ireland. In stories. Not here and now in dusty, hot Australia.

Whatever.

The faery was taking no notice of her. By now it had edged away from the trees and was out on the open path, quivering in a direct shaft of light. Elongating its arms, it tilted its head back and breathed out a lilting trio of notes.

It was so surprising, and so pure and simple, Ellie's eyes pricked with tears. She didn't move, not caring anymore if this was real or she had suddenly, completely lost her mind. A moment, and the song rippled out once more, rising in tone, higher still, before evaporating into silence.

'Hey.' A branch snapped, and Rose's voice cut abruptly through the forest. 'What are you –?'

'Can you see it?' Ellie hurriedly wiped her eyes. She had never seen anything so strange and beautiful before in her life. She turned.

Rose didn't answer. Around them the expanse of trees remained quiet, with not a flicker of wind disturbing the stillness.

'Rose?'

'See what?'

'*Look.*'

It had only been an instant, but when Ellie turned back the faery had vanished, leaving the path with only a few twigs and leaves fluttering in the sunshine.

'Let's go back.' Rose grabbed Ellie's hand. 'I saw you twirling around before, what were you doing? You're such an idiot.'

Ellie flushed and in the embarrassed silence, a series of distant notes sounded through the forest.

'Did you hear *that*?'

'What?'

They began again, this time the notes were more intricate, and they seemed to be moving further into the trees.

'Oh.' Ellie clasped her hands almost begging. 'We have to see what's going on. It could be *magic...*'

'Magic?' Rose snorted. 'What are you on about, you big baby.'

Ellie opened her mouth to protest, but she didn't get a chance as with a hoot of laughter Rose darted away. 'Come on, you'll wet yourself if we don't check it out.'

Smiling, Ellie ran into the depths of the sunlit forest. Ahead she could see her friend's long dark hair in stark contrast with the paleness of the surrounding trees. Without pausing, Rose vanished into a stand of white giants. It was a grove, each tree grew tightly together, jutting up into the sky, edged by a wall of dark granite boulders.

Ellie stopped, her breath dry and rasping in her throat. The notes sounded louder here, she realised. A constant, overlaying tone that seemed to vibrate up through the rocks themselves and out into the air.

Everywhere.

The sound thrummed up through the stone beneath her feet. Rising from the ground, she could feel it spreading through the soil, and seeping into the very soles of her shoes. Frowning, Ellie tried to shift her position, but her feet wouldn't budge; each one felt strangely heavy, weighed down solidly to the earth.

'Hey.' Ellie pulled at them again.

A loud shout burst from the trees and she stumbled forward, her shoes abruptly coming away from the ground. Rose was standing by one of the boulders, grinning and motioning Ellie to follow.

Ellie took in a long wavering breath. 'What had just happened?'

'Come *on*,' Rose gestured, before rushing away through the trees.

'Wait!' cried Ellie as she scrambled after her, trying to keep up on the twisting, narrow path. A step later, and Rose disappeared.

Ellie slowed, around her the air seemed to be shimmering, flashing, like sun-caught water. With each step she took, the shadows between the densely growing trees shifted, becoming lighter and lighter. Ellie's heart pounded, gripped by a fierce elation she propelled herself past the last remaining tree and burst into a clearing.

Music filled her senses. Low tones, as thick as water, brushed over stone monoliths.

A tiny being flitted past, its eyes huge in its face as bright shards of sound streaked to the ground. The very rock itself seemed to shudder.

Eyes wide, Ellie turned around, hugging herself in wonder. Above her, the sandstone cliffs spun in a blur of red and ochre and grey-green trees.

Amazing, Ellie breathed, spinning. *Just -*

A pebble whacked hard against Ellie's hand.

'What are you *doing*?' Rose hissed.

She was crouched low a few steps away by a large rock. In her hand she brandished a second, threatening projectile. Ellie rubbed her skin. Her head felt odd and strangely light, like the day had tilted. It felt hard to focus. Particles of grit irritated her eyes.

'Why are you always so slow?' Rose slapped the rock. Ellie blinked, jolted awake by the sound.

'Check this out. You've got to see this.'

'What?' She crept across the ground to her friend.

Grinning, Rose raised herself and pointed to the centre of the clearing.

The sun had dipped behind a wedge of rock, sending a knife of shadow straight across the ground. Positioned around its tip stood a circle of robed figures. In a single motion, each one took a step back and raised a hand. As they did so, the wind shifted, scattering a flurry of leaves across the rocky ground, and out of the silence came a song as light as breath.

Ellie shivered, the notes lifted, twisting, becoming a layered harmony rising into the ochre red sky. *So beautiful...*

A snort, and Rose slapped her hand on the rocky surface. 'Oh my God. It's just people,' she laughed incredulously. 'It's not magic. It's just ordinary people in awful clothes.'

Ellie stared at them, and the wonder vanished. Suddenly she felt cold, tired, and very stupid. 'Let's go back-'

'No way.' Rose grinned.

In the centre of the circle stood a woman; she was older, but just how old Ellie couldn't see. Her head was down, and grey-streaked hair cascaded down her back. Around her neck hung a loop of long, black feathers. The other voices stilled, and the woman lifted her gaze and sang out a single, powerful note. Shooting into the sky, it reverberated long and hard around the sun-warmed cliffs. The air itself seemed to quake and then, rising like shadows out of the stone, figures emerged out of the rock, tall and fine-boned with huge eyes, and skin the rich red of the cliff face.

Ellie stared, her heart thudding, as with long graceful movements, the strange beings eased free and moved towards the women.

All at once, Rose jumped to her feet. 'Come on!' She turned around, beckoning eagerly.

She couldn't see them. Ellie suddenly knew. Her friend wasn't aware of the creatures towering over the dark-robed figures.

'No stop!' Ellie motioned, frantically.

'No *stop.*' Rose mimicked. Pulling a face, she crept closer to the robed figures. A sigh rippled through the clearing.

'Stop!' Ellie called, suddenly panicked. The woman lifted her hands.

'Stop!'

Voices rose and Ellie jumped to her feet as the woman cried a single spoken word. The sound cracked like a gunshot against the walls of the cliffs. Rose fell to the ground.

'No!' Ellie ran to her friend.

In the circle, the old woman glared at the two girls, her huge eyes piercing the shadows like enormous golden orbs. The ochre-red beings had vanished.

'I'm okay,' Rose laughed. 'I just tripped.'

Pulling away from Ellie, she climbed to her feet and gestured to the motionless figures. 'You don't scare me,' Rose shook her hair back, defiantly. 'You're all crazy, what do you think you're doing? Huh?'

Chortling wickedly, Rose grabbed Ellie by the hand and pulled her back across the length of the clearing. Ellie didn't protest.

After a long pause, voices rose once more from within the circle, like a pulse, quiet and sombre, pushing the intruders away.

Dropping her grasp, Rose scrambled back through the gap in the rock.

Alone, Ellie turned back. The sun had dropped over the cliffs and the entire clearing was now blanketed in shadow. She could hardly see anything save for the ghostly glimmer of the trees and the rock face glowing red in the setting sun. 'I'm sorry,' she whispered. 'I'm really sorry.'

Reaching into her bag, Ellie pulled out her water bottle and tipped the last of it onto the ground, at the base of one of the trees. It wasn't much, but it was all she had to offer.

'Come *on*!'

Sighing, Ellie squeezed herself back through the wall of rock and hurried into the forest.

'You're always so *slow*.' Rose hissed with her hands on her hips and a scowl marring her beautiful face. 'They were weird. Who were they?'

'I have no idea.' Ellie forced out a chuckle.

'And you! What got into you?'

'I don't know.'

'You were scared. You thought they were going to kill us or something.'

Rose handed over her thermos of iced-tea. Ellie took a gulp of the sweet, cool liquid and closed her eyes. 'Yeah well,' she said at last. 'They should've killed *you*. You deserved it. I thought you'd been struck dead.'

'Oh, I was just pretending.'

'Yeah, right.'

'Who cares, they were nothing. They didn't have any magic at all.'

FIVE

A streetlight flicked on and then another. Overhead, the sky was soaked a dull, dark red. Ellie could see Rose just up ahead standing by the kerb in front of her house. It was eerily quiet, with not a child cry or hint of movement within any of the houses, each window closed tight against the dust.

'Do you have any idea what the time is?' Ellie caught up with her friend.

Rose ignored her. 'Do you have any water?'

'No, I'd love some but-'

'Damn, we'll have to just use them dry.' Rose pulled her scarf out of her back pocket and began wiping her face and neck with small meticulous strokes.

'What are you doing?' cried Ellie, grabbing her hand. 'Can't you see how late it is? I have to get home.'

'It's probably not as late as you think,' said Rose. 'You need to just sort yourself out.' She glanced pointedly at Ellie's clothes.

Ellie looked down. Her t-shirt and jeans were smeared with the remnants of leaves and bark caught from the trees. That was easy to brush off - but sticking to her skin, mingled with a layer of damp exerted after the long climb, was a persistent covering of red.

Alarmed, Ellie pulled out her scarf and quickly ran it over her face and hands and neck.

When Rose was satisfied all traces of their journey were erased, Ellie stuffed the soiled cloth deep into her bag and hurried after her friend. Their footsteps crunched as Rose and Ellie eased open the metal gates and slipped as quietly as they could on the gravel path, and down the side of the house. Here Ellie breathed easier. The air was cooler and cleaner, as though shielded from the grit of the day by the sheer weight of the stone walls.

It was dark and hard to see, but turning the corner she stopped, momentarily dazzled by a single light, its beam trained on a figure at the bottom of the garden.

'Hey Dad,' Rose called out, heading along the patchy grass towards him. 'We're back.'

Balanced high on a ladder, the Reverend Matthew Hopkins stood over the mass of ivy that fell from the roof of the summerhouse. A tall, fierce looking man with curly black hair, he was struggling to cut through the last twists of vine. Leaves tumbled to the ground and he turned, his pale blue eyes gleaming in a face that looked worn and bitter in the unforgiving light.

Ellie suddenly felt spooked; Rose's father usually seemed to be the same age as her own, but there were odd moments when he seemed ancient, soured, and beaten with age.

The garden shears clattered onto the roof.

'Do you two have any idea what the time is?' His gaze locked on to Ellie's. 'Your mother has called twice. You were apparently meant to be home some time ago.'

Ellie stared back, gripped by a sudden cold dismay. 'Oh no, I can't believe it.'

'Wait,' called Rose, grabbing Ellie by the hand. 'What's up, surely you don't really have to go?'

'I do,' wailed Ellie. 'They're going out tonight and I promised to cook dinner. She's going to kill me.'

Rose took a step towards her. 'Will your brother be home?' She asked with a sly smile.

'Yeah I suppose so.'

'Well then, let's get going. We'll call her. Dad can drive us and between us we'll be able to whip something up for the twins and anyone else who happens to be around.'

A loud hand slap on the roof cut her off. 'Not so fast, first you can tell me where the two of you have been.'

'Oh Daddy,' Rose murmured, her cheeks dimpling prettily in the light. 'Why are you getting so hot and bothered? It's easy, we've been in the library and then we went to a café and forgot the time.' She paused and asked innocently, 'where else would we go when the weather has been so unpleasant?'

Nervously, Ellie averted her eyes, certain the Reverend could sense the lies, and why did Rose mention the library? Everyone with half a brain knew it was closed on weekends.

'Come on,' Rose reached up her hand. 'You've been out in the garden too long. Let's have some nice iced tea, and then maybe you can take us to Ellie's?'

High on the ladder, Matthew held his daughter's gaze for a long moment then sighed. 'No,' he said quietly and gestured to the summerhouse. 'This needs to be finished, Rose. We need to be faithful to what we have started.'

He paused, his gaze passing from Rose to Ellie, inspecting them each in turn. 'I will take you Rosalind, but,' he added, firmly, 'I do not want to hear that you two have been anywhere but in the town. Hear me?' He stabbed his finger through the air for emphasis.

Against the dark red of the sky, his blue eyes burned. Ellie swallowed, certain that he could see every forbidden step of the afternoon.

The glare softened as Matthew turned back to his daughter. 'Rosalind,' he said softly, and it seemed to Ellie that he was almost begging, his hands clasped together as if in prayer. 'The End is coming. There are things in the forest that are like poison to the soul. They live. They will haunt you, follow you, whisper secrets into your mind through the day and the night until you cannot stand it, and you will fear for your very sanity.'

Rose nodded slowly, never taking her eyes from her father's tormented face. 'Yes Daddy,' she murmured. 'Of course, you're right.'

'Please,' he said, his voice rasped, and he bent closer, so his face was level with hers. 'Do not enter the forest,' he whispered. 'Believe me, I do not say this to frighten you, but it is true nonetheless; there is a war on, a terrible war… Evil is abroad. Within the shadows of the trees live witches and their demons, hungry for our very souls.'

Ellie bit back a startled laugh. She glanced at Rose, but her friend's face was smooth and calm as she nodded seriously, her hand reaching for her father's.

'Yes Daddy,' agreed Rose as serene as an angel. 'That's terrible. Witches live in the forest.' She paused. 'Are you sure you wouldn't like some fresh iced tea? I brewed some this morning?'

'No child,' Matthew held his daughter's gaze. 'Thank you, I must first finish what I started, then I will take you to your friend's.' Reaching for the garden shears once more, he returned to the roof of the summerhouse as a dry and gritty wind rose over the valley.

With his leg braced against the topmost rung, Matthew stopped, his garden sheers poised. On the evening air, peals of helpless, girlish laughter sliced sharply over the garden, painfully loud. Clenching his jaw, he squeezed hard on the shears and the matt of dead vegetation fell into the derelict pond below.

Movement scattered through the trees and the wind shifted, but Matthew ignored both. Unfolding a white handkerchief from his pocket, he carefully wiped his brow and blew his nose. Above him, the sky remained clouded, empty of stars, concealed behind the dark red layering of dust. Further across the valley, he could see the final streaks of the sun disappearing over the horizon.

In the silence, a whistling cry pierced the night. Shuddering, as if cold, Matthew grabbed the shears with one hand and slid off the ladder, stalking across the dry lawn into the back of the house. Another moment and the cry came again, closer and louder this time, but the garden was empty and the doors and windows of the house remained closed.

The skies were huge with dark thunderheads, deep and violet, sweeping up into the night, towering masses, their tops sheered straight, dead flat. Clad in a light cotton nightdress, Ellie sat on her window ledge, her long bare legs dangling almost to the ground. Above her the clouds flashed with light.

She waited, counting the seconds until out of the silence came the low answering rumble. The storm was still miles away, and around her the air remained flat and dead, with no gusts to freshen the day's lingering taste of grit.

Ellie jumped to the ground as quietly as she could, slipping across the shrivelled lawn to the road. Keeping to the shadows thrown by the arc of the streetlights, she ran on soundless feet, past the suburban houses huddled against the night.

She stopped at the park by the edge of the cliff, her breath coming in short sharp gasps, her green eyes open, every muscle in her body poised, as the song rose out again over the waiting forest.

Ellie didn't hesitate. Before her dropped the stairs, each one bolted firmly to the rock, a long, narrow brace of metal, like a ladder, leading down the cliff face and into the dark.

Her hand twitched as she dreamed. Sprawled across her narrow bed, lying exposed, escaping the heat, Ellie's breath came in short hard gasps, and the pillow beneath her face was damp with perspiration.

Help us. Strange faces slipped in and out of her vision.

Help us.

Ellie's mother tipped batter into a frypan sizzling on the stove. Sunlight spilled in through the open back door, streaming over the twins sitting up at the table. With a conspiratorial grin, Annie and Tom banged their hands on the wood, demanding their pancakes in a burst of high-pitched laughter. A swell of gospel music chorused from the radio perched on top of the fridge. Her father wiped his hands and sat down.

Ellie slid into the empty chair opposite. She glared at the twins. God, they were loud. She tried not to wince.

'Morning Ellie, you're up late.'

'Yeah, sorry,' her head ached. 'I had the weirdest dreams.' Ellie gazed dumbly for a moment at the growing stack of pancakes in the centre of the table. The screen door banged open and Ben hopped in, tying up the laces of his boots.

'What's for breakfast, Mum?' With a grunt, he dropped his large frame into a chair. 'I'm starving.'

Brian handed him a plate with a chuckle. 'I heard on the phone this morning that you were getting very friendly with the Reverend's daughter.'

'What were you doing with young Rose?' Claire looked up sharply.

'Don't worry, Mum, we just went to the study group.' Ben shrugged. 'And Ellie stayed here with the twins, doing homework, as usual.' He taunted, rolling his eyes at his sister.

Ignoring him, Ellie poured a dollop of thick maple syrup onto the twin's breakfast. Rose had had a crush on her brother for months. Ellie couldn't begin to fathom why, but last night during dinner, something had clicked and the two of them had driven off, with Rose's delighted giggling hanging in the air.

'It was a great night.' Ben laughed suddenly, the sound ricocheting sharply off the kitchen walls. 'It sounds *really* crazy, but the Reverend sure as hell is right –'

'Ben! Mind your language!'

'Sorry Mum, but it's true,' he said, reaching for a pancake. 'And Rose knows what's going on. 'We've got to be ready,' she says, 'when the End Times come, us Believers have got to stick together …' Ben's voice trailed off, admiringly. 'But you know, Dad, she's changed, seems to have grown up all of a sudden.'

'She listens to her father,' Brian nodded, approvingly. 'You could learn from her Ellie, and start going to Bible study.'

Bible study? Ellie bit back a laugh. Rose had all the interest in Bible study as a rabbit had in knitting.

But before she could say anything, she was interrupted by a sharp intake of breath from her mother. 'Oh that's awful.'

'What?' Ellie asked, swivelling around.

The morning service had finished and news headlines were blaring out from the tinny speakers.

The sea defenses of Kandholhudhoo, a densely populated island in the north of the Maldives, have been inundated by the highest tides ever recorded. Scores are feared drowned, mainly the elderly -

'Oh, turn it off.' Claire said, her eyes filling with tears. 'It's all we ever hear, hurricanes, famine, drought...'

'Mum, sit down for a second.' Ellie stood up and switched off the radio. 'Would you like a cup of tea?'

Her mother sank to the nearest chair. 'No, thank you, love, nothing for me today. Your father and I are fasting for the meeting.' Claire paused and looked up at Ellie anxiously. 'I would really like you to come, please? You hardly ever do.'

'Of course she's coming!' interrupted Ben, finishing his breakfast with a satisfied belch.

Ellie winced. Her brother could be so gross. 'I don't know,' she took his plate. 'I have an essay due on Monday and it's not finished. I have so much more to do.'

'Why are you bothering?' Ben asked, frowning in incomprehension. 'None of that matters, sis. Everything is changing. Look outside; it's meant to be freezing now. Remember? It's almost winter for God's sake.' He shook his head. 'Come to church, Ellie. The world's going to hell in a hand basket, and we've got to be prepared.'

She didn't answer. At the sink, Ellie turned on the tap and waited, studying the old vegetable garden while the pipes thumped, spewing out tepid, tanin-stained water. Spanning half the yard, it used to be the envy of all the ladies in church, with an abundance of thick-stemmed broccoli and long bunches of sweet tasting carrots. But, Ellie sighed, Ben was right. That was then, when the seasons were cool and well defined, and with plenty of rain. Not this continual everlasting heat.

Once she'd finished the dishes, Ellie carried a mug of hot tea back into her room and closing the door behind, sank down at her desk and picked up a textbook, *1944 A Short History of the D-Day Landings*. Ellie opened it at the last chapter.

11:28 a.m. The clock's numbers shone in the corner. Soon everyone would be gone, and there would be enough peace and quiet to finish her paper. Taking a thoughtful sip of tea, Ellie gazed out the window at the enormous red gum spreading its branches wide over the front yard. It looked exhausted, its remaining leaves limp and scorched, its smooth pinkish trunk weathered to grey and struggling beneath the weight of its heavy limbs.

Ben's right, everything's all just going to hell.

Morosely, Ellie dropped the textbook onto the desk. At once, an object fell to the floor with a sharp crack.

Now what? With an exasperated sigh, Ellie peered beneath the chair. There, in a pool of bright sun, lay the strange stone she'd picked up off the forest floor.

At first it appeared perfectly ordinary, but as Ellie studied it, she noticed a hole right in its centre, bored through, white, and pinpricked with a thousand tiny dents, like a small, wonky window.

Curious, Ellie scooped the stone off the floor. It felt surprisingly heavy and cool, and its rounded shape fit perfectly into the palm of her hand. Frowning a little, Ellie traced around the hole with the tip of her little finger. The edge felt odd, soft and hard at the same time, like the texture of weathered bone, or like the surface of sea coral, ancient and gnarled.

It was beautiful, Ellie decided, holding the stone up to the window. And so strange... A light, shimmering like a gentle, iridescent haze, seemed to be swirling towards her from its centre. Breathing softly, Ellie brought the stone closer, her attention caught by the strange pulsing glow, but was startled by a sudden sharp knock at the door. The stone landed in her lap.

'Rose is on the landline.' Her mother peered in. 'I've been calling you three times, why haven't you answered? And don't speak to her for too long,' she added frowning. 'If you're coming, it's almost time to go.'

'What? No. We don't have to leave for another hour.'

'You must have been sleeping over your books, Ellie. It's almost one o'clock. If you're coming, we leave in twenty minutes.'

As her mother closed the door, Ellie grabbed her bedside clock. 12:48 p.m. - the numbers flashed, flaunting the squandered hour.

Through the walls she could hear sharp exclamations of protest as the twins were hustled into the bathroom for a final scrub. Ellie stared at the clock in confusion then, remembering the waiting phone call, she hid the stone deep in her backpack and hurried into the living room.

It was empty; her father's books and papers were shuffled neatly away on the table beside the telephone.

'Rose? Is that you?'

'Of course it's me, you silly. Who else could it be? Anyway, you took so long we can't talk, but I have to ask you,' Rose paused, dramatically. 'Did he talk about me?'

Ellie sank into the sofa. 'Who?' She asked, stupidly. Looking around the room, everything looked the same; curtains still an orange patterned brown, woven with metallic thread. She pressed her head; it felt odd and muffled with a vague, stuffy emptiness.

'Are you even listening?' Rose's sharp tone cut through the fog. 'I'm asking about your brother, silly head, who else? Did he say anything about last night?'

'Oh Rose...' Ellie began rubbing her temples. 'He might've done, but I didn't hear anything,' her voice trailed off. 'I slept really badly. I had the weirdest dream -'

'He's so gorgeous,' interrupted Rose, her voice purring with satisfaction. 'He likes me. I know he *really* likes me. You should've been there, it was so romantic...' She giggled in delight.

Ellie frowned as she tried to focus. 'Rose,' she said at last. 'What were you doing at Bible study? I thought you hated all that?'

Rose snorted, 'Yeah, but I like your brother, so why not? I might as well put what my dad spouts to good use. Anyway,' she added brightly, 'got to go. See you at the meeting – you've got to come, you know, it gets us brownie points. And don't forget to bring your gorgeous brother.'

And with a click Rose was gone. Sitting in the armchair, Ellie sat staring at the mute receiver until her father called her from the kitchen.

SIX

By the time the family car pulled in the church parking lot, it was already full. The gravel road was dry and cracked and clouds of dust billowed over as it jerked to a stop. Ellie's father opened his door and adjusted his tie. Wearing a pair of freshly polished shoes, he walked quickly around the car and deftly opened the passenger side door. Claire gathered her skirt in one hand and rose from the vehicle as gracefully as she could. Glancing up, she self-consciously smoothed down her skirt.

Behind her, oblivious to any heavenly scrutiny, the twins tumbled out of the back, complaining loudly of the heat and sticky vinyl seats. Claire examined them with narrowed eyes. Scowling, Annie fidgeted in shiny pink taffeta, rowed with pearl buttons to the neck and securely tied with a tight white bow. Beside her, Tom scuffed the ground idly, his hair still damp from the shower. She frowned, and in a single manoeuvre rummaged in her handbag, dabbed a tissue on her tongue and wiped a small smear of toothpaste off the boy's cheek. Tom yelped in disgust and ran off up the long gravel path, Annie speeding along in the dust behind him.

Ellie tried hard not to grin. Her mother was determined the family be as shiny clean as possible, presentable, since the Lord may return and claim them at any moment. And the most likely day, her mother always said, would be a Sunday, when they all gathered to praise His name.

The church was old and grand, made from fine light sandstone and watched over protectively by an ornate bell tower. A lone magpie hopped on the ivy-entangled wall as Ellie passed through the gates. She stopped, snared by the smell of moisture rising seductively from the garden. The churchyard was carpeted from wall to wall with a lush green lawn and populated by rows of dark-leaved flowering shrubs watered by contraband hoses hidden under the leaves. There were no trees, but it was cool and still, and so beautiful Ellie longed to stay.

Well, why couldn't she? She was kind of, technically, in church. She could just stay out here and tell her parents she'd been listening up the back. And the grass looked so inviting. But Ellie shook her head, remembering Rose's comment about 'earning brownie points'.

Turning away, Ellie hurried on towards the church and stepped into the cool, dark interior as a hundred voices joined in harmony. Sunlight poured in through the high arched windows, fragmenting colour down over the rows of hardwood pews. The congregation were on their feet, singing with their eyes closed and arms raised to the heavens as a clear high soprano soared effortlessly overhead.

Creeping in as unobtrusively as she could, Ellie found a seat in her parent's row and, smiling vaguely in apology, craned her head up to the front. Through the wall of parishioners she caught the back of the Reverend Matthew's long black robe, his hands raised and his head tossed back as his deep baritone reverberated loudly through the church.

Beside him, Rose was singing with her eyes closed, her warm contralto weaving effortlessly in and out of the main harmonies. She looked as beautiful and as relaxed as always, her long dark hair cascading down the back of her dress. Standing to her right was Ben, his plaid shirt freshly ironed and curly hair carefully neat.

The hymn swept through the interior of the church, swirling though every corner as it soared towards the highest arches. An exalted, crescendo of praise that surged through the stone and tile and on up to the heavens until at last it dropped away to a whisper, and all was silent save for the deep soothing voice of the Reverend Matthew Hopkins.

'My people,' he murmured, his low voice rumbling as he left the front row and stepped up to the dais overlooking the congregation. Light from the stained window behind the pulpit caught and flashed around him.

'My people,' he repeated, 'as Believers we wonder about the world, we wonder about God's plan. We wonder at the weather, the lack of rain and the failing of the very crops that sustain us. Some of us may be wavering in our faith, wondering even if the Creator Himself has turned away, has hidden His face? Every night, on every channel, in every newspaper, in every broadcast, not a moment passes without news of devastation, earthquake, and pestilence. And you may be wondering, where is God in all this?'

Behind him from the air fed organ, music began - a soft questioning tone rising and falling behind his words.

Shuffling in her seat, Ellie stopped listening; she felt agitated and bored. The muscles in her legs twitched and she wished desperately that she had stayed in the garden, or even better stayed at home curled up in her room with her books.

She glanced around. The faces of the congregation were listening with rapt concentration, some eyes wide with belief, while others had their heads down in an attitude of prayer, their hands clasped. Ellie closed her eyes; she could use the time to snooze, she figured, catch up on a few precious moments of sleep. Wriggling, she tried to get a little more comfortable on the hard wooden pew.

'Do not listen!' Thundered Matthew, his deep commanding voice cut through the rhythm of Ellie's quiet breathing. Her eyes flew open. The music from the church organ had gathered in intensity, a soft crescendo of deep tones rising with a subtle, pulsing urgency.

Ellie peered over the bowed heads in front. Matthew had stepped down and was standing on the floor facing the congregation, his hands raised above his head, his eyes closed. The music rose.

'It is all in God's plan,' he crooned. 'As it is written, a great Promise to us his divine and most beloved children.'

Matthew's long black robes swayed in time with the building layer of sound. 'Do not fear. In these Final Days of Tribulation, we shall not suffer, we shall rise in body to meet Him, exalted amongst the heavens.'

He paused. 'Do you want to be left behind?'

His question floated above the people like a wisp of smoke.

'No...' answered the congregation in a sigh.

'Do you want to be left behind?' He asked louder, his eyes piercing blue in the subdued light.

'No!' The congregation shouted their denial to the very heavens.

'No, we do not wish to be left behind.' Matthew dropped his voice to a low murmur. 'But... Hear me well. The words of the prophecies are abundantly clear.'

He bowed his head and read from the large leather-bound book flipped open in front of him. *'The first angel sounded his trumpet, and the earth was burned up, and the trees were burned up, and all the green grass was burned up!'*

Matthew closed the book and a sigh rippled though the congregation, swaying when he swayed, and holding still as he raised his eyes.

'It is written. Before we can ascend,' he spoke quietly, 'the earth itself must burn. Before we ascend to Glory, every living tree, every blade of grass, every forest must wither and die. And believe me, it is happening already, all around us.' He smiled. 'Let us pray for it to continue.'

'Do you want to be left behind?' The Reverend Matthew Hopkins cried out the question in a mighty voice.

'NO!' The people cried as the organ music peaked, a great wall of sound reverberating off the unadorned stone walls and thundering to the sky.

Ellie looked around her in alarm. What was he talking about the earth must burn? The organ surged, deep and tremendous, underscoring the praising, praying rapture of the congregation. Behind her an old man jumped to his feet, his thin wavering voice crying out a prayer driven plea, loud and urgent. Across the aisle a swell of parishioners responded, their bubbling chorus rising ever higher through the incessant wave of sound.

Ellie rose to her feet, fighting the urge to cup her hands over her ears to block out the fevered, emotional outpouring. She glanced to her parents. Claire and Brian were praying with their hands high in the air, their normally closed and strained faces shining with hope and adulation. Beside them the twins stood with their eyes squeezed shut and their small hands tightly clasped. Ellie gazed at her family in mute incomprehension then abruptly looked away, her eyes prickling with tears.

As quietly as she could, she crept off her seat and slipped down the aisle as Matthew's voice rose above the melee. 'We will prevail!' He shouted. 'The earth shall be scorched and we will rise, we will prevail!'

'Not me,' whispered Ellie. She reached the door, pulled on the latch and fled out into the sunshine.

The day was still glaringly bright as Ellie slowed to a walk by the family car. How was she going to get home? Leaning against the bonnet, she sprang away with a cry as the overheated metal bit into her skin. Ellie rubbed her leg and gazed morosely down the road.

The stone church stood near the centre of a village a few miles from home. It wasn't that far if you went straight as the crow flies, but on the ground it wasn't that simple. The road followed the scenic route looping and twisting through the mountains, doubling back to ensure clear glimpses of forest. Tourist buses and day-trippers used to clog it, stopping and starting, and leaning out for photos. But that was back when the air was sweet and cool. Ellie sighed; if she walked it could take hours trudging along on the infernal, heat-trapped tarmac.

Above, a gust of wind whipped through a line of broad-leafed trees scattering the last of autumn red to the ground. Beyond them, swaying haphazardly against the sky stood the darker, grey-green of the eucalypts, their silhouettes etched high over the distant houses.

Ellie hesitated. Those far trees marked the beginning of a way home along the cliff top that was quicker and cooler than the hot, looping roads. But... She forced herself to look away.

On the other hand, Ellie turned back slowly, the cliff top trail didn't go exactly *through* the forest. No... It went only around the edge before

58

ending at the park by their house. And if she left now, she'd be home in time to make for the twins and everyone would be happy.

Leaving a scribbled note on the windshield, Ellie headed off, keeping her eyes trained on the far off dancing branches. It'll be fine, she reassured herself. It's the quickest way, and she wasn't disobeying her parents at all, she wasn'y going through the forest, she wasn't going anywhere near it - not technically anyway.

The footpath began just across from the car park, winding its way from the main street and down into the trees. Wide and concreted, it lay cracked and scattered with dead leaves and brittle grasses. Years ago, before the twins were born, this was the way the family had come to church. It had been one of Ellie's favourite walks. Her father in the lead, dressed in his comfortable shoes and favourite shirt, his voice loud, pointing out odd-shaped trees and tiny flitting birds. But that had been before - before the weather changed, and before the Reverend declared everything in the forest was evil.

Rounding the corner, the path dipped into shadow cast by a row of trees, marking the beginning of the track. Ellie bounded up the stone stairs and, stopping at the lookout perched high over the valley, she peered over into the vast tangle of grey and green tumbling into the depths below.

Exhilaration surged through her being. It was so beautiful here. The air felt cooler, flowing gently across the valley, whisper soft, lifting her hair and unfurling delicately around the exposed skin of her neck. Smiling, she stretched up, and leaning her body against the railing, she flung out her arms wide, her fingers caressing the wind. Ellie exalted in the sense of floating, flying, a tiny speck of weightlessness soaring out on the air.

The sun was shining low across the path when she reached a crossroads. To the left, a brace of narrow metal stairs dropped to the valley floor. Beside it, hung a sign, *Fairy Glen walk*. Its weathered face declared it as moderately difficult, though the paint was peeling and the bottom had fallen into the dust.

Ellie sank to her heels. Her head was beginning to ache, and she rubbed the dull painful point just behind her eyes.

Feeling slightly better, she opened her backpack, searching for her water bottle, and finding instead the smooth, holed stone. Closing her eyes, Ellie held its coolness as a balm against her temple.

Scorched earth… Rose's father couldn't have meant what it sounded like, surely?

Easing down against the rocks, Ellie stretched out her legs. It was so peaceful here, protected by rocks and trees. And the stone was so pretty. Ellie stroked her hand over its surface. 'They've gone mad,' she whispered. 'Why would anyone actually want a world without trees, or grasses? How would anything survive?'

Her breath was coming slower now and she leaned closer towards the stone. A pattern shimmered gently from its centre. Moments passed and the air began to quiver with the chip and flit of insects emerging as the day cooled – and still, Ellie sat with her head down, motionless, her eyes soft, gazing deeply into the stone's iridescent centre.

The sun dipped lower, and a shape appeared; its wings stretched wide, and its mass blocked the light of the sun as it passed. At once the insect hum snapped quiet, and Ellie raised her head and stared, blinking, up into the cloudless sky.

A great bird was turning over the trees above, flight feathers fanned, as though sensing for every nuance and ripple of the wind.

Ellie shook her head too quickly, and the world lurched. She gripped the nearest rock. She felt weird, unbalanced, her mind jangling with odd, limping thoughts. Leaning back against the boulder, she tried hard to focus. 'That's no wedge-tailed eagle,' she murmured.

The holed stone was still clasped tightly in her hand, and Ellie stared at it blankly. Her arms felt oddly chilled, and she rubbed them quickly. Just how long had she been sitting here?

Over the path on the other side, the ground rose to a crest of rocks that angled up away from the edge. Their sides were pock-marked and flecked with grey. They appeared almost grandfatherly in the afternoon light, their faces dipped in shadow, and draping beards of dry, trailing moss.

But kind … thought Ellie, studying them, and sort of cool, surrounded by a thicket of fine, needle-tipped trees. *She-oaks,* she smiled, remembering. She'd always loved them; especially when the wind caught in their soft, feathery leaves and they rustled like a whistling song.

Ellie wasn't aware why she rose to her feet, but with the grey-holed stone still tucked into the palm of her hand, she began clambering off the path and up towards the wall of rock. Ellie moved slowly, her eyes dull, breathing deeply as though asleep.

A cloud followed her. Dipping in and out of the shadows, and flicking to silver and dark and back again, a cloud of countless beings flitted over Ellie like a shoal of light.

She climbed higher, mesmerised by the sway of the needle-tipped trees above, unaware of the wisp of faeries shadowing her every step.

61

The first sign was a light pinch. She stopped and rubbed her arm in surprise, gazing up into the branches. Ellie yawned, and a moment later a second prick of pain burst - this time on her scalp, as sharp and as unwelcome as a wasp sting.

She jolted awake.

Above her head, strands of her red-gold hair were rushing up towards into the trees. It was hard to see what was carrying them - the sun had dropped and was flaring brightly through the needle-tipped leaves. Ellie rubbed her head. Around her, the slender she-oaks were draped in the golden hue of sunset.

As Ellie stared in confusion, light erupted from one of the branches, so bright it dazzled her eyes. As she watched, it melded into another and then twisting into a blaze, it rose higher, streaming away through the trees.

Transfixed, Ellie struggled to piece together what was happening. Then she flung the smooth grey stone to the ground in horror.

Fire.

Desperately she ran back, into the brush searching for a way down, but the trees grew so close, and the rocks angled so sharply they hemmed her, refusing to let her pass. She dropped to her knees and tried to see a way over the edge to the path. Panicked and crying with fear, she scrambled forward, cutting her hands.

Stop! The voice was dry and cracked with age, yet its imperative tone brooked no foolishness.

Ellie froze.

A woman with grey-streaked hair, and a loop of dark feathers around her neck, stood before Ellie. Her hooded eyes were watching the bursts of brightness with great intensity.

'These beings of great beauty and power are not what you fear,' she said.

'What are you talking about?'

'They like to come out in the setting sun. It's their time.'

Behind the old woman, Ellie glimpsed a hint of a track, edging away down through the rocks.

'Listen to me. There is no fire and it is unwise to flee mindlessly into the forest.'

'What do you mean? I know exactly how to get home.'

The old woman stepped a pace forward, blocking any access of escape, and peered down at the ground.

'That's a powerful toy for one so young.' She gestured to the stone. It lay where Ellie had tossed it, wedged within a fracture of a large weathered rock. 'But you must be careful-'

'It's not mine.' Ellie cut in. 'I just found it.'

The old woman said nothing, gazing at Ellie with intense eyes so light a brown, so bright, that they shone gold in the dimming light beneath the trees.

'You do not treat an object of power like that. You need to treat it with respect.'

Ellie stared at her. 'If it's so powerful, here you take it... Just let me go.'

'But it's yours, child,' said the old woman firmly.

'Please... I need to get home.'

Ellie sunk to her knees, overwhelmed by a sudden, frightening thought that she was lost and alone in the forest with a mad woman.

Twigs splintered and she heard the sound of footsteps against rock. 'Get away!' she cried, wildly, clenching her fist. She'd never hit anyone in her life, except her brother Ben and he was much bigger so it didn't count … Ellie tensed. But she was nowhere near, the old woman was squatting down with her hand outstretched towards the wedged stone.

'Do not be so afraid, child. You have a valiant heart, and this tool of being and magic has chosen you for a reason. It is a great honour.'

'Now, get up,' the old woman commanded. 'It is a hag stone. With it you can journey to the very world of spirit itself. But don't be stupid. Do not sit and merely gaze into it, without direction. It is not a toy. It has the power to take you far out of yourself until you are lost on the very edges of being.'

'What are you talking about?' cried Ellie, and she gripped the strap of her bag tight, feeling as though it was her only link with the outside world.

Overhead, the flaring lights had ceased and beneath the darkening sky, she could see nests silhouetted beneath the branches - dozens of them, strange and multi-faceted, strung low from the slender trees. A breath of wind and each one spun slowly, trailing long threads of silk. In the two closest to her, strands fluttered, flashing red and gold.

'What's happening?' A breeze whipped across her skin followed by a shrill click of movement. Ellie squeezed her eyes shut. Yet as she breathed, Ellie felt a quiet flicker of excitement. She didn't open her eyes straight away, and she peered at the old woman through her half-closed lashes.

The sun had set, and a soft blue light had descended over the trees. The old woman settled herself down on a rock, with her feet balanced on a lower one, with the trunk of a tree for support.

'Child, there is much you want to know,' she said softly. 'The questions burn so bright within your heart you fear they will consume you.

Ellie didn't answer.

The old woman smiled. 'Yes, child, be silent. And know it is all within you.'

Minutes passed.

What? Ellie's shoulders slumped. Is that all? She opened her eyes as a sudden spur of anger made her raise her voice. 'What are you talking about?' she snapped. 'My God, I shouldn't even be here. Tell me!' she was shouting now. 'What is going on? I'm listening.'

'Good. That's a start.' The old woman gestured to the ground beside her and once more closed her eyes. 'Sit. And Listen.'

Ellie hugged herself in agony. She had to go home and yet... A sigh brushed delicately across her skin, like mist, emanating from the string of nests turning in the shadows. She shivered; it was all so tantalisingly strange.

The air was warm and still, and the pinching things that had earlier gone for her hair seemed to have disappeared. Ellie glanced at the old woman, hoping for a bit more guidance, but she was facing away from her, breathing softly with her hooded eyes turned towards the darkened trees.

'It'll just be for a moment,' Ellie murmured, leaning herself back against a rock.

Around her the she-oaks grew so tall and slender they seemed to shoot straight into the sky above. Ellie could see where their roots buckled, boring deeply through the mix of rock and soil. *They probably ran for miles,* she thought, the roots, all tangled and spread out with all the others like an upside down forest, bigger maybe than the one on top of the earth.

Startled Ellie's eyes flew open. What a crazy idea.

It took a few breaths for her vision to focus properly, but as clear as day, she saw a tiny being floating in the air before her eyes, dark-eyed, with fine features under a mop of sticky-out hair. Ellie blinked in astonishment. It hovered only inches away, held aloft by horizontal wings flashing light and dark as they whirred.

Ellie didn't move an inch, anxious that if she did so the tiny faery might vanish. Yet… it remained, watching Ellie with a gaze huge and round in its face. After the longest moment, it stretched out a delicate, twig-like hand.

At first Ellie didn't understand. She stared at it for a long while and then it dawned on her. Almost afraid to breathe, Ellie carefully reached up her hand, and, wincing a little, pulled out a few strands of hair and handed them over.

Clasping its prize to its chest, the little faery flared with light, then immediately flicked high, and disappeared inside one of the multifaceted hanging nests.

'You did that very well.'

Ellie turned; she had completely forgotten the old woman, breathing on the rock by her side.

'You're very lucky,' the old woman continued, her golden eyes glowing softly. 'Not everyone has the sight to see them.'

Ellie wasn't listening; overwhelmed by the close encounter, she closed her eyes. *Did it even happen?* As she wondered, a low roll of thunder echoed and a scurry of leaves dropped to the ground.

'You must go.'

'What?' Ellie was startled. 'Oh God, yes. It's so late, my parents are going to kill me.'

The old woman's voice was firm. 'Listen carefully. Use the hag stone. Hold it in your hand and let a picture of your home rise in your mind. Don't force it, simply imagine and let it call you back. Now go.'

Without another glance at Ellie, the old woman rose to her feet. Shaking out her hair, she straightened her spine and stood with her head tilted upwards. Breathing in, she closed her eyes and raised her arms towards the sky.

At first nothing happened and the woman stood with her black cloak lifting in the breeze. Her mouth was moving, but Ellie couldn't make out what she was saying. Then she heard a strange and uncomfortable sound, a low rending noise, like the groan of wood under great pressure. Alarmed, Ellie took her eyes from the old woman and stared up at the surrounding trees. The she-oaks were shuddering; the rough barked trunks and narrow branches were shaking, creaking, as though the whole stand of trees was responding to a great singular force.

Ellie gasped. 'Wait!'

But at that moment, a fierce gust whipped away her cry and an enormous bird leapt up into the sky.

SEVEN

Mrs Beatty's hat was veiled, prim, and quite delicate, the pink confection quivering like a small, fearful animal on her hair of coiled grey. Standing on the threshold of the church, the Reverend Matthew Hopkins nodded, his voice reassuringly calm, despite the impatience hurtling through his blood. 'Yes, you will both be included. Have faith, the tribulation to come is not for you, nor your husband, nor is it for your family. You will all ascend to heaven, whole in body, as has been foretold.'

Mrs Beatty had his hand tightly clasped in her own.

Framed in stark contrast to the delicacy of his elderly parishioner's headwear, a dark bank of cloud was billowing across the evening sky. Thunder rumbled, closer now, and Matthew allowed himself an imperceptible, deeper breath, for riding hard on this ferocious, western wind came the unmistakeable stench of ozone.

Lightning was near.

Beside her, Mrs Beatty's husband patted his wife's shoulder and the couple turned to go, their relief evident as they made their way slowly down the stairs. Matthew beheld their slow congress across the garden as the sky flashed red with heat, and a flare of dirty, sulphurous yellow. They passed beneath the stone arch and disappeared into the night.

Hurrying, Matthew gathered up the folds of his robes and strode through the empty church, his footsteps echoing across the flagstones. Pushing open the door of his private chambers, he stopped. The sun had fallen from the sky. Darkness had settled, but he decided against switching on the light, all the better to witness the almighty storm gathering in the heavens.

Those dark, lightning riven clouds…

Through the high arched windows, crossed with panes of coloured glass, the gigantic cloud massing overhead promised not life-giving rain, but wind, destruction, chaos.

'Sweep away our sins,' Matthew whispered, clenching his hands into a fist. 'Redeem us, my Lord.'

He grimaced suddenly and whirled around. Footsteps, he could hear them tapping a light, bright rhythm through the nave of the empty church. Wood scraped against wood and a squeal of high-pitched laughter erupted as she slumped down on one of the empty pews. His daughter. Matthew heard her feet, echoing off the back of the seat in front and by her excited, careless tone he guessed she was speaking on her cell phone to Ellie. Matthew frowned, listening hard; he didn't feel entirely comfortable with that friendship…

Shaking his head, he tossed the thought aside. At this particular moment the only thing that mattered was this storm. But… Matthew's eyes narrowed as he heard the pew scrape and footsteps tap quickly across the floor; perhaps it was time to show his wayward daughter the truth.

The handle turned and without waiting for permission to enter, Rose barged in and stood before him with her hands on her hips, her dark hair falling down her back. She tossed back her head, laughter shining in her eyes. 'You wouldn't believe who I've been speaking to?' She asked, her tone was mocking. Rose danced around the small room and seated herself on the corner of his desk, her slight frame blocking his view of the window.

'Rosalind.' Her father gestured curtly, indicating his desire for her to move. The window above rattled and shook, a hundred years of stained glass straining in the rising wind. She was so like her mother.

Rose ignored him. 'How do you do it Daddy? She says she might actually have met a witch in the forest,' she stated in a teasing voice. 'And some kind of little flying thing. Ellie's getting as crazy as you.'

Matthew wasn't listening. Jumping to his feet without a word, he pushed past his daughter and stood with his face tilted toward the window. A great section of cloud had separated from the rest, and through the delicate lead frame he could see its dark, almost purple form whipping across the sky.

'Daddy? Dad! Listen to me,' cried Rose, her voice rising in indignation. She grabbed his arm. 'Do you really believe all that stuff about spirits, demons, whatever? You just say it to scare everyone, don't you? And it works!' She laughed shrilly as a whip of lightning flared across her face. Matthew waited, counting the seconds silently in his mind, as the sharp crack of thunder echoed through the stone church. This storm was stronger even than the ones before, and building faster. Ignoring Rose's shriek of protest, he grabbed her hard by the hand. 'Come child!'

Around him, light snapped blue, sparking in the super charged atmosphere of the approaching fury.

'Dad!' cried Rose, pulling vainly on her hand. 'What are you doing!'

But Matthew merely gripped tighter and dragged his daughter out of the chamber and down along the centre aisle of the church. Outside he could hear a sharp crash as a metal bin toppled, tumbling wantonly in the wind.

'Dad!' yelled Rose, digging in her heels and tugging furiously against his grip.

Matthew spun his daughter around to face him. 'Be quiet.' He commanded. 'Stand with me, my child. Praise the Lord and his Holy Ways, for it is beginning. The Darkness is dimming and soon the promise will be fulfilled and we shall Rise up in Full Glory to meet him.'

Lightning flashed.

'It is beginning!'

Strengthening the grasp on his daughter's hand, Matthew kicked open the thick wooden doors of the church and pulled her out into the night, his eyes wide with joy and his arms raised to the sky.

'Come storm!' he cried. 'Come!'

Around him his clerical robes buffeted and swirled, while high above fragments of branches, rocks and debris tore through the sky.

'Oh God, Dad stop it! I want to go inside!'

'Rosalind!' cried Matthew, his voice shaking with conviction. 'Look around you. Open your eyes. Stand and witness! All I say shall come to pass! These are not ordinary storms. They are colossal battles between all the forces of the earth. Good and Evil. Spirits, Demons, against the All That Is. Look around you! And know, the One Truth that will save us.'

71

'No!' Rose tugged, struggling to free her hand. 'It's not a battle; it's a storm, Dad, just another stupid storm!'

'Do not be a fool, and do not fill your ears with silly tales from your silly, ignorant friends.'

Matthew's body jerked as his eyes tracked a point high above the storm. 'Look!' he shouted, his voice trembling with emotion. 'They seek to stop us. They seek to stop the storms, but understand, my daughter, these storms are what we need.'

High above the church, the fury broke and thunder rolled, deafening them both, shaking the windows and slamming the branches of distant trees to the ground.

Rose stared at him, black hair whipping around her face, terror warring with her habitual stance of mockery. But she smacked it away as fury rose in her eyes.

'You're mad,' she shouted. 'It's just a storm! You can try and frighten *them* with your crazy tales. But *I* don't believe you and I never will!' With a fierce cry she freed her hand from her father's iron grip.

Matthew lunged, grasping for her shoulder.

'Get away from me!' she cried and turned to run back into the shelter of the church.

'Evil stalks the earth,' shouted Matthew. 'Harpies, winged devils, and they seek to stop storms such as this!'

He raced after Rose, catching her; he gripped his daughter's arm tight. 'You cannot tell me that is normal.'

Rose stared up at her father's impassioned face, then her eyes widened as she followed his line of sight. An enormous creature was labouring through the clouds, its great wings beating, its body dark. It rose heavily, spiralling upward on massive surges of wild air until it soared at last, high above the squalling storm.

'That *thing* has been haunting me all of my days, since I was a defenceless child.' Matthew shuddered as thunder rumbled long across the valley. 'The embodiment of evil, but she shall not win.' Possessively, he drew his daughter closer to his heaving chest. 'We will ride these storms, you and I. They will scorch the earth, leave it bare and desolate. And then, *we* will ascend pure in form to Heaven. And we shall be free, Rosalind, we shall triumph over her and all of her kind.'

Abruptly the wind changed, knifing in from a myriad of directions, and above them the great bird lost height, plummeting towards the ground. Rose covered her eyes as with a heart-stopping cry, the creature vanished beneath the storm.

'*Yes,*' Matthew nodded grimly, and through the heavy fabric of his robes, pressed his hand hard against the figurine hanging from a chain around his neck. It bit into his skin, a constant reminder of his torment. 'You shall not win,' he said softly, 'and all I have suffered, all the years I have been alone, crawling on this earth amid the dust and filth, will be avenged.'

EIGHT

Southern England 1340

The cart creaked sharply as it rumbled past, its back loaded with a half dozen squawking crates. Twitching the reins, the farmer urged the pony on. Though summer was near, the air was brisk, with the last breath of winter still seeking to chill exposed flesh.

Trudging along the dusty, well-travelled road, the boy grimaced. Eleven years old, his roughly cut black hair fell over light-blue eyes that were normally bright with laughter, but not today. Ahead of him, a pair of traders stood yelling for the other to give way, their heavily loaded carts blocking any progress over the crowded gate bridge. All at once, they stepped back as a pair of black-robed monks appeared, their pates bobbing bare in the morning sun, and without a discernable word or gesture glided unhindered into the town.

A crow streaked overhead, its cries harsh as it joined its companions over the highest point on the walls. Below them hung the ragged remains of a single unfortunate soul, a stark warning to any person foolish or unlucky enough to be caught trespassing on the Lord's lands.

Tey shuddered and dropped his gaze, concentrating on each footfall. *Do not be seen in the forest.* It was the first, and most important rule, and one his mother never let him forget. He increased his pace. Behind him the whirl of beings that had been following all morning dropped to a halt. A pond-green fellow, tubby and warty with a rather bulbous nose, stuck out his tongue and disappeared with a sulky pop, only to reappear with a trailing shower of slimy leaves. With a sudden chortle, the boy ducked as a handful of pond scum sailed over his head and landed behind with a splat. Attempting to appear stern, he folded his arms and addressed the now seemingly empty air.

'Stop that. She said I wasn't to be long, and I can't be.' He glanced at a clump of low growing trees. 'You can stay here if you like.'

A small brown figure with striped skin and hair the colour of moss weed appeared and gave a soft sigh. It hugged Tey's leg tight.

'Don't worry,' Tey murmured, gently prising off her cool, damp arms. 'I'll be right back. You'll see. This will be easy.'

Putting on a wide smile, he lifted his chin.

'Remember Tey, do not be distracted. Do not stop. Talk to no one.' His mother's golden eyes had locked onto his with a fierce intensity. 'Find the spice seller. And hurry.' She'd hissed as she left him alone at the crossroads.

Tey took a deep breath. How he had longed to follow her back into the woods. *I can do this*, he steeled himself, reaching for the strip of leather tied around his neck. A figure hung from it, reassuringly heavy and close to his heart. *I have to…*

Squaring his shoulders, Tey passed under the shadow of the gatehouse and was swept along with the crowd into the town's main thoroughfare. The street underfoot was rutted and treacherous, thick with dry mud and heaving with the throng of people and livestock. A cart jostled him, a dog barked, and a large, flint-eyed man shoved past, swinging a heavy hessian sack close to his head. Tey gave a startled yelp and ducked, almost falling onto the road, but he recovered. He darted away to safety beneath the awning of a small wooden workshop, where he stood shaking. A pale-haired apprentice, about his own age, was sweeping the floor inside.

Panic soon forgotten, the boy from the forest peered into the work area and was rewarded by a glimpse of the potter tossing a portion of clay onto the workbench. Next to him, a stout woman stopped to examine strings of finely sculpted flowers, some no bigger than tiny forget-me-nots, displayed on a small table just inside the door. He leaned in closer for a better look.

'Hey!' The voice was shrill. It cut through the quiet, along with a stone that sliced sharply through the air. 'Clear out, thief!'

Another rock whizzed past, flicking into Tey's cheek. 'I'm just catching my breath!' protested Tey, rubbing his face.

'Well catch it somewhere else, thief.' The pale-haired boy rushed towards him and pushed Tey hard. He tumbled to the ground.

'I'm not a…' he began, but that was as far as he got as a pair of strong hands hauled him upright and Tey recoiled. A crowd was gathering, some were laughing and mocking, others appraised him with narrowed eyes.

The town boy, sensing Tey's hesitation, delivered a sharp blow to his stomach with a ferocious cry. Tey collapsed onto the road, winded and gasping for breath. The young victor stood for a moment with his fist still clenched, then he sauntered back into the shop and resumed sweeping, keeping his gaze fixed on his vanquished foe.

With the show over, the onlookers melted away as Tey slowly pulled himself to his feet. I hate towns, he thought miserably, gazing at the indifferent market day crowd. How would he ever find the spice seller when he couldn't even make it down the street? *I'm useless. I can't do it.* Tey began to cry softly, his early bravado evaporating in a cloud of hopelessness.

At once, a wet belch popped in the air above and a soft sloppy kiss was planted onto his cheek. Through his tears, Tey stared as a protruding pair of twinkling muck green eyes appeared, perched atop a grinning bright red mouth. Next, with his whole body undulating, his best friend in the world eased himself proudly through an invisible hole high above the oblivious townspeople.

'W-what are you doing here?' Tey stammered. Gimbal, the pond-green faery merely grinned, his tubby form pirouetting in graceful circles on the breeze.

A moment later, another pop of an almost fleshy character squeezed into being, and without warning Tey was pushed forward with a rough jerk. Whirling with his fists raised, Tey was about to hit back hard but then stopped. This was no bully defending his patch of turf but another grinning faery, about waist high, splotched all over with yellow and black markings. Strands of reed and the odd bit of rotten food hung off its long tufted ears.

Abruptly this little being shoved him harder.

'What-?' Tey exclaimed, but he didn't get a chance to finish as suddenly Gimbal grabbed him by the hand and pulled with all his might. At the same time, the muddy little fellow behind pushed again and Tey shot forward, lurching a few steps down the road. Gimbal hooted in triumph.

Chortling wickedly, the two faeries pushed and pulled him through the crowded streets. Working in unison they propelled him faster and faster along the road, jerking his arms and legs until his whole body was bobbing and bowing like a demented sort of puppet.

'Stop!' Tey cried, ducking his head away from awnings and throwing his body from side to side to avoid the traffic.

'Look out!' Contorting himself, Tey just missed crashing into a ruddy-faced woman crossing the street with a duckling line of small children. All he could see as he swept past was her mouth, a perfect 'o' of outrage gaping in the flashy folds of her face.

Twisting, he tugged hard at his hand. 'Slow down!'

But it was no use. Giggling with delight, the faeries jerked and shoved him around a crowded corner, dodging a thick-armed man lugging baskets of fish, and heaving him into the writhing chaos of the market square.

'Stop!' yelled Tey again, but the grinning faery ploughed on through the market until, with a final shove, Tey was catapulted out through the other side.

Shrieking with laughter, the two beings jammed their feet down and skidded to an ungainly stop on the cobbled road beneath the Lord's castle.

Tey collapsed on the ground in exhaustion, gasping for breath, when the sharp clattering of hooves on the cobbled road caused him to look up. A black warhorse, with its coat gleaming and eyes fierce under the high glare of the sun, had suddenly emerged out of nowhere. Tey had no time react; he could only stare, horrified as the great beast bore towards him.

At once, the rider pulled his mount under control with a deft jerk - the folds of his red and gold mantle billowing out behind, and the horse halted just inches from where Tey lay cowered underneath.

The knight raised his gloved hand. He was young, with sun-bright hair and proud, grey eyes.

What an honour, Tey thought as he rose to his feet. He blushed with an awed smile and began to raise his hand in thanks, but was suddenly pushed violently from behind by the little splotchy faery. He stumbled and Gimbal jerked him forward. 'Stop that!' Tey shrieked.

The knight's eyes widened in astonishment - seeing not Tey and his forest friends, but a scruffy, young urchin having a strange sort of fit. Quickly crossing himself, he kicked his warhorse and whirled away up towards the castle gates.

Shaking in humiliation, Tey jammed his heels savagely into the road, stopping his momentum with a jerk. The little splotchy fellow, oblivious to his mood, pushed him again with a grin. Gimbal tugged at his hand to continue.

'I said stop!' Tey shouted with all the force he could muster. He pulled back his hand. The splotchy one wilted, its muddy, damp skin seemed to dry to dust under Tey's scorching gaze. 'Why did you do that?' he raged. He glared at the shrinking faery. 'Why are you here anyway?'

The small one hung its head and its eyes stared dejectedly at the ground. It began to fade until only its yellow and green splotches were visible, then with a subdued pop, they too disappeared.

Tey stamped his foot in frustration, fuming over the missed opportunity to greet a real knight.

Suddenly, Gimbal pinched him and then kicked him hard in the shins.

'Ow,' Tey cried. 'Why can't you just leave me alone,' he snapped, rubbing his leg. He glared at the faery until Gimbal the green disappeared with a disdainful pop.

Silence.

A brown bird flitted overhead and Tey watched it pass, his fist clenched, ready for a retaliatory missile or warty slap. A voice of a passerby shouted above the loud clop of a horse's passing hooves, but that was all.

After a long moment standing alone on the cobbled road, Tey's heart began to flutter in alarm.

A squelchy pop quivered above and Tey grinned in relief. Of course his friend wouldn't abandon him. The boy opened his arms in welcome, smiling broadly, but Gimbal merely glared. Hanging high against the stark blue of the sky, his eyes narrowed from their customary bulge, and his bulbous nose began to shrink as his face, though still a pond deep green colour, shifted into a perfect replica of Tey's mother's.

This was one of Gimbal's favourite tricks. He wore her thick, long hair, her elegant cheekbones, and most alarmingly, her fierce, golden eyes. Even though he knew she wasn't really here, Tey shrank away, feeling as he always did - very young and very, very wrong.

'I-I-I'm on my way now…' he stammered to her proud, unrelenting beauty. 'I just forgot, for only a minute.' Too fearful to go on, he dropped his gaze to his feet. The air quivered and Tey looked up to see his friend's beloved fat face bobbing above him once more.

'Oh, I'm so sorry for being such an idiot,' he cried. Rushing to give Gimbal a hug, Tey stumbled as his arms swept through the air. He recovered his footing to see a long, red tongue sticking out, hanging motionless, before that too was gone, leaving only the cool wind whistling in its empty place.

Tey smiled widely, sure his friend was only playing a trick. A sodden belch erupted just behind his ear and he turned with a delighted grin. But it was only a plump old farmer, tankard in hand, waddling towards the nearest tavern.

A series of bells began to peal, marking the noon day hour. In the square below, the bulk of the crowd had long cleared and only a tardy few remained, hurrying over the last pick of the day.

Tey waited, his blue eyes scanning above, yet despite his silent entreaties, the air above the cobbled hill remained stubbornly empty. Clenching his fists, he berated himself for being such a pig-headed fool. Why couldn't he have just let the faeries lead him how they wished?

The boy peered out over the narrow maze of streets, trying to remember the way. Jammed in tight, the roads knotted and crossed over four main thoroughfares, twisting towards the high stonewalls that enclosed them all. The spice seller lived somewhere down in all that confusion. Hidden in a room, in an alley so narrow the sun couldn't show his face. Frowning, Tey tried to think what else his mother had said? And what did that mean anyway? *The sun couldn't show his face?* Tey's lower lip quivered and his eyes stung with tears. He quickly wiped them away and stood staring forlornly over the rooftops. He couldn't fail; his father needed him. Without the spice he would die.

NINE

The high stone towers of the castle dominated the skyline, their banners fluttering red and gold in the breeze.

What had she said? Tey scowled as he approached it, trying desperately to recall his mother's final directions. Did she say something about the spice seller's home being in the alley by the castle, or the alley being in the shadow of the castle?

Coming from behind the castle walls, he could hear the tantalizing, curious sound of scuffling curses and the echoing ring of steel on steel. He bent down low to peer in through a narrow gap.

In a courtyard, several pairs of boys were lunging with all their strength, short swords flaring in the sun with their small forms protected by leather breastplates. On the far side, a figure astride a grey muscular mount wrenched his horse around and with a defiant yell galloped hard towards a wooden dummy spinning in the centre of the practice ground. Forgetting his woes, Tey watched with delight until his attention was drawn to the jingle of metal, and clatter of hooves on the cobblestones behind him.

He turned to see a golden-haired rider seated astride a shadow black horse cantering out of the castle gates, followed by two companions. The rider's cloak was plain without the embroidery or rich colours of his rank, but Tey would know that proud face anywhere.

On impulse, the young boy ran after him through the streets. He didn't know exactly why he was following the knight, but the noble was the only thing Tey recognised in all the noisy confusion of the town. Besides, if the golden-haired knight knew where *he* was going, maybe he'd lead him closer to the spice seller.

Tey didn't think about it much further as a small man, his face pitted and scarred, staggered into his path. Dodging him with a sharp cry, he ran on just as his quarry rounded a corner and disappeared.

Panting for breath, Tey skidded to a halt. This street was lighter and cleaner than most. Up ahead the knight was dismounting from his horse and entering the door of a small stone chapel. The sun glared over the empty street as the warhorse, snorting and pulling on its bridle, was pulled away by the two companions. They passed Tey standing alone on the cobblestones without a glance.

For a long while he stared at the chapel door, until at last he trudged away, angrily brushing away his tears. *Useless.* The word thudded, over and over. *Useless.*

The sky darkened as Tey turned down a thin, mud-rutted alley crammed with wooden, rickety hovels, smelling like rot and sewerage. The air was thick with smoke rising from cook fires burning out in the open, tended by thin, hungry-eyed children. Overhead, through a gap in the wood, he caught a final glimpse of the sun before it dipped low behind the central turret of the castle, cloaking all around in shadow.

Where was he? Tey shook his head, trying to clear it to think, but it was hard; his mind felt clogged by the cloying reek in the air.

Cupping his nose with his hand, Tey took a few short breaths then froze as a lighter, dusky scent lifted on the breeze, like a thread floating, soft as silk. He closed his eyes and concentrated. The scent was deceptive and hard to hold, but it seemed oddly familiar.

Breathing carefully, he slowly licked his lips.

With a half smile, Tey slowly opened his eyes; afraid to believe he could be right. This sharp and pungent scent was a strange mix of smoky-hot and sweet, laced through with something he had smelled once before.

Tey smiled, *last night*. It was last night, in the dregs of a leather pouch. 'Take careful notice, my son,' his mother had said, opening it by the warm embers of the fire. She'd held the pouch for a long moment under his nose. 'This is what will keep your father alive.'

Reaching for his lucky amulet, Tey walked slowly through the shadows, his senses pinprick sharp. A dozen smaller laneways branched off through the gloom, but he ignored them all, his heart beating with excitement as the air thickened with the redolent scent of the spice. He quickened his pace, feeling his way carefully down an ever-narrowing maze of pressed mud and loose hanging thatch. It was impossible to see as the alleys were becoming darker. At last he stopped, bathed completely in shadow, his way forward blocked by a high bare wall.

The castle towered directly above, dark and massive against the distant blue of the sky. Tey took a slow tremulous breath, his senses prickling, fearful he had lost the scent. But no, it was emanating strong and clear from behind a small door buried deep within the gloom.

He hesitated, looking around for somewhere to knock, when he noticed sitting in the corner, as still as a rock and with its eyes closed tight, a large hairy creature. It was as tall as Tey's chest with long pointed ears, and a rather alarming mouth spiked with white teeth.

The creature's eyes opened one after the other and swiveled upwards, each orb blazing a hot sulfurous yellow. Without warning, it released a breathy shriek that punctured the air, reverberating on and on through the narrow confined space. Yelping, Tey covered his ears with both hands. The wooden door swung open immediately, and a crinkled old woman, taller than the creature but not as tall as the young boy, glared at him with deep, almost polished, black eyes. Tey shrunk back into the alley.

'Did you call, boy?' she asked querulously.

'No, I mean yes,' he stammered.

She raised her eyebrows.

'I mean, I would've, I wanted to, but your, your…' Tey gestured lamely at the creature.

'You can see him, can you?' The old woman leant closer, her large hooked nose sniffing deeply across his chest.

Tey stepped back in revulsion, his hand automatically reaching for the eagle amulet.

'What is that?' She pecked forward, her eyes gleaming with curiosity. But as her long fingers clutched at the figurine, the old woman jumped back, shaking her hand vigorously as though it had been bitten.

'Ah… sun metal,' she whispered. 'But why would one so young as you, carry such a thing?' She tilted her head back with a frown and gazed up at

85

him, her eyes cool and speculative. 'Come inside, boy,' she croaked, 'and tell me why you are here.'

She made a quick gesture with her hand and the hairy doorkeeper stepped back into the corner and closed its eyes, dark red fur disappearing into the texture and grain of the shadowed door.

Inside, a subdued light cast a halo of warmth over the bare walls and earth pressed floor. With a slow shuffling gait, the old woman led Tey to a straw pallet lying in the centre of the room in front of the hearth. Tey sank down exhausted, aware only of his aching legs and empty belly. Pushing his hair out of his eyes, he gazed around the room, wondering if there was anything at all to eat or drink.

Above him the old woman stood hunched and stooped, her black eyes glinting as she appraised his every move. 'You would like to eat and drink, eh boy?' she asked. 'How about a nice light poppy cake, or a jug of pomegranate juice?'

Tey's heart leapt. Oh what he would give for a jug of cool sweet pomegranate juice. He was so hungry; he hadn't drunk or eaten anything since the honey cake at dawn.

The tiny old woman smiled, clapped her hands three times and waited, gazing at him steadily. Tey, too nervous to look away, sat mesmerised with her large eyes unblinking in the half-light of the fire. Moments passed. When nothing happened the old woman shrugged her narrow shoulders. 'It seems I'll have to get it myself,' she muttered and shuffled away to a bench hidden by the fireplace. Without speaking, she picked up an empty plate and earthenware jug and slowly carried them back to where he was sitting.

'Here,' she said.

Tey glanced at the plate in disappointment. Taking the jug from her hand, he peered warily into its depths, but the light was so poor and the jug so dark he could see nothing at the bottom. Frowning, he tipped the jug back and took a tentative sip. His eyes flew open. Nothing. The jug was as empty as the air.

The old woman crowed with laughter. 'You should know better than that! The air is never empty. It is as full as you wish it to be. You especially know that!'

Tey stared at her in alarm. This mad old woman knew his mind!

'You think I'm mad, do you?' She snapped, her head abruptly still, cocked to the side. The fire dulled as she waited for an answer, her narrow body poised as if to strike.

Terrified, Tey shrank back against the straw, his eyes darting to the red wooden door behind her. The spice seller snorted back a chuckle, before pushing back a strand of grey-streaked hair, the fierce glow in her eyes gentling.

'Look child,' she said, her voice hard to hear above the panicked thudding of his heart. 'You don't have to have magical powers to be powerful. Power is often nothing more than taking the care to see.' She looked at him closely. 'Remember that when you need to.'

Hobbling over to the table by the fire, she shuffled back clutching a plain wooden cup.

'Here,' she said, 'you should find this more to your taste.'

With a suspicious frown, Tey took the cup and held it to his nose, wondering what trick the old woman was playing now. He breathed in as an unexpected sweet smell of honey, mixed with something deeper and sharper, filled his senses. The boy took a wary sip, and then another and another, until the cup had completely drained. Tey glanced up in wonder. The delicious drink seemed to both ease his thirst and slacken the exhaustion that gripped his muscles.

The spice seller eased herself down onto the edge of the pallet with a creaking sigh. Taking the cup out of the boy's hand, she placed it on the floor then pointed a thin bony finger. 'Just what is that hanging there?' Her eyes glinted in the glow of the fire.

Tey's hand flew to his neck. The old woman scared him as she sat motionless, studying him, her grey-streaked hair pushed behind the black hood of a cloak; her shoulders hunched; and her fragile hands clasped together tightly. Behind her, the fire danced patient shadows on the wall.

His hand shook as he untied the leather thong and handed the eagle amulet over without taking his eyes off her face. 'My mother said you would know her if I showed you this.' Tey whispered at last.

The old woman giggled a strange high-pitched sound that scratched uncomfortably at the edge of his hearing.

'Ha,' she crooned softly, 'you don't burn me now.' The golden figure lay in her palm, burnished in the light of the fire. Fashioned out of pure gold, it was small and perfectly made, a winged female form, each feather outstretched for flight above fierce extended talons.

'Ah,' the spice seller sighed, as though she'd been holding her breath for a long time. 'This is what's known in my country as a soul flyer.' Her deep black eyes were filled with reverence. 'In the land of heat and endless sands, these talismans are very rare and precious.' She stroked it once more, slowly shaking her head. 'They fly souls to the underworld and sometimes,' she whispered, 'very rarely, they are in the possession of those whose very being vies with the Gods themselves for immortality.'

Without warning, the old woman locked onto Tey's gaze, her eyes a deep bottomless black. The dark, airless room seemed to spin, stringing swirls of light and a low moaning wind, a breathless song...

There was a roar as the fire flared high in the grate and the old woman released her scrutiny. 'Tell me, boy.' She had somehow moved and was standing closer to the hearth, her gaze trained on the warm embers of the fire.

'Is your mother still fierce and proud? Is she still with the falconer, your father?' She turned towards Tey. 'Such a good-looking man.'

Tey felt light-headed and slightly sick, but he didn't want to seem a total dim-witted fool. 'Yes, of course,' he declared with more confidence than he felt. 'But ... my father hasn't been well. Please,' he took a deep breath, 'that's why my mother sent me. She said he will die without your spices.'

The old woman whooped and cackled with laughter, the sound beating off the walls and deadening the fire until it diminished into a single spluttering glow.

'Oh she did, did she?' She grinned gap-toothed at him. 'Of course he'll die. We all die, even you, my boy, though it seems a long way off to one so young.' She paused and looked down at the golden eagle, balancing its weight in her palm. 'It's only a matter of when.'

Tey flinched as she turned quickly and held out the amulet.

'Give your mother a message, boy.' The spice seller said sternly. 'Tell her to come herself next time. There are too few of us left who know the old Gods and Goddesses. They will fade away if not given the proper reverence. Especially from one such as she.'

Tey looked down at his hands. 'My father was too sick to be left,' he said softly.

The old woman frowned, then without another word she turned and shuffled back through the room, pausing at the hearth to light a rough tallow candle. Tey heard her soft groan as she bent low, her knees cricking in the silence, and heaved open a chest.

Spice swirled, rising pungent and scarlet above the spluttering, animal stink of the candle. Tey craned his head to get a better look, but he was too far away. He crept across the room quietly to stand at the shoulder of the old woman, holding his ground should she try and send him away. But the spice seller merely nodded.

In the fluttering light, the chest appeared ancient and stained with use, its golden-hued wood smooth from the oil of many hands. The lid was inlaid with a creamy white shell, carved with the markings of creatures in flight, while inside the chest were many tightly-bound pouches.

Muttering to herself, the old woman quickly pulled out each one and placed it on the floor beside her, until all that was left was dust of mustard yellow, burnt orange, and a dark congealed red. She then raised the empty shelf to reveal further pouches secreted away on the bottom of the chest, licking her lips.

The spice seller selected one and peered at it for a long time. Her long nose twitched as she sniffed it carefully. Tey found the scent overwhelming and his head was swimming from the ever thickening cloud surrounding him; but still the old woman hadn't found what she was searching for. She examined each pouch, closely sticking her nose in, tasting and weighing it in her hand, before placing it on the table with a frown.

When at last it seemed to Tey as though there were no more spice pouches; no more small shelves; the chest empty of all its treasure; the spice seller reached her bony arm into the depths and pulled out a worn leather pouch secreted in the furthest corner of the box. She put her nose to it and, with a look akin to worship, took a slow deep breath and closed her eyes as if in prayer.

Tey shuffled his feet. Will she ever hurry up? At this rate he wouldn't get back home to the forest before dark. With an impatient sigh, he pulled his gaze away, drifting over the empty plate and around the quiet flickering room. He stopped in surprise; the room was as still and dark as ever but nestled in between the shadows he could see a pair of small, bold-eyed beings. One yawned and looked away as though unconcerned, while the other seeing him watching, dived into the fire, its serpentine body flaring amongst the flames. Tey grinned, and without thinking lifted his hand in greeting. The being emerged from the fire and gazed at him, its face glowing in response.

'They come to you, do they, the hidden ones?' The spice seller's voice was curious. 'That talent is not so valued by you Eagle people. I wonder what your mother makes of you?'

Tey said nothing, but the old woman was watching him closely as though waiting for an answer.

'She thinks I'm nothing, just a silly dreamer.' He said at last and then looked away, his throat caught by the familiar, searing hurt.

'Ha, she would, wouldn't she? She spends so much time up in the clouds herself that she doesn't care for the talents of others. Pride, that's what will get her in the end if she doesn't learn her lessons.'

The spice seller handed Tey a single small pouch tied securely with a leather thong. 'Here, take what you came for. But I wouldn't take it myself.' She cackled loudly, her eyes shining in a face lined and spotted with age. 'Endless life, what a curse that would be, just imagine.'

She stared at the young boy sombrely. 'Tell your mother, she can try and cheat Death, but she will never succeed. Death will be ever watchful, biting His nails, biding His time, just waiting to take what is rightfully His. And when He does, you can be sure it won't be pleasant.'

The spice seller sniffed and chewed her protruding lower lip thoughtfully, then slapped Tey hard on his shoulder with her bony hand.

'And don't forget to remind her of her duties! Just because she's fooling around with her young lover in the forest, the Gods and Goddesses must be served!'

Abruptly, Tey found himself pushed out of the house and back into the alley outside.

The sun was low by the time Tey reached the crossroads on the edge of the forest. His body shook with exhaustion, but nothing could dampen his soaring spirits. He had done it. The precious spice was safely tucked under his tunic, and amazingly he'd made it back before dark without mishap.

The long valley stretched out before him, lit with a glowing, burnished bronze and bordered by densely wooded hills. In the distance on the surrounding strips of freshly ploughed fields, Tey could make out a team of oxen plodding along the rutted road toward a farmhouse, through a low curl of smoke obscuring the far off walls of the town.

His belly gave a loud rumble. Back home his mother would be preparing the evening meal around the fire, stirring the pot full of thick stew flavoured with herbs from the forest. He smiled, imagining her crying out in happiness as he returned bearing the leather pouch filled with spice.

A loud, squelching pop rudely interrupted his daydream and a shower of leaves fell with a splodge onto his head, and ran oozing down his cheek. Tey wheeled around in search of the culprit. Another splat landed with an insolent slop on his legs. It was like a signal, as all at once a hail of forest debris and lumps of mud flew at him from all directions. He dodged and dived but it was no use; within moments Tey was covered top to toe in smelly muck.

'All right, stop!' He dropped to his knees, flinging his hands up in surrender. Above his head, the last bundle of sodden leaves wavered for a moment before drooping and falling to the ground.

Tey grinned, 'I'm sorry for being such an idiot!' The air quivered, seeming all at once full of wide-open ears.

Without warning, Tey jumped to his feet and lunged for the wet pile of leaves, throwing them hard at a spot that seemed particularly thick. There was a satisfying splat and Gimbal materialised, dripping goo from the top of his bald head to the end of his large bulbous nose, and his wide grin showed that all was forgiven.

Tey felt a shiver of cold as a pair of thin stick-like arms wrapped themselves around his legs. A small faery had crept closer and stood hugging them tightly, its huge eyes closed. Grabbing the little being with both hands, Tey reeled it high in the air and it shrieked, its nutbrown face shining with glee. Faster and faster, Tey and the little faery whirled, careening off the crossroads and into the wide shadowy forest. The world spun, a wild blur of sun-glinting land, swirling green, and spindly legs.

Tey let out a peel of laughter. The air rushed past, clean and cold, scattered with leaves and twigs whipped up by their wild spinning dance. Flapping his long feet hard against the ground, Gimbal joined them, whirling Tey and the little faery even faster, around and around under the trees.

High above in the canopy, faces gazed out from behind spindly branches. Leaf-like forms peering, captivated by the spontaneous laughter rippling through the forest. Further into the shadows, deep within the trees themselves, the eyes of ancient wizened beings watched.

After a moment, using their elongated twig-like fingers, they carefully pushed back the rough bark to reveal bodies as brown and as textured as the wood itself. Satisfied all was safe, the huge oak faeries prised themselves free in angular, creaking movements and ran in great jerks to the dance.

All at once, the leaf folk released their grip.

Delicate and pale green, with hair as fine as a spider web and fine dots patterning their skin, they abandoned themselves to the spinning, dancing updrafts.

And others came.

Rising up from the earth and tumbling down from the hills, emerged great beings of rock and pebbles, as different as the myriad of stones they inhabited. The very air seemed to shake with each mighty footfall, and they all responded - some joining the wild chaotic dance; others standing quietly with their great faces raised in homage to the glow in the west.

For it was sunset, the very edge of the day when beings of magic and spirit met to farewell the fading energy of the light.

It was the time when, at home, Tey would rush to finish his chores before hurrying deep into the forest, following the song of the birds as they roosted in the trees. As the birds rested, the faeries gathered either quiet and still, or swooping and wheeling in the air.

TEN

Galloping alongside the forest on his way back to the town, the rider cursed the infernal setting of the sun. What a fool he was. He bellowed his frustration out loud to the sky, but the sound was lost behind him in the swirling dust of the road. With his rich brown travelling cloak and golden hair flowing behind, the knight urged his great horse on faster, muttering a quick and heartfelt prayer. It would take a miracle to make it back to safety before the town gates were shut for the night.

He grimaced and dug in his spurs; his warhorse lunged forward its neck slick with sweat, its breath laboured, but the rider showed no mercy. This was not the kind of land one would wish to spend the night, no matter how strong the mount or well sharpened the blade. He'd heard enough tales warning of the demons and ghouls that haunted the forest, stealing souls and driving strong men mad.

The crossroad between the town and the forest lay some way ahead; if he narrowed his eyes he could just about make out the marking in the distance. Clenching his knees, the knight leant across the horse's muscular neck, whispering words of encouragement. They must pass this place before the sun dipped below the horizon. All Christian folk knew that crossroads at sunset were no place for God-fearing folk.

Ulrick cursed himself again for being such a fool. Dazzled by hearsay, he had ridden to the secluded hills searching for an old hermit. This holy man was rumoured to be so pure of spirit that he had been blessed with visitations from the very angels themselves. But to see him, his old tutor had said, that very afternoon, one had to be pure and worthy of God's grace.

He had failed. After hours of searching he had found no sign of habitation, no secluded chapel or even an abandoned wooden hovel. He had found nothing but empty trees and a sighing wind. What a fool.

By the time the knight reached the crossroads, the sun had vanished beneath the horizon and darkness bit at his heels. Ulrick wavered, then pulled the horse to a stop. Surely just a moment's rest, even here would do no harm.

Reaching for his water flagon, he unstopped it and took a long, slow swallow before closing his eyes. A small bird twittered as it flew overhead towards the trees, and he could hear the great forest sighing in the cooling wind. Ulrick patted his horse's shoulder. It was steaming hot and slick with sweat; they had to stop, even if only to let his mount ease its trembling. Ulrick felt a chill run up his back and he shivered. The wind was rising with no light remaining to warm it.

Gathering his cloak, he gazed upwards while the horse grazed; the greying sky was riven with wisps of gold and orange cloud arcing across the heavens. All was quiet save for the rhythmic munching of his steed.

Suddenly Ulrick blinked and jerked up in his saddle, as there on the breeze a strange tone was rising and falling in the silent air. The knight whipped around, his skin prickling, but the rock-strewn road behind was empty, shimmering pale in the shadowy light. An owl hooted, and after a moment a dark shape flew low across the road. Ulrick laughed out loud. 'You're getting soft from spending too much time in the town, jumping at the sounds of the hunting night,' he muttered to himself in disgust.

A sigh and the air beside him stirred. His horse quivered and lifted its head, pricking its ears forward. Rising from the darkness of the forest ahead came a soft sweet music, its harmonies intertwined with the low sighing of the wind. The tune was simple, a lilting, calling phrase soft with longing, the last note hanging before it was whipped away by the breeze. The young knight held his breath and waited, gazing across at the great dark trees.

A trick, he wondered ... it could be a trick, sent perhaps by the Hound of Darkness – the Devil himself, determined to lure *him*, a newly sanctified Knight of the Cross, off the safety of the road. Ulrick sat taller in the saddle, listening intently as the wind picked up and ruffled the soft fabric of his cloak. The music came again, fainter this time but heartbreakingly sweet.

Ulrick hesitated, his heart torn, but the desire to follow overwhelmed his senses and drowned out any half-remembered warnings. He stared mutely, his eyes tracing the narrow line of the forest path. Perhaps the holy man was *here*, bringing the gift of the Creator's light into the endless darkness of the forest.

'But if it *is* the work of the Evil One', he whispered, gripping his sword as valour rose in his veins, 'I will not shy away. I will rid my father's land of its malignancy and bring honour to my house.'

With his mouth set tight and grey eyes hard, the young knight kicked his heels and the horse responded with a defiant snort, charging away from the crossroad and into the trees.

Great gnarled trunks soared overhead, huge and cloaked in shadow. Ulrick slowed the horse to a walk, its hooves muffled by the thick layer of leaves covering stretches of the rocky road. The air was calmer here, protected from the cold wind gusting outside by the surrounding trees. Through them and louder now, lilting through the stillness, Ulrick could hear a series of rippling notes so pure and sweet, he felt as though his very heart would weep. He urged his horse on as the road ahead slipped through the trees and disappeared around a sharp bend.

Muttering a quick prayer, the knight cantered into a stand of bushes, their sharp thorns snatching at the wool of his cloak. Pulling his up mount, Ulrick saw a sight so astounding that his heart leapt. In a small clearing under the vast dark trees, a figure stood, small, his arms outstretched, his face bathed in light and glory. Surrounding him was the most wondrous of miracles.

Angels, they must be angels, countless shining angels of all sizes - from the smallest blessed with luminous, transparent wings, to towering seraphs. They encircled the clearing, moving and swaying or standing in complete stillness in silent homage.

In the centre, the figure brought a small wooden instrument to his lips. The smallest angels grasped hands as a breath of expectation quivered through the gathering, and a lilting poem of praise rose up quietly through the trees. Gradually it built in strength, drawing power until the clear notes soared above the circle. A beauty without peer, eclipsed only by the shining majesty of the angels sweeping up on the sound into the heavens.

With a cry, Ulrick slid off his horse and sank to his knees on the forest floor. It was the hermit - the hermit he'd searched for these last hours. Never before had he heard music so blessed, nor witnessed a man so holy. The radiance from the angels bathed the old hermit's face in light. His eyes were closed and, like a miracle, his skin was smooth, fair and entirely without blemish.

Reverently, Ulrick inched himself forward, desiring only to be closer to this beloved of the Divine. As he crept across the undergrowth, the figure breathed out unadorned series of notes. Low and sweet, they undulated around the surrounding trees and floated away into the darkness. Ulrick stopped, his breath caught in wonder. He leant forward, his gaze intent, but his expression soon turned to horror as his knee slipped on a mossy branch and he fell, snapping the wood with a crack that reverberated throughout the forest.

In an instant the angels vanished, leaving empty branches and scattered leaves fluttering mutely to the ground.

The music trilled then stopped. *Where did everybody go?* Tey gazed about him in incomprehension. The air fell thin and empty, with not a blur of movement or the company of teasing devilish grins. There was a sudden crunch of leaves and he turned as an agonised moan rose out from beneath the underbrush. Tey recoiled in fright as a stranger rose awkwardly to his knees, his head down and long golden hair obscuring his face.

'Please, please, forgive me, my Lord,' he wept. 'I am a fool, such a fool. I had no idea - my foot slipped...'

He fell silent, hanging his head lower as his shoulders slumped. Tey stared, wondering who he was. The man's cloak was dark and smeared with mud and leaves, so it told him nothing, but he had a horse that stood tall and unafraid under the trees. The boy's heart began to pound. The animal was huge and dark, and what he could see of its saddle was well worked and too fine to be that of an ordinary traveller caught after dark in the forest.

The man spoke again, his voice subdued and trembling, though its well-rounded accent rang clear enough in the stillness of the night. 'My Lord,' he repeated with his head still low, 'please forgive my intrusion, I beg of you, I only seek your blessing.'

A twig snapped as Tey backed further away and fear rose to his throat, almost making him gag. What was one of the highborn doing in the forest and at this hour, he almost moaned out loud. What should he do? The boy whirled around to the trees. *I could just slip away*, he thought. Even if this stranger was hurt, he spoke far too well for safety. He could one of the highborn, or even worse, he could be in their employ.

At the sharp sound of a snapped twig, Ulrick swallowed his fear and glanced up, fully expecting to see the wrathful face of the old hermit. Instead he beheld the frightened face of a young boy, simply dressed in a grey tunic belted over saggy leggings. The knight jumped to his feet at once, as the humiliation of being seen prostrate by a mere child surged through his veins. 'Where is the holy man?' He demanded, his voice abruptly harsh and unforgiving.

Tey's legs buckled at the sudden change in the stranger's demeanour. Mute with fright, he stared up at the great towering stature of the golden-haired man.

'I demand you answer me, where is he?' Ulrick strode towards him with his fist raised in a clench, his earlier shame and remorse discarded.

'What holy man?' cried Tey.

'Don't lie to me,' Ulrick growled, grabbing the boy's narrow shoulder. He shook him hard. 'The holy man, here, communing with angels, where is he?'

Gasping in pain, Tey struggled hopelessly in the man's iron grip. 'I don't know what you mean,' he cried, through a sudden blur of tears. 'There's no one, only me.'

Ulrick glared in silence, his hold never slackening. Tey moaned, his gaze never leaving the man's vengeful face surrounded by a halo of golden hair. The boy's heart thudded; he knew that face anywhere. Horrified. He struggled hard against the young knight's rock hard grip, but he was too late.

Ulrick's eyes widened, 'I know you,' he cried. 'You are the idiot boy by the market.' He paused, his voice tightening with suspicion. 'What are you doing here on my Lord father's lands?'

Tey struggled, but the knight gripped his shoulder harshly. 'What is going on? First you accost me in the town. Then I find you here in the forest, where no one, other that than those my father permits, are to tread.'

Looking desperately down at his feet, Tey wondered what he could say that would satisfy the furious noble. 'I-I-I was just resting,' he stammered at last, 'playing my flute.'

The grey eyes above him hardened in contempt. 'Don't lie to me. How could one such as you play music such as that?'

Tey stared mutely up at the harsh, angry face. Silence filled the clearing, broken only by the sound of the tallest branches above knocking in the wind. The boy gulped, his heart pounding in terror. Slowly he lifted his rough wooden pipe and, without taking his eyes off the knight, placed it slowly to his lips.

With as much care as he could, Tey breathed out a simple series of notes. They were quiet and so delicate that the air itself seemed to wait, then closing his eyes the young boy poured out his fear and longing into a single melody. The harmony rose and fell echoing through the forest before dying away in a heartbreak of loneliness.

The boy stopped playing and dropped his head as tears welled and dripped one by one down his nose.

The grip on his shoulder loosened, and Tey heard a loud strangled cry and a sudden thud on the ground. His eyes flew open, and through his tears he could see the knight had dropped to his knees on the forest floor.

'It is you!' he gasped, his eyes shining. 'You are the holy one.' Ulrick dropped his head and tore at his cloak with his hands. 'Oh forgive me,' he cried, beating his chest. 'I am such a fool.'

But Tey, not waiting for another chance, and not knowing why the knight was now on his knees crying like a madman, dropped his flute into his pocket and fled without a backward glance into the safety of the forest.

Wiping tears from his eyes, Ulrick stared in reverence after the small retreating figure. *What a miracle,* he thought, his heart bursting with pride. And he, Ulrick, the lesser son of a minor Lord had witnessed it.

The knight struggled to his feet, his body trembling with joy and amazement. Who would have believed such a miracle had occurred on this day? What folly it was to seek after an old hermit when a Holy Child, blessed by the Creator himself, lived deep within the bounds of his father's land.

'Yes, a miracle,' he whispered out loud. Ulrick crossed himself and lifted his face to the heavens, offering up a prayer of thanksgiving. Tomorrow he would tell his father, the abbot, and all the nobles of the town about this boy who dwelled in the forest, communing with the very angels.

ELEVEN

Blue Mountains, Australia, present day

The sky was as black as sin. A thin remnant of dust dulled the streetlights below and smothered the stars above. In the distance, over the sweeping depths of the valley, an edge of brightness shimmered faintly on the horizon, the new moon rising without fanfare through the darkness, its edge weak.

Inside no one turned to look. The night was warm, hugging the grand stone house close. The curtains were drawn and windows shut tight. Inside the smallest of the rooms on the top floor beneath the eaves, a fire burned in the wrought iron grate, and a lone shadow moved.

Grimly, Matthew loosened the rope cincture around his waist. He slipped off the darker, outer cassock, revealing the simple white tunic beneath, which he slipped over his head and laid neatly on the bed. The undergarment was heavy and coarse, reaching down over his torso and fitting tightly over the top of his bare legs.

As he moved, the hair shirt rubbed his skin raw - the thistle-like texture catching on the delicate area of his underarms and over his ribs. Matthew swallowed, welcoming the stinging pain as a friend, a faithful companion. He had been wearing it long enough to feel its rough hand, but not so long as to be inured to the discomfort. A few weeks of the year, that was enough, for a true penitent's flesh must remain soft - soft enough to flinch at the garment's bite.

Against the wall, thrown by the single wax candle on the bureau, his shadow rose, oversized and angular, following the line of the room's sloping roof. The Reverend Matthew Hopkins reached for the thick gold chain coiled on the top of the opened desk. A figure swung from his hand, finely made, about an inch high, a female face atop feathered wings stretched wide.

Matthew studied the necklace, his finger hovering over its winged form, as though poised to touch. The amulet glowed, lit by the flickering flame, staring up with ancient calm eyes as though it saw everything, and judged nothing. He stroked its head as the shadows of the outstretched wings, thrown on the wall above, reached for the window as though merely waiting for the word to fly free.

Through the glass he could see clouds stretching out across the valley, great flourishes of them, streaming as the storm moved on across the valley. Matthew watched with his eyes narrowed; from this vantage point he could see deep into the forest itself.

Bowing his head, he listened intently making sure all was well in the house before he began his night-time ritual of prayer and mortification. The tool of flagellation waited patiently, hidden in a nook under the eaves. But still Matthew waited.

His daughter's room was directly below and he could hear her moving quietly. Other nights, and at other times, she would be singing as she readied herself for sleep. But now her voice was silent, and her footsteps were slow and careful. All that sounded through the stone house was the scrape of her cupboard door and an occasional light cough.

Rose, wearing a simple pair of grey gym pants and a light t-shirt, studied the neatly folded dress with a critical eye before adding it to the growing pile by her bed. She stifled a yawn. Her chest ached and a dull queasiness sat in the pit of her stomach, but she pushed the discomfort away.

Rose reached for another item of clothing - a light top, festooned with delicate flowers and laced in silk. Holding it up, she draped it against her body and turned to the full-length mirror now pushed to one side of the bed. Her face was pale with her hair pulled up into a demure bun, and her eyes were wary.

Rose cocked her head. In the reflection she didn't look too bad, she thought leaning forward, interesting maybe, and a little tortured. Pouting her lips a little, she turned back and laid the top out on the bed, ensuring that the sleeves lined up, and the embroidered tassels were each of the exact same length.

Rose didn't want to go to bed and she didn't want to think. But the image wouldn't relent. A creature battling the storm, a *thing, straight out of a nightmare*… She closed her eyes. *Why did he show it?* Rose shook her head, anger battling with the horror of what she'd seen. Moving carefully, she placed the top on the pile of casuals before reaching for a pair of black cotton pants. She sighed; these were hopeless - a consequence of being strewn across the floor with everything else.

Rose glanced up, briefly wondering if she could be bothered to head downstairs to the kitchen and find an iron. But no, she didn't want to see her father, or leave the safe confines of her room. Snapping the fabric to ease the worst of the wrinkles, she set about folding the black trousers, keeping the seams straight and smoothing the rest out with her hand.

As Rose bent to her task, she winced and reached up to rub the line of muscle and tendons running across her shoulders. They ached, every morning when she woke, her shoulders, and the muscles running down her back and up along with her arms, ached, as though she'd been lifting weights in the gym, over and over.

She shook her head. The taffeta dress didn't really need folding; it would be better to find a hanger and place it with the others in her cupboard. She thought for a moment but then reached for it, and carefully began folding the intricately pleated fabric.

From deep within the house, the hall clock began to chime. The full sound resonating up through the wood panelled rooms. Rose waited. Ten... eleven... She counted them out by habit.

The last chime was swallowed by a series of sharp, hard knocks.

She stared at her bedroom door. 'What?' she answered at last, and her voice bristled with irritation.

After a pause, it swung open, revealing her father dressed in a simple black dressing gown. His feet were bare and pale against the wooden flooring, and dangling from his hand was a fine chain with a simple golden crucifix.

At the threshold, Matthew hesitated. His daughter's dark hair was pulled off her face, and behind her the bed was hidden beneath piles of neatly folded clothes. *Like her mother*, he thought. She looked so young, and so beautiful.

'Rosalind,' he cleared his throat, 'why are you still awake at this hour?'

Rose didn't reply. She glared at him.

For a moment neither of them spoke and Matthew could feel the heat of her eyes as they slid past him and stared pointedly back out into the hallway. Her meaning was clear. Go away.

Matthew held up his gift. 'I thought you might find this of comfort.' His words were careful. 'I saw your light was on, and thought, perhaps, you may be having trouble sleeping.'

Rose hesitated; her anger at seeing him was softened by his feeble attempt at a peace offering. Sighing, she stepped towards the door and, turning around, allowed her father to place the chain around her neck. In the mirror, she could see how the gold of the little cross glinted across her skin as it caught the light.

It *was* pretty, she would give him that, but what fat lot of good would it do to help her sleep?

'Dad,' she turned, her eyes downcast, and her voice was just a whisper. 'Do you have any pills or anything?'

'Are you sick?' Matthew felt a snap of alarm.

'No,' Rose murmured, hiding a small yawn with her hand. 'It's nothing really.' Her tone was quiet and she stood in an uncertain pose with her hands clasped together like a child's. 'It's just that you're right...'

Her hands shook.

'If you don't have anything, it's okay.' She turned away. 'But you know.... Can you help me, Dad?'

Suddenly Rose laughed, a strangled, uncomfortable sound. Her father was actually right... she wasn't sleeping...

'It's so weird,' she spoke softly more to herself, disregarding her father's proffered hand. 'I'm having dreams.' She laughed again but the sound was tight, laced with suppressed hysteria. 'It's ridiculous, but I don't know what's going on. I'm dreaming and I don't know where I am. I look down and my body is weird, like really wierd… and I hate it. I'm rushing through the night sky. And you know how I hate heights!'

Her laughter was harsh and grating.

'It's just a dream', murmured Matthew, unsure if she would let him touch her.

'I have them every night...' her voice trailed away.

His daughter seemed so young, so fragile.

'They can't hurt you.' Matthew whispered, fiercely. 'Dreams are nothing. They're not real, nothing can hurt you.'

Yet even as Matthew spoke, the lie of his words rose bitterly in his throat. Dreams had power, he knew, and some never let go. Once in, they could reach, twist, and consume one's very soul…

'Oh,' sobbed Rose as he gathered her into his arms. 'I'm just so scared.' She leant into him, shaking like a lost child.

Matthew hugged her tighter. *She's so tiny*, he thought. Her bones under his embrace felt so slight and fragile.

'Don't.' She cried, and she pushed him away. 'Please… be careful. My shoulders really hurt.' She stretched out her narrow arms and shook them gently, almost like a bird cooling its flight worn feathers.

Matthew froze, as a click of warning became a deadening thud.

'They feel really pathetic.'

Suddenly she tossed her head back and laughed, the sound bouncing painfully off the walls. Stretching out her arms again, she shook them fiercely not once but two, three times, laughing louder each time before raising them high above her head to the ceiling.

'Enough,' commanded Matthew.

Rose stopped at once, and stood posing with her hands outstretched, her fingers long and tapered. She regarded her father with a hard smile, her eyes older now, no longer a child's bright tawny brown; now they seemed more knowing, and riven with a glowing, fierce gold.

'No', he whispered, 'we still have time. She's just a child...'

Abruptly Rose blinked and yawning widely she lowered her arms. 'Ah Daddy,' she whispered, 'please, do you have anything to help me sleep? I'm just so, so, very tired.'

TWELVE

The air felt soft and warm rushing over Ellie's cheeks and hands as she freewheeled down the long winding back road into town. Gripping the handlebars, she leaned low, urging her bike on faster as the few squat houses secluded amongst the trees reduced to a mere blur. She grinned, breathing in the smoky, delicious scent of evening barbeques curled over a sharp hint of menthol.

Ellie half closed her eyes; the smell of the trees was always stronger in the late afternoon, bursts of scent, hanging in fat airy clouds. She had no idea why. Maybe it was the trees' last long exhalation before they settled in for the night - like a yawn or something, released slowly into the sky.

Tightening her grip, Ellie dared herself to ride blind down the long hill. Breaking, the bike slowed and she sat up straighter in the saddle, feeling every bump and loose pebble scudding beneath the wheel.

'Hello!' Ellie shouted out loud and laughed again in exultation, as she sensed a cluster of small pointy faces laughing with her from within the blurred passing trees.

'I'm talking to the trees!'

Grinning, Ellie pedalled faster, while the streetlights arced on as she passed, throwing a bright orange glow over the road ahead.

Moments later, Ellie arrived at Rose's house, out of breath and with her heart pounding from the exertion of riding up the last tortuous hill. Jumping off, she lugged her bike up the last few steps of the gravel driveway, the white pebbling scrunching under the weight of the tires. Ignoring the front door - there was no point as Rose never answered it anyway, Ellie pushed round to the iron gate at the back.

'Hey,' she yelled, breathlessly. 'I'm here!'

Ellie lifted open the latch and awkwardly shoved her bike through into the back garden.

At first Ellie didn't take too much notice of the quiet, she was too intent on propping her bike up against the side wall and wrangling with the buckle of her helmet. Gritting her teeth, she fought to unlatch the idiotic clasp, sure her friend would be flinging open the back door in welcome at any moment.

The grand stone residence loomed dark against the grey of the early evening sky. It appeared empty. Not a single glow of light shone from the arched windows and every curtain was drawn tightly shut against the gathering night.

Ellie hesitated, and then knocked on the door. *Come on, hurry.* She shuffled her feet impatiently as a long chiming reply echoed from within the house - the standing clock in the hallway marking the afternoon hour.

Ellie glanced back at her bike dropped against the gate. She loved that old thing, but its paint was chipped and scratched, and the stuffing in the saddle was coming out through the stitching.

'Hey you.'

113

The voice rasped like sand against stone.

Ellie whirled. Rose stood against the edge of the open door. In the dimness of the hallway, her face appeared pale and her normally shiny hair hung dishevelled and twisted down her back.

For a moment she could only stare. 'Rose,' Ellie blurted out at last. 'Are you okay?'

Her friend shrugged a curious, wincing movement. 'Yeah, of course I am. Don't have a fit.' Disregarding Ellie's outstretched hand, she stepped back from the entrance and with a theatrical bow, gestured for Ellie to enter.

But Ellie didn't move. She hadn't seen Rose for a couple of weeks, but her friend seemed smaller somehow, as though her normal, bright vitality had been diminished, turned down from its normal searing flame.

'Are you coming in or what?' Rose smiled, and a hint of light returned to her eyes. 'God, you're always so slow.'

Relieved, Ellie smiled back; perhaps she'd only imagined it? 'Is your dad here?' she asked as she stepped into the wide panelled emptiness of the hallway. She hoped he wasn't.

Rose shrugged and without waiting for Ellie to reply she turned and hurried through the formal living area, heading for the hardwood staircase curving up to the second floor. Ellie followed along behind. The shrug could mean anything; no, her father was out, or yes, he was in. Or more likely that Rose couldn't care less. Ellie knew better than to ask again. Rose and her father had a curious relationship, they lived in separate worlds, on separate floors, each one both placating and protecting the other.

The door to the bedroom was already open, and low sultry music streamed from a music system hidden under a pile of discarded clothes.

114

Imperiously, Rose directed Ellie to the stand directly in front of the mirror.

'Have I got a dress for you!' She declared, sashaying over to the pile. With a teasing grin, Rose lifted up a long gown draped on top of the pile. Rich forest green, it was layered with silk and featured two delicate shoestring straps.

Ellie stared, dumbfounded. 'But we're just going to the movies.' She blurted out at last. 'I'm okay in just these,' she gestured at her jeans. They were her favourite, dark blue, almost black, and she'd added a silky silver blouse borrowed from her mother.

'Oh…' Rose smiled one of her deep, most effective smiles showing both her dimples. 'I forgot to say that Ben's coming too.' She added, taking the dress and waltzing with it around the room with the length of the fabric flowing behind.

'What?'

'Oh don't be like that, it's a Friday night,' Rose pouted, dropping the garment in a heap to the floor. 'And I've been feeling so tired and crappy I thought it would be fun, and when Ben phoned, asking me out, I thought of you first.

Ellie looked away, disappointment colouring her cheeks. *But I've got so much to tell you!* She wanted to shout. And besides, she especially didn't want to hang in the background while her best mate canoodled in the back row with her older brother.

Rose took her hand. 'Come on, Ellie, please, we can both dress up and look beautiful.'

All too aware of Rose's powers of persuasion, Ellie closed her eyes and said nothing. A waft of a movement and a moment later her friend's fine-boned hand clasped her own.

'Open your eyes,' Rose whispered, her voice quivering with excitement. 'See what else I've got to show you.'

A loop of something cold and heavy dropped into her hand. At first Ellie thought it was just another show off bit of jewellery, then her heart skipped a beat as an unexpected longing began to course through her blood, doubling her heart rate, calling to every nerve and fibre. Opening her eyes, Ellie gasped out aloud.

Glowing softly, a golden rope lay coiled in the palm of her hand. From the centre hung a heavy intricately fashioned charm, an eagle body with fine outstretched wings topped by the carefully crafted head of a woman. It quivered in her hand as though alive.

Ellie stared, words dying away in her throat. The air around her felt heavy and hot, and around the necklace sharp halos of light crackled like short bursts of static.

'Where did you get this?' Ellie's voice was dry and strained. She looked up at her friend. Rose only smiled, her eyes glittering with pride and excitement.

Ellie's heart thudded in shock. 'My God,' she croaked. 'This has got to be worth a million dollars, at least. Where did you get this?'

She stopped speaking. Ellie was finding it hard to breathe and around her the room was wavering, the edges of the mirror and chair and even Rose were undulating, rippling almost. She felt very weird, as though some kind of power was rising, gaining strength from the glowing figurine.

'Rose, answer me.' She said, shaking her head and trying to maintain a sense of equilibrium. 'Where did you get it?'

'Oh it's nothing,' she said lightly. I just found it.' Rose looked away but not before Ellie caught a brief spasm of guilt.

'Where?'

'Oh, Ellie stop grilling me it doesn't matter.' Rose grabbed the necklace from Ellie's hand. 'It's mine.' She declared as she held the figurine tightly, the chain looping out from her grip spiralling freely into the air and waving like the coils of a segmented serpent.

'I found it a few days ago when I was feeling really crappy.' Rose's voice was tight and defensive, and Ellie could just make out the rushed jumble of words. 'I was up in Dad's room, feeling weird, looking for a headache pill or something, and I just found myself you know, just wandering around looking. Remember his old bureau? That old ancient thing he keeps still in the corner?'

Ellie did know it. It was like something from a storybook, all polished wood inlaid with ivory and onyx tiles. They'd been caught once when they were young, Ellie couldn't remember the exact age, but she could still remember that guilty feeling of excitement as they opened every one of the tiny secret drawers and doors. Like an intricate puzzle, each hidden drawer contained smaller further drawers. Some held delicate vials of glass, some held rocks, and others held fragments of claw, skin and feathers.

'No, you didn't...' Ellie whispered, remembering how the curious, shrivelled specimens had frightened them. 'Why?'

'I don't really know,' Rose answered softly, her habitual, teasing manner evaporating. 'I haven't been sleeping, Ellie, and Dad won't get me anything to help. Just drink warm milk,' he says, 'and pray.' But it was so weird, Ellie, it was like I could hear it…'

Rose leant closer, gazing up, her tawny eyes gleaming gold in the light. 'The first few drawers I opened were empty, which was odd; you remember how full of useless junk they used to be?'

Ellie nodded, frowning.

'Well, I noticed a smaller, tinier opening in the middle of one of the bottom ones. It was just big enough to get my little fingernail under it,' she smiled. 'It took ages as though it was on some kind of spring, but then the wood just popped off like a lid.'

Rose looked down at the gold figure in her hand. 'It was like it had been calling me.' She said softly, her voice imbued with a new tone of longing. 'It's mine. I know it. I can feel it. This is why I haven't been able to sleep. It's like it's been calling out to me for weeks and weeks.' As Rose spoke her fingers were gently stroking the small finely wrought figurine. 'It's like it's magic.'

Warning flared, painful and hot, in the pit of Ellie's stomach. 'Put it back,' she said firmly. 'You don't know what it is, and what if you lost it? What if your dad found it was missing?'

'I don't care,' said Rose, placing the necklace against her cheek, she closed her eyes. 'You're always going on about magic, why aren't you excited?'

Ellie didn't know what to say. As she studied the golden figurine, a thought stirred in her mind, but it was so crazy, so unthinkable, she could barely grasp it.

'Rose…' She began slowly, testing the words on her tongue. 'You know the last time we spoke, on the phone; I didn't tell you all of it… That

118

woman, when I saw her in the forest that time, she said to get home all I needed to do was wish on the stone. I didn't really believe it would work but then... somehow I was there, at home, just standing on the front porch, and it was like no time had passed at all...

Rose shrugged. 'Maybe you were just dreaming.'

'No, I wasn't...' Ellie shook her head. 'But Rose, what if magic *is* real, like really real, like things *happen*. That old woman...I've seen her a couple of times, down in the clearing, just sitting like she's meditating or something.'

'You've been back there?'

'Yeah well, I'm just kind of curious,' Ellie shook her head, 'I know it's nuts, but sometimes she's in my dreams, and she changes... You know that eagle we saw –'

'What?' Rose cried out, backing away. 'Stop, I don't want to hear it.' She clutched the necklace to her chest. 'Anyway, why are you always obsessed with the forest? Who cares about it? It's just a bunch of stupid trees, and dead dirt. It's boring. I wish you would just shut up about it for once.'

Ellie stared at her friend. 'I thought you liked going there.'

'Well, there's nowhere else for us to go that's private, and *you* like it. But for God's sake, stop going on about it, you're just giving me the creeps.'

Rose flopped down on her bed, and arranging her feet prettily beneath her, she looked up, her face suddenly serious. 'But, if it *is* real, Ellie, that weird stuff you're seeing, and that awful woman...' She shuddered. 'She's got to be evil, why else would she be just hanging down there.' Rose paused. 'You know, sometimes my dad's right –'

Ellie couldn't believe what she'd just heard.

Rose glared at her. 'Think about it, the things you're seeing in the forest really have to be bad because they're sending you crazy. Flying things? My God!'

'Come off it, Rose, the forest is amazing and you know it, and those tiny faeries are the most beautiful things I have ever seen. I see them all the time now, how can they be evil?'

'Well, what's her name then?' Rose snapped.

'Who?'

'That old woman, the witch?'

'I don't know, I haven't asked her, we don't talk. But not knowing her name doesn't mean she's bad or anything. She's not really a witch. God, now *you're* talking crazy.'

Rose jumped to her feet. 'You don't know anything.' She snapped, pacing around her room. '*We* don't know what's evil or not, it's not like they've got signs on them, like 'ooh I'm bad.' Beautiful things can be wrong too, you know. How does anyone know?' She stopped. 'But, I know my dad. And there's stuff he's right about.'

'Well you should ask him about that necklace,' Ellie snapped.

'Why? It's mine and I want to wear it tonight.'

'Rose, you can't be that stupid!' Ellie shouted.

'Don't call me stupid!' Rose flared and she whirled away to the other side of the room near the bay window, where she crouched to the floor shielding the figurine with her body.

'It's got nothing to do with you. I want to wear it,' she whispered. 'I have to wear it. God, Ellie you don't understand. I bet it was Mum's.'

The room fell silent. Ellie gazed at her friend, lost for words.

Rose held the necklace possessively, closer to her chest. 'Yeah,' she crooned, 'I bet it was Mum's.' She stroked the little figure's head gently. 'It feels like it's a girl thing, like it comes from a long line of girls, like it doesn't want to be with Dad at all.'

'Ellie,' she whispered. 'I don't care about magic or all that rubbish you go on about. This belongs with me and has been waiting for me for a long, long time.'

THIRTEEN

Monday after school, Ellie strode along the narrow forest path, head down and hands shoved deep into the pockets of her jeans, her long hair tied back high off her neck. Abruptly, she scowled and batted away a dry branch that dared block her way. It whipped into the air, scattering dry twigs and dust onto the ground below. Ellie only hurried on, her heart thudding in sync with each footfall.

What the hell was going on? She kicked out at a rock in the path. And what was up with Rose?

The thought wrenched her to a sudden stop. Ellie glared at a small quartz riven stone that lay wedged in the dirt at her feet.

My God… Ellie exhaled sharply in frustration.

The pebble was kind of pretty, in a small white sort of way, and ordinary.

Her foot twitched, eager for the signal to give it a hard, satisfying whack.

Above her the sun glared hot and unrepentant through brittle, grey-green leaves. The trees hung mute, their branches swathed in ribbons of dry bark so low they trailed down along the ground.

Ellie hesitated then gritted her teeth and turned away. It wouldn't have helped anyway, not now. Not when everything and everyone around her was going completely nuts. She hurried on once more through the trees, heading back to the clearing. She sped, almost running further down into the valley, the heat following close like a wraith, pressing in on her bare skin from all sides - thirsty, hungry, and desperate for any lost drop of moisture. Ellie tried to ignore it but her throat hurt, and the air itself was so dry that each intake of breath was like sucking up a straw of old stale dust.

'It just needs a wash,' she muttered hoarsely to herself. 'It's almost winter … please, a little bit of rain, that's all anyone needs.'

When the path at last reached the edge of the fern gully and the base of the stairs, Ellie dropped her backpack and sank to the bottom step, her legs shaking.

Leaning back, she reached into her pack. The water bottle was easy to find, and quickly Ellie gulped down a few mouthfuls before pouring the rest of the contents onto the base of the nearest fern.

'At least that'll help a little,' Ellie muttered as she dropped the now empty bottle into her bag and jumped to her feet.

Ignoring the path, Ellie slipped under a low branch, her footsteps crunching as she clambered over a heap of dry bracken. Overhead, the high glare of the sky began to dim as furls of cloud began to reach out across the valley. Ellie frowned; from here she could just make out the grove of pale trees, their white branches in stark contrast to the deep red of the cliffs beyond.

She hurried on, they were so close and Ellie didn't intend to take the slow way to the clearing, bogged down by the convoluted twists of the path. She wanted to get there, and she wanted to get there now.

It was impossible. After squeezing past the last picnic table, and stepping over the dry creek bed, Ellie stood staring up at a wall of rock, high and impenetrable and made of the smoothest grey granite. Incredulously, Ellie ran her hand along the speckled face.

It was quite pretty, she supposed, the rock dark flecked with silver specks. She pressed her hand against its surface. 'Let me in!' She muttered. 'Let me *in!*' she cried again louder this time and, frustrated, she slapped it hard with her hand.

Nothing happened. The barrier jutted high against the sky. Faceted and sharp, the rock face angled away, as though she didn't matter, as though she was too small, too insignificant, too young to be attended to by a being as ancient and as immoveable as this. Leaf shadow danced over the stone, light interplaying with the heaviness of rock. The wall held a silence that had faced down the challenge of the eons.

But Ellie was sure she'd never seen it before.

'How can I be lost?' she wondered, 'I'm *not* lost, I've just come a different way.' Ellie suppressed the urge to kick at the wall with her foot. She slid down its face to the ground. Behind her, the sun-warmed rock cradled her back. She closed her eyes, reaching for her drink bottle. It was empty, of course. With a sigh, Ellie opened her eyes and noticed the edge of the hag stone peeking out from the top of her bag.

She pulled it out. 'I want to talk to her,' she whispered, holding it close against her cheek. It felt like an egg, she thought suddenly, a warm smooth egg, and oddly comforting. 'Please', she whispered, 'take me to her.'

She waited staring into it, willing herself into the clearing. But nothing happened, no light, no weird pulsing, nothing.

Disappointed, Ellie dropped the hag stone back into her bag. Then not knowing what else to do she reached up under her scarf and, wincing, pulled out a couple of strands.

At least I can leave these somewhere, she thought morosely. The afternoon won't have been completely wasted.

Pulling herself to her feet, Ellie trudged back along the length of the wall holding the strands of red and gold aloft. They trailed softly from her fingers, long and light like spider silk. After a few minutes, Ellie stopped. 'This is stupid.' She muttered, dropping the strands on the ground.

'You can have them, okay!' She shouted up into the wall, cursing herself for getting lost. 'But I'm not lost.' She said out loud. 'This thing shouldn't be *here*.'

Turning, she stopped, staring in disbelief. Straight ahead right before her eyes lay the narrow, twisting forest path and just beyond it, she could see a small gap exposed in the wall.

'Oh that's too weird, I just came from there before. I know I did.'

With a shake of her head, Ellie squeezed herself into the grove of towering ghost white trees.

'Hey!' She called, a moment later, bursting into the clearing.

Her voice echoed, ricocheting uncomfortably off the face of the sandstone cliffs.

Ellie swung around. The clearing was unchanged, a space, hidden and sheltered beneath the cliffs. Dotted throughout were pale trees, each one reaching for the light, their roots edging into the cracks of fallen sandstone.

Ellie tilted her head back, and from the branches above a row of angular nests trailed from beneath the trees. Made of twigs and woven grasses, they hung empty, like puffed up paper bags or wonky Christmas decorations, delicate, and abandoned.

Nothing moved.

'Hey,' Ellie tried again, her voice wavering fearfully in the silence. 'Hey, please, is anyone there?'

Clasping her hands, Ellie waited as her last syllable echoed away to nothing, absorbed by the sheer walls of sandstone. Opening her mouth to call again she stopped. Why should the old woman be here at all?

Ellie winced. How stupid, stupid to even imagine…

'Child.' The voice was older, calmer, and close.

Ellie whirled around.

Only a few feet away, the old woman stood, her eyes were bright and shining, her slight form concealed in the shadows of the surrounding rocks.

'Young woman, I should say,' she corrected herself, peering up at Ellie. 'You were taking so long muddling to get here I was afraid you wouldn't make it. Stopping and starting… Why did you leave the path? Don't you ever read folk tales? Anything can happen at all.'

'I-I-I-' Ellie stammered, 'I-' She stopped, tongue tied as embarrassment flushed her cheeks hot.

126

The old woman regarded her with her head cocked to one side. 'It doesn't matter in the least, you did what had to be done to get back on the path and you made it.'

Confused, Ellie stared at the old woman before she too smiled, surprised by the surge of warmth that flashed between them.

'Well, come,' said the old woman firmly and gestured to a small clump of rocks protruding near them. 'If you are ready to learn the way of Heka, first we need to introduce ourselves properly.'

Ellie didn't move, the old woman was so tiny, she realised studying her, that her head barely made it to Ellie's shoulder. And though her dark hair tied back in a bun was streaked grey, she didn't seemed old or frail at all. Instead, she stood calm and firm, radiating a feisty impatience.

'What is your name, child?'

'Uh, sorry, I'm Ellie.' She held out her hand.

The old woman nodded and shook it, her bony grip firm and sure. 'Pleased to meet you, Ellie,' she answered formally, 'You may call me Ba Set.'

Not sure if she'd heard rightly, Ellie leaned forward. 'I'm sorry, did you say Bast?'

'No,' said the old woman sternly, 'Ba *Set*, it's an old family name. You need to pronounce it clearly. Speak correctly when you say it. Words have power you know and names even more so. This is one of the first things to understand if you would learn the ways of Heka.'

Ellie slowly tried again. '*Ba Set*.'

The old woman smiled in approval, her huge eyes glowing against nut-brown skin. Ellie's heart skipped a beat. She may be old, she thought, but power radiated out of the depths of her being, and her face spoke eloquently of past beauty with her high cheekbones and delicate bones. As Ellie stared, the spaces through the air around them seemed to quiver and sizzle, like a bending mirage in the heat of the day. She gasped, sure for a second Ba Set held a hint of someone she knew.

The thought evaporated as Ba Set lowered herself down by one of the largest rocks and arranged her long skirt carefully around her feet. She gestured to Ellie to sit.

'Heka,' Ba Set repeated, 'takes us into the very centre of creation.'

She waited while Ellie settled herself against one of the lower rocks. 'Follow me.' Ba Set commanded and closed her eyes.

'Wait. I don't understand.' Ellie said quickly. 'Ba Set, please, we need to talk. I need to know about faeries, what are they? And the hag stone, it didn't work-'

Ba Set shook her head firmly. 'Quiet. If you would learn more, follow me.' Ba Set sang a deep tonal note.

The air around quivered, and a cold shiver tingled on Ellie's skin, prickling up along her arms and the back of her neck. Shuddering, Ellie looked up and gasped in a mixture of fright and wonder as out from the lopsided nests dropped a dark, rippling cloud, swirling and changing direction on a whim. It streamed towards her and then turned, revealing a mass of spidery, spiky-topped beings flying out and around the tops of the trees.

'We don't compel them, Ellie, or command them,' said the old woman, her golden eyes watching closely. 'It is the song, the language of Heka, the language of magic, which connects us all. It bypasses our minds and goes straight to our hearts.'

Ba Set repeated a deep tone, and then stopped. 'They like this time of day best, as you've found,' she smiled as the tiny faery drew closer. 'It's the edges; when the light drops or rises at dawn or dusk. The edges of the day are the best time to work with these ones, the mighty workers of the forest.'

'Join me. Breathe out a sound from deep within. All edges; land to sea, night to day, girl to woman, are powerful.'

The old woman held Ellie's gaze and didn't look away. Ellie's head began to spin, drawn into the great shining orbs.

'Magic works best on the edges because when one is neither one thing nor the other, all things are possible.'

Ellie swallowed, she didn't know what the old woman was talking about.

'Sing.'

It was no longer a request.

Opening her mouth a fraction, Ellie made a tiny round 'o' shape. At first the sound she made was just a mere puff of voice. She stopped, feeling silly and self-conscious. God, what was she doing? She couldn't sing, she wasn't like Rose or even like her mum.

Ba Set waited.

Frowning, Ellie bleated out a single strangled note, it began high up in her throat before evaporating into the air around.

A small faery hovered closer. It seemed be smiling, its dark eyes shining, eager for Ellie to try again.

It couldn't really be that hard. Ellie shook her head willing her embarrassment away. Closing her eyes, she breathed in until her lungs could hold no more, then she opened her mouth and exhaled, letting her breath vibrate out through her throat. It sounded less like a strangled cat this time.

'Again,' said Ba Set.

It actually felt good, realised Ellie in surprise. She could feel her normally stiff shoulders relaxing as the air rushed in through her throat and out into sound.

'Again,' said the old woman. 'Follow me. Drop it lower, breathe from your belly.'

How can you breathe from your belly? Ellie almost laughed out loud, but she was concentrating now. She shifted her position, mimicking the deep tones of Ba Set.

The sound seemed to come from somewhere deeper than the old woman's throat, deeper even than her belly; it seemed to come from somewhere even further down below.

Ellie grimaced, imagining her own voice slipping down into the ground, following worm holes, animal burrows, any opening that led into the earth. Her voice dropped beyond the tangled roots of the trees, through layers of bedrock, through huge underground caverns of crystal clear water; it dropped so far down, deep into the hot centre of the earth, it disappeared.

All was sound.

Contracting and expanding sound. The song filled Ellie's senses, becoming louder and louder, filling her chest, her throat, every cell, every muscle.

Elated, she dropped her head back as the tone coursed back up through her body, taking her higher and higher until it felt she was floating, conscious only of a singular lightness of being.

Soft fingers, as light as air, caressed her cheeks. Warmth, light and soft, danced over her skin. The scent of eucalypt, tantalising on the wind.

Ellie opened her eyes wide with a smile, then bit back a cry of shock.

The ground, it, the land, the earth, was gone. Far below, a faint smudge of colour fell away to the horizon, while above, high against a dazzling sky, the sun sizzled and crackled, its glare eased with streaks of cloud.

Dumbstruck, Ellie peered down. She felt herself drop until she saw a small familiar shape nestled against a rock in a clearing, encircled by red folds of stone jutting towards the sky.

Awareness shot through her body. She was flying. Oh my God, she was flying.

As though pierced by the realisation, the air around her abruptly collapsed and Ellie fell, dropping through the layers of scent and wind and lightness, landing into the hard reality of flesh with a juddering, mind numbing shock.

All was quiet around. The singing had stopped. She opened her eyes. Ba Set was gazing at her, her golden eyes bright with merriment.

Ellie stared at her, speechless. Terrified, she checked her body gingerly, flexing her hands and wriggling her toes. Her neck? Anxiously she checked each vertebra and moved her head carefully side to side. She was fine. Unbelievably she was fine, no bones were broken. Her back wasn't shattered.

'What happened?' She whispered, her voice small and trembling.

'Child, you should take more care,' smiled Ba Set.

'What just happened?' repeated Ellie louder as a wild excitement began to bubble up though her blood. 'Wow, I can't believe it.'

131

Ellie began to laugh as a wild happiness filled her being. *I flew,* she thought. *Oh my God, I can fly!* Elated, she laughed and threw her head back, opening her eyes wider to try and cram in as much of the immense sky as possible.

'Wow!' She shouted up into the trees. Clouds scudded; it looked just all so ordinary when viewed from down here, tethered to hard, solid ground. 'I can fly.'

'A Soul Flyer.' Ba Set murmured, watching. 'I haven't met a Soul Flyer in over a hundred years.'

Ellie wasn't listening. 'What actually happened?' She asked, patting her body to feel if it was real. 'Was that really real?'

Ellie stared at the old woman, and then abruptly dropped her face in her hands as doubt, cold and remorseless, clenched her being. 'That's impossible. I'm an idiot.' She reddened, embarrassed by her earlier baseless joy. 'That always happens. Oh my God.' She closed her eyes, fighting the urge to run away; fighting the urge to pound her fists into her head, so mortified that someone had witnessed her be so stupid.

'Ellie,' interrupted Ba Set firmly. 'Soul Flyer. It is real. At last the old talents are returning, just when the need is greatest.'

Ellie took in a shaking breath. Ba Set seemed to be surrounded by some kind of haze, sparkling and riven with swirling changing colours. Grimacing, Ellie shook her head. 'I'm going nuts,' she whispered.

'Ellie, you are not going nuts, as you put it. Believe me, you are very sane, and very, very talented. And I would teach you,' Ba Set whispered softly. 'Oh, I have waited age upon age for one such as you.'

But Ellie didn't respond. 'I'm an idiot.' She whispered, hugging her knees tight, trying to hide.

'Pull out the hag stone,' commanded Ba Set.

Ellie didn't move. Ba Set waited, patient as though impervious to time. Reluctantly, Ellie turned to her backpack, opened it and pulled out the stone.

'Look at it closely. Take a long careful look. This stone, this Old One, is your anchor to the world of truth. Any time you feel as though you need to be brought back down to earth, fly too high or fear for your mind, use the stone. It is a being of great power. Ask of it and it will answer. But do not be flippant, have respect. It will not respond if there is no need.'

'Now. Look through it.' The old woman gestured to the trees above.

Ellie pointed the hole, like a lens, towards the multifaceted nests trailing from the branches above. She gasped as she watched the faeries, framed through the stone, noting they had changed. Their tiny beings sparkled as they flew under the canopy, shining, shot through with colour as iridescent as falling water caught by the sun. 'Wow,' she whispered.

'That is their true form,' Ba Set smiled.

The stone in her hand pulsed with warmth and, without thinking, Ellie raised it towards the dark clad, old woman.

Ba Set sat before her, as regal as an ancient queen. Around her, rippling like a star, was a golden outline glowing so bright that it hurt the eye. And yet there was more. Wavering through the brightness, flickering from human form, was the figure of a huge dark eagle and resting on her head was a finely beaten circlet of gold. A small puff of wind rippled through the clearing and Ba Set raised her arms, the air ruffling the tips of her vast outstretched wings so she resembled a living breathing goddess, glowing like a golden winged idol.

Ellie dropped the stone to the ground. 'What's going on?' She cried as shock coursed through her body.

Ba Set didn't move. 'Ellie,' she breathed. 'Do not let fear and ignorance rule your heart. Look at me and tell me what you see.'

'What are you? Tell me!'

All the earlier warmth and elation that had flooded through her, evaporated as though it had never existed.

'How do you do that? Are you a d-d-devil?' Ellie choked the word out. *Oh my God, Rose was right, and so was her father. Oh my God.*

'Do not call us devils.' Ba Set hissed the word out and it hung, small and toxic, coiling in the air. She stood straight, the earlier vision vanishing. 'Do not call us devils.' She repeated, quieter now. 'For those such as I, have naught to do with puny, frightened superstitions.'

'You ask what I am.' Ba Set paused and closed her eyes, as though searching carefully for the right words.

Ellie backed away, poised to flee away into the trees.

'I am of the Old Ones.' Ba Set's voice was low yet it held great power. 'Do not let yourself be ruled by fear,' she said. 'We are not devils. We protect the earth. That is our calling. That is our great work.'

Ellie stared. Ba Set stood taller, her arms reaching for the sky. 'Go now, while the winds remain calm.'

Gone was the tiny old woman - instead she looked ancient and powerful, wrapped in a cloak of long dark feathers crowned with gold. Holding back the storm, the old woman was no longer alone. Behind her in the shadows, stood a line of black-haired, golden-eyed women, winged and eternal, stretched back through the ages, all gazing implacably at Ellie.

'Go,' repeated the ancient one that was Ba Set. 'And return only if you would join us. Protecting the earth at this time of great peril is not a game. You are needed, Ellie Soul Flyer, but if you join us, you will leave behind all you have ever known.'

FOURTEEN

Southern England 1340

A rich, mouth-watering aroma filled the forest clearing, spiralling lazily up into the night sky. Breathing deeply in the chill air, Ba Set stirred through the swirls of marrow fat that seeped from the bones resting on the bottom of the pot. A meal fit for a king, deep and nourishing, made with chunks of tender venison, and herbs picked from the forest that morning.

'Ach,' she snorted in frustration. Her husband needed his strength, but he had managed only a few sips of the broth that evening, and had laid his spoon on the table, unable to eat anymore.

Frowning, Ba Set dropped the lid back onto the blackened pot, the loud clang cutting into the silence of the camp. Wiping her hands on her gown, she reached for a log of cut oak and dropped it onto the fire. The heat licked its way along rough-edged bark, tasting the beads of moisture sizzling down its sides, before all at once bursting alight, the bright flames twisting with coiling, dancing forms.

A sharp cry rent the air. Her husband lay in the hut behind, muttering and jerking as he slept. Ba Set listened intently. A hiss from the fire flared up into the darkness and a scamper of tiny feet scurried away into the trees, but that was all. Whatever had disturbed her man had eased, and he had settled back into an uneasy rest.

She sat motionless, strain and worry etched on her lovely face. She knew with every heartbeat that the gift of life was leaching out of him, slowly and steadily. As sure as the sun would rise on the morrow, and the harsh grip of winter would follow the softness of summer, her beloved husband would die.

'No,' she whispered, tightening her fists in defiance; not while the breath of life still remained in his body. She would not let him go. She would fight the whispering thrall of death that enticed from the shadows, calling from the edges of his dreams. Ba Set pulled her cloak around her shoulders and turned back to the dancing fire. The intense heat made the delicate skin of her face burn and tighten, but she didn't flinch, anything to relieve the chill of fear that rasped at her soul.

'He will survive,' she whispered. He had to. Shuddering, she closed her eyes as the memories of her life gone by rose unbidden into her mind. The long years, empty, her heart barren and scored with loneliness.

She had waited, each day as the sun had risen blazing in the sky and dropped quiet and subdued in the west, performing her duties to the Goddess, following her mother and sister, healing those in need. But after years upon years had passed, bitterness dulled her eyes and the bright beat of her heart slowed to the low thud of lost hope. She was alone, only half alive, waiting for the one who would bring her soul to life.

Then on a day like any other, though the cold air sparkled with the fresh promise of spring, he had appeared, his spirit arcing like the first flare of light on the dawn. His great booming laugh split the silence of the forest, scattering birds and beings alike. Yet they had followed him, watching, mesmerised by the stranger's joyous, virile spirit.

And so had she, soaring above the sea of trees. She had descended as night-time fell to appear before him naked, her dark hair falling to her waist and her pale skin hot with desire. His laugh of surprise and delight had crackled through the forest, and when they came together she had felt as though her barren, stricken soul was now filled and overflowing with life.

By the glowing fire, Ba Set smiled. *No,* she vowed. Death could not have him, not *her* man. The great Goddess Herself knew he belonged to her, and only to her. Time would not take him.

'Hold on, my beloved,' she whispered fiercely. 'Hold on, for the spice is coming. It will give fire to your veins and the strength of twenty lions to your heart.'

Picking up a twig that lay by her feet, Ba Set began to trace an intricate three-sided symbol into the soft soil, whispering ancient, clicking words known only to a few, and passed down through the ages. The spice was coming, but her husband needed to be strong, and for strength he first needed to rest. This song was potent, and as the chant rose above a whisper, the air began to quicken, drawing closer, gathering in the dark.

In the forest, power gathered, a silvery blue, dappled with bursts of light and shadow. Ba Set raised her hand, and with an arc of movement sent it deep into the hut where her husband lay. She could see it in her mind's eye: a light-flecked covering, a web of magic and protection, keeping him safe, soothing him into a deep, dreamless sleep.

When it was done, Ba Set placed the stick on the ground, and gazed over the glowing coals into the inky blackness of the trees. Now, where was her son, and where was the spice? She frowned; she had expected Tey back soon after the sun had set, tired and clamouring for his supper. Beyond the clearing, the trees surrounding the edges of their home stood motionless, their bark gnarled and ribbed. The moon had not yet risen. Only the stars moved, sparkling brightly against the dark sky.

Where was her son?

Ba Set sat staring into the dense wall of trees, ignoring the glare of the fire while her irises, huge in her golden eyes, adjusted to the pool of darkness beyond. In a heartbeat, every distant leaf, blade of grass, and nervous tremble in the undergrowth became crystal sharp. A light scampering of padded feet was followed by the sound of bracken snapping in the silent forest. Tilting her head, she caught a muffled cry of dismay and the splintering crack of a large dry branch.

It could only be Tey. Who else would be crashing through the forest with all the grace of a wild boar? Ba Set shook her head. Still, at least he was close. Now at last she was free to gather the other vital ingredients.

Rising to her feet, she stepped away from the fire and into the centre of the clearing. She was a handsome woman, strong and lean with high cheekbones and hair that fell thick and dark to her waist. With elaborate care, she unfastened the bodice of her long gown and stepped out, letting the folds of fabric drop in a heap at her feet.

Naked, Ba Set stood bathed in light, her skin caressed by the dappled light of the embers. Shaking out her hair, she stretched out her muscled arms horizontally to the earth and planted her feet firmly on the ground. The soil felt cool and moist beneath her feet. Ba Set adjusted her stance, finding her centre, until her body felt poised and balanced upon the earth. Taking a deep breath, she closed her eyes.

The air rushed cold and sharp in through her nostrils, scented with deep notes of wood smoke overlaid with the fresh tang of the surrounding trees. Pausing for a moment, she savoured the held scent before slowly letting it out, releasing her breath to the forest beyond. Drawing her hands over her heart, she breathed in again slower, letting the coolness fill her lungs, and dropping it down into her belly. Holding it a beat longer, Ba Set sent it lower still, imagining the warmed air flowing down her legs, to her feet and into the earth below.

Her lungs emptied and in the quiet, above the slow beating of her heart, Ba Set became conscious of another pulse, thudding quietly, almost imperceptivity deep.

Like a beam of light, Ba Set dropped her awareness to meet it; the powerful, molten heartbeat of Mother Earth. Shaking slightly, she sang out a low tone of reverence, calling in an ancient tongue to the rhythmic tide far below.

At first nothing moved and Ba Set waited, breathing quietly, standing patiently above the layers of soil and rock, deep silent caverns, and hidden pools of clear cool water.

A quiver, and every cell and nerve of her being began to sizzle and crackle as warmth surged beneath.

Her heart thundered. Her blood sang out in exaltation as heat rose up through the crust of earth, flooding her arteries, her veins, her blood, with molten surging power. Clenching her fists Ba Set drew in a shuddering breath as searing energy flowed up into her legs, up into her belly, expanding into her chest, melting into the crimson layers of her heart, every cell swelling, every drop of blood becoming golden and glowing.

Trembling, Ba Set fought to contain her awareness as the song of the earth burned up against her throat, pushing, building, and crying out to be voiced. Her body shook, tipped on the edge of control, but she held her ground and with her next breath drew in more of the pulsing, roaring heat.

She raised her arms to the sky. The power increased, surging in the narrow confines of the throat, demanding escape. She clenched her jaw for a moment more, her whole body engulfed in heat. Then when she could hold it back no longer, Ba Set opened her mouth and, with a mighty word of power, released the surging heat out into the night sky.

She leapt into the air.

The wind felt cool and sweet, the night air clear. A pinion feather dipped and stretched combing the currents. She turned effortlessly, catching a strong updraft spiralling above the trees, her magnificent black wingspan moving barely a whisper.

In her eagle form, the shapeshifter gazed down at the forest spreading out far beneath her - her keen sight able to discern each bright line of energy emanating from each living thing. A vast web, illuminated with every foraging insect, every creature that scurried, every tree that stretched its roots far beneath the surface of the earth. It was a pattern glowing with life.

Her wings beat slowly. Her golden eyes flickered. Movement stumbled, as far below a large figure crashed through the undergrowth. Tey, blundering along, was stopping and starting like a confused, overgrown mouse, and the bright aura of his spirit was being trailed by the usual gaggle of childish over excitable sprites.

Ba Set circled slowly, silently watching as he narrowly missed the last turning point, and stopped, cursing in frustration. She dipped lower. He took a deep wavering breath, and leaned towards the larger of the luminous spirits that surrounded him. They appeared to be arguing, the sprite streaming lines of agitation into the air. Abruptly Tey turned and stomped away, showering great sparks of temper as he went. After a few more steps he stopped and bent over, his hands furiously scraping leaves off the path to reveal the stone marker hidden beneath.

The eagle's keen eyes flickered as she circled once more, then with a strong beat of her powerful wings, she swooped down over the trees above him, crying out once before flying on into the night.

'You could have helped me!' Tey watched as the dark shape soared away, each wing beat blocking the glow of the stars. Resentment clutched at his throat. 'You could have waited!' Furious, he stamped his foot, his eyes stinging with bitter tears.

He dropped his shoulders and sighed, turning to look for Gimbal. The fat faery lay floating in the air ahead, his big silly face gazing at the path with a satisfied grin. Running to catch up, Tey grabbed his friend's hand. At least now he knew that home, and more importantly dinner, was not much further away and that was a huge relief.

He'd missed his way, like any brain-addled fool. 'But it wasn't my fault,' Tey muttered to himself. The forest path wound its way through the forest, as though it didn't care if a young traveller became lost or confused by its frustrating, twisted turnings. Tey rubbed his eyes tiredly; there was a more direct route home but he had missed it. He had been so frightened by the strange lone knight that he had run past the start entirely.

Scowling, Tey clenched the eagle amulet around his neck. Why didn't his mother ever come to help him, instead of always leaving him to find his own way by himself? It wasn't fair, he sighed, his flare of resentment dying away to a resigned exhaustion.

Eyes down, the young boy let go of the necklace and trudged along the narrow track, his way lit by the light of the faeries shining above. Reaching a small rise, he stopped. Floating overhead in the trees, Gimbal was grinning in triumph, his large bald head like a beacon against the dark sky.

Tey frowned, puzzled, as one of his friend's twiglike fingers was inching, worm like, in the air, pointing in the direction of a large clearing half hidden in the trees.

Home.

Smiling in relief, Tey waved the troops on, but the leaves overhead merely fluttered, empty.

'Where are you?' he whispered.

The air quivered as a translucent being materialised, hovering above the ground, its small body radiating a gentle glow under the trees. However, before he could even take a step forward towards it, the faery raised its twig thin arm in a wave and winked out like a light.

'Oh don't go,' Tey cried, whirling around in the sudden darkness. It was like a signal, as at once a cascade of shining beings streamed from the heights of the forest, their silky hair glistening behind them. Laughing, Tey reached into his pocket for his wooden flute, eager to begin another merry spinning dance. But as he raised the instrument to his lips, each incandescent being vanished into darkness.

'Please don't go. She's nowhere near, you saw her.'

Tey sighed in defeat. This edge of trees, with their smooth bark and soft green leaves, seemed to mark some kind of invisible boundary the faery never, ever crossed. His mother terrified them and no matter how much he begged and cajoled them to stay, nothing could entice them one single step closer to the camp. Not even another spinning dance.

Tey looked up into the glittering sky. Why hadn't Gimbal stayed around to say goodbye? Hugging himself, Tey waited in the darkness for a few moments longer before turning with a shrug and trudging down towards the camp. A low branch blocked the path in front, and beyond it he could see the top of the old oak tree that protected the camp from view. Clearing the branch, Tey was hurrying on when without warning, it sprung back, giving him a sharp whack.

'Ow!' Tey whirled around.

Gimbal popped into view, a delighted smirk splitting his face.

'I'll get you for that!' Tey yelled, shaking his fist in mock fury. He stopped. 'Hey, come into the camp with me. You're not scared, are you?' he taunted.

But Gimbal only shook his great bald head and with a final tumbling bow, disappeared in a burst of sparks that streaked, crackling up into the night. What a show off. Grinning, Tey ran down the grassy slope and into the camp beyond. He was ravenous and already he could catch the unmistakable, delicious warmth of dinner.

The dwellings faced each other across the clearing, each one nestling close to the trunk of a tree. Constructed from pieces of fallen timber, they seemed as much a part of the woods as the shadowed outlines of the undergrowth. Tey skidded to a walk as he came to the largest hut built around the foot of the oak. His stomach rumbled.

First some dinner, then he would give his father the pouch of spice.

The cooking fire was piled into a bed of glowing red embers. A blackened pot hung from the tripod. Tey breathed in. The rich scent of meat and broth filled his nostrils making his mouth water. He glanced around hopefully, but no movement or calls of greeting heralded him from any of the other huts. He shrugged; he should've known.

Turning back to the fire, Tey lifted off the lid with a stick and peered inside, inhaling the thick rich aroma. The night was dark and he was alone in the immense silence of the forest, but he took no notice. For the whole of his young life his family had lived under the trees, far from the watchful eyes of the Lord's men, coming and going as carefully and as cunningly as any wild creature of the forest.

Tey sat down on a wooden bench and ate slowly, dipping his spoon for a dumpling that bobbed lazily in the fatty broth. He sighed and took another mouthful, happy to be home at last, safe, far from the stink and confusion of the town, and far from the knight shouting threats at him from beneath the trees.

Tey froze. 'What have I done?' He moaned as the images of the tortured, swinging remains he'd seen that morning, flared in horror in his mind.

Do not be seen… Slowly Tey placed his half eaten bowl on the bench, his appetite gone.

The trees encircling the clearing trembled as a breeze caught the leaves. Beyond them, the forest waited, dark and peaceful in the night. An owl hooted, but no wild-eyed knight crashed through the undergrowth, nor howled any slavering, red-eyed dog hot on the scent of trespass. All was calm.

Swallowing, Tey's fears eased down a notch.

At least I have the spice, Tey thought, scrapping out the remains of his dinner. This spice would save his father's life, it would give back his sunny strength and once well enough, his father would again take him out into the forest and show him the secret ways of the fox and the hare.

His heart now bursting with hope, Tey watched as the heat of the fire writhed with the glowing, undulating beings playing in the embers. Nothing bad will happen. His father was the best woodsman in all the forest, everyone knew that, and all Tey had ever wished for was to track the wild deer, charm the birds from the sky, and to live his life in freedom under the trees forever. With that thought, he rose from the fire and turned into the hut to sleep.

Straining with every muscle and wing, and with his heart surging in exultation, Tey dreamt he was flying, the wild folk by his side. His head forward and his arms outstretched, he swooped fast through the sky, the forest a blur of dark green beneath. Just ahead, glimpses of dark black flashed through the trees, just out of reach.

Tey fought to catch up, to pass, to win. Then without warning his flight faltered and with a great shriek he fell tumbling out of the sky, the far distant stars glittering high above.

His bed thudded as Tey fell back into his body with a jerk, and his eyes flew open. He reached for his blanket and shifted position, and could hear out of the quiet a heavy rhythmic thud and a low murmur of voices.

Shyly, Tey peeked out from under the covers.

His parents were on their own bed, silhouetted against the greying sky that seeped in through the cracks of the hut. His mother, back in her human form, was naked - save for a drape of cloth tied around her shoulders, shielding her from the dawn chill. She was pounding vigorously with a large wooden pestle. Clouds of amber dust, rich and pungent, cut into the early morning air.

Tey licked his lips, then grimaced as a sharp bitter taste filled his senses.

Pausing, Ba Set added a pinch, then stirring carefully, poured in a small amount of water while his father lay beside her calmly watching, his head a mass a dark curls with a streak of grey at the temples.

'How long, my beloved? You have already stretched my allotted life for years beyond belief.'

Ba Set stopped mixing and gazed at her husband with eyes full of a fierce possessive love. 'Time will not take you from me,' she murmured. 'No matter the length of years, they will always be too short for me.' Ba Set's golden eyes held her husband's for a heartbeat. She looked away and spooned a mixture of spice into a large wooden mug before adding a measure of water. Stirring the contents twice, and careful so as not to spill a drop, Ba Set handed her husband the cup.

Hew hesitated before accepting the spice mixture. He held the cup carefully in his hand and, with a half almost self-mocking smile, drank it down in one swallow. He placed the cup on the floor and looked at Ba Set for a long moment.

'Another lifetime,' she whispered.

Hew held her gaze then shook his head and drew her into his arms. Ba Set laughed softly.

Embarrassed, Tey turned away, drawing his covers over his head. The rough linen scratched his cheek and he closed his eyes, claimed by the deep pull of sleep.

FIFTEEN

The next morning Tey lay very still with his eyes closed. His muscles ached and he was finding it hard to breathe under the covers, but he didn't care. Frowning in the darkness, he scrunched his eyes tighter, trying to recapture the exact way his body had swooped and soared through the night.

Painstakingly, he flexed each finger and straightened his arms, marvelling at their strength and power. They were invincible, sweeping him high with an exhilarating speed, soaring over the land, his heart singing in delight, the night air prickling his cheeks as it rushed past his face. His golden eyes stung in the sharp cold, missing nothing, as his gaze scoured the land below.

'I am the Eagle King,' Tey whispered proudly. 'I am the ruler of the air and all the folk of the forest. Heed me!'

Imperiously, he threw back his head and stamped his right foot down - his leg hitting the wall with a hard thud. Pain flared and he cried out, opening his eyes.

Sunshine streamed in, throwing bright, striped patterns across the floor of the simple one room hut. Around his bed were the clothes he'd discarded and his wooden pipe. Tey rolled over in disappointment; he was no Eagle King, he was just a boy lying on his straw bed at home.

With a sigh, Tey glanced over to the far corner of the room. His parents' bed lay empty. Their woollen covering, handwoven by his mother, tossed carelessly to the side as though it had been kicked, the under blanket trailed to the floor. 'Oh no.' Tey sat up in alarm. What if the spice hadn't helped?

Through the cracks in the wall there was a blur of movement. Tey could see figures gesturing, dark against the bright green of the trees. At once, Tey jumped to his feet and ran towards the door.

A man was working in the centre of the clearing. A leather apron tied around his waist, and his face was obscured by thick, loose hair. Tossing his head back, the man let out a sudden laugh and the merry sound boomed loudly through the camp. Tey gasped, it was his father!

Laughing, Tey grabbed his flute and dashed out into the sunshine.

A metallic hiss rent the air as Hey drew a blade along a slab of oiled stone. Near to him, where Tey longed to be, stood a wiry figure with thinning hair and a darting, bird-like manner. Martin, the woodsman, was speaking with one hand on the knife belted to his waist. Between them lay a deer, its dark eyes open and its delicate hooves dangled. The broken shaft of an arrow still protruded through the skin above the animal's heart.

Tey swallowed, ambushed by a wave of shyness. All he wanted was to run and bury his face in his father's chest - hugging him, revelling in his strength and his earthy, familiar smell, but now… Tey shuffled his feet awkwardly and looked away. Across the ground, shadows moved and a warm breeze brushed past his cheek, carrying the soft chirrups of birds flitting through the branches. A note of urgency rose above the birdsong.

'No, *with* them,' Martin was gesturing emphatically towards the trees. 'The abbot, with a dozen black-robed monks, followed by four armed sheriffs.' He turned to Tey's father, his narrow face strained. 'The question is, what is the Lord, his brother, and a litter carrying the ladies, doing with such a retinue in the forest?'

'They are most likely simply passing through,' answered Hew as he continued to sharpen the blade. 'You know the Lady's brother has lands on the other side.'

He stopped and ran his thumb across the blade, testing its edge. Martin shook his head, staring back towards the trees, his hand hovering over the knife tied to his belt.

Seizing his chance, Tey crept forward and slipped in as quietly as he could beside his father, his head down. He swallowed, anxious he would be sent away. A hand descended onto his shoulder and Tey jerked, his heart leaping in panic.

'Your mother left those for you,' said his father, his green eyes crinkling in welcome. Tey smiled shyly and reached for one of the freshly made honeycakes. He took a small bite, conscious of a heavy silence stretching in the air above.

There was the sound of a footfall, and Ba Set - her hair tied back under a loose scarf, threw a bundle of slender, green juniper branches onto a pile by the fire pit.

'Did I hear you say there is a party of nobles in the forest?' She wiped her hands on her apron.

Martin nodded. 'Aye, not only the nobles but men of the cloth following close behind, though their doleful chanting would dull even the brightest spirits.' He spat onto the ground with a sour grimace.

Ba Set's eyes narrowed. 'Are they passing through?'

'I don't know, but it is very curious,' said the woodsman, glancing back to the trees. 'They have neither dogs, nor falcons, but they move as if searching, loudly and with much merriment and excitement.'

Without a word, Ba Set caught the gaze of her husband, her mouth set and eyes piercing.

But Hew only shook his head. 'It is probably just a party looking for a meadow in which to eat out of doors,' he said soothingly. 'You know how these nobles are.' He ruffled the top of Tey's head. 'They have nothing better to do with their time.'

Tey nodded and leaned closer to his father's steady warmth.

'Yes perhaps,' interrupted Martin sharply, 'but there is one stranger thing still. Leading them is the Lord's youngest son, do you know of him?' He paused, 'Sir Ulrick, the one who was first marked for the church, but it is said he caused such a ruckus as a child, he was sent to be a squire in his uncle's household.'

'Ah yes,' Hew's eyes narrowed in distaste. 'And now that he's won his spurs, he's joined the monk's protectors, all aflame to win glory in the Holy Land.'

'What is one such as this doing here?' Ba Set glanced down at her son with a frown. 'This one would fight a rock if he thought it would brought him glory.'

Tey placed the last honeycake back on the table, his appetite vanishing. He pressed even closer to his father. *It couldn't be?* With his heart thudding anxiously, Tey reached for his father's hand. Huge and strong, its familiar warmth soothed the sharp spikes of Tey's rising fears.

'If they are merely travelling through the forest, they pose no threat to us,' Hew said quietly to Ba Set. 'Do you agree, Martin?'

'Of course,' said the woodsman, 'but they are not going in the straight line of the forest road. They are searching through the deep wood that runs in from the crossroad. The Lord's son drops to his knees as if in prayer, they wait, and then they search on.'

As the adults talked, a sickening fear crept up Tey's spine. He remembered the hungry fury on the knight's face, and the strange elation as he'd watched him in the forest. He swallowed. 'Fa-Father…' Tey began, but stopped. His throat hurt as though dry, and crammed too full of sharp-edged words. 'La-La-Last-' Tey tried again, stamping his foot in frustration.

Unaware of his son's turmoil, Hew stared into the forest, his eyes grim. Their attention was fixed on the trees.

Ba Set tossed her head back in defiance. 'I need to see them,' she stepped back, gazing up into the still blue sky. No breeze disturbed the calm and the midday sun shone bright and clear. She smiled proudly and stretched out her slender muscled arms, shaking them impatiently as though she was already a creature of flight tethered for too long to the ground.

Hew stopped her with a frown. 'Be careful, my beloved.' He murmured, taking her hand. 'These nobles may not be hunting, but one such as you would be a great prize indeed.'

Ba Set slid her hand away. 'They'll never see me,' she shook her head scornfully. 'They'll be like little rats sniffling along the forest paths, too blind to look up.'

'Perhaps. But we mustn't be foolish.'

He gestured to Tey. 'I'll take the boy along the hidden paths, and we'll hunt out any broken stick, or sunken footprint that may betray our presence.'

Ba Set nodded. 'You'll have a lot to do', she said. 'Our son crashed through the forest last night with all the sense of a crazed boar.' She looked at Tey sharply. 'Why,' she asked quietly, 'were you running through the forest, without heed, as though being hunted by the Lord's dogs themselves?'

Tey's eyes faltered then slid away, unable to meet the intensity of his mother's scrutiny. He swallowed.

Frowning, Ba Set looked at him closer as he fought for the right words that would explain his panicked flight through the trees.

'I-I-I-' he began at last, blushing painfully; how could he tell her without sounding like a dimwitted fool? 'La-La-' he stammered, his eyes welled stinging with tears of frustration, but still the words refused to come. 'B-b-b-'

His father's hand descended on his shoulder. 'Leave him be, my love,' Hew said gently. 'Young ones do strange things for their own peculiar reasons, particularly in the dark.' He ruffled Tey's hair. 'Leave him, we have enough to do.'

Ba Set considered Tey for a long moment, then she nodded and kissed her husband briefly before striding towards the trees without a backward look. Wilting in misery, Tey stared down at his feet. No wonder she thought him such a fool. And he was, he was useless. Agonised, he stamped his foot on the ground.

Movement shuddered at the edge of the clearing and a dark bird rose above the forest canopy, sunlight rippling lazily along the length of her wide black wings. Rooted to the ground, overwhelmed by a sense of wonder that never ever changed, Tey watched as the eagle swept low, her flight feathers deftly caressing the wind, and her shadow blurring along the ground. Banking left, she caught an updraft, spiralling higher into the dazzling brightness of the sun. And with one last flick of her powerful wings, his mother was gone.

Head down, Tey trudged back to the table in the centre of the clearing. Martin had finished cleaning and dressing the venison, and the flame-coloured skin lay draped across the bushes, its pale markings darkening as it dried. There was a metallic hiss as the woodsman hunched over the whetstone and sharpened his long steel blade.

Tey hesitated, not sure what to do next. Near the fire pit, a pile of fresh branches lay stacked neatly on the ground. He brightened; this was one of his favourite chores, helping preserve the prized meat in the fragrant smoke. It took hours of careful work feeding in the green wood to keeping the fire smoulderingly hot, but afterward came the reward of tender, delicious meat. Tey licked his lips, his stomach growling.

'It won't happen any time today, boy,' Martin stopped, the knife glinting in his hand. 'We'll have to rid ourselves of the vermin first.' He grinned, anticipation brightening his coal black eyes.

A bulging leather pouch dropped onto the table in front.

'When you've finished here,' his father nodded to Martin, 'go by the river and release all the snares and traps. Be sure they find no signs to betray us. And here,' Hew handed the woodsman a wrapped parcel of food. 'Take this, and go quickly.'

Tey and his father worked their way down along the looped and twisted path. It was a bright day, unseasonably warm and Tey's neck was soon flecked with a prickly red rash from where his undershirt rubbed damply against his skin. Uncaring, he brushed the irritant aside, and smiled up again at his father.

The sun had dropped lower by the time they came to one of the oldest and most secret parts of the forest. Dark and quiet, the air lay unmoving in the wide-open spaces between the trees, and beech trees towered overhead, their dense leaves blocking out all but the most direct shafts of light.

There was a quick chirrup, and a tiny bird flitted up towards the heights. Its wings blurring as it hunted for grubs - its sharp beak ignoring the delicate whirr of forest beings working on the sun struck branch above. If he squinted, Tey could see them silhouetted against the bright glare - hundreds of tiny, finely limbed forms darting back and forth.

Intent on their task, the faeries lifted their hands to the sun, their nimble fingers working quickly, gathering the brightness before pouring the threads of sparkling light into the leaves.

Grinning, Tey reached into the pocket of his tunic for his flute, a tune already forming to help the tiny beings with their work.

'Son, what's keeping you? We've got a lot to do.'

Tey spun around startled.

His father was standing a little way ahead of him, his head on his side watching him closely. 'What are you looking at?' he asked.

Dropping his flute back into his pocket, Tey hung his head down. 'Oh ... well,' he mumbled, tongue-tied and embarrassed. 'You know…' Unsure of what else to say, he hesitantly gestured up into the tree.

Following his direction, Hew looked up into the branches, his eyes curious. Tey shifted his weight, not daring to hope if this time his father would at last see for himself the wild spirits that powered the forest.

After a moment, his father ruffled Tey's hair. 'Ah son,' he smiled ruefully, 'I don't have the eyes for it, you know, no matter how hard I try.'

Tey shrugged, and without another word took Hew's hand and together they turned back to the path through the woods. His father never saw them; he said he could feel them sometimes, but he never ever saw them for real. Tey didn't understand why, when the beings were all around, all different sizes, living and working in the trees, the rocks, the shadows, everywhere.

They toiled in companionable silence, covering the path with soil from the woods and carefully erasing any footprints that remained. As the afternoon dimmed, they came to a section of ravaged forest, the low growing bushes broken and torn, and the carpet of forest bluebells beneath crushed and strewn haphazardly over the ground.

His eyes widened, and Tey stifled a giggle that threatened to burst out of his throat. It looked really terrible, like the land had been trampled to pieces by some maddened, furious beast.

'I don't think there is much we can do here,' said Hew with a raised eyebrow. 'Save trying to plump it up like a fine lady's pillow.'

Tey laughed out loud, then whipped his hand to his mouth in alarm as his eyes darted in panic around the woods.

'Don't worry,' murmured his father with a smile, 'if any of these nobles were close by, we would've heard them by now. See', he pointed to the trees, 'even the shy ones are calm.'

Around them, a handful of finches were flitting amongst the shadows, their bright golden crests bobbing in the falling light. Tey swallowed, his eyes dropping guiltily to the carpet of ruined flowers.

'Father, it was me,' he confessed quietly. 'La-last night-'

Taking a deep breath, all the pent up words streamed out at last. '...He saw me. I didn't know what to do. I was playing my flute near the crossroads and a noble just went crazy, chasing me, yelling...' Tey's voice trailed off, 'I was so scared … so I ran … and ran.'

He stared down at his feet, his heart in his throat, waiting for an explosion of fury.

His father smiled. 'Ah, so we have a mad man in the woods. It wouldn't be the first time, I wager. But no matter, there's nothing about a scrap of a boy like you that would truly interest one such as that.' He clapped his hand on Tey's shoulder with a smile. 'I promise, the knight last night had too much strong ale, and more than likely thought you were a ghost or some such thing. Do not worry, there is nothing you, or I, can do about that now.'

Tey grinned, feeling quite giddy with relief. Of course his father was right. Strong ale - why didn't *he* think of that?

Smiling, he bent to the forest floor where a single bluebell stood unbowed among the wreckage, its violet petals half opened and edged in white. Picking it carefully, Tey placed it in his pocket by his flute. Maybe he'd give it to his mother later, his heart bursting at the thought. She loved that sort of thing.

A thick pop split the air and Gimbal appeared, twirling mindless somersaults high above the ground, broken stalks and bluebell heads raining down around. *He's the idiot*, smiled Tey and threw a handful of broken flowers over his capering friend.

Oblivious to the faery's antics, Hew gestured to the leather satchel open on the ground. He had one of Ba Set's seed cakes in his hand. 'Sit down, son,' he mumbled, 'you've been working hard and you must be ravenous.'

The mottled green faery made a pleading motion of mock starvation, but Tey ignored him. He sat on a clump of grasses and took a bite; the cakes were a little stale, but they were still delicious. The faery vanished and reappeared on the ground, his body curled as if asleep.

As Tey sat chewing he looked up at his father. Leaning against the base of an old gnarled tree, Hew's hat was down over his eyes and a small smile of contentment played across his face. Tey relaxed; it was all going to turn out fine. Nobles had been in the forest before, of course, and besides they owned it so why shouldn't the Lord and his family enjoy a day out? Nodding, he took another seed cake from the satchel.

A few crumbs scattered and a nose poked out from beneath a tight-leaved bush, its delicate whiskers twitching. Breaking a smaller piece of seed cake, Tey tossed it lightly onto the ground. The little mouse hesitated, sniffing the air. Tey sat as still as he could, scarcely breathing, willing himself unseen. However, the little creature wasn't fooled; it sniffed once, then twice, before whirling around and scampering into the undergrowth, its tail held high.

Tey smiled. He and his family had to be as careful and as clever as the little mouse, ever vigilant, hiding in the dense woods while the highborn foxes roamed the forest.

SIXTEEN

The light was failing as Tey and his father made their way down the incline into camp. In the centre, parcels of milled wheat and other foodstuffs were sprawled across the surface of the table, but Ba Set was paying them no heed.

With her were two other women. Tey rushed into the clearing with shout of greeting rising on his lips. *They were back,* he grinned. But his grandmother, Au Set flicked her golden eyes to him and gestured him sharply to be quiet. She was tiny - as small as a child and as light as a bird. She sat unmoving between her two, dark-haired daughters.

Tey skidded to an abrupt stop. Confused, he glanced at his mother and her twin sister, Ash Kit. They stood poised by the table, their bodies trembling and muscles quivering as though they were listening with every cell in their bodies.

Tey gazed at his mother in wonder. Though her bright eyes were open, it seemed as though Ba Set was far away - her senses roaming past the chattering birds and creak of the nearby trees, along the whisper of the wind to the rustling sounds of the great forest beyond.

Beside her, Ash Kit's eyes were closed, her brow furrowed in concentration. Watching her closely, Tey marvelled at how alike she was to his mother. Being the younger twin, his aunt stood smaller but she shared the same hawk-like intensity and slender muscled frame.

Careful not to disturb them, Tey ducked his head and crept past the table as his grandmother nodded and closed her eyes. Yet a few feet away, a tree root lay barely visible in the afternoon light, its knobbled edge poking up through soil. Tey didn't have a chance and, with a painful whack, his foot hit the tree root and he stumbled, crying out as the momentum flung him hard into his father's arms.

At once, Ash Kit's eyes flew open and her head swivelled towards him. He flinched, grimacing in quick apology, but the piercing tawny stare didn't change, so intent was she in listening for danger.

'Come, son,' whispered Hew. 'We'd best stay out of their way.'

Miserably, Tey followed his father into the family's hut.

'We may be needing this after all,' Murmured Hew, his eyes narrowing. A sword, lay in a shaft of brightness, still encased in its leather scabbard.

With a single practiced move, Hew unsheathed the weapon and felt the sword's weight and balance with a straight arm, his eyes peering critically along its length.

Longing gripped him, and Tey almost moaned aloud. His hand quivered, desperate to hold it and try a few good parries and thrusts. Setting his jaw, Tey narrowed his eyes. *I, Sir Tey of the Good Forest will challenge any man. And I will vanquish all foes.* He leapt into the air, imagining a sharp thrust dealt into the shield of his enemy, and with a fierce cry, Tey grabbed for the sword. Take that!

'No, it's not for you son, not yet,' his father firmly whisked the weapon out of reach. 'When this trouble is over, perhaps then we'll practice swordcraft.' He paused, his eyes stern. 'Maybe it will help teach you some sense.'

His father stood without another word, his huge frame filling the hut, and then he was gone.

'Stupid, you're stupid, stupid.' Tey hit the bed with his fist, trying to pummel away the hanging words of rebuke. The empty wall space mocked him; teach you some sense...

But... Tey looked up, his mood brightening. His father had said he was going to learn *swordcraft*. With an excited laugh, Tey jumped to his feet. He was going to learn to dash and parry. The boy made a few quick practice moves at a phantom foe, before opening the door with a grin and dashing outside.

A light wind had risen in the camp. By the table, Ba Set had his father by the arm. Hew was listening and nodding, peering out into the trees. A moment later, he embraced Ba Set and together they left the camp, following the narrow winding path that led into the heart of the forest.

Tey sagged as he watched his parents go. Why didn't they ask him to go too? He kicked listlessly at a rock in the ground.

'Hey,' the voice was light and teasing, 'Tey, come over here, we need to find you some wings. You trip over so much, you'll need some just to stay on your feet.'

Startled, he looked up. His aunt Ash Kit was smiling by the table, her long dark hair falling unbound to her waist and her tawny eyes warm with humour. She gestured to the parcels. 'Come and help us, lazybones, we could use the help of a big strong boy.'

163

Trudging over to the table where his aunt was sorting out the parcels of food with his grandmother, Tey began to smile in spite of himself. Other than his father, Ash Kit was his most favourite person in the world.

'Do you really think so?' He asked, his voice catching with hope. 'Do you really think I'll get wings?'

'Well I don't see why not.' She said giving him a quick hug. 'I wager you'll end up soaring for miles under the sun, so quick not even I could catch you.'

Tey sparkled. Imagine zooming fast, in real life, freer than the wind racing high through the trees! Raising his face to the air, the boy closed his eyes, remembering dreams of cool air rushing past his cheeks.

'Shush, daughter,' Tey's grandmother murmured quietly, her voice whisper dry. 'Do not torment the boy. The gift of flight is only handed down through the female line, as you well know. This one,' she uncurled her ancient hand and patted Tey on the arm, not unkindly, 'he will never take to the air. Never.'

Tey flinched, his skin burned under the weight and he ached to throw it off, but her hand remained, holding him firmly still.

'As you say, Mother, but I am not so sure,' objected Ash Kit, her voice questioning. 'His talent still remains hidden, and we do not know his strengths - he can see the wild ones after all.' She paused, gazing at Tey in all seriousness. 'He could still be one of us, why else would the Goddess not bless my sister with a daughter. Tey is her child. He must be born with her gifts.'

Feeling emboldened and with a surge of love for his aunt, Tey pulled his arm away from his grandmother. He grinned. Of course Ash Kit was right, he would really fly someday in the sky, and not by some other pretend way, soaring and swooping in his dreams.

'My daughter!' cried Au Set, her golden eyes blazing with the authority and power of the ancients. 'Do not get the boy's hopes up. He has no talent. He will live as his father does, without Heka, without the magic power of Word and Wind. Seeing the spirits of the forest is a small thing, a minor talent that even the uninitiated can possess. It is nothing. I do not presume to know the will of the Goddess, and I do not know the reasons why Ba Set was not blessed with a daughter to carry our birthright. Yet he *is* her son, for that, and if he is worthy,' Au Set paused and her bone-like fingers patted Tey's smooth soft cheek. 'We will increase his time spent on the earth with the power of the Spice, like his father. But that is all,' she added with a final pat, looking sadly at Tey. 'Boy, you have no magic, no talents, and you will never fly.'

His heart plummeted like a struck bird. Tey looked away, seeing nothing, his vision blinded by sharp, bitter tears. He brushed them away. Why should he care anyway? He swallowed. All this talk of flying and magic wasn't for him. This was women's talk. And anyway, he thought, clenching his jaw in determination; he'll grow to be like his father, skilful with the sword, living free in the forest with the wild ones.

A long line of shadow snaked its way across the clearing as birds darted through the crisp air, hunting the whirr and glint of tiny insects. The towering forest was dipping to grey and cool blues, while high in the tallest trees the leaves tipped to gold in the setting sun.

On the ground, Tey winced and rubbed his face where a sharp twig had scratched it as he peered through the leaves. He was hiding, crouching at the base of the old oak, its low hanging branches sheltering him from searching eyes. The boy shivered, the air felt chill and he rubbed his arms, longing for the warmth of his woollen cloak. But it wasn't here; it was stuffed uselessly into the chest by his bed. Scowling, Tey peered again out through the branches. How long, he wondered, would it take for his father to look around and realise he was missing out in the cold?

They had been standing - his parents, grandmother, and aunt by the table, talking for an age, ever since they had returned from the forest, but no one seemed to have even noticed he was gone. After a moment, Ba Set turned and wound her arms around his father and closed her eyes. Tey frowned. *Let him go. Let him go so he can come and find me. Please...*

Sighing, he shifted his position. His back hurt where he had scraped against the rough bark, and his legs were beginning to go numb. Miserably, he struggled to his feet and stood squeezed behind the branches of the ancient oak. In the quiet, the boy could hear his mother's voice rising on the evening air.

'I flew higher,' Ba Set was facing her sister and mother, and to Tey her voice sounded strained and thin. 'It is as we feared. The Lord and ladies have returned to the castle, but the rest, they are not letting go, not even for the dying of the day.'

Tey squinted through the overhanging leaves and his breath caught. His mother looked exhausted, her shoulders were trembling and she hid her face in his father's chest. Sitting on the bench beside, Ash Kit gently stroked her sister's hand. Anxious now to hear more, Tey extracted himself from the tight clasp of the branches as carefully as he could, and tiptoed closer.

'What they search for, I wish I knew,' continued his mother. 'For then we could recreate it, summon their intention with illusion, dream and desire, and send them seeking far beyond our own sanctuary. But,' she paused and said quietly, 'we do not know what it is... They are not interested in the oak wood by the river, nor the open heath land where the deer graze, but are circling the hidden paths of the old forest through the woods of lime and beech.'

Ba Set took a deep, steadying breath and tilted her head back, watching the flight of the swallows as they flashed through the clearing. 'Hear me well,' she said, her voice rising and her gaze dropped to her son as he crept toward her. 'They are not giving up,' she said flatly, her face tight with strain. 'They are getting closer with each and every moment.'

Tey shuddered and stopped dead in his tracks. *Was he coming?* He wondered, staring into the surrounding forest, gripped by a violent urge to flee. Was the mad knight coming or had he too returned to the castle?

Panic thudded through his body as he stared up into the leaves. They had lost their sharp red glow and were swaying calmly in the blue-grey light, a light breeze rippling through the very top of the branches.

He blinked; half hidden in the darkening shadows of the trees, a bald tubby being with protruding eyes and a wide grin was beckoning to him furiously. It was Gimbal, and his long knobbly fingers were gesturing to a stream of lithe figures racing though the branches above.

Impulsively, Tey took a step towards the darkening woods, his fears forgotten, imagining the tunes he would play to the whirling dancing faeries.

'Tey,' a firm voice stopped him in his tracks and he turned. His mother was watching him carefully, her body still enfolded within the warmth of her husband. 'Do not go,' she said, 'not this night. The sprites you follow would be no protection should these searchers find you alone in the forest.'

Without stopping, the boy scowled. *Of course they would,* he thought indignantly. *She doesn't know everything.* And he quickened his pace towards the trees.

'Son,' his father's voice cut sharply behind him, 'heed your mother and do what she says. The knight, Ulrick, remains in the forest.'

Tey felt the blood drain out of his face and his delighted mood vanished. He whirled to his parents in alarm.

'Yes,' said his mother evenly, 'the young knight stays, leading the whey faced abbot with a retinue of dour monks and a handful of armed foresters at his heels. Do not be so foolish as to run off into the woods tonight.' She looked hard at Tey. 'This noble bodes us ill, I fear, and I don't know why.'

The first star sparkled as the men disappeared into the darkness of the surrounding trees, each with a sharp blade in their possession. Tey's father and Martin were seeking branches, thick and tipped with leaves, long enough to conceal the cluster of huts scattered across the clearing. The women were elsewhere, walking the edges of the camp in single file through the greying light. They stopped every now and again, and laid their hands palm down on the earth, their low song spiralling quietly around them.

Tey crept along behind as quietly as he could, with his head down, careful not to be seen. He was meant to be in the forest with the men hunting for smaller branches, but he had run off across the clearing after his mother, anxious to know more about the magical seals the women were setting to protect their home.

They set them morning and every night as regular as the sun rose and fell in the sky. *But how?* Tey wondered, frowning and staring at the ground. *How did they work and how would it ever be enough?* The question circled around in his mind and tonight, no matter what he did, it wouldn't let him be.

A shudder of cold air rippled across the boy's back, and he looked up with a start. The three women had stopped and were standing bunched together in the shadows, their hair long and loose and identical golden eyes watching him closely under the trees. In the centre stood his grandmother, small and fragile, though as she spoke, her voice rang hard with disapproval.

'Go back,' she said and her gaze was unrelenting. 'Boy, this is not for you. You do not have the eyes for magic. Go back to the men.' She said no more but turned and walked away through the trees with her back straight and her chin held high. His mother and aunt followed without a backward glance.

Tey crumpled and his eyes stung with tears; his need to know draining away to a hollow empty ache.

Why wouldn't they tell him? He wondered miserably, and who cared if he couldn't see? Why couldn't they at least tell him something? Hurt filled his eyes and slipped down his cheeks as he sank wretchedly to his knees.

'Those of us who work with power,' came an unexpected voice. 'We can see it.' Hesitantly Tey looked up. Through the blur of tears he could see his aunt Ash Kit a few paces away, crouching down with her back to him, her hands splayed out firmly on the earth.

'We can see it spiralling up from the ground like smoke. This is the energy of the air and of the earth, and we weave it, shape it, sing it to our own design and set it in a great circle of protection around the camp. Thus the magic happens.'

'But how does it work?' whispered Tey, his heart in his throat, not daring to believe he would hear an answer.

'We weave first a pattern of distraction,' she said softly, turning around with a smile. 'If any stranger should find themselves coming too close for safety, a deer bark or a bird call will distract them, compelling them away to another, more distant part of the forest.' She paused, gazing away into the trees. 'But if someone is directly hunting us,' she said softly, 'then we need a working that is far stronger, something that will need the energy of us all.'

'But what? And how does it work?' Tey stood, his heart lifting in hope. 'Can you teach me?'

His aunt stared at him, as if weighing up how much to reveal, then rose to her feet. Ash Kit was the same height as her mother and sister, and her tawny eyes were level with his as she stood straight beneath the trees.

'That level of working magic is difficult to understand,' she said at last, and raised her hands as though feeling for the very fabric of the air itself. 'You need to see it,' she murmured, 'sense it, taste it, feel it with every pulse of your being, but if you don't …'

Pausing, his aunt looked at him sadly before shaking her head. 'Go child, it is not for you. Your grandmother has spoken, you do not have the Sight,' Ash Kit lifted her chin. 'Help the men with the last of the wood and leave us to finish working the land.'

Without waiting for a reply, his aunt turned and walked away with her hands outstretched, sweeping them over the ground as if she were caressing the weave of the air before her. Deflated, Tey watched her go, a small figure melting into the shadows between the trees. As she walked, a line of light flared behind her, rising, like a faint bluish haze looping up from the earth.

Tey blinked. 'Hey,' he cried out loudly, 'hey, I can see it!' But his aunt didn't stop, and after another breath, the swirling brightness winked out as though it had never been.

By the time Tey sat down at the table to eat a cold supper, the first star had risen and the work was finished. All that could be seen of the wooden huts was a dense line of slender trees, waving against the dark of the sky.

His father and Martin ate in silence, each lost in thought as their eyes stared blankly into the heart of the unlit fire. At the far corner of the table, the women were talking in quiet tones, their long hair obscuring their faces.

Tey forced down a few mouthfuls of stew before laying his spoon on the table. Around him he could hear branches knocking gently in the wind, like they did every night as the sun edged below the horizon. The sound should have been comforting, but Tey knew this night was nowhere near normal, as a madman was out there in the darkness, searching for him and not giving up.

Moaning in fear, Tey lay his head down on the table and squeezed his eyes shut. The wood felt cold and rough against his cheek, but he pressed his face into it harder, trying to force himself inside, hoping it would swallow him up and make him disappear.

At the murmur of his name, Tey's eyes flew open. His mother and father had risen, their faces grim. Motioning to join them quickly, Hew hurried after Ba Set, who was now striding across the clearing. Following a few steps behind was his grandmother, Au Set, while, deep in conversation, Martin and Ash Kit brought up the rear.

The adults stopped on a secluded piece of ground. Above them the sky was clear and fringed by a circle of trees. At a nod from his mother, they joined hands and waited, their eyes trained on Ba Set standing alone in the centre, her arms outstretched with palms facing up towards the heavens.

With a cry of alarm, Tey raced over to join them, squeezing his body into the gap beside his father. He breathed out a loud sigh of relief; he couldn't face being left out, no matter what was going on.

Hew nodded at him. 'Got here just in time. Now let's show these women who can sing.' And smiling grimly, his father squeezed Tey's hand tight.

Under the glittering sky, the trees stood tall and straight, like sentinels towering high above him. Titling his head back, Tey let the delicate shimmers of starlight wash over his upturned face. Out of the corner of his eye, a streak of silver flashed leaving a trail of bright song in its wake, the final notes of faery singing farewell to the sun.

With a deep breath, Ba Set raised her open hands higher into the air, followed a beat later by Au Set and Ash Kit. With closed eyes, the women began a soft, undulating tone, creating a layered triad of sound. Their voices rippled, seeming to rise and fall, and then repeat, as though waiting, cycling, ever patient.

A husky cough erupted above his head and Tey glanced up. His father was pulling breath in hard through his nostrils, his eyes were closed and his brow furrowed in concentration. Adjusting his stance, Hew coughed once more before breathing out his own gravelly tone. Low and quiet, the note skimmed over the boy's head before falling away to silence. Tey waited, gripping his father's hand, but then it came again. His father's voice gathered strength, becoming louder and more assured as it warmed beneath the layered harmonies of the women.

The pace changed. Picking up speed, the voices throbbed and pulled, becoming a wordless chant that swept around the circle, enveloping the singers in a rush of power. Martin tilted his head back, his voice booming out in a wide-open note of abandon. Laughing, Ash Kit matched her tone to his and their voices merged, rising in harmony to the heavens.

With his chest vibrating and his head lurching as the sound around him swelled in intensity, Tey's breath came quick. Gripping his father's hand hard, he tried to calm his trembling. Next to him, his grandmother sang out with a passion that belied her age. Her head tipped back to the sky, her arms were raised, and the sound rippling in her throat, poured out in exaltation, seeming to crackle and spark with colour.

With each breath the song spun faster; with each breath the separate voices mixed and merged. As Tey watched, Ash Kit sang with all her heart, her silvery tone mixing with the rich brown tone of the woodsman, and the deep shadowed green tone of Hew.

A cool blue note shot high overhead, cutting through to the apex of the circle. Ba Set stood with her feet bare and toes splayed, as weighted and as rooted as the trees. Pausing for a moment, she drew in a lungful of air and closed her eyes before singing another stream of energy up into the night. The sound hung, illuminated, as the circle of voices below rose to meet it.

173

'Shield us, cover us, hide us from this night!' Shining with joy and defiance, Ba Set cried out a stream of words. Indecipherable, and with a clicking, rhythmic cadence, they burst into the sky.

Tey stared, his heart pounding in fright. Blue licks of flame were rising up through the earth beneath his mother, engulfing her feet and flaring up her legs.

His eyes darted wildly around the circle, but no one else seemed to notice. The others were standing as one - their heads tipped back, their mouths open, streaming out a torrent of colour and sound. Tey whirled back to his mother. Bursts of iridescent blue were searing out of the top of her head and through her outstretched fingertips, towards the sky.

Abruptly his heart dropped with a deep internal thud and his body flashed hot and cold. A sudden numbness gripped his feet. Tey looked down. Loops of golden, molten heat were scorching up out of the ground, up through the soles of his bare feet, clutching him to the earth. A beat later, and it flashed up into his legs, up into his bones and muscles, gripping his limbs.

Tey struggled, frightened beyond measure, as bolts of energy shot up his back and into his neck, where it thudded and pounded on his vocal chords like a live thing trying to force its way out of his throat. Terrified, he opened his mouth to scream but out poured a fierce stream of sound that vibrated with all the might of the earth herself.

Tey shut his jaws tightly with a snap, mortally afraid of the power surging through his being. It felt as though the very earth had woken up beneath his feet and was pushing her will through the tiny vortex that was himself.

His body shuddered; this had never happened before. The last time the family had met in the circle, he had stood hand in hand with his father, taking part, respectful, at times lending his voice but sometimes not, content to let the voices of the others swirl and build above.

There was a jolt from the ground and Tey jerked. The energy was building now, stronger, as though more confident of him as a vessel. His feet began to throb, as power, now pure and blue in colour, surged up through his legs, scorching them from the inside. Frantically, Tey closed his mouth and opened his eyes, then opened his mouth and closed his eyes, panicked, not knowing what else to do, sure that he was too small to contain this immense rising energy, terrified it would split him apart.

Tey wrenched his eyes open, frantic for help, and reached out his arms in desperation to Ba Set. His mother stood crowned with a deep blue flame, her long dark hair sparking, spitting with power. She didn't respond. As the adults in the circle sang louder, Ba Set swept her hands across the sky, and a flame rose from the crowns of both Au Set and Ash Kit, arching overhead.

Tey widened his eyes. From each arc, an immense curtain of energy was forming - like a transparent cloak, gathering, ready, poised to drop down over the circle.

He gasped. *Mesh them in. Cut them off.* Panicked, the boy dropped to his knees, unable to breathe.

Ba Set, oblivious to the terrors rocking her son, stood transcendent and glowing with power. With a cry, she called on the energy of the song to rise even higher, to shield them, to protect them, to set them free forever from the terrors of the world.

She felt for the shape of the song swelling around her, preparing to draw the apex closed when the voices peaked for the final time.

At the bottom of the circle, Tey was shaking violently, his eyes glazed in terror, blue-white flame surging up his spine, pounding on his clenched teeth, trying to force them open to meet the call of his mother. Above him the song vibrated, calling to every nerve, every cell, every sinew of his body.

Silence held as the circle drew in a final collective breath, readying for the surge of sound, which would be shot like a great, single act of magic up into the sky.

Power knifed his body and Tey shook uncontrollably, his teeth almost cracking with the strain of clamping his jaw shut. He felt the earth below urging the song to be released. Teetering, almost completely overwhelmed, he felt like he was drowning, suffocating. He knew he was about to be split asunder.

'Now!' cried Ba Set.

Power jolted, an ice-hot searing blue and Tey could hold back no longer. He screamed.

A howling, piercing sound ripped through with fear and confusion as it shot past his aching jaws, up through the unclosed apex of the circle, and out into the darkness. A sharp angular red, the sound stabbed at the night sky, frantic, crying, calling desperately for help.

The circle collapsed.

His father and Martin dropped at once to the ground as though dead. Ash Kit and Au Set clutched each other, staggering, falling, their golden eyes dark with shock.

Only Ba Set remained standing, incandescent with fury, power pulsing still from every fibre and cell of her being. With one step she flew across the circle and hauled her son to his feet, shaking him, wordless with rage.

'I saw, I saw,' sobbed Tey, his teeth chattering.

Ba Set released her hand and the boy tumbled to the ground. He lay still, inert with misery.

A shrill of light. A shudder of movement. Out of the darkness a cascade of bright eyes and fury streamed into the clearing. It was a silvery whirlwind of massed faeries with hackles up and sharp teeth bared. The stream split in two - one to cover the cowering boy, while the other plunged through the night towards Ba Set.

She swotted them away.

'Seen what?' she demanded, full of rage. 'You can't have seen anything. You, a mere boy, have seen nothing.'

Tey began to sob, a great body wracking sound. His head was cast down, and his arms were wrapped tightly around his knees. Ba Set seethed, energy crackling around her. More faeries emerged from the deep forest, drawn by the young boy's cry. Gimbal swooped down from the heights to stand protectively, as tall as he could, the fat faery's bulbous eyes glaring up at Ba Set in defiance.

From behind the trees a shadow emerged, its great eyes blinking, joining other mighty spirits rising out of the rock and ground, streaming towards the stricken boy. Within a moment he was surrounded by a glow of beings, shielding him and lending him strength. Tey gulped a breath and gazed up into his mother's fierce golden eyes.

177

'I did See,' he said, in a trembling voice. 'And I still See. You have fire all around you.'

Ba Set took a step towards him. 'How dare you,' she began angrily. 'You are of your father's line. You cannot See.'

Wilting, Tey shrank away from his mother's unyielding denial.

'It's impossible.' She stated flatly.

A hand touched her lightly on her shoulder. 'It is not impossible, sister,' murmured Ash Kit, gazing at the massed wild folk, her eyes soft with wonder. 'Look how the spirits come to his aid,' she whispered. 'It's a mighty talent. I have never heard of such a thing.'

Ba Set brushed her sister aside. 'They're nothing, they're mindless, senseless creatures,' she snapped with a wince. Ba Set shook her head as if in pain.

'Sister, place your hands on the ground. You crackle with unreleased energy, it can do you great harm if you do not let it go.'

Ignoring her, Ba Set reached to pull Tey to his feet, but as she did so, a tall angular spirit rose to shield the boy. Elegant and luminous, the figure gazed at Ba Set with such a serene, implacable energy that she faltered.

Another taller faery appeared - a transparent, liquid being, it rippled with light and its soft radiance covered the forlorn boy. Elsewhere, spilling from the trees, more wild spirits emerged from the heart of the forest, from the ancient groves, from the tumbling waterfalls, and from the hidden silence of the deep caves. They appeared until Tey lay surrounded by beings of untold beauty and strength.

'No,' declared Ba Set, as radiance danced over her face. She raised her hand, golden eyes flashing with pride. The beings waited, each one as cool and serene as a deep-water pool. A breeze danced, lifting her hair, releasing sparks of pent up energy into the night air. Abruptly Ba Set laughed, a high incredulous sound, and lowering her palms, she breathed out a long, loud sigh and the ground around her flashed as loops of pent up energy melted back into the soil.

Then in the hushed clearing, from the massed spirits of fire and water, earth and air, came a song, spun from the very fabric of the forest itself, a song that descended over the boy and his mother as gentle and as light as the wind.

Tey lay quiet, his earlier terror and confusion forgotten. He turned his mother, and her face was bathed in light.

'My son,' she reached for his hand. It felt cool and dry and surprisingly small. 'I never…'

Tey bowed his head, too overcome to meet her eyes, his heart trembling, waiting.

But Ba Set never completed her sentence as a mighty shout ripped through the clearing and a horse, its huge chest lathered with exertion, charged into the circle, dashing sparks from the flint that lay embedded in the ground. A tiny faery with thistle-topped hair and delicate limbs flared in fright and vanished. Ba Set, swept aside by its bulk, stumbled to the ground.

On the beast's back, his gold and red cloak billowing majestically, was a single knight. His fist was raised in the air, and his ice blue eyes were blazing with fanatical fire.

'Rejoice! The Blessed Child is found. Rejoice!'

SEVENTEEN

Blue Mountains, Australia, present day

The streetlights blinked on as Ellie hurried up the driveway, her parents' car was parked in its usual place by the back gate. From the house, seeping out through the living room curtains, a blue and white flicker cast a ghostly glow over the front step. The blue switched to a more soothing yellow as a shadow swept through the room. Her mother, Ellie guessed as she quietly turned her key in the lock, changing the channels. It was a Saturday night and it looked like the family were home.

Taking care not to creak the floorboards, Ellie slipped in as quietly as she could and crept down the hallway into her room. Dropping her bag on the floor, she sat in the dark, catching her reflection in the small oval mirror on the wall.

Did any of it really actually happen?

Her face stared back, serious, her green eyes wide. It looked the same, pale and freckled with wisps of untidy hair sneaking out beneath a wrap of brightly coloured cloth.

Soul Flyer … Ellie mouthed the words, tasting them on her tongue. They felt weird yet zinged and exploded through her senses like fragments of space rock or sweet, fizzy sherbet.

Pulling off her sandals, Ellie pushed them under her bed and then, on impulse, jumped to her feet. She lifted her arms and whirled around and around on the spot, her hands out wide and her hair flowing soft and loose.

'Soul Flyer,' she whispered, and her bed, bookcase, cupboard, and desk blurred as she spun faster and faster. My God. What could it all mean? Dizzy, Ellie sat down with a sudden lurch, the room wheeling and tilting around her.

And Ba Set… My God. Ellie shuddered as she remembered the disquieting vision of an endless stream of women, ancient and crowned in gold. *Was that even real?* Ellie sat for a long moment with her eyes closed, before taking a deep breath and tiptoeing down the hallway to the kitchen.

She checked her clothes were straight, with no twigs or leaves to give her away, and fixed a smile on her face as she opened the door to the brightly lit room. 'Hi Mum,' she called. 'I'm back.'

Claire wiped her hands on her apron and turned around. 'Ellie, how long have you been home? I didn't hear the front door.'

'Oh, just now.' Ellie shrugged. Opening the pantry she peered in, looking for some biscuits. She was starving. 'Where are the twins?' The house seemed unnaturally calm.

'Ben has taken them out. Ellie,' she paused, 'did you find what you were looking for at the library?'

Something in her mother's tone made Ellie look up. Claire was standing with her hand on the bench, watching her closely.

181

'The library?' Ellie flushed, thinking hard. She hadn't gone to the library, or anywhere near it. Ellie had been so focused on confronting Ba Set, she hadn't considered her parents would wonder where she'd been all day. 'Yeah Mum, I ducked in and found a few books,' Ellie replied, uneasily. 'But then I didn't stay,' she added. 'I just took them out and found a quiet little place to study-'

'Where was that?'

'Um, under a tree, in the shade, in the park.'

'For the Lord's sake, do you think we're stupid?' her mother cried out, slapping her hand down hard.

'What? No!'

There was a crash of wood on the wall as the door to the kitchen burst open. Her father strode in, his tall frame filling the kitchen, and his anger even more frightening because it was contained and directed solely at her.

'Where have you been?'

'I-I-In the park, Dad.' Ellie stammered, 'I was just reading. You know I like to read outside.' Ellie couldn't think of anything else to say, but it wasn't a complete lie; she did like to read outside...

He glared at her. 'What book, from where?'

'Just a textbook from the library, my God Dad, why are you both having a go at me? You know I have to study and its just too loud here with the twins always going mental!' She was shouting now, anxious to deflect the conversation away from the dangerous subject of where she'd been.

Without a word, her father hauled Ellie by the hand and pulled her down the hall and into her room. Behind them, following closely, Claire was crying. 'Ellie, why do you lie to us, why do you lie to us all the time? Where is God to you, what is God to you? Where is truth?'

Ellie shut out the anguished torrent, her heart was thudding, and she almost tripped as she stumbled into her room and fell onto her bed. Her father loomed over her, his anger as sharp as a slap.

'You're grounded. Now. Forever. You are not to go out. You are to go to school and come back within half an hour of the end of the school day. You are a liar, Ellie Malone. You habitually, and wilfully disobey us. And we are sick to death of it.'

'What? That's not fair!'

'Don't even bother, Ellie.'

The streetlight fell in stripes of orange as her mother silenced her with a look, and closed the door behind her, making a point of turning the handle so the catch locked it shut. *Like bars,* thought Ellie, standing alone in the centre of the room. Morosely, she gazed at the pattern of shadow and light on her bed.

I'm jailed. Forever.

Outside, the old red gum bumped against the wall of the house, wood on wood, its rhythmic thudding marking the first intervals of her sentence. The window was open, and as the curtains rose and fell, the dry warmth of the night, tinged with the dusty traces of the forest, swirled and eddied through the gap.

Numb with shock, Ellie pulled off her jeans and t-shirt and, opening her closet, searched until she found her oldest and most comforting nightdress. Made of soft cotton, and only slightly too small, Ellie slipped it over her head and climbed into bed, pulling the covers right up to her chin.

Cocooned the darkness, Ellie lay as still as she could, her arms folded across her belly, her eyes open, trained on the shadows cutting sharp across the ceiling.

What had just happened?

From the living room, laughter buzzed, followed by a burst of tinny music and a rapid-fire voice. Over the blare of the television came the clink and scrape of cutlery, her parents eating their evening meal in the kitchen. But they weren't talking, Ellie realised, and for a long time she lay wondering, listening to the familiar sounds of the house. What was going on? Her parents never normally looked for her, and besides, how had they known she wasn't in the library?

On the lower shelf of the desk lay Ellie's cell phone, its face reflecting the soft green glow of her bedside clock. She hardly took it anywhere, it was way too expensive, and besides it was only ever used for emergencies.

Kicking off the covers, Ellie picked it up.

'Oh what?' she groaned.

Its normally blank screen held a list of calls missed from today, two from home, and a single one from Rose.

Ellie leant back against the wall. Of course, how could she have been so stupid? If her parents were looking for her, they would've called Rose first to ask where she was, and Rose would've said 'the library' out of habit.

But … Ellie winced. Oh God … she was so busted. Saturday … today was Saturday, and everyone knew the library was closed.

The clock clicked and Ellie had just rolled over, closing her eyes, when the floorboards creaked and her door swung open after a single knock.

Ellie's mother entered, carrying a small tray covered with a cloth. 'I've brought you some dinner.' Her voice sounded tired.

The mattress dipped as Claire perched herself on the edge of the bed.

Ellie didn't respond, her breathing was slow and steady as if she was already deeply asleep.

Placing the tray on the floor, her mother sat for a long moment in silence.

'I wish I could understand you.' She said at last. Her mother's voice trembled, and the tone was soft, but the unmistakeable note of reproach settled over Ellie like a net. 'Why do you disobey us? Why would you choose a life of sin over the love of your family? Why Ellie?'

Ellie didn't move, but her heart began to beat louder, and she was sure her mother could hear its rising rhythm of alarm.

'We don't forbid you out of malice,' her mother was still speaking. 'We know you love the forest, you always have, but we have to protect you, and we will. Even if we have to chain you to the bed.'

What? Ellie couldn't contain herself any longer and her eyes flew open. 'You wouldn't do that!'

Her mother sighed. 'You *are* awake.' She clasped her hands in prayer and looked down. Her eyes were red and painful looking, as though she had been crying for a long time. 'Ellie, we would do whatever we needed to. You are our responsibility. How could we stand before God, and say we let our daughter go?'

'But you haven't let me go.' Ellie's heart thudded as the enormity of the thought filled the room. 'You haven't, I just ... I don't know...'

They stared at each other.

'Where did we go wrong? Where?' Her mother dropped her head.

'Mum,' Ellie whispered desperately. 'Don't. Please.'

'It's just so important, and you just ignore us.'

It was awful. Ellie felt helpless as her mother hid her face in her hands, her shoulder's shaking, as though she couldn't bear anyone to see her tears.

'Please don't, Mum.' Ellie sat up and placed an arm awkwardly around her mother. ' Please don't cry. I won't go back, I promise, I really won't. I'll be good. Mum, I promise, please.'

And she meant it. Ellie really meant it.

The tears didn't stop immediately, but after a long moment Claire retrieved a tissue from her apron pocket and gently blew her nose.

'That's better,' she murmured, scrunching the tissue in her hand. She patted Ellie's leg. 'Are you hungry? I've brought you some dinner.'

'No…Thanks.' Ellie shook her head, relieved the emotional storm was over. 'I have a bit of a headache...'

'It's all that studying you do,' said Claire, handing her a glass of water from the dinner tray.

Ellie drank the contents down.

'Now let me hear your prayers.'

A burst of laughter caught in Ellie's throat, but she coughed, forcing it back down. She'd promised to be good. Her mother waited, her hands folded.

'Please God,' Ellie began, 'bless my Father, bless my Mother … bless Ben ... bless Tommy, bless Annie...' On and on the list went, a prayer of blessings for her family, her friends, her town, her country, and it ended in a plea for forgiveness for all her sins.

Claire smiled. 'I won't let you forget your promise, Ellie. Especially in these End Times, we need to be together as a family. You need to put your doubts aside and trust us. We're your parents and we know what's best.'

Ellie could only nod, she felt exhausted. It had been a crazy, confusing day.

Her mother laid a hand on her shoulder before taking the dinner tray and closing the door tightly behind.

Now what? Ellie rolled towards the wall. She closed her eyes and settled into her bed, waiting for sleep to take her away.

But it was no use.

Ellie pushed the covers off and stared up at the ceiling. How could she keep that promise? And Soul Flyer ... was that sinful? Was it? Was Ba Set a devil? How does anyone know what's true?

Ellie's backpack lay in the centre of the room, abandoned where she'd dropped it. Its zip was open and from its depths, a hazy light seeped up into the darkness.

Ask the stone ... ask it anything at all.

'Should I?' Whispered Ellie, her heart was thudding, in fear or excitement she didn't quite know.

Lying back down on her bed, she placed the stone carefully onto the soft area of her belly. Despite the covering of her nightdress, Ellie's stomach muscles recoiled as its smooth coolness seeped into the warmth of her skin. Shadows played, dancing on her walls, a dog barked outside, and the branches of the tree knocked gently against the side of the house.

If she did this, Ellie thought slowly; if she entered the strange world of magic by her own choice, she probably *was* sinning and she may well damn her very soul forever. Ellie's heart jolted in fear.

Through the walls, Ellie could hear the final strains of a guitar and applause as the credits rolled. Her parents would soon turn the TV off, brush their teeth, and say their bedtime prayers, dedicating their sleep to the safety of the Lord.

'But it feels right…' Whispered Ellie, her hand hovering over the stone. 'And I have to know, I just have to know.'

Ellie clasped the stone to her skin, and its cold moved from her belly down to her spine, spreading like a mist up into her chest, and out through her limbs.

'Soul Flyer…' The words hung soft and sibilant above her. 'What is it, what is a Soul Flyer?'

Breathing softly, Ellie waited. She wasn't sure what for. She shifted her position. Beside her in the darkness, the green numbers of her clock clicked over a single minute, then another, and another. The bathroom door, down the hallway, closed with a quiet snap of the lock.

Ellie wriggled her toes. How would she even know if something was happening? She clenched the hag stone firmer against her skin.

Just ask…

Had Ba Set suggested anything else?

Ellie tried to think, but it was hard, her thoughts felt weird and gooey, and thick, like her brain was stuck - stuck, stickity stuck, and old, like a jar full of melted sweets.

Ellie shook her head, or tried to, but nothing happened. It refused to move, as though it was a lump, weighted on the pillow. Frowning, Ellie tried to think of something, anything, but it felt an impossible task. Her thoughts were disjointed as though her mind had given up, and was now floating high and free, like a balloon.

She giggled. What a mad idea. On impulse, Ellie reached up, trying to pull her mind back. But the next thing she knew, she had the weird sensation of floating, stretching up high above her bed, with her feet the only things keeping her tethered to her body. Without really meaning to, Ellie yanked at them and the sudden momentum pushed her so hard that she slipped free and banged up against the underside of the ceiling.

Below, Ellie could see the outline of her body on the bed. It was lying perfectly still and peaceful, with one hand over the hag stone and the other resting by her side.

How did I do that? She wondered. Her thoughts, thankfully, now felt free and clear. As Ellie hovered she wasn't sure if she should go back down and ask the stone for help. She could sense it, an ancient, solid piece of earth weighing down the centre of her stomach.

As she considered it, Ellie felt herself begin to sink lower, down towards the bed. 'No, no,' she whispered. 'No, not yet.' Immediately the descent eased.

Elation surged though her being. *Soul Flyer.* She grinned. My God.

The bedroom ceiling was the only barrier between her and the open sky. Ellie hesitated, wondering how to get through. Trying not to think about it too much, Ellie simply willed herself upwards. She didn't know exactly how, but a breath later she was floating high above the roof outside. Her home lay below - a dark, squat shape surrounded by a sea of dried out lawn.

It was weird. Ellie could feel, acutely, physical sensations running over her body - the warm air streaming over her skin, the prickling cold of distant starlight - every cell felt energised and wide-awake. But she couldn't see it; she couldn't see her body at all, she could only *feel* it, like she was dreaming - but wide, wide, awake.

Soul flyer, that's what it all means.

Hugging herself in delight, Ellie let her vision settle on a fine line of brightness spanning the darkness. The sun, she realised with a shock of surprise, the last edge of the sun before it disappeared over the distant ocean. High above the horizon line, specks of light glittered in the inky blackness - stars, beckoning her still further upwards into the wide embrace of the heavens.

I could just keep on going... Ellie realised, as she considered the vast cool expanse of space, and a frisson of fear trembled though her heart. Then she laughed and, turning on a whim, Ellie soared down and away, her flight as light and as ephemeral as thought.

Effortless, all it took was a simple arching of her back and Ellie executed a flawless looping circle. Delighted, she looped higher still, dipping and tumbling in the vast wonder of the sky. With a flick of an idea, she swept above the sleeping landscape, over the cliffs, and on to the dark forest beyond, her eyes wide and her hands outstretched.

A shimmer brushed her skin, and then another. Ellie turned to see a gathering cloud of beings, of all shapes and sizes and brilliance, swooping toward, above, and beyond her.

For a long time - Ellie didn't know quite how long, she flew through the open night, but after a time her exhilaration calmed and she slowed, circling in wide slow arcs back above the trees. Darkness, the canyons below held quiet shadows of night and rest. The rocky edges were mere ghostly shapes jutting through trees and meshed so closely together they seemed a single wave of deepest black.

Ellie breathed, mesmerised by the calm and depth of the sleeping valleys. But as she gazed down, studying the forest, she began to be aware of something else, a faint silvery glow running through the land itself, connecting tree to tree, rock to tree, rock to rock, delicate, overlapping, its rhythm as constant as a heartbeat. Lines as fine as lace were intersecting through the forest like luminous strands, looping around, beneath, and through the trees, fanning on through the soil, connecting them all.

Beautiful. Ellie thought, floating motionless above. *It is so beautiful, I wish Rose was here too, and then she would understand. Nothing this beautiful could ever, ever be wrong.*

EIGHTEEN

The stone house on the edge of the cliff was dark.

A full-length mirror stood in the centre of the bedroom on the first floor, its smoky glass edged with an antique wood, red cedar perhaps or mahogany. Arranged at its base in a half semi-circle were coloured candles of different heights, each one freshly lit.

Blowing out the match, Rose casually flicked it into the wastepaper basket by her door where it hit the tissue paper, crackling and hissing. At her feet a dress lay crumpled in a heap on the floor, the price tags still showing, its silver satiny delivery box kicked near the wall.

Facing herself in front of the mirror, Rose pursed her lips to a pout. She turned and stood side-on, studying her profile illuminated in the flattering, fluttering light. She arched her back to a rebel pose and raised one hand, tapping out an imagery cigarette, with the other poised, cupped under her chin. Smiling, she blew herself a kiss. Her reflection smiled back, a slow full movement.

Rose licked her lips. *I'm beautiful,* she thought, her eyes travelling over the curves and swells of her body.

She felt so good, gone was the cloying heaviness that had been pressing in on her for weeks. She could breathe again. The air in here even felt a little cooler. It danced around her skin and from the open window she could smell a sweet hint of freshness. It might even rain. Parting her lips, Rose licked them again, slowly, how she longed for moisture.

'What is with me tonight,' she murmured, trailing her fingers down her arms. She shook them out, watching her hands as they fluttered prettily in the light. Her skin felt hot to touch and she closed her eyes, enjoying the feel of her hair as it fell against her fingers.

Rose was alone in the house. Her father had left for a service hours before, and the day had since lengthened into darkness.

'I don't feel well,' she'd explained sleepily that morning, her father waiting outside her door. Later she had heard his feet echo as he paced up and down the hallway, waiting she supposed, in case she changed her mind. But as the clock in the hall marked the hour, she'd heard the back door bang shut and the low roar of the car as it faded away into silence.

She had let out a long, slow breath in relief.

In the quiet of her room, as the sun streamed in through the chinks in the curtains, Rose had slept. The afternoon silence was broken only by the chimes of the clock, and her dreams were free of disturbing, frightening images.

Now her dreams were much more fun.

Rose frowned, watching the pretty lines crease her forehead.

Ben could've come over, she pouted. Later. She'd call and convince him to climb up into her bedroom.

She giggled softly. He wouldn't be able to resist. And she would wear nothing… Except -

Rose paused as a hot flush burned across her skin, tingling across her cheeks. She imagined Ben climbing up into her darkened bedroom, lifting her window, pushing back the heavy velvet curtains, and finding her lying, draped sinuously over her bed. Lit by the gentle glow of the candles, she would be wearing only her own soft satiny skin and….

Her tawny eyes shone golden. *Oh yes it would be perfect.*

Smiling, and enjoying the feel of her swaying hips, Rose padded over to her dressing table. Humming softly, she opened the top right drawer, and searched through the mass of tangled silken scarves. Her fingers brushed metal. It was there, just where she had hidden it. She lifted the heavy roped chain high, and the feathered wings of the amulet wavered in the soft light of the candles.

'Oh…' Rose sighed in wonder at its priceless, mesmerising beauty.

Stumbling over the intricate workings of the clasp, she lowered her head and secured the thick chain around her neck. She shivered as the golden body of the amulet fell heavily between her breasts. Clasping it between her hands, it felt solid and vital. Unthinking, Rose pressed the figurine right to her skin, close to her heart. Her pulse raced. Her legs trembled and, unnoticed, a crackle of heat began to flare over her skin.

A warmth she'd never before experienced, a rich golden heat as molten and thick as honey, began to spread out from her chest, melting down into her belly, curving along every hidden swell and surface. Expelling a low moan of surprise, Rose closed her eyes as her body began to sway in response, her legs trembling as the warmth melted through every cell of her being. Rose moaned again, enjoying the sensation as the warmth rose higher and higher up her spine, up into her throat. It begged to be released. Smiling languorously, Rose tipped back her head and sang out a low rich tone.

Oh that felt good, thought Rose in surprise.

She breathed in again, her belly felt warm and soft as if the sound was made of liquid. Rose moaned again, letting her voice stream out from the base of her throat. Unstopped, unfettered, she sang it out, long and loud. Undulating with power, the moan of sound filled the room, before slipping through the window and soaring out into the night.

Rose moaned again.

On the gravelled drive outside, the Reverend Matthew Hopkins slammed the car door shut and stared up at the darkened face of the house. The windows were drawn and the sky behind was lit with a haze of stars. He waited, his body tense, but whatever had made that infernal, ghastly noise had ceased. Frowning, he turned away. Some night creature, he supposed, scuttling back into the darkness from whence it came. Brushing it from his mind, Matthew walked quickly across the path to the back gate, his robes flowing in his wake.

A good night, he smiled, nodding to himself as the metal latch creaked open. The congregation gathering around him were rich and fervent with belief, especially that young Ben. He smiled again, such a good choice for his daughter.

Matthew let the gate bang behind, feeling his heart clutch in regret that his Rosalind hadn't felt well enough to join them this evening. *May she find peace,* he prayed softly. *May she be sleeping well and safe.*

His footsteps crunched as he rounded the back of the house and entered the secluded peacefulness of the garden. As he always did when he returned late, Matthew glanced up towards the second floor, his daughter's window; it was the largest, double cased and situated behind a small balcony in the centre.

Matthew stopped. A single spot was glowing within the vastness of the dark stone brick. Rosalind had retired, her high window draped with cloth emitting only the faintest of wavering lights.

So like her mother, Matthew smiled. She too had preferred the gentle soothing flicker of candles. In this modern world, he mused, the old ways were still best.

Relishing in the peaceful quietness, Matthew turned back from his daughter's window and headed towards the back door. Pulling the long brass key from under his robes, he had turned it only once in the lock when the terrible sound erupted once more into the night.

Fear hackled across Matthew's skin. After a dreadful pause, in which it seemed the very heavens drew breath, the sound came again - louder this time, rising in tone and urgency, on and on and on, a wanton lowing shattering the stillness. Staring up into the centre window, Matthew whispered a single desperate word.

'No!'

The wretched noise erupted again as Matthew rushed into the house.

What was happening? He stopped on the first landing, trying to gauge its direction. A lull, and then it came again, from somewhere on the first floor, gathering in strength and intensity.

Where was Rosalind?

His heart pounding, Matthew flew up the stairs as the sound gathered intensity.

Reaching his daughter's room, Matthew threw his weight against the door.

It was locked. Inside the moaning was reaching a fevered crescendo, wailing higher, shrieking now its desire for release.

Gathering his strength, Matthew hurled his body against the door once more and burst open into an abruptly silent room.

Darkness waited.

Desperately he searched for the light switch, his fingers draping the wall behind the door. He flicked it on.

The light glared, dazzling his eyes. Blinking rapidly, Matthew rushed into the centre of his daughter's room.

'Rosalind' he cried, his voice hoarse with fear.

Her bed opposite lay open and exposed, unmade and empty, the covers pushed against the wall. The new dress she had pleaded for so eloquently lay discarded, crumpled on the floor. In the centre of the room, in its habitual pride of place was the mirror she loved so much, but pooling at its base were puddles of coloured wax and the misshapen remains of burnt out candles.

What had she been doing?

Shaking, Matthew turned. 'Rosalind.' He called softly. 'Rose.'

The room remained mute save for a hushed whisper. Matthew glanced over at the window. It was open, a gentle unconcerned breeze lifting and lowering the fall of the curtain. But beneath it hidden, unnoticed in the shadows, a figure stood hunched beneath the folds of the drapes, its head turned as though it was staring up into the starlit night. The curtains lifted, and the ripple of air ruffled the dark feathers along its crown.

Horror and shock tore the breath from Matthew's throat. 'No…' he gasped, refusing to believe. Cautiously, he stepped forward, his tread creaking the floorboard as he moved. The thing turned, its deep yellow eyes pinioning him with the intensity of its gaze.

'NO!' The sound wrenched itself out of his heart, out of the pit of his deepest nightmares. With a bellow of revulsion, Matthew threw himself forward and slammed the heavy window shut. He bolted it, locking it tight.

The creature reared in alarm, its dark wings unfurling, its sharp talons scraping along the bare floors. But it couldn't flee. Ungainly, it scrabbled further into the room away from the window. Away from him.

The thing could not escape

His Rosalind could not escape.

Agonised, Matthew moaned, his hands shaking, tearing at his hair, his face, his eyes; the desire to scratch them out to blind himself from this horror was overwhelming.

No! No! No!

How could this be happening; she was still just a child! She was an innocent. She didn't know the ancient ways.

No wait. Agonised at what he might see, Matthew opened his eyes. Hanging around the creature's neck, looped around the abomination of its form, was a string of gold - a long twisted chain. From it, hanging insolently over its chest, was a golden figurine, boastful in its finely wrought detail - an idolatrous half eagle, half woman monstrosity.

Matthew's heart quaked, and if he hadn't been holding onto the wall he would have fallen, crashing to the floor.

With a howl he sprang for the golden amulet, and in a single swift movement wrenched it off the creature's neck. Clutching it between his hands, Matthew ignored the intense heat searing into his palms. The creature reared, flexing its dark wings out to their full span. The tip of one swept over his head into the centre of the room, while the other bashed against the confines of the wall. The creature hovered, lopsided for a split second, held aloft by the strength of a single wing before it toppled, crashing to the floor, unused to the limits of its new-found form.

Matthew ran from the room.

'She is an abomination!' The agony in his voice knifed through the shadows of the house. She was a thing to be shunned, a thing to be destroyed, a monstrosity to be cast into the pit of everlasting torment along with all others of her kind.

'Oh why didn't I have a son?' shouted Matthew, his eyes staring up towards the apex of the house. 'Why Lord, why? Why did you not give me a son?' The questions flung into the silence were answered only by the pounding of his footfalls as he fled from the nightmare in the bedroom above.

She was cursed. *He* was cursed. She was a monstrosity. *He* was an abomination. But no, Matthew's heart whispered, refusing to permit him to deny the love he felt for his only child.

'Do not damn her,' it whispered. She was still his beautiful daughter, his own sweet faced Rosalind and he would protect her if he could.

Muttering a delirium of prayers, Matthew dashed into his room and without hesitating, flung open the doors of the scroll-topped cabinet standing in the corner. Down low he searched, nearest to the floor for the tiny drawer hidden within a nest of others. With his heart in his throat, and hope flaring, his fingers unlatched a silver clasp and he reached down deeper into the maze, and drew out his greatest treasure. Small, only pebble sized, it lay almost lost within the palm of his hand.

Matthew stared at it, fear and grief paralysing his muscles. The stone shone obsidian, its dark surface reflecting the feeble light of the moon outside.

It had kept him safe for centuries, for nigh on eight hundred years.

NINETEEN

Southern England 1340

Ulrick pulled the reins, forcing his mount to rear with a shriek before it dropped heavily to the earth, its nostrils snorting and eyes rolling in fury.

'Here he is!' He cried, brandishing his staff in triumph. 'The Holy Child whom I saw commune with angels and does so again!'

Jumping off his horse, the knight dropped to the ground. His eyes bright with glory as he gazed up at the towering, luminous faeries. 'Bless me, child.'

Tey recoiled. Behind the knight, six hooded monks too had fallen to their knees and, with fingers bone white against the black folds of their robes, they were gesturing the sharp sign of the cross. Behind them all, watching silently from the shadows was the abbot - his face hidden and his jewelled staff glinting in the afterglow of the luminous faeries.

The boy shuddered, then felt his mother's hard hand grasp his own, tightly. At first Tey couldn't see what had caught her attention. Concealed on the ground, his grandmother was crouching low, shoulder to shoulder with Ash Kit; the two women's hands were face down, and their eyes were closed.

An armed figure slipped between the bushes.

Shadows danced, and from the throats of the monks a chant of devotion began smoking its way up into the trees. Like a grey and torpid thing, it rose over them all. Tey shuddered.

A light winked out.

'I ... I didn't know...' the boy stammered fearfully. 'I didn't mean for him to see me...'

His mother didn't move, her eyes were seeking any hint of movement from between the huts.

'What are you saying?' She gripped his hand tighter.

'He was following me,' Tey whispered, tears springing to his eyes, 'I didn't know what to do…'

'Who?' asked Ba Set turning. 'My son, tell me. Who was following you?'

'Him,' whispered Tey. His gaze shifted to where Ulrick was kneeling, his eyes wide to the heavens. 'The knight.'

Ba Set stared. She dropped her son's hand and in one fluid motion rose to her feet. 'It's you? You? This… This… Knight of the *faith,*' she spat the word out, 'has been searching for you, and yet you kept silent?'

She stared, incredulous. 'Why Tey, why didn't you say anything?'

Tey hung his head in shame, thinking of all the reasons but not one of them made sense anymore, not now.

Ba Set raised her chin at the mournful, chanting monks, her mouth twisted, appalled. 'What have you done? They seek to destroy us, and all we hold dear.' She said flatly as she gazed into the cold eyes of the black-hooded abbot.

Tears stung his eyes. Around them, movement shuddered as the monks' song rose and settled thickly over the camp. A spark of energy flared through the soil then was still, suffocated by a devotion that would negate any belief but their own.

Behind, a single wild spirit sang out a bell-like note of sorrow and evaporated into the chilled air of the clearing. A delicate being standing close to Tey shivered and winked out. Then another larger, flaming faery leaned in low from the shadows, its great eyes begging for forgiveness, before it too vanished.

One by one, as the monks' fervour and chanting increased in intensity, the great beings disappeared back into the hidden shadows of the forest, until Tey was left on his knees. His small, crouched form watched over zealously by Ulrick, Defender of the Faith.

'Search the camp!' A shout erupted from out of the dark, as a forest warden – a great bear of a man, emerged from the trees with a whetstone brandished high above his head. 'Search the camp,' he bellowed once more. 'This is no haven of the holy.'

Hew and Martin had been lying stunned in a pool of shadow, far from the torchlight. Now, they stirred.

'No,' Tey breathed, terrified, as his father struggled to his feet. The woodsman was beside him, moaning and clasping his head in pain. Hew clutched the trunk of a small tree as if to stop himself from falling and shook his head. Lifting his eyes to Tey, he smiled gently, and then turned his gaze to the direction of the storehouse.

Hidden well, the grey slab hut resembled a slender grove of saplings. Leaves stirred gently amid lengths of struck branches. All were dark, silhouetted by the light thrown by the fires. Tey moaned; it was hard to see, but a figure was heading towards the shadows, swinging a double-bladed axe with nonchalant ease. A few steps ahead, came another, a sharp-faced wiry fellow. He gripped a thick cudgel in his hand and in his other he held a flaming torch that he plunged into the shadows, searching for evidence that would damn them all.

Energy flicked, cool and sure as Ba Set crouched to the ground. She raised her hands towards her husband, moving them as though she was pushing her beloved away, willing him to melt into the safety of the forest. Her breath was loud; the in breath sucked in like it was never enough, and the out breath was long and urgent.

Tey clenched his eyes shut. 'Please, please, *please*,' he whispered desperately. 'I am not afraid…' Gritting his teeth, he willed the energy of the earth into his hands. But he was too late. As his palms touched the soil, fire erupted from the camouflaged huts, searing high into the night.

Crowing in triumph, the rat-faced warden swung his cudgel hard into the burning saplings and knocked them to the ground. The weathered walls of the storehouse gaped, exposed in the flames.

Hew leapt to his feet and with his sword held high, ran towards the hut, slashing at the warden, driving him away from the door. The man spun sharply, and with a laughing sneer, smashed his weapon towards Hew's head. Tey screamed, but his father dodged and struck, whipping up the edge of his sword. Stepping back, the warden wiped his face with the back of his hand and it came away sticky with blood. Smiling disdainfully, he raised his cudgel and aimed a swift blow to Hew's kidneys.

Tey shrieked and jumped to his feet, but before he could take a single step, a hand grabbed him. Tey tugged with all his strength but Ulrick, his face calm and full of the glory of the divine, forced him to his knees.

'This is not for one such as you,' he whispered, his light-blue eyes glinting in devotion.

'Help me!' Tey cried to his mother, but Ba Set seemed to be entranced. Her beautiful face was still, and her golden eyes dulled as she watched her husband fighting for his life.

Tey kicked hard, but Ulrick only held him tighter, calmly ignoring the blows against his shins as though taking the pain as penance. Tey kicked until his bare feet ached and all he could hear was the ragged sound of his own breath, as a shriek rent the air.

Lit red by the flickering of a torch, Martin lay against the wall of a second hut, pinned down by the huge bear-like warden. Blood seeped unchecked down the side of his head.

The man raised his powerful arm, his sword flashing in the light ready for the final blow, but Martin, with a quick lithe movement, twisted his body away. He almost made it to safety, but for his foot catching on the twisted tree root that snaked its way through the clearing. He stumbled, and the big forester took his chance. He plunged his sword into Martin's chest and twisted it with a satisfied grunt.

The woodsman shuddered, his eyes finding Ash Kit. He smiled, revealing his love and adoration, before falling forward, impaled on the forester's bloody sword.

Tey screamed for help and the sound tore the night air. Horror clouded his vision, but this time no beings came to his aid. The faeries of the forest were powerless against the hard, thrust of iron.

Ba Set stood frozen, mute with dread as Ash Kit fell to her knees, moaning in agony. Tey's grandmother, Au Set, keened an ancient word of power into the air. Rising to her feet, she grabbed Ash Kit's hands and snarled, jerking both of the women into life.

'Daughters!' she roared. 'What are we doing? Are we not of the Blood? Why do we lie defeated and powerless!'

Ignoring the frailty of her tiny body, hobbled and twisted by the vast years of her life, Au Set stamped her foot on the ground, crying out, demanding the earth heed her call. With a sharp hiss at the still chanting monks, Tey's grandmother shouted a single bright word into the sky.

In the shadows, Hew was tiring. His breath was coming in rasps, and he favoured his left side where his tunic was stained dark with blood. A clink of movement, and the fight was joined by the bear-like warden, his eyes gleaming with victory. Two on one, the men circled Hew, closing in for the kill.

Tey's father clenched his fist on his sword, holding it steady and chuckling as though it was all a huge joke. The dark of the trees flickered with the watchful eyes of the few faeries that remained. They streamed through the air as though desperate to lend their magic, twisting their light-filled bodies to avoid the odious chants that were still rising from the throats of the monks.

Below, the air quaked as the rat-faced warden darted in to attack Hew's exposed left side.

'Ah. Kah. Neh. Mah!'

The word erupted. Au Set raised her hand, her body quivering with a word as ancient and as powerful as the earth herself. The cry prickled the hair on the back of Tey's neck; he saw no blue-light energy this time but he could feel it. Each time she uttered the word, molten, turbulent fury gathered from the earth beneath.

'Ah Kah Neh Mah!' Ba Set's voice joined her mother's, crying the great word to the heavens.

Grunting with exertion, the fighters' weapons were a blur of light and blood. Hew slashed and parried for his life, with the huge warden forcing him back.

'Ah Kah Neh Mah!'

Like a charge of lightning, radiance blazed upward, thick and sure, enfolding Tey's father in a wave of protection as strong and as unstoppable as the tides.

He seemed to grow twice in size and twice in strength. With blood seeping from a fresh wound in his side, Hew attacked his opponents with his movements strong and sure. Laughing his bellowing, vital laugh, he struck the bear-like warden with such ferocity that the man fell lifeless to the ground. Giving no quarter, Hew surged forward, and the smaller warden staggered and hit the earth. In the coiling brightness of the flames, Tey could see the skin exposed on thc back of the warden's neck. Smiling grimly, Hew raised his sword and, with a single blow, his opponent's body fell to the ground.

Ba Set and Ash Kit screeched their triumph to the heavens, their bodies contorting in the darkness, their fingers raking the sky. In the wavering heat of the fire, the womens' forms shuddered, changing, appearing huge and feathered one moment, then flicking back to human the next, with only their huge golden eyes remaining the same.

As one, they turned with their mother, three powerful priestesses gathering all the terrible powers of the earth. Wind surged through the branches overhead as the women clasped hands, locking in as one, readying for another surge of power.

'Harpies!' A shriek cut through the clearing as Ulrick stormed towards the women, a thick branch flaming in his hand. 'Harpies!' He screamed again, his mouth contorted in revulsion.

With a cry, the knight lifted the torch and brought it down on the women with all his strength. Tey's grandmother took the full force of the blow. Her body crumpled, her bones shattered and she collapsed, broken, to the ground. A brace of a dozen tiny faeries hiding in the branches above, flared in terror and vanished.

'Bless me, Holy Child!' cried Ulrick, dropping to his knees in supplication. 'For I have ridden the world of a great evil.' He bowed his head.

'No, no, no.' Tey stared, stricken at his grandmother's shattered body.

The circle of protection collapsed. Hew dropped down to his knees, his hands useless by his sides. It happened so fast. Tey tried to shout, but the words of warning stuck fast, unable to push past his terror. Agonised, he could only watch as the one remaining warden emerged from the woods. Over one shoulder he gripped the carcass of the spotted deer, and in his hand the double-bladed axe swung free. In two strides, he was upon Hew, and without pausing he raised the blade high and severed his head in a single stroke.

Praise bolted, exultant, towards the heavens. The monks crossed themselves, their faces glowing beneath the dark fall of their hoods. Dazed, Tey watched his mother scream her agony, her fingers clawing into her skin until great rivulets of blood coursed down her cheeks. Crawling over the ground to her husband's body, she gathered his head from where it had fallen and cradled it lovingly in her arms, her eyes dark with horror.

Tey couldn't move, his heart frozen, trapped in this nightmare without end.

Strong arms grasped him in a punishing grip. He struggled weakly. Under the oak tree, Ulrick climbed onto his warhorse, his mouth grim. 'Bring the Holy Child to me.'

'No!' cried Tey. Finding his voice, he kicked, lashing out with all his strength.

The face of his father's murderer bent down and hissed. 'I'd stop that if I were you, *boy,*' he spat. His foul breath washed over Tey's face. 'You're not so holy to me.'

Tey lunged, but the warden caught him and hauled him roughly to his feet. 'Mother,' he cried, his voice choking in sobs, 'Mother. Help me!'

But Ba Sat said nothing as she huddled, crooning and rocking, surrounded by the twisted body of her mother and her fallen husband.

'Mama!' With a final twist, Tey slipped out from his captor's grasp and ran across the clearing, throwing himself at his mother's feet. 'Mama!' he cried, 'Help me.'

Ba Set said nothing, locked in her own world of pain.

Grabbing her, Tey shook her arm desperately. At last she looked up and her eyes flared gold.

'This. Is. Your. Fault. Foolish. Unthinking stupid *boy!*' She hissed. 'Curse the day I bore you!'

Her voice rose to a shriek so agonised that it seemed it would crack the very sky. Raising her arms once more, Ba Set tipped her head back, and with her long hair rippling and crackling with power, she keened out a stream of heartbreak. Ignoring her son, she rose to her feet and, tearing off her grey woollen gown, she tossed it disdainfully to the ground.

Proud and naked, Ba Set stood in the dying light, her body lean and powerful. She glared at the watching gaggle of monks and men, her great eyes raking each and every one as though marking each face for retribution through the eons.

Then, crying out one last divine word of power, Ba Set leapt into the night sky, her body shuddering as she transformed, her golden skin darkening, her dark hair feathering behind her. On powerful wings she climbed into the wind, into the blackness, into the very arms of the sky itself.

Soundlessly, a sparrowhawk, the fastest of all the birds of prey, sprang up banking higher and higher until, without a sound or cry of farewell, Ash Kit vanished, following her twin into the night.

Tethered uselessly to the ground, Tey stared with his arms raised up into the darkness. A heartbeat passed and out of the night a rough hand hauled him to his feet, but Tey no longer had the will to struggle. In a blur, the warden half dragged, half carried him, and hauled him onto Ulrick's muscled horse.

Unseeing, unfeeling, Tey sat in shock, aware of nothing - not the sweep of faeries undulating in misery in the air, nor the urgent voices around him gathering the bodies of the fallen wardens.

Nodding in satisfaction, Ulrick gathered his mount's reins and climbed behind into the saddle, his bulk dwarfing the stricken boy. Clicking softly, the knight rode from the clearing, his head held high, leaving the embers of the huts and the slain bodies to the night, and a single bluebell lying in the dirt.

Trailed by a fleet of shadows, the party rode at a swift pace - the abbot on his red mare and the monks following as fast as they could on foot. Tey slumped against Ulrick; his eyes were clenched shut as he was pummelled by the jolting gait of the horse. The road was fast and straight, mirroring the watercourse that cut its way through the trees. Tey moaned, leaning to the low gurgling sound of the river, and if the knight's arms hadn't gripped him so tight, he would have thrown himself into its depths to drown.

A quarter moon rose above the trees as the priory gates opened. Metal jangling, the horses cantered into the receiving area. A stone gargoyle leered from its high vantage point.

At once, a door swung open in the walls and a trio emerged, clad in simple white. Hoodless, the novices bowed low, and in the flare of the torchlight, Tey wondered dully at the blooded nicks in their freshly shorn crowns.

He flinched as hands reached for him, lifting him off his mount. Ulrick dismounted with a flourish. He bowed low, dropping to one knee, and brushed his lips reverentially against the abbot's proffered ring. Tey gazed at them blankly, his legs shook and his shoulders sagged; he felt as though at any moment he might crumble, collapsing to the straw covered stone.

Ulrick turned, his size looming over the boy as he crossed himself, clasping his hands together in an attitude of prayer. The young knight waited, but Tey did nothing. After a long moment, Ulrick bowed sharply and swung back up on his mount. He rode out into the night, his proud back framed by the grand arch of the gateway.

Tey moaned, the sky was empty of stars and the air was cold. Unexpectedly, a hand clasped his, warm and narrow and with dry rough skin. He couldn't see the man's face, but he was taller and older than the novices, and his abbot's ring gleamed in the light. A torch flared and a youth emerged out of the darkness and ushered them through the double doors into the heart of the monastery. In single file, they swept through the maze of silent passageways, the stone walls absorbing every scrape and thud of their footsteps.

At last, the trio halted in front of a door like all the others - solid wood and braced with iron. At a gesture, it opened, revealing a simple straw pallet and a narrow window that was cut high within the whitewashed walls.

The abbot gestured Tey inside. 'They left you,' he crooned, his voice was soft and unexpected, rising like smoke through the quiet of the enclosed space. 'Didn't they? The harpies, the witches, sooner or later they always show their true colours.'

Tey didn't reply. He dropped onto the bed and lay unmoving with his eyes tightly closed.

'Bless the Lord we found you, Holy Child, nested within that patch of adders you surely would have perished.'

The abbot patted his shoulder and blew out the candle on a single breath. A moment later, the cell door thundered shut.

Left in the darkness, Tey lay as still as he could, trying hard not to even breathe - knowing that if he let himself move, even by the slightest amount, he would be cracked open by a grief so overwhelming that he would surely be lost forever. He lay with his arms locked by his side and his fists clenched, as the abbot's footsteps faded to silence.

A whimper escaped as Tey squeezed his eyes tighter shut, huddling as deep as he could into the pallet.

Outside, the crescent moon rose higher, its faint light angling in through the cell window. In the quiet, a soft, almost soundless pop erupted and a faery appeared, his great warty face ashen with the strain of being caught within the heaviness of the stone walls.

Gimbal turned a single, sad somersault before straightening his body out flat, and floating down with the lightness of a leaf, he landed beside the stricken boy. Curling his length around Tey, like the warmth of a comforting puppy, the forest faery hummed a single vibrating note and, imperceptibly, a glow hinting at the cool green of summer filled the tight confines of the cell. Still with his eyes tightly closed, Tey sighed, his fists relaxed and he slipped into the relief of dreamless sleep.

Later, in the hour before the dawn, the abbot returned and stood with his hands clasped by the door of the cell. Eyes lowered, his lips were moving as a hundred soft soled feet moved through the vaulted passageways. The brothers, roused by the milky veil of predawn light, were heading to the chapel for first prayers, and the rhythmic movement of their footfalls echoed dully against the monastery walls.

Murmuring his own prayers, the abbot pushed back his cowl, and opened the latch to the cell window. He peered in, and the abbot's breath caught in awe. Sprawled beneath his blanket, the boy slept a sleep as deep as any innocent child. His body lay pressed against the wall, arms clasped across his chest as though in an embrace, but what was astounding was the boy's face. It was upturned and it appeared alight, illuminating the darkness of the simple cell with a glow like the halo of an exalted angel.

A miracle made flesh. A Holy Child who drew the very angels to his side. Truly, he would be an Instrument for the Lord.

The abbot bowed his head. 'Thank you,' he prayed, 'thank you for bringing one such as this to our humble lives. He shall be cleansed. We shall sprinkle his brow with holy water, and he shall be baptised, and be given a new name… a blessed new name.'

Nodding, the abbot turned the key and with the barest scrape of sound, the cell door swung open across the stone floor. At once the brightness illuminating the boy's face flared hotter, before vanishing with an almost imperceptible pop of outrage.

The abbot was too intent to notice the abruptly dimmed light and, reaching into his robe, he pulled out a stone, black and about the size of a man's thumb.

A priceless treasure. He bowed his head. This stone was the last tear ever shed by the Saviour made solid. A holy relic brought with much suffering back from the Holy Lands, and here he held it, in his own unworthy hands. Brushing his lips reverently against its cool obsidian surface, the abbot dropped to his knees and placed the treasure in a small cleft in the floor at the foot of the narrow bed.

'This shall keep you safe, child,' he whispered. 'It will protect you from the sight of those…demons, harpies…' The word was hissed out in sharp vehemence. 'It will shield your dreams and neither your mother, nor any of her kind will ever find you.'

The abbot made the sign of the Cross. 'Keep it close, and as you grow, my child, as you enter fully into this life of Servitude to the Lord, you will be forever free of them, and be blessed.'

Closing the cell door behind, the abbot clasped his hands and walked reverently through the vaulted passageways as a high, sweet voice rose from the chapel, singing praise to the rising light of the new day.

TWENTY

Blue Mountains, Australia, present day

The black stone was a comfort and, gripping it tight, Matthew fled back up to the second floor. Perhaps it was untrue - perhaps he had only been dreaming and this nightmare he had been trying to avert, ever since his daughter first drew breath, was not really happening, and she would be sleeping in her own bed at peace beneath the soft covers of down.

But the thing was still there, crouched in the middle of the room, facing the window and staring out at the night sky. As he entered it turned, its wings lifting higher off the floor, its gaze pinning him to the spot, fierce and glowing with an increasing fiery strength. Shuddering, Matthew pulled his eyes away and dropping to his knees, he flung the black stone across the floor. It rolled on its side, wobbling for a couple of metres, before toppling beneath his daughter's dressing table.

Muttering a prayer, Matthew rose to his feet and left, closing the door tight behind. It was done, she was in the Lord's hands now and the hallowed stone of protection was no longer his.

'I do not need it.' Clenching his fist, he rushed on through the cavernous house, darting into each room, making sure each window was locked securely until finally he was on the porch outside. Matthew pulled the front doors closed and locked them fast.

Whatever she was, whatever she had become, his Rosalind wouldn't be able to escape.

Stepping back to the top of the wide marble stairs, he looked up to the second floor. The sky glittered, studded with distant stars while darkness hung below, shadowing the window of his daughter's room. Matthew waited, but not a sound could be heard.

He clenched his fists tight and cried out as the sharp claw of the eagle amulet bit, unexpectedly, into the palm of his hand. The pain was intense, spiked and red hot.

'No!' Matthew roared, lifting his head to the sky. He swept his gaze over the horizon to the dark outline of the forest. 'No. You will not have her. She is mine!'

Swinging open the door of the black 4WD, he leapt into the driving seat. Gunning the engine, he roared along the winding, forest-edged road towards the highest cliffs, his eyes wide glaring in hatred at the spectral forms of the trees guarding each side. The car bounced and lunged until at last Matthew wrenched the car to a stop. Jumping out, he ran straight towards the ledge overhanging the highest point.

The forest spread out before him, dark and sinuous, lit only by the thin light of the crescent moon. It was a mass of writhing, twisted life, each branch, each stem, each root, a horror conspiring to draw him closer, to trap him, to bring him to his knees.

But tonight he wasn't here to berate the forest. Matthew climbed over the safety rail bolted to the rock and stood balanced at the edge of the cliff; silence and darkness engulfed him. Matthew flung his arms up towards the sky, the necklace dangling from his fingers. Thunder cracked.

'Lord! Let us not be too late! We need to Ascend as You promised. Those that are worthy will Ascend, full in body. Let me be worthy, Lord. Let my daughter be worthy for she is just an innocent.' As his cries rang out across the valley, a flare of white-hot light forked overhead.

'Take us. Take us. Now! Help us escape this earth. Help us escape this damned curse of our blood. Take us!'

With each agonised plea, power crackled through the night. At first it was tiny, white-hot sparks and spits. And then with each entreaty he poured to the sky, it swept closer, a gathering force. Unaware, Matthew stood crying out into the night. In one hand he gripped the amulet. 'Curse her!' He screamed. 'Curse my mother and all her kind!' With a bitter cry, he flung the necklace from his hand.

At once a wind tore over the valley, snatching at his robes, twisting them around his body as the amulet arced high, before falling, looping and spinning down into the darkness.

'It's yours, witch! Damn you to hell!'

His voice was lost as a ferocious roar ripped towards him from all directions. It swooped over the trees, pulling out from the rocks, crackling though the air, gathering in strength, booming with thunder across the sky.

Matthew opened his eyes and scrambled back, his hand clutching the rail in shock. Above him, a huge storm front was massing overhead, and within the blackening clouds loomed columns of luminous beings, translucent and towering with majesty. They spiralled, swirling though the darkness.

What are they? Angels… Faeries…. Or worse…?

For a heartbeat, he stared in horror. But suddenly, Matthew didn't care what they were - if they were angels or fiends from the darkest pit of hell.

'Help me!' For what he didn't know, for what action he couldn't fathom. All Matthew was aware of was the rage surging through his being, and the river of bitterness and grief that he had kept damned his whole life long.

'Help me!'

Surging on a rising wave of wind and fury, the spirits coiled upwards. Incandescent with power, and riven with great sparks of light and dark, they swept up into the clouds, lending them their energy. The moon hid, as vast fingers of white snapped across the night.

'I hate her!' Matthew, his eyes wild, abandoned all restraint. 'I hate her! Help me!' His need was now a command. It lashed out into the sky, a wild defiant call to arms. 'Help me!'

The thunderheads turned from white to black, then to the deepest, darkest red.

Energy crackled and exploded.

Lightning crashed, forking over the forest.

The temperature plummeted as ice, as hard and as bitter as nails, began to fall, lashed from the sky by angry, driving winds. The force hit the valley below, the canopy writhed and buckled, unable to resist the violent onslaught of freezing air.

With a great tearing roar, a tree fell, a forest giant, its heavy limbs torn clear from its trunk.

'Yes.' Cried Matthew as lightning slashed the sky above. 'Yes. Come to me, obey me. Destroy them all!'

Ellie's eyes flew open. Her room was shaking, a great howling wail ripped through the night, hollow and tormented with anguish.

'Brian, Brian!' Through the tempest, Ellie could hear her mother's voice echoing shrilly through the house. A moment later, the front door opened and closed again with a crash. Silence.

Ellie scrunched further down and pulled the covers over her head, desperate to escape the terrible shrieking of the wind. But it was no use. Through the walls she could hear a moaning tearing sound, as though the wood was tensing and flexing, and the house itself was battling the storm's relentless fury.

It was hard to breathe; opening a gap, Ellie poked her nose out.

'Brian!'

A sound of rushing feet and a beam of torchlight shot through the window, before vanishing into sudden silence.

Alarmed, Ellie pushed the covers back and climbed out of bed. Her head felt fuzzy, and she looked around trying to work out what was going on. The wind had eased, and for a moment the house was still. Then the curtains snapped and a blast of air sliced across her bare skin.

Ellie stared in shock. Her window was open as usual to catch any hint of breeze and ease the night-time heat, but now the curtains were jerking and a bolt of icy cold wind whipped through the room. For a moment she stood, unable to register what was going on, then a shiver wrenched her spine and Ellie sneezed, her throat aching in the frigid air.

Hauling her duvet off her bed, Ellie staggered out into the hallway.

'Mum?' she called. 'Dad?' In the answering silence, Ellie anxiously flicked the wall switch on and off, and on again. Nothing. Shivering, she pulled the duvet tighter around her body, and inched her way through the gloom. In the twin's room she could see their closets were open, and a trail of clothes lay discarded on the floor. Where was everyone? Biting back a cry of fear, Ellie careened through the empty house like a demented mummy, her bulk knocking against the walls as she struggled to the front door. Pulling hard on the handle, it flew open and Ellie was hit by a blast of freezing wind.

It hurt. As she breathed, Ellie's throat felt pricked as though the air was hiding a thousand tiny shards of ice.

'Hey! Where are you?' she rasped, though her voice felt too weak and thin to be heard.

'Ellie! Ellie!'

From out of the darkness, a small running body threw itself onto her, knocking her back into the wall.

'Wait, wait...' She croaked, pushing the figure away with one hand.

'Where have you been?' Tom's face shone in the darkness, his eyes bright with excitement. A heavy, adult-sized woollen sweater enveloped his small frame, its sleeves knotted snugly over his hands.

'Ellie!' A small hug seized her, and Annie - her blond ringlets hidden beneath a knitted tea cosy, buried her face deep into the duvet.

'Oh, thank God you're still here.' Ellie closed her eyes in relief, and drew both the twins in close, hauling the thick covering around them all.

'What took you so long?' whispered Annie, her voice muffled in the warmth. 'We've been out here for ages.'

'Why are you by yourselves? Where's Mum and Dad?'

221

'Come and see.' Tom pulled impatiently at Ellie's hand.

'It's awful,' muttered Annie.

The two children, united for once by a common purpose, pushed Ellie across the flat expanse of front lawn as the wind rose and shrieked around them.

Above them, the starless sky hung low, bruised and sore, with a twist of white cloud falling sharply away to the horizon. Ellie stopped abruptly, and the twins, close behind, lurched hard into her back.

It was way too dark, she realised. Pushing the covers off her head, Ellie searched for the familiar orange glow of the streetlamps and saw nothing. A bank of thick freezing cloud had settled over the land and not even the shape of the neighbour's house, just metres away, could be seen through the gloom.

'It's not natural,' muttered a reedy voice.

Torchlight arced out of the night. 'It's dropped another ten degrees. It's got to be twenty below by now.'

'That can't be right,' answered another, deeper and slower further away. 'The thermometer must be broken.'

'Hey,' called out Ellie, anxiety leaping out of her throat. 'Please, who's there?' The light paused and then sliced upwards, dazzling her eyes.

A face emerged, soft and older, its small dark eyes squinting. 'Oh it's you, my dear,' wheezed the family's neighbour, her small voice puffing out warm and visible in the icy air. 'We were just heading back indoors.'

'Don't know what's going on.' She was joined her husband. The two of them were huddled together, wrapped in faded terry towelling dressing gowns, with their feet clad deep in sheep skin slippers.

'What's happening?' Ellie meant everything. She gestured with her hands still wrapped under the duvet. *What's happening with the weather, why was everyone outside, what was going on?* She felt panicked, and she fought the urge to run back inside with the twins, close the door and hide.

'Don't know,' repeated the old man. 'There was no warning on the telly, and there's us watching it all day you know, for the cricket. The day was stinking hot, as usual. And then out of the blue the storm came you know, but different, wilder, and freezing. I've never seen anything like it in all the years we've lived up here in the mountains. It's not right. The weather shouldn't be doing this. Shouldn't change so hard, so fast. Why Cheryl here was just saying -'

'Sorry dear,' interrupted his wife with a firm shake of her head. 'Ellie honey, you better go to your mother.' She gestured into the gloom. 'She's down there, by the road... Be quick. She's had quite a shock. And we've got to get inside where it's warm.'

Nodding her thanks, and bundling the twins close, Ellie hurried across the lawn. More shapes appeared - people moving on the road in groups of twos or threes, their presence visible within the point and glare of torchlight. Others were merely standing, their torches pooling on the road, alone, wrapped in layers of clothing, and their thoughts.

'Mum?' Ellie called out tentatively. 'Where are you?'

'She's down there.' Tom lifted a gloved hand and pointed.

'Just there.' Echoed Annie.

On the kerb and wrapped only in a thin dressing gown as protection against the freezing air, Ellie's mother sat with her arms hugging her knees, staring blankly out over the road.

'What are you doing down here?' Easing herself onto the ground, Ellie unravelled the warmth of the duvet and draped it over her mother as quickly as she could, before gathering the twins in close.

'It was here when we were still young,' Claire murmured sadly. 'It was one of the reasons why we bought the place, when you were still little. It was a lovely thing.'

'What was?' Ellie didn't understand, but before she could ask anything else, a shard of light shone into her eyes before slicing out over the road - illuminating carnage.

The massive red gum tree was lying with its bulk splintered, and its great height spanning the road. Chunks of debris were scattered across the opposite neighbour's lawn, propelled by the force of the fall. But far worse, the giant's higher branches, as sinuous and gnarled as any ancient beasts, lay cracked and torn, their great weight crushing the front porch of the weatherboard house opposite. Black and white shards of 'For Sale' signs lay shattered across the grass.

'Oh no,' choked Ellie. She turned in horror to her mother, 'was anyone hurt?'

'It's a miracle, but your father is over there making sure,' whispered Claire. 'The young family moved down to the city a few weeks ago, do you remember them? They'd had enough. Their youngest child would scream whenever the storms came, he'd be terrified.'

'This is going to happen more and more, you know, Ellie,' Ben appeared. He flashed his torch over the wreckage. 'It's what the prophecies have been saying all along. Storms, chaos, all this has been foretold.' He smiled grimly. 'It won't be long now.'

Appalled, Ellie could only stare. She loved the tree. For years it had graced and shaded the front of the house, its long sinuous limbs perfect for lying on, for reading, dreaming, dozing, while the leaves brushed the sky and the sound lulled her to sleep.

'I hate it.' Her mother's face was set with an expression Ellie had never seen. 'I hate it, and I don't see it getting any better soon.'

Later, after helping put the kids back to sleep, Ellie reached for the hag stone lying on her table and crawled back into the warmth of her bed. Burrowing down deep under the covers, she closed her eyes, wishing only to escape into the oblivion of sleep. Yet the suppressed hiss of voices wouldn't let her.

'How can you say that?' Her mother's voice, thin and trembling, snaked through the quiet of the house.

Ellie tensed, listening in the dark.

'Brian, that could've been one of us. That tree could've landed on our house, how could *that* be God's will?'

Her father's response was softer, too distant to hear. Ellie turned her head.

'No Brian, it's too much, it's too close,' retorted her mother, her voice tightening, as though she was spitting out each syllable. 'We should leave. What's here for us now?'

Ellie stopped breathing. *What?*

'Where would we go?' demanded her father, his tone clear and flat. 'Where Claire? And why?'

Ellie didn't quite catch her mother's murmured answer, but she heard a garble of angry words and her father's explosive reply as he slammed his

225

hand hard on the table. 'We remain here under God's grace, Claire. The weather, this house and all that is here is under His dominion, under his Will.'

'No, Brian, you may believe this is the Lord's will, but I don't believe He could be so cruel.'

The kitchen door slammed and Ellie flinched as she heard her mother run weeping into the bathroom. Silence descended, broken only by the increasing howling of the storm.

'No.' Ellie whispered beneath the covers, 'No, please, we can't go.'

A pulse of warmth stole unnoticed through her hand. 'I need to be here...' she murmured. *I need to be here...*

Breathing softly, Ellie's voice faded as sleep crept undetected over her senses. She sighed, snuggling deeper into the warmth of her bed and then, as light as thought, as if in a dream, she slipped out of her body as lightly as a hand slipping out of a fine, silk glove.

Still holding the shape of the hag stone under her cheek, Ellie rose up from her bed, passing up through the ceiling and out into the night. Floating on higher, warmer currents, she drifted, weightless, as the storm cloud massed high over the sleeping land.

Light pricked over her skin. Cool and soft, and as fleet as a moth wing.

Ellie.

A delicate hand traced a single line of cold fire across her skin. She shivered.

Soul Flyer.

Help us.

Ellie slowly opened her eyes, and a thousand beings held their breaths around her.

The land beneath her fell away to the horizon, but she had no time to be afraid, as around her came a wave of sound. At first it sounded like the hum of countless bees, but lower, deeper, more desperate, like a quiet, keening lament.

Ellie still wasn't sure if she was awake or dreaming. But at once, as though it had been waiting for her to respond, a tiny being flared diamond bright, its eyes huge and as dark and as deep as the sky. It hovered close.

Help us.

From its head spiked a mass of sharp, sticky-out hair.

Recognition jolted and Ellie gasped as her favourite little forest faery darted before her, its true form as iridescent as a jewel.

Now fully awake, Ellie rose higher into the darkness, following the flare-bright shape as it darted over the land. At last the faery stopped and, together with its fellows, keened out a single tone, high pitched and full of sorrow.

Tumbling in the air, it gestured wildly down towards the ground. Beneath them, the great forest slept. And through it, threading through the soil, Ellie could see the clear network of blue-white light flaring from tree to tree, leaping from branch to branch and fanning outwards in an infinite, beautiful pattern.

What's so wrong? Ellie looked up confused.

The tiny being gestured again.

There.

There.

At first Ellie couldn't see what was agitating the faery. There!

She dropped lower, following its brightness as it skimmed closer over the trees.

And there! The faery turned to her, its eyes were imploring, its tiny hands pointing to an area of the sleeping forest.

Hovering in the darkness, Ellie stared as around her the cloud of faeries broke into a heartbroken cry.

What? What's so wrong?

Beneath her, a single line of brightness traced the contours of the landscape, an illumination emanating from tiny, hiding creatures and countless scuttling insects. She watched as it ran on through the earth, picking up speed, and winding out from tree roots and on through the night. And then abruptly the line stopped. Its jewel-bright light snuffed out in sudden darkness.

Another great lament rose from the surrounding beings.

Ellie gasped as she finally understood. It was not a thing that was distressing the faeries, but an *absence, a* void, a blankness creeping through the pattern. As quick as thought, Ellie rose higher and then see saw it. Holes were spreading through the valley of light; deadening pools of darkness seeping across the vital web like a vast unchecked cancer.

As she watched, another light winked out, and another, and another, as a great icy silence gripped the forest.

TWENTY-ONE

Rose woke, curled in pain on the floor. A deep chill gripped her bones. Her room was dark, her curtains drawn tight, blocking out any intrusion of the day. She was caught, her body pinned between her chair and the bay of the window. Stretching her legs, she stopped, her heart beating faster as she ran her hand over the hard wooden surface beneath her. What was she doing lying down here?

Her stomach heaved.

A dream. *It had to just be a dream.* Warily, she touched her naked skin; it felt hot, burning under her fingertips, but… smooth, human, and thankfully, just skin. Rose shuddered, remembering the heavy, horrifying feel of wings dragging her body down.

A horrible dream… She lay back down on the cold floor, hugging herself tight.

Her eyes flew open, and her hands flew to her neck. *Where is it?*

In the middle of her room, dark and angled away from the door, stood the mirror, surrounded by the gutted remains of the candles. Panicking,

Rose jumped to her feet, searching among her clothes, yanking off the covers on her bed. Looking through every inch of fabric.

When she was done, it looked as though a storm had thrown the contents of her room to the wind, but she didn't care; it was nowhere to be found. She shuddered, as fury as hot and bitter as bile surged through her. Fighting the urge to howl her loss to the sky, Rose ran to the window and yanked open the curtains. A burst of cold spilled into the room. She shivered once, but didn't care, her skin still felt hot to touch and… she stopped, remembering the silky feel of the necklace draped over her bare skin, and Rose frowned. Shaking her head furiously, she batted that memory away. *No! It was just a dream.*

The necklace was all that mattered.

Where was it?

Thinking hard, Rose stared out over the garden stretched below. It looked different; the light was a dull, dense grey that draped the length of the garden, concealing the trees and the summerhouse in a dank cloud. Rose shivered again, as cold from the bare glass seeped into her skin.

She frowned. *Someone, somehow, in the night had entered her room…*

Scooping up a grey hoodie, she pulled on a pair of long, loose trousers and avoiding the mess of puddled wax, stepped cautiously to the mirror. From the window, a shaft of light sliced across the floor and ran up its darkened surface.

She tilted her face to one side.

Am I still beautiful? Her reflection stared back, not answering, her long dark hair curled seductively over her breasts. She felt different, she realised. Strong, and the ache in her muscles had eased; her arms felt supple, poised, as though she could leap into the air at any moment.

Revulsion gripped her heart.

No. It was just a nightmare.

Matthew was crouched low in the kitchen, feeding fuel into the cast iron stove that dominated one corner. Fire roared from its heart, sending heat billowing up into the vaulted ceiling, and chasing away the bitter chill. As Rose entered, he rocked back onto his heels. He was in civilian clothes, wearing a black shirt tucked into a pair of black woollen trousers. Nodding at her, Matthew resolutely snapped a branch with a single hand.

Lifting her chin, Rose smiled a faint *good morning* to her father and padded on bare feet to the fridge. The trousers she was wearing were long, but they didn't protect them from the cold rising from the hard stone floor. *I should've worn socks,* Rose realised belatedly, rubbing her soles with her hand. The nightmare she pushed to the back of her mind.

She was all right. Turning back to the fire, Matthew tossed the wood into its centre and breathed the thought out loud. 'She is all right.' Thank the Lord, his Rosalind was here, whole, perfect once more, without blemish. But…

Rose flung open the fridge door. 'You look awful, Dad. Do you want some eggs?'

Matthew wiped his hands and eased the metal grate shut. A fire sprite curled away with a serpentine flick. He ignored it.

Cautiously, as if afraid of startling a forest creature, or the most timid of his parishioners, Matthew rose to his feet.

'I'm starving. I think I'm going to make us both a fry up.' Tossing her hair back, Rose scraped some butter from the butter dish and cracked a couple of eggs into a pan. 'You look as though you need it.' She commented, looking up. 'And you get angry with *me* for staying out late.'

He didn't answer.

Silence filled the room, save for the rhythmic beating of the old clock in the hallway, and the sizzle of the butter in the pan.

She was all right, but for how long? Forcing himself to look away, to not be so obvious in his appraisal of her, Matthew sat down at the wooden table. He clasped his hands and began to pray. *Hear me Lord. Hear my prayer; let us Ascend now Lord. I have been Your good and faithful servant. I have served Your Church for many, many years, please. The blood-curse is manifesting … the abomination of her heritage is rising. I beseech You. Let us Ascend quickly, take us now, before my daughter-*

'Dad! Did you hear me? Would you like some tea?' Rose's voice snapped. 'Come on, wake up sleepyhead, or else I'll have to send you to bed.'

She pushed a plate of yellow eggs towards him. Matthew blinked. His breakfast sizzled hot on the plate, sunny side up, and the odour of salt, butter, and sulphur filled his nostrils.

But he took no notice. *When will they be free?*

Grimly, he gazed out through the arched window and down to the bottom of the garden. Streaks of cloud, ice-white and luminous, were racing against the frozen sky. The mist had lifted and Matthew could see down to the boundary fence – a line of thin trees were bent low, like a brace of impotent old men struggling against the bitter wind.

They're in such pain, he mused. The trees' limbs were gnarled and twisted, and their individual branches whipped and jerked, wrenched into the air by each icy gust until the leaves were shredded and they fell to earth, mute, and as grey as ash.

Nothing could ever triumph against such an onslaught. The storm he had unleashed was born of power and fury, and it would never, ever end.

Matthew froze.

He stared at the tortured trees. *Of course...*

The storm *he* had unleashed...

Rising to his feet, Matthew strode over to the window, his mind racing.

The abbot in the monastery all those years ago had recognised this skill. 'A Gift from God' the old man had called it. Spirits. They came to his aid. Always, whether willing or not, they loved him. They couldn't help it.

Angels, they came too, as light as prayer, and as towering and as implacable in strength as any of the faery in the forest.

Matthew closed his eyes.

Of course.

What a fool he had been to not realise. This was his *talent* ... a talent brought before the glory of God. A talent used in service of the Lord. And now...

It was so clear.

'In the name of the Lord,' he whispered, 'spirits, you are mine, as you have always been.'

Slowly he breathed out a familiar name.

Gimbal...

He leaned forward, his eyes intent, and lifted his hands. He quietly called again.

Gimbal...

233

Deep in the garden, a shimmer began - a slow sort of twisting, a colouring-in of the air beneath the eaves of the summerhouse. It somersaulted awkwardly, and abruptly fell towards the ground. But at the last minute, it checked itself, and a being appeared - green, warty, with large bulbous nose. It looped slowly in the freezing light.

Gimbal.

Matthew didn't smile.

Faery, spirit, or angel, he knew they were all the same in essence. Powerful beings, free from the longings of the flesh, each put here to serve the Lord Almighty in their own way. He could command them. This was his strength.

And now…

Matthew gazed into the garden.

First this cold, and then he would call on the angels of chaos to come to his aid. He would call on spirits of unbridled hurricanes, and desert winds. He would call entities of the air, he would call fire, he would call destruction, and the damned forest below would turn to dust.

But that was only the beginning.

Not just this forest, but also the next, and the next. On and on, until all the forests, the grasslands and the oceans, and the whole world was scorched, from pole to pole.

The prophecies were clear, and he, the Reverend Matthew Hopkins, had the power to make it happen.

Peace flooded his soul. 'I see it now, Lord,' he whispered. 'I see what must be done.'

It was written in the holiest of books. The earth will be scorched and then the Faithful will ascend to heaven. Every one of them, free at last, whole and perfect. *And myself and my daughter will be first amongst them.*

'I am the Instrument.'

'What the hell are you doing?' Rose's voice cut into Matthew's thoughts.

The fire had burned low and she was sitting across the table, studying him. Her plate was untouched, and the eggs were congealing in the centre. She slapped her hands on the wood, not hard, but enough for the sound to echo against the empty spaces in the kitchen.

'What are you doing?' She repeated.

'Rose,' began Matthew.

'Don't pretend you're innocent.' She almost snarled.

As she glared at him, Matthew could sense power rippling off his daughter. Like smoke, it looped up from her shoulders, in bright fits and bursts. But she seemed unaware...

Matthew swallowed.

'Rosalind,' he began carefully. 'Calm yourself. Do not take that tone-'

'Don't, "Rosalind" me, Dad,' Rose snapped. She stood up. 'Where is the necklace?'

Heat radiated through the kitchen. Matthew tensed as she walked towards him. Her stance was light and powerful, and she flexed her arms to their full length. 'Did you come into my room last night?' She shook herself.

'Rose, you must calm.'

'Did you?' Her head loomed forward, and her eyes gleamed hot.

'Where is it?' She demanded, and her voice screeched, loud and coarse.

235

Matthew's heart began to thud. She's changing, and she is unaware.

'In the name of all that is Holy,' he began to pray.

Rose slapped his hand away. 'Where is it?'

'Dear Lord,' whispered Matthew, 'Stop this-'

"Where is it. Tell me!' She cried.

'Rose, you do not want that accursed thing.'

'Where is it?' She cried again. Power now was streaming off her in waves.

Matthew thought quickly. The obsidian stone was upstairs. It shielded her from magic, but to be effective it needed to be close.

Outside ice fell from the sky, lashing against the glass as hard as stone, and the wind howled. Through the window he could see Gimbal still somersaulting, twisting his tubby form as though trying to avoid the driving rain. Sensing Matthew, the faery looked up to the sky and lifted his hands in mock-horror, as though begging to be allowed inside.

Ignoring the faery, Matthew pushed open the back door.

'Do you know what it happening to you, Rose? Do you?'

'I don't care,' Rose shrieked. 'No! I just want my necklace.'

'Rose you do not want that accursed thing.' He snapped. 'It is evil. It is the stuff of nightmares!' Matthew glared at his daughter. Then he knew what he had to do. He grabbed her hand and pulled her outside, dragging her down into the garden towards the summerhouse.

He called to the faery.

Gimbal glared at him, sticking out his tongue, then he began gathering ice and packing it into his hand.

'Not now.' Matthew turned away. 'Follow us.'

'Who are you talking to?' Rose pulled at her hand, struggling against his grip.

Matthew gripped it tighter. 'Rose, there are…' He paused, 'secrets in our family that you need to know.'

'What things? Where are we going?'

'In here.' Matthew unclasped the summerhouse door and dragged her inside.

'What are you doing, Dad?' For a brief moment her voice wavered as if afraid, then her eyes gleamed, and she tore at him with her other hand. It struck him like a claw.

'Gimbal,' he shouted. 'Show yourself.'

With a defiant pop, Gimbal appeared and, with an exaggerated carefulness, began shimmying-in through the wall.

Matthew twisted his daughter's face hard towards the faery. 'Look Rose, see! You are of the Blood, and you do have the eyes to See.'

'See what?' She cried.

'Look.'

'I will not! There is nothing to see. Give me the necklace. It is mine. I can feel it. My blood sings to it, I want it!' With a loud shriek, Rose pulled herself free. Power hummed, it looped off her, a rich molten gold, warming the freezing summerhouse, reaching to the sky, and coursing down to the ground. She shook herself as though released from a pent-up cage, and tilted her head back, moaning out a loud, unearthly sound.

'Rosalind, stop!' Beneath him, Matthew felt the earth stirring in response; a deep vital thrumming, a vibrating heat reaching up through the wooden floor. His daughter moaned again.

'Rose, stop, before it's too late. Rose!'

Heat flared, and Matthew watched in revulsion, as smooth skin shifted to feather, as her long, dark hair shimmered changing texture.

'Dad!' she cried. Her eyes widened and Rose's whole body shuddered. She raised her arms, beating them as though trying to ward off the horror befalling her. 'Help me!'

'Look to Gimbal,' shouted Matthew. 'Look at him, he is a fool, he is harmless. Let your mind be filled with him. Calm yourself. You must. Hold on!'

Matthew raced back into the house and up into Rose's bedroom. Dropping to his knees, he jammed his hand beneath his daughter's dressing table. *Please God let it still be here...* Yes! He exalted as his fingers connected with a cold, hard shape. Breathing a prayer of thanks, Matthew ran back to the summerhouse as a long, eerie moaning tore into the storm-wracked day.

'Rose!' Matthew howled his daughter's name.

Lightning flashed bright against the sky and, prising the door open, Matthew had time to roll the small black stone inside before the icy wind whipped the door from his grip. It banged shut.

Matthew yearned to howl his frustration. Gathering his strength, he kicked the door of the summerhouse down. Trees grated incessantly, banging against the roof as the winter storm increased its intensity.

Inside, the obsidian stone lay free, surrounded by splintered wood. In the centre of the summerhouse, Gimbal lay curled into a ball on the wooden floor. His eyes were tightly shut, and his body rose and fell as though the faery was deep asleep. Opposite, Rose was seated on the floor in the corner, her long hair draped down across her face and her arms were wrapped tightly around her legs.

In the silence, Matthew retrieved the obsidian stone from off the floor and warily handed it to his daughter. 'Wear this,' he commanded roughly. 'Always. Do not take it off, ever. It will keep you safe.'

She did not respond. Gimbal opened one eye.

'Take it!'

Rose gazed up at him through eyes that still held a deep, unearthly glow. 'What is happening to me?' she whispered.

Her face was delicate, beautiful but softer, Matthew realised. Not as proud as his mother's was. But still, he could not deny it. The blood link, the resemblence to his witch-mother was clear for all to see.

'Dad, please, tell me what's happening.'

Matthew hesitated as his centuries-long hatred of witches, harpies, followers of evil, rose like bile in his throat.

'Dad…' Silently, Rose began to cry. Without another word, she took the obsidian stone and buried her face in her hands.

Oh Lord, Matthew clenched his fist. *Help me now. Help me find the words to reveal the truth to my daughter.* His breath felt jagged and raw in his throat, clutching a lifetime of secrets and silence that waited to be wrenched into the light.

'Rosalind,' he began. 'Listen carefully and do not interrupt.'

Afterwards, with the storm still shaking the house, Rose sat in the kitchen, leaning against the back of the chair. Her hand cradled a mug of milky, honey-sweetened tea. She could feel the shape of the stone in the pocket of her hoodie.

Firelight from the stove illuminated the lines in her father's face.

How old is he? She wondered. She couldn't even imagine. Behind him, shadows danced as a burning log fell, and sparks burst against the glass of the fire. From the hallway outside, a series of chimes marked the hour passed.

Slowly, she traced a finger down her arm, and watched as the muscles and tendons flexed. *I am a monster…an abomination,* she mused. Her hand clenched. Clawlike. Frightened, Rose pulled it back within the sleeve of her hoodie.

Outside, the tops of the trees lashed against a sky as dull and grey as the dead. She glanced at her father. *And he wishes to die. My father wishes to die but can't, for he carries the curse of endless years in his blood. How old is he?* She wondered again.

Rose dug her fingernail into her arms, again not enough to draw blood, but the sharp pain was a relief somehow. *And I'm a freakin' monster.*

Matthew turned to her. 'Rosalind. Do not give in to despair. The Lord has not abandoned us. For is it not written, that at the End Times, the faithful will rise, full in body to meet Him? There is hope. We will rise. We will be free. We can ensure it will happen.'

Matthew watched his daughter closely. Her face was pale, and her golden eyes were dull with fear. 'Listen carefully, Rose - the end of the forest heralds the beginning of our salvation.'

'But Dad,' her voice cracked, as though she hadn't spoken in a long time. 'Ellie won't let it happen.'

'Ellie?' Matthew barked out a laugh of surprise. 'Why do you speak of Ellie? What has your mindless little friend to do with anything?'

Rose looked up. 'She will never let the forest die. She's met that … that thing, your mother … *that monster -*' Rose closed her eyes as a wave of revulsion roiled through her stomach. 'She's been meeting with her in the forest. Ellie didn't say her name, but I know who she means now.'

Turning, she looked out of the window. 'Dad, Ellie sees her all the time. She's learning from her. Ellie loves the forest, she loves it more than her family, more than God, more than anything.' Rose lifted up her hand, and gazing at it, she slowly flexed it. 'They will fight us. Your mother and my best friend, they'll fight us together. They won't give up.'

Leaning over the table, Matthew gripped his daughter's hand. It felt so delicate, each finger bone so fragile, so fine, it would snap if he held it any tighter.

'Neither shall we, Rosalind.' He said firmly. 'We will not give up. The *witches* will not win.' He spat the word out. 'Our lives, our very souls are at stake. We have the Lord, we have the angels and we have the prophecy on our side. Do not despair. Our success is foretold. The forest, and the earth will die, and die quickly. It will happen. It has to - for it is the only way we can be free.'

TWENTY-TWO

The sun was barely over the horizon when Ellie stepped off her bike, stones cracking underfoot. Shaking out her hands, she blew over them quickly, trying to warm her bare fingers in the freezing air. It didn't help. Shivering, she shoved them back into her jacket pockets and glanced back. Ice fell from the sky. Behind her lay miles of exposed gorse and wind-swept trees.

Ellie hesitated. She may be a Soul Flyer and all that, but she needed to be able to talk, walk, and act. For that, she needed to be in the flesh. She grimaced; flying was much easier.

Up ahead, somewhere further beyond this twisting foliage, lay the highest cliffs in the area, unfenced against a sudden, terrifying drop.

She shouldn't be here. She'd promised her mother.

Ellie gripped the handlebars. She was way out of bounds, and the expanse of high, wild scrubland lay desolate with not a mark of civilisation - no signs, no houses, no roads.

An urgent impatience tugged from her bag.

'Okay, okay,' Ellie muttered, and heaving the front wheel forward, she pushed further into the bank of dense, silent trees.

The path was narrow, twisting its way through the bush. It was more like an animal track than anything constructed for people. Ellie inched her way forward. A twig scraped her cheek as her feet crunched on the ice-covered ground.

Hurry…

'This is mad, why would anything be here?' she muttered. But a few moments later as Ellie pushed the bike through the last stand of wizened, low growing trees, she saw it.

Nestled by an outcrop of granite and painted such a soft dove grey it seemed to waver in the muted light, the wooden cottage was almost imperceptible against the dull, cloud-covered sky. Shivering, Ellie pulled her coat tighter.

Maybe no one was home? She wondered, caught by a sudden shyness. She half hoped so, then she could just turn around home and no one would ever know she'd snuck away.

But no, plumes of very real smoke rose from the solid brick chimney.

Heaving her bike to the ground, Ellie slung her bag over her shoulder and headed towards the cottage. As she hit the first step, a shape toppled to the ground, clattering loudly as it hit the wood. Ellie froze. Around her, balanced precariously on the rickety stairs, were slender towers of smooth round stones. They were quite beautiful, Ellie decided as she inched past. Each one a different size and shape, but if she knocked any, they'd all topple, rattling loudly down the stairs like the fall of ninepins.

Like it's all booby trapped, Ellie thought, stepping onto the porch. Swiftly, she ducked her head to avoid being hit by a string of cylindrical shapes.

The contraptions were everywhere. Hanging about head height, they emitted a light tuneless whistle as they spun haphazardly in the wind.

Carefully weaving between them, Ellie made it to the front door without mishap. A stone gargoyle leant insolently against the wood. She stopped, aware of the fierce racing of her heart. Hadn't it been in a different pose a second ago? 'Oh God', she whispered and her breath steamed into the frigid air. 'What is this place?'

Hurry.

'Okay,' muttered Ellie, and lifted her gloved hand to knock.

The door opened before she made a sound, and Ba Set stood at the threshold.

'Hello?' began Ellie.

The old woman gestured for Ellie to enter as the shrill whistle of a kettle filled the air.

Bending low so she didn't bang her head, Ellie stepped straight into a tiny room. In the corner a fire blazed, illuminating a wide picture window overlooking the tree-covered valley below. Heaped on the mantelpiece, and on every surface of the room, were strange little sculptures and piles of curiosities - glinting stones, heaped feathers, and oddly shaped seed pods. On the floor by the fire, a fan of delicate bones lay drying in the air.

Crockery jangled, and Ba Set appeared bearing a teapot and a plate of biscuits on a tray. Settling herself on the sofa, she poured out a rich steaming brew, and gestured for Ellie to sit beside her. They sipped their tea in silence. It was spicy, sweet and hot.

'I had to come,' Ellie set her cup awkwardly on the floor. 'It was this,' she reached into her bag. 'It showed me how to find you.'

As she held it, the hag stone gave off slight tremors, flinging out small, surprising shocks of electricity.

'It was insisting, over and over, that we come and find you. God … what's happening?' Ellie closed her eyes, remembering her anxious ride through the icy, pre-dawn streets. 'This,' she gestured, suddenly to the open fire, and the frightening coldness outside. 'I mean, I know it's almost winter, but this change is just *insane.*'

She gazed straight into Ba Set's golden eyes. 'And another thing - I know what's happening. I've seen it. I've been flying - they've shown me, the spirits, or whatever they are.'

Ba Set said nothing, but she held herself still and listened, her very being taut.

'It's dying. It's all dying.' Ellie caught her breath as a tide of grief and despair threatened to submerge her. 'The drought was bad enough, but this weird, extreme cold, it's killing everything.' Her voice trailed off. 'We need rain,' she said quietly. 'Warm, clean rain, it would at least give us all a little time. Can you make it rain? Can you?'

Ba Set took another sip of tea and lay down her cup. She reached for the hag stone and traced her finger around its glowing centre. 'What you seek is something that requires great skill,' she said after a moment, and her voice shook. 'Weather working is a great and rare talent. Now, one of the rarest of them all. In the old days, every village had its healers, its weavers of magic, but only the most fortunate had the ones who could call the breeze, master the storm, shape the very weather itself.'

Ba Set closed her eyes. 'But the talents were snuffed out when we died by the thousands in the fires. Witches they called us. Their priests declared us evil and so we were hunted almost to extinction.' She shuddered.

245

'Those of us who survived scattered to the four winds, and the secrets we keep are carefully guarded. We do not share what we know easily. I am sorry. Ellie, the talent you seek is outside my knowledge. And child, it is true what you are saying. The forest is dying, as is the earth herself.'

Ba Set's gaze shifted past Ellie to the window. 'The signs are clear to any that have the eyes to see. And it is up to me, and to those like me, to ease Her passing. To prepare, and midwife this forest, this land, this world, on into the next life.'

'What next life?' cried Ellie. She didn't quite understand what Ba Set meant, but she could see the fatalism etched on every line and plane of the old woman's face. 'And on what planet? This is all there is. If the forests die, we all die!'

'Ellie, calm yourself; it is all we can do. Sing the last Songs and prepare ourselves.'

'No!' Ellie snapped; she couldn't believe what she was hearing. 'This is the Mother you said so yourself. My God, everyone is just giving up, or else saying '*bring it on.*' Come on, please, Ba Set, you must know someone who can help!'

'I cannot help you. We all have different talents and mine,' Ba Set's eyes flashed proudly. '*My* talent was to fly free and Sing the truth of the earth. Sing Her alive, and I have been doing that for a long, long time.'

'But you said the earth is dying,' interrupted Ellie bitterly.

'And so the Wheel turns, and we too are dying, dying out. We used to gather and meet by the dark and light of the moon, we would sing and dance and honour the gods, the spirits and the cycles of life, death, winter, summer. But that stopped. The one god religions came to dominate, to burn, to destroy.' Ba Set spat the words out. 'We had to hide,' she snarled, rising to her feet. 'We had to deny who we were. We were hunted and killed and our very existence ground to disbelief.'

She shuddered. 'So few of us remain.'

Silence filled the room, bitter and acrid. Ba Set turned and walked to the window.

'There *were* weather workers, Ellie,' she said quietly. 'But they were so short-lived, a single life span quickly snuffed out. Unlike us. My family, we go on and on, and what knowledge we have we pass onto our daughters and so the line continues down the centuries, but in my case it stopped with my son. The magic died.'

Ellie looked up. 'You have a son? Where?'

Ba Set, lost in reverie, didn't answer. 'We, blessed with the longest lives, can have only one child, it keeps the balance I suppose, but I never had a daughter to train. And then you came. Ellie, you are rare indeed. I knew from the moment I saw you in the forest, kicking the stones in anger, power ricocheting off you in great streams.'

She turned from the window and regarded Ellie steadily, her small dark form silhouetted against the grey light of the day.

'You are born out of the line, but you are one of us, that is certain.' Ba Set nodded. 'Perhaps those who died in the fires are being reborn in this time of great peril for a reason. But it's too slow, the Mother will die before enough of us can gather to save her, so I fly and ease the pain of her passing.'

'Don't give up, please,' begged Ellie. Everything the old woman was saying was so strange. 'Look, Ba Set, please. If I'm one of the ones that's been reborn, or whatever, well, I wasn't born to just watch it all die, was I? It doesn't make sense. Come on. Think. What about in other places?

247

There has to be others like us in the whole world. Don't you talk to them? Isn't there some kind of social media group or something?' Ellie laughed, suddenly almost hysterical. 'Don't you just hang out and chat?'

Ba Set watched, her lined face impassive, then abruptly she seemed to crumple, exhaustion etching out each and every one of her years. She turned back from the window and eased herself onto the sofa.

'I am tired, young Soul Flyer,' she said, taking Ellie's hand in hers. 'I work with others, yes, they are powerful, but they are not what you seek. And all I can do is tell you what I know. But you, you have the hag stone. It is the only one of its kind in all of existence. It stayed with me for hundreds of years and then it left me for you. If you wish to help, Ellie, now is the time. The stone led you to me. And I say ask the stone and let it take you to where you need to go. Do it now.'

Ellie swallowed. Ask the stone? But she didn't know how or what even to ask?

Rising to her feet, Ba Set pulled the curtain across the window, shutting out the morning, dropping the room into shadow.

Ellie hesitated. *Okay,* she thought, *now is the time.* Taking a deep breath, she lay herself down on the sofa.

Ba Set sat by her feet. 'Concentrate,' she said firmly, 'breathe to the earth, ask the stone and you'll know what to do.' The old woman closed her eyes.

Panic flared and Ellie fought the urge to run out of the cottage and back to the safety of home. No, she clenched her fists; she was the only one who could do this.

Settling the hag stone on her belly, she could see its faint outline of luminous blue, pulsating gently from its centre as she breathed. Ask the stone what?

Ellie felt stupid and self-conscious, and quite alone in this little room with only the glow of the embers for company. At the end of the sofa, Ba Set was so still she seemed like a rock, or a carving.

But what if nothing happened, what if it didn't work? Ellie shifted her body, trying to straighten out her legs without disturbing the old woman. She shook her head; she could at least *try,* something, anything. Quietly, Ellie breathed out a soft, experimental sound.

Pathetic, more like a croak than a note. But, barely perceptibly, and Ellie thought she may be just imagining it, the light from within the stone seemed to brighten in response.

Encouraged, Ellie sang another note, this time imagining herself with a line connecting her down into the earth. The stone on her belly shimmered and pulsed with heat. Ellie stared elated, and abruptly she knew what she had to ask.

'Help me,' she whispered. 'I know it sounds nuts. But I need to save the earth. And I need help. A weather worker...' *Can you help me find a weather worker?*

A tone rose out of Ellie's being, as if by its own volition. Becoming louder, it surged into the dark and an eye-dazzling brightness flared out from the centre of the hag stone.

Ellie didn't quite understand how it happened, but she simply stood up and stepped out of the confines of her body. With the hag stone tightly in one hand and her arms raised, she leapt high up into the vast emptiness encircling the earth.

Later, Ellie could only remember it in snatches of sensation, like the tantalising wisps of a dream.

Ships.

A great fleet. Sailing boundlessly, caught in the slipstream of time.

Square sailed. Huge and creaking, they swept across the universe, every detail, every texture etched in starlight.

Ellie dropped onto the deck of one, the first.

All was empty.

The wood creaked, the sails flexed, tugging on the ropes, holding the tension between flying free and flying forward.

On soundless feet, she entered the captain's cabin.

Spinning, lit by the flame of a single candle, was a globe and a golden spiralling orrery. Each orb, each planet, complete in its own singular motion.

A lone figure stood with his back to her, a slim shape leaning out to sea.

But before Ellie could move, the figure turned.

'Who are you?' Said the young boy. He had the face of an angel, symmetrical, beautiful, perfect.

'I am Ellie,' said Ellie simply.

'I am the Last Soul,' replied the boy.

Ellie opened her hand.

In it the boy dropped a ring. Bulky and huge, it was set with an oversized green orb. It flashed brilliant white as it hit her palm.

'Take this,' he said, his eyes solemn and glinting.

With tears? Ellie wondered.

But the boy was talking still.

'It opens time,' he said. He turned the orb once.

250

Ellie dropped to earth, landing back on the sofa so hard that her body jerked, her jaw snapped, and the springs jumped and creaked beneath.

TWENTY-THREE

Ellie didn't want to open her eyes. She winced; a light source was nearby, but she feared if she opened her eyes it would stab without mercy. Groaning, she shifted her position and pain cramped the muscles of her back. What happened? Gingerly, she raised one hand and stopped, surprised as a hard round object clattered onto her chest and onto the floor. She opened one eye.

A large ring, with a clear, deep green stone, uncut, a perfect sphere set in beaten yellow gold, spun to a stop.

Dazed, Ellie raised her head. An ache throbbed at the base of her skull and dropped sickeningly down into her stomach. She swallowed.

'Please,' she croaked…

The room seemed empty. A chink of light pierced the curtain and she flinched, but Ba Set was nowhere to be seen.

Warily, Ellie scooped the ring into her hand and lay back onto the cushion. What just happened and why did she feel so horribly weak?

Footsteps hurried into the room and Ba Set appeared carrying a tray, with a fresh pot of steaming tea and a plate of fruit.

The scent of honey filled the air and Ellie ate and drank as though starved. All the while Ba Set studied the ring gripped tightly in Ellie's hand. A pinprick of light pulsed deep from within its green centre. The old woman hesitated, a worried frown creasing her face.

'Ellie,' she said at last. 'I have heard the faintest of whispers. I heard tales, tales told in the temple which were already ancient when I was a mere stripling of a child. You hold an object of power, unfathomable power, that much is certain.'

The ring felt heavy, and so hot it almost burned Ellie's palm, and her arm trembled. Yet she couldn't let it go. It felt so beautiful, and full of promise as though it held all the possibilities that could ever be imagined.

Ba Set's eyes softened. 'This is out of my knowledge. Go child. You have asked the hag stone for guidance and it has answered. Take the ring and go home.'

The old woman rose to her feet and stood by the open picture window, gazing down at the ocean of trees below. 'Trust the hag stone and your own inner knowing, for I feel you will go on a journey that I cannot follow. But I will be here waiting, with help, when, and if you need it.'

Her mind felt blank, and Ellie was scarcely aware of the long miles as she cycled. The cold bit into her flesh, hungry, ravenous, chasing her back to her family. At last, she rounded the corner to her street and pushed her bike past the wreckage of the fallen tree and up the driveway. Thankfully, no one was awake to witness her return, and once in the safety of her room, Ellie collapsed into bed.

Her chest and her head ached, and after some time her door creaked open and her mother entered with a bowl of steaming soup. But Ellie didn't hear; she slept on with one hand stretched beneath her pillow, her fingers wrapped around a bundle of cloth, with the hag stone and the ring hidden safe within.

Later, a day, a week … Ellie wasn't too sure, she woke after what seemed to be a long, dreamless sleep. Stretching out her cramped legs, she tentatively opened her eyes. Light filtered in through the curtains and she flinched, waiting for the usual stab of pain, but none came. Warily, she took an experimental breath. The air was bitingly cold, but that was all; gone was the thick, soupy wheeze that had gripped her lungs.

What had happened? Ellie sat up, bewildered, her mind felt blank and empty. She shook her head trying to clear it, but it did no good.

Shivering, Ellie wrapped herself in her dressing gown, and shuffled down the cold hallway to the kitchen.

'It was just a regular day', seeped a voice, nasal and incredulous, *'and suddenly for about 20 minutes there was just a white-out blizzard, you just couldn't see anywhere. And then 20 minutes later - sunshine…'*

She opened the door. Sprawled around the table, her dad sat over a bowl of cereal with Ben beside him, listening to the radio with his spoon poised midair.

'It's not right, I tell you; the last few days have been really hot – 25 degrees yesterday when it should only be six or eight degrees, but now it's way below freezing again.'

'It's happening,' nodded Ben, banging the spoon hard on the table.

'What is?' At once Ellie wished the question away; she didn't want to know, she felt too lightheaded to deal with anything at all. Biting her lip, she edged past them both as inconspicuously as possible, and opened the fridge door.

'Ellie.' Her father pushed his bowl away. 'How are you feeling?'

'Fine,' she answered after a pause - and she was, she realised, turning around. 'I'm feeling much better… thanks.'

'Good, good, that's good.' Her father seemed on edge, his fingers tapped nervously on the top of the table, and his eyes were an intense green as they studied her. 'Ellie, your mother and the twins are out shopping. I don't expect you to be too aware of what's going on, especially while you've been so sick, but it's been decided that the four of you will go up north to stay with your uncle.' He paused. 'It is for the best, just while things sort themselves out here.'

'What?' Shock jolted through her body.

'As if they will,' muttered Ben.

'But Dad, I can't go, I love it here.' And much to her shame, tears welled up in her eyes.

'Well love won't make it safe, and your mother has decided.' Her father said tersely. 'Besides, there's nothing for you here. The school has closed; the pipes have burst in the cold-'

'Yeah, but Dad it'll open again,' Ellie interrupted. 'And until it does, I can study online, that's what everyone else will be doing. And besides, I have to stay here, who else would look after you and Ben?' She flicked her brother a conspiratorial grin, then stopped, thinking of something else. 'Hey have you seen Rose?'

Her brother didn't answer; pushing his chair back, he grabbed his jacket and headed to the door.

'Ben, wait, have you seen her?' Ellie asked again, louder.

He stopped. 'Yeah, I've seen her, at the meetings. There's one tonight, and every night, if you care to come.' The door banged behind him as he left. A moment later, Ellie heard the guttural sound of the truck as it roared down the road.

'What's all that about?' Ellie tried to smile, but her eyes burned with sudden tears.

'Ah Ellie,' her father had moved and was standing by the window, looking up into the sky. 'The prophecies are coming true, that much is certain. Your friend Rose is standing firm with her father. And you need to decide where you stand.' He paused. 'Two weeks,' he said firmly.

'What?' asked Ellie confused.

'You have two weeks to regain your strength and then your mother will be back to get you.'

Claire left with the twins the next day - Sunday morning. Their faces were smiling from the window as the weekly train disappeared beneath the flat, grey sky.

Two weeks, Ellie thought morosely. Just two weeks and I have to go too. It was still freezing cold, and her breath steamed as she opened the front door to the empty house. Inside, Ellie tossed her bag onto the sofa in the living room and cranked on the portable gas heater. The flame flared once in the grate, and sputtered out.

'Damn,' she muttered. 'Dad must have forgotten to fill it before he left for church.'

Ellie shook her head. Her father had let her stay home and catch up on the schoolwork she'd missed, and she'd planned to curl up nice and warm in front of the fire. But now it was just way too cold.

Shivering, Ellie hurried down the hallway and into her room. There, she pulled on a pair of tracksuit pants and a long-sleeved jumper and climbed back into bed. Through the window, she watched as a band of darker cloud gathered against the sky. The wind picked up, and a gust of icy air whipped in through the cracks beneath the glass. Ellie snuggled further beneath the covers. She could always read in bed, she supposed, but even with an extra blanket and the blankets pulled tight over her head, it was still stupidly, utterly, perishingly cold.

If only the wind would stop, Ellie thought miserably, rubbing her skin, hoping the simple friction would warm her up. If only it would stop being so cold … if only the weather would just go back to normal.

The weather…

Ellie's eyes flew open.

If only someone could just fix the weather.

Sitting bolt upright, she reached out behind her to her pillow. A tight bundle was hidden deep beneath the softness. Carefully, and with her heart thudding, Ellie unravelled the bound cloth. A single ring tumbled onto the bed beside her and after it, fell the smooth, grey shape of the hag stone.

Ellie gasped as the fog clouding her mind evaporated.

How could I have forgotten?

Ellie didn't wait. Slipping the ring onto her middle finger, she turned it so the emerald green orb was nestled, protected by her palm. With her other hand she reached for the hag stone.

Outside, the storm began to howl.

'Weather workers,' she whispered. Ellie brought both objects to the centre of her chest, close to her heart. 'Please.'

Help us.

Lightning flashed.

Flared, crashed, spat.

A whirling cacophony of blackness and noise.

'I conjure thee!' a dagger of light shot up into the night sky.

'I *command* thee!' a louder voice shrieked once.

Thunder rocked.

Beads of rain pelted the swaying forms down below.

'Wind! Come to *me!*'

A stream of ice-cold air whizzed past Ellie where she hovered, somehow, in the sky. It surged down to the sodden earth below. Below her, Ellie caught a glimpse of sturdy boots, imperious eyes, and a couple of long dripping noses.

'Earth, I stir thee, and I call thee forth!'

At once a force pushed Ellie right between the shoulder blades. She tried to resist, but it was useless. Against her will, she was propelled from the vantage point in the sky, her arms flailing, down towards the milling, black clad personages.

Inches above their heads, Ellie's descent halted. Framed between her dangling feet, she saw a circlet of quizzical faces, turning up to her like the petals of an opening flower.

Rain lashed down.

A crackle of lightning burst past her cheek.

'What is your name, spirit?' queried a thin, but well modulated voice.

Ellie peered down in confusion. She opened her mouth, trying to think of the best way to respond, but before she could answer a figure bustled forward.

'We do not know this entity!' Cried a loud, regal tone.

With a firm flourish, Ellie was banished with two words.

'Be gone!'

She fell, squashed flat.

A shape, hard and lumpy pressed into her cheek, and her foot hurt where it had landed on something solid.

Groggily, she opened one eye.

Whiteness, and a dark hulking shape careened lopsidedly into view.

Oh God.

Blinking, Ellie shifted her head and tried awkwardly to sit up. Everything was spinning and her shoulder was shoved up hard against something cold and unmoveable. Frantically, she pushed against it, again, and then stopped, as a bolt of realisation brought her desk, cupboard, and bedroom into crystal clear focus.

It was a wall and she was back in her room.

'Ha!'

Elation surged through Ellie's being.

Grinning, she untangled her body from its position wedged at the foot of her bed and gazed down at the emerald ring. It had worked, unbelievably, it had actually, unbelievably worked. Tendrils of light drifted carelessly across its dark surface. *Like clouds,* Ellie thought, tracing her finger in wonder.

Across from her bed, the curtains were open, revealing a wide, grey cloudless day. It was still morning and freezing.

Where, she wondered, looking out to the dry, frigid sky, *exactly did I go?*

Leaning back, Ellie closed her eyes. A minute ticked by, and she reached for the small, smooth shape lying beside her.

'What were they doing?' she asked, cradling the hag stone in her hands, those women with the proudly jutting bosoms, and long dripping noses? Smiling, she brushed the stone against her cheek. Whoever they were, they seemed right at home in the flashing lightning, yelling and commanding the thunder and wind.

Ellie gazed down into the centre of the hag stone. 'Oh my God.' she whispered. 'I've found them.'

TWENTY-FOUR

New Forest, England, 1944

'Over the wide churning sea
Comes the white Lady glory be
Calling a spirit with gold-red hair
A jewel, an emblem, a fine face free of care.'

The grey-haired lady sniffed and pulling a dainty handkerchief from the front of her ample bosom, she carefully wiped her nose. 'Queenie dear, what do you think,' she asked, peering down at the page. 'Should I change the last line?'

The fire crackled behind and before her companion could answer the old woman sneezed. 'Oh dear…' she muttered, reaching again for the hankie. 'Kept out at all hours with that lot,' she blew her nose delicately. 'What a bother.'

As Dorothy Clutterbuck adjusted her reading glasses, a rumbling emerged out of the distance until, gaining in volume, it roared overhead, shaking the walls and swinging the pendants of the crystal chandelier as it passed. Dorothy took no notice; executing another small sniff, she squinted through her glasses and set back to work.

Only the nib of the pen scratching across the paper broke the quietness. Minutes passed, then she laid down her pen and cleared her throat.

'Over the wide churning sea,
Came the white Lady glory be
Calling a spirit with gold-red hair,
Attempted contact … but none so fair.'

'No, that isn't right,' she muttered. 'It's got more to do with … hmmm…' Pursing her lips, Dorothy picked up her pen.

A ring…?'

'Ha! That's it!'

Without taking her eyes from the page, Dorothy Clutterbuck took a deep sure breath.

'Over the wide churning sea,
Comes the white Lady glory be
Calling a spirit with gold-red hair,
A ring.
A stone.
And a face so fair!'

With a dramatic flourish, Dorothy cried the words out into the quiet of the room. Lightning flashed, its remnant brightness arcing across the dark window. This was swiftly followed by a hiss of alarm from the cat, and a booming crack of thunder.

'That's it!'

The chandelier shook.

The old lady clapped her hands together in delight. 'That sounds right. At last! How do you like it, Queenie dear?'

Dorothy turned with a triumphant smile, her bright blue eyes shining in her soft round face.

'Oh!' She gasped in shock. Her reading glasses slipped out of her hand and clattered loudly to the floor. 'Where did you come from?'

'I-I-I-' Ellie wobbled. Her throat felt scratchy, and her knees like jelly noodles. She wasn't quite sure how long she'd been standing there. From its position on the sofa an overfed white cat with wide orange eyes was studying her. Its tail twitched as it blinked and disdainfully looked away.

'I asked, what is your name, spirit!' Scooping her glasses up off the floor, the grey-haired old lady thrust her large bosom toward Ellie as though it was an armoured tank.

'I-I-I-' Ellie tried again, but the words were stuck fast in her throat.

In one hand she still held the hag stone, and in the other she could feel the icy coldness of the ring. The room was dim, the only light coming from a small fire glowing in the hearth, and the flame of a single gas lamp illuminated the glaring face of her inquisitor.

Ellic swallowed. It was hard to breathe. The air was thick with the sweet, damp smell of drying wool and lavender. Pegged out along a line by the fire, were a pair of tights and beneath them, filling a china bowl, were stems of budding purple flowers. A pair of black and white portraits glared down on the scene from the wall above.

It was just like the antique shop in town, Ellie thought, looking around - right down to the funny old sewing machine in the corner, and the pair of leather bellows lying by the fire. She stared. Why would you have something like that, all shiny brass and decorated, lying around on the floor? Shouldn't it be on a shelf or something?

Ellie frowned. 'Where am I exactly?' She asked, as politely as she could.

'Where do think you are? You are in my house. And *I* am doing the questioning here, since *I* am the one who summoned *you*.'

The lady looked around sixty; she was tiny and round in a light grey woollen skirt and grey cardigan, pulled tightly across her ample chest. She stared up at Ellie with fearless eyes. 'Spirit, I command you tell me your name!'

'I'm sorry.' Ellie sighed, she felt overheated. 'I am not a spirit. And you didn't summon me, not really.' She paused. 'Do you mind if I take off my jacket?' Ellie reached for the zip of her raincoat.

'I command you to stay right where you are!'

The door to the room banged opened.

'Miss Dorothy, where would you like these?' A young man of about eighteen hobbled in. He smiled, but as his eyes swung round to Ellie his foot tripped on the rug. He stumbled and the armful of wood fell to the floor with a resounding crash.

Dorothy clicked her tongue in annoyance. 'Well, Gerald,' she said tartly, 'where else but in the middle of the carpet of course.'

A great roar swept low and deafening overhead. Grimacing, Ellie covered her ears, though the old lady and the boy ignored it.

'Oh I am terribly sorry.' He cried, reaching awkwardly for the fallen wood. She could see his weight was balanced on one leg, while the other leg, smaller and twisted, lagged behind, encased in a bracket of metal.

Dropping the hag stone and her jacket onto a side table, Ellie darted forward to help.

'So you are not so incorporeal, it seems.' The old lady leant closer, her gaze taking in Ellie's faded red t-shirt and jeans. She squinted through her glasses. 'But just what are you, then?'

Pursing her lips, Miss Dorothy leant into a stack of books on the floor by her writing bureau and examined the titles of the top few volumes with a studied frown. She selected a worn leather volume from the centre and, shaking her head, the old lady licked her finger and slowly turned the thin pages.

The only sounds in the room were the rustle of paper, and the loud ticking of the wooden clock on the mantlepiece. Picking up the last of the wood, Ellie handed it to Gerald. Smiling shyly, he placed it on the fire and sparks flew. The cat watched them, its eyes blank with disinterest as it morosely swished its tail.

Ellie reached forward to pat it.

'Oh miss, I wouldn't do that,' exclaimed the boy. 'Queenie is likely to bite and scratch strangers. Not that you're a stranger,' he added quickly, 'but she just doesn't know you yet.'

Immediately, Gerald blushed bright red.

'Oh,' said Ellic, 'Ellie, you can just call me Ellie.'

The boy smiled, and Ellie, unsure of what to else to say, began fiddling with the emerald ring on her finger. Pull yourself together, she told herself sternly. Primly, she brushed a strand of hair and looked away.

Miss Dorothy was staring at them both, stock still, and her mouth open in a perfect 'o' of astonishment. Ellie had forgotten all about the little old lady. Her eyes were fixed directly onto Ellie's hand, staring at the ring. Light shimmered across its perfectly spherical surface, a rainbow of multi-hued green splashed across the ceiling.

The book dropped to the floor with a bang. 'Who are you?' She asked, and her voice had lost its imperious, commanding tone. 'And what do want from us?'

The fire hissed sibilantly in the grate.

'I'm just a person like you. I'm Ellie, I'm not a spirit at all.' But she stopped, unsure of how much more she could say in front of Gerald. The boy still lingered on the doorstep, one hand on his cap, as if waiting to be dismissed. 'Ah, if that will be all, Miss Dorothy?' he asked after clearing his throat politely.

Dorothy, her eyes clouded with thought, simply waved him away with her hand. The door closed.

The room fell silent.

Wondering how to even begin explaining who she was, Ellie crept forward and retrieved her hag stone from its spot on the side table. She felt better immediately, its weight warm and familiar in her hand, and now, whatever happened, it didn't really matter; she could get back home whenever she wished.

'Ah a hag stone,' Miss Dorothy had relaxed slightly and was gazing up at it with interest. 'You are very fortunate, child. They only go to those they choose.'

Nodding, the old lady rose to her feet and pushed back the scroll top to her desk. She pursed her lips, before clicking open a series of smaller, interior drawers. From one, she pulled out a small cloth-covered object.

'My hag stone' she said, uncovering it with a gentle flourish, 'has been in the family for generations.' It was very much like Ellie's - smooth and gray and small enough to fit snugly in her hand, but what made it all the more similar was the hole worn through at its centre.

'But mine is the only one in existence,' Ellie stared at it in astonishment.

'Oh no,' said Miss Dorothy serenely. 'They're quite common around here on the beaches. They're gifts from the sea god, you know, Mannanon? Oh how I adore him, he's very good looking you know.' The old lady smiled, lost for a moment in reverie. 'Oh yes, the hag stone,' she blinked. 'What was I saying? Only some though have power and yours, it's true, has an uncommon amount of power. And you do too, if I may say so.'

Ellie didn't know how to respond. The cat, all at once jumped off the sofa and brushed past her legs before settling itself at Miss Dorothy's feet. A low, vibrating purr filled the room.

'Ah, Queenie, what do you think?' murmured the old lady, reaching down to pat the animal's head.

'Please, may I look at your ring?' she asked, her face creased with concern.

Ellie, not sure if she wanted to take it off, reached out her hand and turned the stone side up to face Miss Dorothy. The vibrating purr ceased, and the cat leapt at once onto the old lady's lap. Both pair of eyes, one deep orange and the other a bright inquisitive blue, stared into the dark green centre. Ellie watched them as a pinprick of light flared so abruptly that the old lady and the cat recoiled.

'Tell me why you are here, young Ellie?' Miss Dorothy asked quietly. 'Is it something to do with the War? I have felt huge forces swirling in the ether. The spirits are frightened and uncontrollable. The weather is hard to manage, it fights us.' She paused and lifted her frightened blue eyes into Ellie's. 'We are on the cusp of something huge - Gladys saw it in her mirror. Are you here to help us? Are you?'

And Ellie said, 'I don't know ... I really don't know anything at all.'

Sunlight fell onto the crumpled cotton sheet. With a sleepy moan, Ellie rolled over and opened her eyes to a sea of pink. The walls were papered in light rose pink wallpaper. A crocheted throw, pink and patterned with small furled white roses, covered the bed.

A knock tapped on the door and Miss Dorothy entered carrying a wooden tray. Her stomach rumbling, Ellie could see a pot of tea and four slices of thick cut toast, richly buttered, with honey on the side in a pot. Dorothy placed it on a side table before sitting herself down.

'Sorry, there's not much. What with the war on, but we do have our own cow and we are lucky, there is plenty of butter and milk for our tea.'

'Wow,' breathed Ellie, and she quickly sat up, the rich sweet smell of honey and butter almost made her swoon.

'You must be tired after all that flying,' Miss Dorothy commented as she watched Ellie eat, 'and hungry. That happens to me too. Once I came back and nearly ate a whole buttered teacake to myself. Can you imagine?'

Ellie stopped chewing, 'What?' she asked, her mouth still full of toast.

'A teacake, you know, with apples and raisins. But of course we don't make those for ourselves anymore. Must think of our boys.' She smiled up at Ellie, her eyes twinkling in the sun.

Behind her, through the open window, a flock of small birds descended on the tree outside. It was delicate and shaded a light, gentle green. So different, Ellie thought, as she watched them flitting and

268

quarrelling through the branches - different than what we have back home. All at once they whirred away into the gentle blue sky.

'Miss Dorothy,' asked Ellie slowly, 'can you tell me where I am exactly. Of course, I know I'm in your home, but where is -?' Ellie gestured towards the window.

The old lady smiled. 'Why dear, you're in Burley village, in the New Forest, of course.'

'Where?' Ellie stopped in shock as a huge armoured vehicle, squeaked and clanked past the cottage, its square outline visible through the delicately laced curtains. 'Is that a-?'

Miss Dorothy only nodded and smiled; conversation was now impossible, drowned out by the rattle of the windows and the engine roar of the passing tank.

Oh. My. God. Thought Ellie.

'Yes they had to widen all the roads, imagine that! Cart tracks widened too for the huge beastly things. It's bad for the forest ponies. I don't know how many have been killed, or run over, it's awful.' She paused, her eyes misting with tears. 'But,' she said dabbing her eyes with a handkerchief, 'must not complain. They're here to get rid of that horrible, horrible man and his frightful armies. We all know, even though it is an awfully big secret,' she added solemnly. 'That's why there are so many Americans here and Canadians too. They're so very good looking, lovely and polite. Why-'

'Miss Dorothy...' interrupted Ellie faintly. My God this old woman could talk. 'Could you please tell me what the date is, I'm sorry, I really don't know what's going on?'

'Oh dear, I do blather on, I get so carried away.' Cheerfully the old lady patted her grey curls and pursed her lips. 'Now the exact date is...' she paused. 'Let me get the grimoire.' Dorothy stood and left the room. Ellie could hear her rummaging about in the living room.

'It was a dark moon last night in Taurus,' the old lady returned and eased herself onto the chair with a cloth covered book in her hand. 'Today, it's in Gemini, so that makes it May the 23rd in the year of King George the VI of England, 1944.' She smiled briskly at Ellie. 'Would you like some eggs, dear, they're very fresh, from our own chickens?'

But Ellie couldn't hear her, all she was aware of was the panicked thudding in her chest, as shock coursed through her body.

England? 1944?

Breathe, she ordered desperately, *just breathe, connect to the earth and breathe.* Closing her eyes, she felt for the roots of the trees branching out underground and the calmness of the forest. Quickly she breathed it up, letting it fill her being until there was only silence and peace.

Ellie opened her eyes.

'That's a useful little trick.' Dorothy was looking at her closely. 'I always have trouble, you know, with getting overexcited. If you could instruct me how, I would be ever so grateful. But not now.' She glanced at her watch. 'Why don't you rise, and we'll go over into town and we'll meet Gladys. She's the bossy one who shooed you away the other night. Ooh, I could've bitten her head off.'

Standing up, Dorothy tidied the breakfast things on the tray. 'But Ellie,' she added, 'you'll have to borrow some of the clothes my niece left last summer. We can't have you gadding about in your own things. They are very peculiar.' Dorothy laughed, a wide pealing sound of delight.

'They'll all think you're a Nazi spy.'

TWENTY-FIVE

Blue Mountains, Australia, present day

A select group gathered in the narrow room under the eaves. A single candle warded off the dark. Mrs Beatty's hat lay on the low chair, hidden beneath a tumble of woollen scarves and heavy coats. Ben's boots sat neatly by the door. Outside, the storm had eased, and the constant moan of the wind had dropped to an occasional gust that lashed through the skeletal remains of the trees.

Rose shivered despite the fire burning in the grate. Against the window she could just make out the shape of her father's bureau. Tonight a velvet cloth hid its secrets, and on its surface eight small glasses and a plate of unleavened bread waited, the Holy Sacrament, bread and wine, to seal the commitment of the faithful.

With a flourish, Matthew selected a page from the large leatherbound book. As he read, Rose watched him closely. Her father looked different, his face was tight with exhaustion, yet his hands were firm and his eyes blazed bright as he stared deep into each and every one of them in turn.

'... You've heard the promise, it is clearly written. Purified souls can never sin. Do not forget this, we are pure and we can never sin. When we are in the service of the Lord, our actions are exalted, for we do His Will.'

'Let us pray.'

Rose quietly slipped her hand into Ben's. His skin felt warm, and the calluses on his palms scraped roughly against her skin. She didn't mind. Closing her eyes, she eased herself closer, breathing in the sharp scent of the herbal soap he liked to use. Unfussy, direct and clean... Rose allowed herself a small smile, rather like Ben. She had decided.

Ben.

He would be her world. She would wrap herself in his love, hide in it, like it was a thick warm blanket, and think about nothing.

Nothing.

She squeezed his hand.

Everything else was just a nightmare.

TWENTY-SIX

New Forest, England, 1944

The bike was built for comfort and not speed. Clad in a dusky pink dress with a rounded collar and buttoned all the way down the front, Ellie cycled with her back straight and her hair swept up off her neck. Cool air brushed her legs and the sun flashed through small rounded leaves.

A bird sped ahead, tiny, with wings flashing the brightest gold. The scene was almost unbelievably perfect, like something out of a child's storybook, spotted deer with white tails flouncing, forest ponies with wide trusting eyes…

She squeezed on the brakes and glared irritably at the road ahead. It would have been perfect, except for that continually, teeth clenchingly, irritating, squeaking, groaning, lumpy *thing* shaking the very ground beneath.

Miss Dorothy didn't seem to notice. She was way ahead, pedalling serenely, eyes straight forward, taking no notice of the armoured monstrosity clanking a few turns behind.

'Oh God. Go away!' Ellie threw out her hand. At once, the tank careened off to the left without slowing, and headed out across what looked to be an open field. Ellie stared open mouthed, then she laughed out loud. 'That will teach you!'

Energised by her unexpected success, she sped up the road until she caught up with Miss Dorothy. The old lady had stopped and was now deep in conversation. The man had an open smiling face and silver hair and was standing by an open cart. His small pony tore eagerly at the long grass at its feet.

'Do you say yes to an extra chocolate, Miss Dorothy?' A bar, wrapped in silver glinted in his hand, 'Or are you sweet enough?'

She giggled and blushed as bright as a girl. 'Well, the Americans eat so many they wouldn't miss one more, would they?'

Ellie turned her bike back to the road, thinking she'd just wait for the old lady a little further on.

But Miss Dorothy waved at her quickly. 'My dear! Where are you off to?'

'This is my young friend Ellie, er, Smith,' said Miss Dorothy as Ellie walked back slowly towards them. 'Ellie, may I introduce you to Billy Buckland. He and his family have been a treasured part of this forest for generations.'

Ellie smiled.

'Her family are stuck abroad,' Dorothy was confiding in a low, concerned voice. 'And she needs to stop with me - imagine! She's all by herself.'

'The war,' Billy frowned, 'everything is such a terrible mess.' Then he brightened, 'but it could be worse. Would you like some chocolate Miss, or are you sweet enough?'

Dorothy pealed with laughter. 'Ooh Billy, you do spoil us.'

He winked. 'I'd better be off,' he said, placing his hat back on his head, 'no rest for the wicked.'

'Gladys said we meet tonight, an hour earlier,' Dorothy said softly as Billy climbed back onto the cart. 'And the girl is coming too.'

What? The chocolate bar almost fell from Ellie's hand.

Tilting his hat back, the older man considered them both for a long moment; his dark eyes were no longer so welcoming. He clicked to his horse. 'Is she now, Miss Dorothy,' he said quietly. 'I do hope you know what you're doing.'

Dorothy and Ellie rode into the centre of the town and halted their bicycles on the grand avenue hugging the curve of the bay. Ellie studied the house; it was high, white and double storeyed, with wide windows staring out over the foam-tipped waves. The wind was up, and she shivered as Dorothy lifted the brass ring and knocked loudly.

After a pause, the door opened and a large, hooked nose followed by a pale, distrustful face peered out.

'Yes, Dorothy Clutterbuck?'

Ellie shrank back. This must be Gladys. Tall and thin, with a pinched mouth and grey, distrustful eyes.

'We had arranged to meet tonight, yet the mirror said you were arriving imminently. And here you are. Both of you.' Gladys sniffed as she regarded Ellie. 'We do not often meet other witches.'

Ellie baulked, and bit back a bubble of laughter as she realised the grim-faced woman was serious.

'I'm not a witch,' she tried her friendliest smile. 'I'm Ellie.' Politely she offered her hand.

Gladys took a step back. 'Oh', she said. 'If not a witch, what are you then?'

'Oh Gladys, stop it,' muttered Dorothy. 'Let us in.'

Gladys hesitated, and seizing her chance, Dorothy grabbed Ellie by the hand and bustled into the house. 'Ellie is one, aren't you, my dear? She just doesn't call herself one, very sensible I say considering the laws.' Dorothy marched straight into the front living room. 'I'll vouch for her, if she isn't a witch I'll eat my pointy hat.'

The room was simply furnished with white walls and high, airy ceilings. A brown leather sofa commanded the central space. Despite the chill, the windows facing the sea were open, and cold, salty air was gusting into the room. A dark standing mirror was by the wall opposite and, as the curtains lifted, grey thick cloud danced across its polished, ovoid surface.

Ellie stifled a yawn; the sofa looked good, so soft and welcoming. Would it be very rude, she wondered, if she lay down and had a little nap? Behind her, the two women were discussing something quite urgent. Ellie's ears pricked, sure she heard her name spoken once, then twice. She yawned again.

A nap would be fine, she decided quite suddenly. All I need right now is a little catnap. Ellie's eyes drooped and, quite unconscious of what she was doing, her feet shuffled forward along the floor, taking her, not towards the sofa as she'd intended, but away down the length of the room.

It's quite handsome, Ellie thought dreamily. Handsome, what a funny word to describe a mirror, she almost giggled. Freestanding, and almost as tall as her and almost as wide, the mirror's ornately carved frame was patterned with leaves, flowers, faces…

Hello, Ellie thought stupidly, standing almost nose-to-nose with her own hazy reflection.

Clouds scudded.

Hello…

Around her the light in the room began to fade.

'Step closer, child.' The voice held the resolute steel of command.

Was that Miss Dorothy? Ellie wondered. The question rattled around in her head. But there was no time to chase it as a moment later, Ellie tipped forward into inky blackness.

She blinked slowly as she woke; around her everything seemed to be white, a stark featureless white. *Am I in heaven?* Ellie giggled aloud.

'We have been given a task to keep the skies clear - each and every night. We do not know why, or for how long.' Gladys's voice was cool and precise. 'The vision was clear. We must delay the storm that is approaching, and we cannot deviate from our task.'

Ellie shifted her gaze and the white solidified into a tall, thin figure, straight backed and silhouetted against the window. Ellie felt around with her hand. She was lying stretched out on the sofa, her bag placed beside her. Miss Dorothy was sitting perched by her feet; she looked as pleased as punch.

'The mirror welcomed her that much is true,' sniffed Gladys. 'She has not been rejected, but we do not know how her energy will affect the balance.' Gladys peered sternly at Ellie. 'You can attend tonight, but you must be silent, you are to observe only. You are not to act, and above all, you are not to perform any magic. The work we do is too important for us to be concerned with the proficiencies of a mere child, an unknown one at that.'

Ellie didn't know quite what to say, so she said nothing at all, and nodded, hoping that was the right thing to do.

Drops dripped through the darkened trees as Ellie and Miss Dorothy wheeled off the forest road. Leaning her bicycle against a fence post, Ellie smoothed the heavy woollen fabric of her coat and turned the thick collar up against the drizzle. A few steps away, in the gloom of the evening, a group of cloaked, hooded figures were moving slowly over a wide grassed area, and a bank of trees grew off to one side.

They were circling around a central stone, Ellie realised. It looked like a monument of some kind - tall, weathered, and ancient. Above them thunder rumbled and a burst of rain fell from the sky.

No one stopped to greet them as Miss Dorothy and Ellie drew closer, no one smiled or even seemed to notice their arrival; all seemed too intent on their task.

Ellie frowned. What were they doing?

'Blessed water!' muttered a thin, feminine voice. 'Tumble and turn and do my bidding!'

'Come to mine!' A shadow passed. 'Know me, know my family, know my line. I bid you!'

Ellie turned; she knew that one. Sure enough, she caught a glimpse of Billy, his face scrunched in concentration, his mouth moving. Smiling,

Ellie waved, but the deliveryman only whipped his hood down low and averted his eyes.

Across the circle, a voice cried. 'I do quell thee!' And a sudden whip of air, chill and sharp, cut through the gathering before escaping into the night.

'Heed me!' A dark figure raised a hand, flourishing a stick, polished, and set with stones. They glistened in the wet, and an intricate pattern flashed in the darkness. Seconds later the flurry of rain stopped.

Ellie fidgeted, she wasn't sure what to do. Miss Dorothy had raised her own hood and left her at the edge with a whispered reminder to just watch, and be quiet. Ellie could just about see the old lady weaving in among the others, each figure following their own invisible path.

It didn't seem to make much sense. Overhead, a sizzle of lightning spat through the clouds and the hairs on her arm prickled.

'Spirits of the South, workers, weavers of the forked flame, I command you, depart!' Gladys, her bony fingers scrapping white against the night, threw forth her arms.

Ellie gasped as a sudden flicker burst into sight around the thin woman's hands. They looked like wisps of tiny faeries, working hard, their mouths open in effort. Around them light sparked.

'Go back!' barked Gladys, her brow pressed together in concentration.

Unthinking, Ellie stepped forward and raised her hands, ready to sing out a tone to help. At once, Gladys whirled and tossing back her hood, furiously shook her head.

No. Ellie was not to interfere.

Afterwards, Ellie and Dorothy rode back to the village in silence, the rain still dripping from the broad-leafed trees arching over the road. Miss Dorothy seemed exhausted; her small stout figure sagged as she pedalled the last mile. A pop of distant gunfire sounded. Flinching, Ellie stopped, her eyes wide.

'Don't worry, it's just the shooting range,' murmured Miss Dorothy. 'There's all sorts of goings on during the night. Keeps their eyes sharp, I imagine.'

'I wonder what the time is at home?' Ellie tilted her head up to the cloud-covered sky. 'Dad will be reading, I guess, and Ben, I don't know, probably out with my friend…' She sighed, overwhelmed by a sudden surge of homesickness. 'I wonder how long I have to be here.'

They had reached the corner of the village high street. Houses slept silently on either side and, intermittently, the ground shook as rolls of thunder boomed on the horizon. 'Oh child, no matter how long you're here, when you get back you could have been gone for years, or merely a flash of a second and your loved ones none the wiser.'

Ellie squeezed on the brakes. 'What?'

'Of course you know time behaves differently when you work magic. It's in all the fairytales.' The old lady had seemed to have recovered her good humour. She nodded at Ellie. 'A hapless traveller enters the hall of fairy, eats, drinks, and is merry, and on their return a hundred years has passed.'

Ellie stared at Dorothy, 'but that can't happen to me?'

As she spoke, the air quaked as an enormous shape swooped towards them out of the darkness. It was so close, Ellie could see the four engines under its wings glowing an unearthly red. The bomber was so huge and so dark, its shape blocked out the entire sky, leaving an acrid smell of hot oil in its wake.

'We don't really know do we, child?' Miss Dorothy cried over the noise. She gestured to the sky, 'But you could hardly call *this* fairyland.'

'I have to go home! Oh no, I had no idea'.

Dorothy walked ahead and unlatched the front gate to her cottage. 'Are you planning on coming back, to here I mean?'

'W-w-well, I don't know.' Stuttered Ellie, she hadn't moved; she stood glued to the footpath, frozen with horror. 'I think I have to.'

'Well then, you'd best keep something of yours here.'

'I don't understand.' Ellie stared at her. 'What do mean?'

'Come on in, quickly.' Dorothy gestured her into the garden. 'Just what are you being taught?' Her lips pursed in disapproval. 'Well, it's not like that around here. An apprentice learns the art and science of magic and knows just what's what. They're put in their place, and don't just go gallivanting around the countryside on their own. Why if you were mine –'

Ellie put her hand on Dorothy's arm. 'Please...'

The old lady sniffed. 'Well, come inside. We don't want to be having this kind of conversation where *anyone* could hear.' She pointed to Ellie's bicycle. 'Put that in the lean to around the back, mine too if you please, and I will tell you what to do. It's quite simple, something a first-year apprentice would know. But as I said, if you were mine, I would not let you leave in the first place.' Miss Dorothy declared, jutting her full bosom forward and bustling up the garden path.

Wheeling the bikes around to the side of the cottage, Ellie heaved them into the narrow space and closed the gate behind her. Her heart was thudding, panicking. She tried to breathe, and the ground shook as another bomber roared overhead.

In the living room, Miss Dorothy was bent low in front of the fire, working the bellows; the flames rose brightly as puffs of air blew over the hot coals.

'We don't know exactly *how* Time works,' she began as Ellie entered the room. 'That's for the science mages to work out, but the mechanics seem to be relatively straightforward, dare I say even simple. The answer is hidden in what the fairytales *don't* tell you.' She sniffed. 'It's all in there, you know, if you care to look. You simply leave behind something of your own. That way, of course, you won't get lost.'

'But how do we know what will happen when I get home?'

'We don't, none of us have tried a two-way portal, in fact none of this has been tried at all to my knowledge, jumping all over the place. But needs be as needs must, so they say.'

Ellie rubbed her head, none of it made any sense at all.

'Ah. This would be perfect.' Miss Dorothy had stood up and was now regarding Ellie's waterproof jacket. It was hanging over the armrest of the sofa by the fireplace where Ellie had left it. 'But it is very peculiar.' Dorothy commented, examining the mesh lining and strips of Velcro fastenings. 'What is all this used for? But, no matter,' Dorothy gave a satisfied nod. 'If it is yours, it should do the trick.'

Ellie took the jacket without a word. It had been a gift from her parents a couple of years before, back when the rain had been as regular as clockwork.

She'd scarcely worn it.

'Oh and Ellie, one more thing, if you do leave it here,' Miss Dorothy looked up, a tiny dimple showing in her apple-red cheeks. 'Would you mind terribly much if I wore it to tomorrow night's circle, if you're not back by then? It looks like it should me keep jolly well dry.'

TWENTY-SEVEN

Blue Mountains, Australia, present day.

The heat was suffocating and a thunderhead was building, rising into an otherwise cloudless sky. In the canyons, trees stood huge, careful and completely still, their limbs so dry and brittle any movement could cause one to crash heavily to the ground. Beneath them, the forest floor was covered with litter, dead branches, and shattered, fallen giants.

In the canopy, narrow leaves turned to catch the sun as it arced across the sky, absorbing precious energy even as their tips burned, and what moisture was remained sucked dry.

Matthew stood at the cliff edge, clad in his full clerical regalia, surrounded by the select few from the congregation. The storm roiled, a deep angry bruise against the glare of the midday sky. Magnificent, the cloud towered straight up into the heavens and its base flashed bright with heat, like a beacon - with lightning shards of energy bound deep within the body of the thunderhead itself.

Matthew raised his hands to the sky.

'My people…'

In response, the followers standing before him raised theirs, the fumes from their torches mixing with the menthol of the eucalypts, spiralling upwards in the heat.

'Listen, turn your eyes to the storm and know a mighty truth; as one we are feeble, but joined in a single-minded purpose, we are mighty.'

'Are you with me?'

Matthew clenched his fist as they roared their affirmation; the rush of his people's faith was like a jolt of concentrated power.

The storm cell surged and fingers of black cloud descended like daggers to the earth, sparking with the fury of the spirits.

He smiled. They were so simple to call, and so powerless against his will.

At his gesture, Ben came forward and the Select fanned behind - his flock, his resolute band of faithful warriors.

Matthew laid his hands on Ben's head and began to pray.

'We are your Instrument, oh Lord. We hear your call.'

'We are your Instrument, oh Lord. We hear your call.' Ben repeated.

As he spoke, the people swayed when he swayed, and prayed when he prayed.

'We do your bidding.' He raised a single hand.

'We do your bidding.'

'We fulfil your desire.'

Matthew glimpsed at Rose at the back, behind Mrs Beatty and her husband, and Ben's father, Brian Malone. The man's eyes were open and he gazed heavenward, awash with belief. Matthew nodded. Yes, the Malone family, all of them stalwart believers, firm supporters of the doctrine of ascension and the scorching of the earth, all of them ... except...

A vision of Ellie's face flashed before him, pale and asleep in her room, ill with the fever that had settled in days before. Matthew indulged a minute nod of satisfaction. There would be ample opportunity to deal with her later, and now, whatever influence the rebellious girl had over his sweet Rosalind had faded. Here was his daughter standing before him, her beauty and steadfastness shining like a beacon.

Exalted, Matthew cried out in a mighty voice. 'The End has come!' and the people shouted in turn.

'The End has come!'

In response, the cloud roiled as the spirits dropped lower, their incandescent forms bright against the massing darkness. Only he, the Reverend Matthew Hopkins, the Instrument of God, knew they were there - a vast reservoir of power poised to heed his command.

He smiled, and his voice became a whisper caressing the wind, so soft the Select had to lean in close.

'As the forests burn, and as the earth is scorched, then we shall be lifted up.'

The words were as rhythmic and as powerful as any incantation.

'As the forests burn, and as the earth is scorched, then we shall be lifted up.'

As the people repeated the phrase, a wind began to stir - hot, dry, and merciless.

'As the forests burn, and as the earth is scorched, then we shall be lifted up.'

The voices increased in intensity, and Ben reached into the top of his chequered shirt.

'As the forests burn, and as the earth is scorched, then we shall be lifted up!'

The chant rose louder and louder, and the spirits responded, snatching the words and pulling them high into the sky. Thunder cracked, and from the monstrous cloud a shard of lightning burst free.

'Now!' cried Matthew.

His face ablaze with faith, Ben struck a match and his kerosene-soaked torch burst into flame.

The chant dropped to an expectant silence, as sharp as a cut.

Below stretched the forest, a maze of tree-filled canyons rich in combustible fuel - fallen leaves and dry branches, and something else; the agent of its own destruction. *Oil.* It had evolved over eons to aid survival; protecting slender eucalypt leaves from the ravages of hungry predators. Matthew smiled even as the menthol scent burned his nose. This cloud of vapour, rising from countless leaves, bore thousands and thousands of tiny droplets, sharp, pungent, and highly flammable.

It was his daughter's turn. Eye's downcast, Rose dipped her torch into the flame. Matthew nodded, his heart filled with fierce pride as she took her place beside Ben and the others, her slender arms raised out over the lookout, her dark hair curling down her back.

He didn't need to say a single word.

Matthew bowed his head as the Select lifted their eyes to heaven. In unison, they flung their blazing firebrands high over the edge of the cliff. Flames streaked, first orange, then flaring blue as each one tumbled over and over, down into the tinder dry depths.

Ellie snapped awake. The night was dark and quiet; the only light was the green glow of the clock spilling over the wall above. Warily she turned her head just as the set of electronic numbers flipped over in the night. 00:04 the digits hovered before her. Ellie expelled a sigh of relief. Just past midnight. She paused, bracing herself for any discombobulating sensation of her room lurching and spinning. Yet, despite a distinct queasiness, nothing happened - her desk, cupboard, and window remained anchored securely to the floor.

Thank you, she smiled, still tasting the tang of the dark, bitter concoction Miss Dorothy had handed to her the night before, 'Drink it, child,' she'd insisted. 'The recipe has been in my family for generations - it'll help keep your wits about you.'

The old lady had been right, for despite the mixture's foulness, Ellie felt pleasantly sharp and very awake. She looked to the window closed tight on the other side of the room, and a shiver of warning flicked across her skin. Tossing back the covering, Ellie tiptoed across the floor and pushed back the curtains. It all looked okay. The remains of the fallen giant had been mostly carted away, and beyond it the road slipped away down the hill and into the night.

The houses slept, even the wreck opposite. Above its jutting frame Ellie could see a tiny sliver of moon, shining clear in an ocean of stars. She frowned.

With a hard shove, Ellie pushed open the sash of the window. Where were the clouds?

She took in a deep breath and almost choked as the air tore into her throat; close, dead, and hot - like the final exhalation of an exhausted beast. Coughing painfully, Ellie slammed the window shut, and stood stunned in the centre of her room.

The freezing winds had vanished, and heat had returned to the mountains, heavier, drier, and more desolate than before.

'It's not right,' she gasped. 'What's going on?'

Ellie shook her head, trying to ease the alarm that was thudding through her body. Thinking quickly, she hauled off the heavy jumper she'd been wearing and, clad in just a t-shirt and her tracksuit pants, quietly opened her bedroom door. Peering around, she tiptoed down the hallway towards the kitchen. It was the middle of the night, and the house should have been dark and sleeping, but before the closed door Ellie stopped, surprised by a chink of light that cut along her feet and the swell of braying voices.

What's going on? Ellie hesitated, and then hurried back through the hallway to her bedroom. *There.* The hag stone and the green-orbed ring were lying on the bed where she'd left them. Ellie closed her eyes. They both pulsed quietly, two magical tools of immense power, and they were hers. Feeling stronger, Ellie shoved them both deep into her pockets. Now, whatever happened, she was ready.

No one noticed Ellie as she surveyed the room. The kitchen was full, humidity dripped from the yellow walls, and in the centre the table was laden with glasses, mugs, a pot of coffee, and a can of kerosene. Voices were loud, and Ellie recognised most of the guests. Mrs Beatty was there with her husband from the congregation. Near her, Ben stood within a circle of young men, talking with shining eyes. Ellie heard an exuberant chink of glasses.

A party maybe…? Ellie wondered. But it was so late - maybe they'd had a midnight prayer meeting or something…

Catching her father's eye, she gave a hesitant wave. He nodded in response. By the stove the steam had cleared enough, and she could see Rose examining the contents of a large pot with a frown.

Smiling now, Ellie began easing through the knot of guests towards her friend, when a hand reached out and gripped her arm tight.

'Ellie, it is good to see you.' The Reverend Matthew Hopkins greeted her, 'I apologise if we woke you. How are you feeling?' His pale-blue eyes glinted with questions.

Ellie pulled at her arm. It hurt and he frightened her. Matthew seemed to have changed. Gone was the bitter, defeated air that had hung around him like a shroud; instead he seemed taller and somehow stronger, energy sparked off him clear and sharp and it sizzled into the very air.

Quickly, Ellie averted her eyes.

'We have been worried. Your father reported that you had succumbed to some sort of flu?'

'Uh-oh, I'm better now thanks. What are you-' confused, Ellie glanced around.

'What are we doing here?' Matthew chuckled.

Ellie flinched, the sound was weird, she doubted she'd ever heard him chuckle before.

'But you know know why we're here. Don't you?' He glared, his tone changing.

'I-I don't-'

Matthew cut her off. 'Don't lie to me Ellie Malone. You have seen our work.'

'What work?' She stared at him.

'Ellie,' Matthew's grip burned. 'You cannot win.'

'Let me go! I don't know what you're talking about.'

'You don't? Tell me, who are you seeing in the forest? I know you pretend to be ill. But the truth is revealed with every lie you utter.'

Ellie shook her head. The kitchen was becoming unbearably hot. Someone brayed with laughter right by her ear.

'Let me go.' She snapped again, louder this time. She fought to free her arm. 'It's none of your business who I see.'

The kitchen door was only a few steps away, but it may well have been a mile as Matthew moved his body, blocking any avenue of escape.

He smiled. 'It *is* my business when you consort with known witches.'

Ellie froze. 'You don't know what I do.'

'Oh yes I do.' Matthew bent closer, his breath hot on her skin. 'Ellie, I know evil when I see it.' He whispered. 'I know you sneak down into the forest and consort with the devil himself, *and* his harpy.'

'That's a lie!' Ellie couldn't contain herself. 'You are insane!' She pulled her arm free, shouting in a white-hot blaze of anger.

'I do not lie.'

'You do.' The hum of party chatter fell abruptly silent, but Ellie was beyond caring. 'Everything you ever do and say is a twisted version of the truth! You have them all believing you, but it's a lie-'

'Hey,' a hand dropped on her shoulder, small and light. 'What's happening, Ellie?' The voice was soft. 'You've been sick.' Rose glared up at her father. 'What did you say to her, Daddy?'

291

'Leave me alone.' Ellie shook her friend away. 'All of you are being duped by everything he says. It's crap. Rose, you of all people should know it's all lies.'

'But Ellie,' Ben appeared by Rose's side. He held his hand out. It had been such a long time since her brother had looked at her so gently. 'Stop freaking out, none of us are being duped.'

'Yeah,' Rose smiled. 'We're winning. All of us. And Ellie we've been promised so much. Don't fight it.'

'But it's all bullshit!' Ellie cried in frustration. 'You never believed any of this!

'She does now.' Brian's deep voice rumbled over her. 'Ellie, Rose has come to her senses. She has left childish rebellion behind.'

Rose was standing with her hands clasped, clad in a light brown cotton dress buttoned tightly to her neck, her deep golden eyes were warm with concern. Ellie stared, sometimes her friend reminded her of someone else, someone different but… Ellie shook her head.

'Are you even listening?' Her father snapped.

'I'm sorry.' Ellie raised her hands, bracing herself for a familiar burst of anger. 'Look, Dad…'

'No Ellie, you look.' He cut her off. Her father's eyes looked red and raw, and his voice wasn't angry. It sounded deeply sad. He was dressed in his Sunday best, freshly scrubbed, despite an inky black smudge on one side of his cheek. He took a step towards her.

'Dad...'

'Ellie, we don't want to leave you behind.'

Her heart dropped, and Ellie knew suddenly, right now, she had to choose. She swallowed, and her heart fluttered with panic.

'We have been promised. And it is coming.' Her father's voice tightened. 'We the faithful will be taken fully in body. Ascension is nigh.'

'Join us,' a voice murmured.

'We don't want to do this.' Ben advanced, as did other men in the congregation, closing in on her like a net.

'You can't fight us, Ellie.' Rose smiled, reaching out her hand. 'Join us.'

Around her, the small group from church began to join hands.

'Join us.'

Mrs Beatty stepped forward from behind her husband, leaving a space opened wide behind her.

Ellie clenched her fists. 'I can't.' She whispered, 'Oh Dad, I'm so sorry.'

In less than a heartbeat, Ellie bolted through the backdoor and ran out into the garden. With her heart thudding in fear, Ellie wrenched her bike out of the shed, and tore off the driveway and onto the road.

Ellie glanced back.

The front lawn was bathed in light. Matthew stood on the centre, his expression creased into a tight smile. Beside him Rose was huddled into his side, and Ben was close. Ellie couldn't see her father's face; he was in shadow, standing alone, with his arms folded over his body.

TWENTY-EIGHT

The road blurred beneath her wheels. Ellie gripped the handlebars tight and leant forward. Her eyes stung and she squeezed them, blinking rapidly. Her throat ached.

At the top of the hill, Ellie lifted her feet off the pedals and free-wheeled down the long road out of town. As the last of the houses fell away, she began to cry, great gulping sobs for the family she had left behind.

Miles later, the streetlights petered out and the paved road gave way to a dirt track. Ellie brought her bike to a stop and wiped her eyes. She was on the final crest, scrubland stretched out before her, miles of gorse and windswept trees. The moon edged up into the night, its leading edge just visible over the expanse of darkness. Ellie shivered.

She felt exposed out here, alone on the high plateau. No one knew she was here ... no one knew where she was headed. Ellie swallowed. In the shadowed growth, she could see shapes reaching out to the sky, like animals frozen in pain, their sinuous, misshapen limbs thrown in stark silhouette.

Quickly, she turned her bike lamp away. 'They're just gorse bushes,' Ellie murmured. *Calm down...*

Steadying herself, Ellie had her foot on the pedal, when something else stopped her. She listened hard, but she heard and saw nothing. Around her the night held not even a light breeze to disturb the calm, and yet a distinct sense of unease prickled over Ellie's skin.

In the distance, the moon rose higher, its belly almost full. A gibbous moon, Ellie remembered its name - though instead of having a gentle radiance, its face was dull and lopsided and its shape was obscured behind a thin, hazy veil.

Ellie frowned, that was weird too. Despite the lack of wind, the cloud layer appeared almost alive, rising, twisting out of the dark, and becoming denser with each passing moment.

Ellie didn't hesitate; she rummaged through her backpack and pulled out the hag stone.

'Show me.' She whispered and held it up to her eye.

At first Ellie didn't see anything different, but as her breathing calmed and her vision cleared, she saw an enormous eagle above the strange, coiling cloud, flanked by a pair of shadows – a trio, black on black, flying high against the night.

Ba Set.

Ellie stared in surprise and two things seemed to happen at once. A quick and sudden gust of wind barrelled towards her from the darkness and the three beings dropped - the eagle first, straight into the centre of the cloud.

Ellie only had time to cover her face with her hands as the tempest burst through the surrounding gorse, splintering the brittle branches. It was chaos. The wind snatched at her hair, pulling at her clothes, propelling a sharp rain of twigs into the sky. After only a few moments it was over. The fierce outburst streamed away over the scrubland, trees bending and swaying in the onslaught.

Crazy... Ellie dusted off a handful of twigs. The weather was just crazy. With a sigh, Ellie hauled her bike back to the path. She should be used to it by now.

In the distance, the layers of billowing cloud had thickened and the moon now shone a baleful, ugly red. That was weird. Frowning, Ellie licked her lips; the air smelled different, like the sudden squall had brought with it a sharp, acrid stench she could almost taste.

That smell... Ellie hesitated.

She studied the gorse for a moment and then dismissed the thought; gorse didn't smell like that. Intrigued, Ellie watched the cloud swirling over the moon for a long moment and closed her eyes, as the sharp scent caught at the back of her throat. She coughed.

Of course...

Kerosene. The bite of kerosene overlaid with the bitter stink of burning. Ellie watched as the amber tinged cloud undulated above the moon, its slow curves seeping into the darkness of the night.

That's no cloud,' she whispered. *No...* It was smoke - manmade smoke, and it was coming from the forest.

Ba Set's cottage was unlocked. Ellie let herself in and as she closed the door to the living room, the gust of air caused the candles in the window to blaze.

Shadows of magnified patterns - feathers, twigs, and pillars of stone streamed across the walls. Ellie dropped her rucksack on the floor and sank wearily onto the sofa to wait.

When she opened her eyes, sunlight flared through the trees. Ba Set was seated in the smaller chair by the window, a black robe wrapped tightly around her shoulders, and her golden eyes trained on the day outside. A jug of water sat on the table, with a plate of food.

'T-they're burning the forest,' Ellie burst out, fear making her voice shake. She struggled to sit up. 'Ba Set, what are we going to do?'

Ba Set didn't respond at first, then she turned and Ellie gasped in horror. The old woman's honey-brown skin was disfigured, swollen by an angry red mark that cut from the top of her hair line, down the side of her face to her jaw, and disappeared into the folds of her cloak.

'Oh my God, are you all right?'

'Ellie, calm yourself.' Ba Set murmured.

'No, we should get you to a hospital.' Ellie cried. She'd have to get home, to raid her mother's well-stocked first-aid kit. *But oh God if I'm caught...* Ellie's heart sank at the thought, but the burn was puckered with blisters - she had to help, she had to do something...

Ah. She could get back in a flash.

Ellie reached into her pocket.

'Stop.' Ba Set's tone was firm. 'You need to rest. This is not the hag stone's function. The hag stone *focuses*. But, Ellie, any splitting of space, time and matter, the sacred trinity of all corporeal existence, draws enormous amounts of energy - energy from both spirit and one's very essence. And *your* essence is already depleted. Sustain your body, or your mind will slip so far from it, it will not be able find its way back.'

'But Ba Set-'

'Sit down, Ellie. You are not here to look after me. The best treatment for a burn of this kind is rest, and fluids. My skin will heal, and there are many plants that will ease the worst of the discomfort. We're not invincible, Ellie,' She gestured to the plate of food. 'None of us are. Please … eat.'

Gathering her cloak, Ba Set rose from her seat. As she moved, Ellie could see the tightness in her gait, and the way she favoured the left hand side of her body.

Ellie reached for a sandwich.

'It is true.' Ba Set's voice was quiet as she stood and gazed over the forest below. 'Those who seek to destroy all we love have a new tactic. Most fires are easy to put out. But there are times when embers catch in the hollow of a fallen tree and lie, gaining in strength. That fire is more difficult to check. And this is my work.'

The air shimmered and two sinewy creatures, as insubstantial as smoke, appeared on either side of Ba Set. They seemed to be supporting her, propping her up, their knotted forms as black as char, as though burnt in a raging fire.

She smiled at them. 'And as you can see, in that I have allies.'

'I saw them,' Ellie gasped. 'Last night. My God, what are they?'

Ba Set thought silently before she answered. 'Powerful magical beings, of the kind I casually dismissed in the arrogance of my youth.' She smiled softly. 'I was so proud, I made so many mistakes… But they forgave me.'

With a sigh as muted as shuffling paper, the black-hued faeries crowded in close.

They are so beautiful, Ellie thought, gazing at them. *The Watchers,* as she thought they should be called, kept close to Ba Set, focused on the ancient shapeshifter like a pair of faithful companions.

'But Ellie, we have little time.' Ba Set turned and eased herself onto the end of the sofa. 'Are you rested? You have had less time to recover than you need. But events are moving quickly. Are you ready to return and continue your work?'

Ellie looked away, shielding herself from the sudden intensity in her teacher's gaze. 'But Ba Set, what work exactly? I don't know what I am meant to do? I've found them, I've found the weather workers, but so what? They didn't know what they were doing either!' Ellie bit back a hysterical giggle, fearing if she let herself laugh that she would never be able to stop. 'It's chaos there!'

Remembering something, Ellie reached into her pocket and pulled out the hag stone. 'And what about this?' She thrust it forward, almost angrily. The Watchers tensed. 'Miss Dorothy has one just like it and says they're very common. You said this was special,' Ellie's voice rose. 'But it's just the same as her's.'

Ba Set answered softly. 'Calm yourself, child,' she said. 'The stone is one of many, but it is also unique, and the only one of its kind. As we all are. Magic works better in paradox, don't try to prise it open with your mind too closely. Feel from your heart and you will know the answers.'

'But I don't have the answers, Ba Set.' Ellie blurted out, desperation making her voice sharp. 'How can I? I need to bring back rain, and save the forest, but how?' She dropped her face in her hand. 'It's impossible.

How am I meant to do it…?' She gasped for breath; and to Ellie it felt as though she was floundering, being sucked under by an enormous pitiless wave.

'There is no easy answer, Ellie, trust, this is your task. The hag stone has chosen you.'

'But why me?'

'Perhaps because there is no one else.'

Ba Set settled back on the very edge of the sofa and seemed to sink into herself, dimming her energy down until her outline seemed to waver, black on black, cloak to feather and back again. She closed her eyes. 'You have a choice, Ellie,' Ba Set said softly. 'You could turn away, even now.'

Ellie swallowed, her belly knotting painfully, overwhelmed by the sheer weight of expectation. Her heart skipped erratically in her chest, almost painfully, as the chatter of self-mockery redoubled in her mind. *Stupid … what if I fail?*

Ellie clenched her fists.

It took a long moment, but at last her breathing had calmed and she felt stronger.

Ellie reached for the hag stone. 'Okay.' She whispered quietly. 'You are unique and you are just one of many.' *And we're in this together.*

Ellie lay back and held the hag stone to her body. It felt cold and its chill hardness seeped into her skin and spread through the muscles of her belly. Breathing slower now, Ellie lifted her hand and shifted her attention to the ring she wore securely on her middle finger. Trembling, acutely aware of the spectres of anxiety prowling at the edge of her consciousness, Ellie peered into its deep green centre.

Her heart pounded. The ring stone loomed large, its emerald orb beckoning, drawing her closer. The pinprick flared and Ellie tumbled into the dark.

TWENTY-NINE

New Forest, England, 1944

The sky was black. The moon, mottled and three quarters full, hung low, one edge swallowed by a bank of rolling clouds. A crashing sound, like a large hollow pot being hit, echoed into the night. Ellie hung in the air, high above it all, her hair streaming, buffeted by a wild, squalling wind.

Miss Dorothy, a blur of bright red, careened in and out, her short arms outstretched waving, while other figures, dark cloaks flapping behind, whirled about in directions of their own.

Voices shouted a fevered cacophony of commands, and somewhere someone banged a drum. Just above the witches' heads, faeries were twisting, all different colours and shapes, their luminous forms weaving a tight pattern of light before fraying apart and vanishing in the cold and biting wind.

Lightning cracked, and Miss Dorothy ground to a halt.

'Come spirits of earth!' She cried, her voice thin but sure.

Energy, like a sharp snap of electricity jolted Ellie in the centre of her back. It didn't hurt, but it was enough to drop her like a stone, halting a few feet above the ground. She sneezed.

'Ellie!' cried Miss Dorothy. 'I knew you would come back. Welcome!' At the invitation, Ellie's height collapsed like a ruptured umbrella and she fell to the ground, just avoiding a figure spinning in the centre of the circle.

'Water!' The voice was high and undulating, the syllables long and strangely gurgling. 'Water, heed my call.'

A stream of water sprites whirled in response and hovered lightly, their liquid forms flaring an iridescent blue. The voice called out again and Ellie saw it was Billy. He had his eyes closed and his hands raised in supplication.

Immediately, Ellie opened her mouth and copied him, seeking to match his high pitch. At the same time, she breathed out a quick strand of connection down into the earth. 'Water, Water, hello.'

A hand grasped her own and Ellie turned to see Miss Dorothy beaming, encased in Ellie's red raincoat. Its hood covered her hair, though it was too large, and below it her nose dripped.

Miss Dorothy sniffed. 'Whatever you're doing, I shall have a go too.' Her eyes twinkled as she opened her mouth and exhaled a high, operatic note. It shot up into the air as though it was alive and fell in graceful harmony over Billy's wavering call.

Ellie joined in again. As Billy's eyes were tightly shut, he seemed to be unaware of his singing companions. He raised his hands and threw his voice even higher into the heavens. A light flashed out of the night, and a stream of movement burst around him before abruptly vanishing.

'Come spirits,' sang out Ellie, her breath catching with hope. 'Come liquid beings. Come dancers of the deep, of sweet summer rain.'

As Ellie, Miss Dorothy, and Billy called out and sang with their arms outstretched to the elemental beings, more faeries appeared. It was as though they condensed out of the very air itself, in all different sizes, shapes and densities. Some with a form like liquid silver, some insubstantial, others appeared cloaked in a mist so fine they refracted light - sparking shards of rainbow.

'Come...' Ellie sang in amazement, elongating the word so it stretched into a single, singing tone. *Come...*

In response, the beings seemed to solidify, building into a layer that swept over her upturned face, blowing into her eyes, and her hair. Shivering, Ellie kept calling, and the movement intensified. She could no longer see, but she could feel the faeries swirling faster and faster around the three of them.

'Water,' cried Billy in a sharper, more imperative tone, his eyes still closed. "Waaater!'

It was like a command. In a single surge, the faeries shot up into the sky, and the whirlwind vanished, the air sagging behind them as though a pressure system had abruptly eased.

A drum beat loudly, and individual voices called and cajoled behind her, but Ellie tuned them out. She could feel a great gap in the circle. The power that was water had completely vanished. Mystified, she stood staring up at the night sky. Miss Dorothy was still singing out in joyous abandon and Billy still cried out his repetitive singular word. But where were the water spirits? Ellie didn't understand it.

'Water?' she whispered. 'Water...?'

Where have you gone?

She waited staring up into the night. *Come to us.* She sent the call out.

A finger of wind tugged at Ellie's hair, she shivered, hugging her arms to herself in the cold.

Water?

Air gusted overhead, a tempest, bursting with flashes of a silvery liquid light.

No one else noticed.

Ellie didn't understand what she was seeing. On the tail of the wind, a vast, mirrored substance was moving, coming in swiftly from the west. It was following, or being pulled… The only hint of its immense size was the reflection and distortion in the sky as it moved.

Was that rain?

Hope surged through her being and Ellie focused on the sky. Streaming above the circle came countless spirits of water, dragging behind them an immense, trailing sheet of silvered currents.

Ellie threw back her head and shot her voice high above the circle. 'Water, come, come, please come!' She cried. The sky seemed to hold its breath.

'Just what do you think you are doing?' The outraged voice hit her like a slap. 'Stop!'

Miss Dorothy gasped. Billy opened his eyes. At once the gigantic sheet collapsed and a torrent of water flooded out of the darkness.

Miss Gladys shrieked, her face a mask of fury. 'Look what you've done!' Shocked to silence, Ellie watched as figures, racing in sopping wet cloaks, tried to push away the streaming rain. Some whirling where they stood, some attempting to smack it, to beat it back with their hands. Billy,

305

his face aghast, stood stunned as water and fierce wind surged out of his control.

'You have broken the circle!' Hissed Miss Gladys, her cloak flapping behind. 'I don't know why you're here, but…' She pushed back her sodden hood, her protruding eyes fierce as she glared at Ellie. 'The mirror wants you, that much is clear. But you are here to watch, and watch only. Do not interfere again or you will have me to reckon with!'

Storming back into the centre of the circle, Miss Gladys began to hurl commands up into the heart of the hammering rain. Lightning flashed and Billy, his face still bewildered, lifted his face into the night. 'Water,' he croaked. 'Be gone!'

You're an idiot, you're an idiot, you're an idiot. The singsong voice looped taunting, poking, jabbing, around and around, in her mind. Ellie winced; she was drenched through and beginning to shiver. Overhead, branches creaked as another load of wind and rain splattered across the road.

'It's not your fault,' repeated Miss Dorothy as her bicycle squeaked alongside. The old lady had wanted to walk, though her saturated shoes squelched with each step and her drenched skirt dragged along the road. But Dorothy didn't seem to mind at all; the rest of her was wrapped snugly inside Ellie's raincoat.

'Anyway, it's been quite unsettled for weeks,' she added dryly, peering at Ellie from within the hood. 'The weather has its own mind, and don't we know it. For the last week, especially, even before you came, mind you – it's been impossible to manage.'

Miss Dorothy's words didn't make Ellie feel any better. Dejectedly, she brushed another dripping strand of hair from her face. Why, why, why had she interfered? With a sigh, she gazed up into the water drizzling through the trees. It fell onto her face, cold and wet and horrible. You might as well try and push it back with a net, or something else just as stupid. Ellie ached to kick a stone.

'You can't control it!' she cried out. 'It's all stupid, how can anyone think they can actually control this?!' Ellie flung her hand up to the dripping sky. 'It's crazy!'

'Crazy, you say?' Miss Dorothy looked up sharply. 'It's not the weather we control, dear, it's the spirits; we each call our weather spirit and tell it what to do. It's quite simple really, and not at all crazy.' Her blue eyes twinkled as though quite unperturbed by Ellie's outburst.

It didn't make sense. 'But why would they obey you?' Ellie hadn't seen evidence of anything obeying anyone.

'It's in our families, they come with our families, some bring rain, some wind. It's all very secret, but I know I can trust you not to tell.' Dropping her voice, Miss Dorothy glanced around and said very quietly. 'We don't usually work as a group, as you no doubt have gathered. We like to keep to ourselves. But for something like this we have to pull together.' Miss Dorothy sighed. 'It's for the war, you know. The skies must be kept clear over the Channel, but it's been very difficult.'

Ellie felt even more confused than ever. 'What channel?'

'Oh, the English Channel, of course.'

Ellie looked away, it didn't make any sense.

The two walked on saying nothing much for a while. Ellie dragged her feet. Rain dribbled down the back of her neck and the wind picked up strength, the sound pelting on the leaves.

Wearily, they pushed their bikes around the last bend to the village. From out of the night, lights shimmered, like a mirage emerging out of the gloom. Ellie hadn't heard a thing, yet as the road straightened she saw the Burley village hall glowing in the darkness. Brightness spilled out from its windows and glinted over the rain-soaked ground. Figures moved, sheltering between rows of canvas covered trucks and jeeps, cigarettes burning like hot pinpricks in the night.

A trumpet wailed over a quick muffled rhythm. Inside the hall, pairs of men and women were dancing. Ellie quickly pushed the bike towards the dark side of the road, closer to the bushes. She didn't want to be seen; the pink dress she'd borrowed from Miss Dorothy's niece was drenched, it scratched her skin and her hair flapped wet and sopping down her back.

'Come on,' she whispered loudly.

But Miss Dorothy had stopped and was standing spot-lit in the rain, her red hood up, grey curls framing her face and droplets glistening in the wet. Starstruck, she looked like a little gnome bedazzled by the grandeur of fairyland.

Clapping her hands, Miss Dorothy hurried forward. A young man stood out from the others, about twenty years old, the buttons shining on his forest-green uniform. Following at a safe distance, Ellie noticed the word 'Canada' emblazoned on his shoulder.

'Are you coming in, Miss?' He tipped his maroon beret with a smile.

Miss Dorothy stepped forward, 'Why yes we are, we would love to.'

'Oh no,' gasped Ellie, horrified. 'I can't. Really, I don't dance –'

'It's Saturday night.' The young Canadian smiled and his eyes were a dark chocolate brown.

Ellie felt a small hard tug on her hand.

308

'There's a war on,' Miss Dorothy whispered. 'We all have to do our bit.'

Ellie woke in the pink room to a loud purr. Queenie lay across her legs, his heavy weight warm and comfortable. Outside, the sky remained overcast and through the partly open window she could see leaves trembling, spattered by a crisp, light rain. Ellie closed her eyes again, lulled by the rhythm of the gentle sound and the soft, sweet smell.

'Oh dear what dreadful weather,' Miss Dorothy bustled in carrying a tray. She set it down on the table.

'It's beautiful,' said Ellie sadly. 'At home it hasn't rained for so long, I've forgotten what it's like.'

'Well, you're welcome to it. What I would give for some lovely sunny days to dry my washing and keep Gladys happy.' The old lady sniffed.

'Well it's not fair!' Ellie hit the bed with her hand. 'Why can't we just swap?'

Unperturbed, Miss Dorothy handed Ellie a piece of buttered toast. 'No reason why we couldn't.'

Ellie stared at her.

'Now don't get excited it might not work.'

'What do you mean?'

Miss Dorothy busied herself with the teapot.

'What do you mean?' repeated Ellie, louder. She sat up. The old lady was up to something. Usually she would be talking a mile a minute by now, but Miss Dorothy was studiously avoiding Ellie's eye.

'You mustn't laugh.' She sat on the edge of the bed and handed Ellie a cup. 'But I was musing about it last night while dancing with that nice young man. He's here, in the UK, his family is back in Canada, but they still hear from him, every now and then, through letters and so on and I got to wondering - we could do that.' She looked up with a pleased grin.

'Right. Mail the rain.' Ellie took a bite of toast.

'No, not mail it exactly, my dear,' Miss Dorothy huffed. 'That would be silly. But…' She smiled slyly. 'When I was a girl, I was a clerk in the department store in Southampton. Wonderful it was. Great brass tubes ran across the ceilings, like tunnels, that connected us to the office. We would put the customer's money in and whoosh, it would disappear and thirty seconds later the change would come whooshing back. It was like magic, great fun. Though some of the sillier young men would put their arms down it, all the way to their armpits and they would get stuck. I remember one, I think his name was Harold, he –'

'Miss Dorothy!' cried Ellie exasperated, 'Please, it sounds all very interesting, but what are you going on about?'

The little old lady blinked. 'Oh, well, where was I?' she pursed her lips. 'Ah yes. That's right. I was thinking we could, of course, try to do it again now. Create some kind of tunnel but using *real* magic, you know, like a great, invisible brass tunnel.'

Miss Dorothy leaned forward. 'I have a feeling if we left one of my things in your time and one of your things here…' She stopped, frowning. 'But I'm not quite sure what we would need to leave? They'd need to be linked somehow…' Miss Dorothy stood up. 'If we could find a way, Ellie, I do believe it might just work.'

Starlings erupted from the hedgerow as a convoy of trucks rattled along the back lane. Twittering in outrage, the birds wheeled high above the garden, hundreds of them, blackening the sky.

Secluded in the bottom corner, Ellie sat beneath the branches of an ancient beech. Cool air filtered though its leaves. She breathed quietly, her hag stone clenched in her hand, and a spot of rain fell on her upturned face.

'Trees are such big beings, but people don't really pay them much attention,' remarked Miss Dorothy, looking up. 'If they were animals, we'd all be standing in awe, don't you think?'

Ellie didn't reply.

The damp ground beneath the rug was seeping into the woven fabric. The land felt different here, just as powerful, but not quite as ancient as home. It was like the song felt newer. Ellie shook her head. What was she going on about? Feeling self-conscious under Miss Dorothy's quizzical gaze, Ellie gripped the hag stone tighter and strove for a deeper, slower breath.

'Wait!' The little old lady jumped to her feet and dashed up the length of lawn into the house.

Ellie gave up and opened her eyes.

Beyond the garden, a picket fence opened onto a patch of meadow covered with blue, bell-like flowers. They swayed, bright against the rain soaked green. A few steps further on and the actual forest began for real. Ellie felt a shiver dance up her spine. The earth may not be as ancient as home, but the woods here were full of dark, spreading shapes, watchful, and alive.

Ellie shifted her attention. Faeries. She could sense them, huge and gnarled, standing half in and out of the trees. The air shimmered as though they were waiting for her call.

Feeling a little unnerved, she closed her eyes.

Breathe. Connect with the earth.

Ba Set felt close, very close...

'Here!' Wheezing for breath, Miss Dorothy returned brandishing a smooth, grey object. 'I've never used it,' she admitted, easing herself down on the ground. 'Oh that's hard, my poor old knees.' Smiling, she placed the second hag stone on the rug between them. 'It has just sat in that drawer for years. My father never used it either, but his mother, now she was very powerful. In the village she was known as the wise woman. They loved her but feared her, I -'

'Miss Dorothy! Please, you can tell me later…'

The grass felt soft, the air moist and rich. Ellie tentatively breathed a low deep tone, holding her own hag stone tight in her grasp. 'Breathe into the earth,' she instructed Miss Dorothy. 'Breathe and sing and follow me.'

The rain held off, and in the hedges the birds settled once more, their excitable twittering fading into the morning. The wind shifted, fresh and sweet, carrying the gentle scent of the English summer. Softly it brushed against Ellie's cheek and lifted the hair around her face, bringing before it a scent of something else. Something deeper, earthier, like freshly turned soil, damp bark, and the brown scent of mushrooms, all overlaid with the deeper scent of shadowed forest.

A scrape etched down along her spine and Ellie shivered. It wasn't sharp, it didn't hurt, but it felt defined, light, made with something hard and real.

Curious, Ellie opened her eyes.

The sky had vanished into darkness. It loomed overhead, created by a single, unimaginably huge being. Its face was a woody strip of trailing bark; its great limbs were gnarled and twisted. Very slowly, the enormous faery was inching itself out of the beech tree above them, its body crinkling. One of its fingers, stick thin - its joints elongated and rickety, jerked again along her back.

Ellie almost lost the song. Her heart thudded in shock, but still she sang out another wave of rising notes. A hard tremor hit her leg. Miss Dorothy had noticed the being, emerging joint by joint. The old lady shook, her chin quivered, and her blue eyes widened in astonishment, as the faery, slowly, and with much care, unfolded its strange, extended form from within the tree. At one point it leant forward as though resting, and without missing a note Miss Dorothy waved a delighted gesture of welcome.

All the while Ellie's hag stone pulsed, sending a single coil of brightness through the covered darkness.

This wasn't the only faery responding to the song.

Wisp-thin small ones edged forward from the grass. Others - blue with tetchy frowns etched across their tiny faces, crept in from the meadow. These ones stopped just inside the fence as though they couldn't bear to be away from their bluebell homes for long.

'Oh my...' Miss Dorothy fell silent as she gazed at the vision of creatures surging into her garden. They emerged from the trees, from the sky, and from the ground. Some were huge, some silent, some crooning softly, some not quite seen at all. Feeling more confident, Ellie gathered in her breath and streamed it out across the open ground like smoke. A call, sent out to the forest beyond.

The hag stone responded by flaring brighter.

Ellie closed her eyes as dozens of faeries gathered in around them both, and rain began drizzling from the sky.

Miss Dorothy quivered and trembled with excitement. She shifted her position and quietly sang a new low, experimental note. As it gained in volume, her voice rose up the scale, becoming more operatic and rich with emotion. The beings pressed closer, and the air around them began to trill and heat as Miss Dorothy's note rose higher and higher, becoming a single exhalation of sound soaring overhead. A crackle of sound, and the tone ended abruptly with a high, sharp shriek.

Shocked, Ellie opened her eyes, certain she would find Miss Dorothy crumpled to the ground beside her.

'Ellie dear, what's happening?'

Light was flaring up into the trees. The old lady didn't look afraid; her round-cheeked face was glowing - reds, blues, greens - reflecting the changing colours that were streaming out from the hag stone she held clutched between her hands.

'I don't know!' Ellie cried. Her own stone flared with heat and Ellie dropped it onto the rug, startled.

'Oh my,' murmured Miss Dorothy. Carefully, as though she was in no great hurry, she placed her stone down next to Ellie's.

The hag stones touched and immediately an incandescent flash arced into the cloud overhead. Thunder cracked, booming so loud it shook the ground like a cannon.

'Oh my,' repeated Miss Dorothy gazing upwards, the red hood of Ellie's raincoat bright against her face. 'Oh my, oh my, oh my...'

Around them, more faeries surged closer, pressing down, leaning on them both, drawn by the brightness coiling from the centre of the stones.

'Oh my –' whispered Miss Dorothy, smiling up at Ellie. 'Oh my, oh my... this is wonderful.'

Lightning sizzled and, as Miss Dorothy and Ellie looked upwards, the heavens opened and a deluge of water fell from the sky. It drenched their upturned faces, saturating the tree and all the beings crowded around them in the garden. Miss Dorothy giggled and tipped back her hood. In a second, her tight grey curls were plastered against her skin. Ellie grinned and together they began to laugh and laugh, the delighted sound lost in the noise of the pouring rain.

THIRTY

Blue Mountains, Australia, present day

The black stone, hanging from a long, silver chain, thudded against her skin with every downward step.

A bellow echoed up from the trees below, and Rose slowed. She contemplated stopping altogether, but Ben was behind her and she could hear the pace of his breath and the laboured groan as he wrestled with the weight of the jerry can.

'Hey.' Rose turned. 'We could rest for a bit.' Just ahead, an outcrop of rock jutted out at an angle above the stairs, sending a pool of shadow over a single seat carved into the cliff face.

Brushing her hair up off her neck, Rose stopped. Moisture beaded, sliding between her breasts, causing the light fabric of her dress to stick to her skin. Rose sighed. Overhead the sun glared in the white-hot sky.

'Rosalind!' Her father's voice snapped with impatience. It sounded further away.

'We'd better get going.' Ben urged, hefting the jerry can to his other hand.

Smiling, Rose traced her finger along his arm as he adjusted the load. 'We don't really have too...'

'Rosalind, Ben!' Her father's voice shot up like a command.

With a careless shrug, she tilted her head back for a prolonged kiss before sauntering down the stairs again, her hips swaying with every movement.

At the bottom, her father was pacing along the path, clad in a simple white shirt and black trousers, thudding one hand hard into the other. A tree fern trembled with each footfall, its fronds gone and its trunk blackened and crumbling. At its base were the charred remains of a torch.

'How did this happen?' Matthew roared. He looked wild, his eyes drawn as though he had spent too many nights awake. 'Look!' He struck the torch forcibly with his foot and it crumbled to ash.

Rose glanced away, having reached the lower steps. She stood gripping the handrail, while Ben squeezed past and dropped the jerry can to the ground. She closed her eyes. At least here at the base of the cliff the temperature was cooler, out of the sun and shadowed from the worst of the freakish heat.

But they weren't here for a day trip into the forest. Scattered between the shaded rocks, and hanging precariously overhead where they'd landed, were the ruins of their once blazing torches.

Rose didn't want to look, but still, she couldn't help seeing the wide circle of blackness fanning out from the cliff base and into the forest itself.

That was all.

The fires hadn't sustained.

'She did this. Everywhere, it's the same, all our work for naught.' Matthew trembled with fury. 'She, and your faithless little friend Ellie, we have to find them. We have to stop them, or we'll never be free.'

'But Dad,' Rose swallowed and set her mouth into her most encouraging smile, 'it's working, look around you at the trees, everything is about to keel over anyway.'

'No,' Matthew snapped. 'It's not fast enough. We cannot stumble at the first hurdle. To be faithful, we must be true in life, and in action.'

'But Dad -' Exasperated, Rose jumped off the step towards him and landed in a pile of blackened fronds. They disintegrated into a cloud of soot. 'We don't need to-'

But Matthew wasn't listening. Gathering his robes, he strode down the narrow path and into the silence of the forest.

Ben held out his hand. 'Come on. He's right. We've got to finish it.'

Rose shook her head. She considered tracing her hand across Ben's face, or pressing the warmth of her body into his. Smiling, she peeked up at him through her lashes, but Ben had lifted the can of fuel. Rose hesitated; his eyes mirrored the same flare of conviction as her father's.

'I am not going back in there!' Rose cried and turning, she ran away up the first flight of stairs, dramatically stopping only when the steps were high enough to hide her from view.

'Ben,' she called softly.

She paused, a leaf dropped from overhead, its brittle form turning slowly in the stillness. 'We can wait for Dad here, just the two of us...'

Silence.

Frowning, Rose crept back down the stairs, peeking over the edge into the forest below.

'Ben?'

A footfall cracked.

Tossing back her hair, Rose quickened her pace. Her thoughts fixed on an appropriate punishment for her lover. Haughty silence. Or maybe she would just sidle up to him and kiss him – but, only if he was truly contrite.

Clasping the handrail, Rose reached the bottom of the steps and jumped to the ground.

Ash swirled, with flakes as soft as snow falling in the stillness of the blackened trees.

Like a crowd of haggard men, weighed down by their scorched brokenness, the dead and dying tree ferns stood in hunched and skeletal poses. They seemed to press in closer, waiting. Waiting for her to move, to react.

A shadow trembled and Rose whirled around, her heart thudding in fright.

The ferns shrank back, exposing the narrow forest path that twisted its way further into the trees.

Ducking her head low, Rose ran. Twigs slashed against her skin. The path looped around gigantic boulders and fallen shattered giants. Furious, Rose smacked at a branch in her way.

The path widened into the picnic area and ahead Rose could see the two of them, her father and Ben, their heads together, talking by one of the low, broken down tables. Her father didn't even look up as she walked towards them.

'Is this where you first saw her?'

'What?' Rose glared at him.

'You heard me, Rosalind, we need to know.'

Rose stopped, her father's face was paler than usual, and his hands shook as he studied the tracks branching away from them through the trees.

'Why didn't you wait?' She placed her hands on her hips, glaring at Ben, and sank angrily onto the bench. 'I hate it here.' She muttered.

'Rosalind,' Matthew's voice was brittle with impatience. 'Calm yourself. You were here. Is this where you and Ellie first saw -'

Rose cut him off with a sharp slap on the wood. She dropped her head onto the table and lay with her eyes half closed, as all around sharp bands of sunlight slashed across the forest floor. Moisture had fled, and any hint of dappled softness had vanished.

'Rose?'

Memory flared. A tone, a shape... Ellie spinning, round and round like an idiot.

Rose shuddered.

'Tell us.' Ben's hand felt hot on her skin. 'We need to find her. We need to find Ellie. We know the witch has trapped her. Tell us, is this the place?'

A dappled wood, a tree, and a shadow turning its face to hers...

Fear thudded through her chest and Rose slapped it back, hard. No, she did not want to remember.

She jumped to her feet. 'I'm going home.'

'Rosalind,' her father snapped. 'Do not be such a fool. You are not a child. You know what we search for, and why.' His blue eyes were piercing.

A fool...? Abruptly Rose laughed out loud, the sudden sound piercing the stillness of the forest. She lifted her arms, stretching her muscles out, and raised them, once, twice into the air.

'I'm not a fool ... *Father.*' She hissed, dragging the word out. 'Of course I know why we are here. And what we have to do. But it doesn't mean I want to be here, or want to remember.' Rose shook herself, her eyes gleaming gold in the harsh light of the day. 'I never had a choice!'

She didn't wait for them. Turning on her heel, Rose marched out of the gully with her head up, leaving her father and her lover to scurry behind. She didn't need to think, she didn't need to remember. With her perfect sense of direction, she could see the land stretched out before her like a map - every turn, every fold of the land clear, and marked, like she was flying high above with a perfect, bird's-eye view.

The cliffs jutted stark against the sky, rich red against blazing blue. Sunlight scorched the clearing.

Rose leaned against the nearest rock, the rough surface scratching against her leg. She ignored it; she held her gaze trained straight ahead onto Ben, only Ben, and nothing else. Her skin prickled, but she was ignoring that too, prickling as though a thousand, tiny eyes were tracking her every move.

'My God.' Ben held up a lumpy bunch of twigs. 'This is where she got it from. I had no idea she was in so deep, all this time...' His eyes narrowed and, aiming with his foot, he kicked the woven nest out over the wall of boulders.

Come on. Rose gestured impatiently to the jerry can. Behind him, her father was in the centre, standing with his eyes closed and his arms wrapped tightly around his middle.

It was revolting, she shuddered; it felt like ants crawling up her back, focused on her, watching her.

'Ben,' she hissed in a loud whisper. 'Ben! Just get on with it. And then we can go.'

He shook his head.

Raising his hands, her father lifted his eyes straight to the heavens. 'Hear me,' he shouted, his voice echoed through the clearing. 'Hear me. You know I am here.'

Rose felt a sharp contraction of terror. It was like it was a physical thing, falling straight out of the sky, settling over her heart, squeezing her guts. She could barely breathe.

'Hear me!'

Rose tried to push it away. 'Who's he talking to?' she managed to croak out the words. 'He's not praying, is he? Who is it!'

Ben shrugged and picked up the can of kerosene.

Matthew stared upwards. Ba Set had been here. He could feel remnants of her presence - her evil, lacing the very air. It raced along his nerves like fire.

The abbot, God rest his soul, had forewarned him. He had counselled him about this unnatural linkage, this blood bond between his witch mother and himself, and had gifted him the holy stone as protection. But without it he knew he was naked, visible, his pure shining spirit laid bare to this being of corruption.

A howl of fury rose in his chest.

'Mother!' He shouted. 'Damn you! Where are you hiding?'

Stillness and silence answered. Heat shimmered over the trees. No reply. Yet. He could feel *them*.

There was a sliver of movement and Matthew beheld a clutch of small faces up high, peering down at him through the leaves.

There.

'Be gone!' He roared. At once they vanished, leaving only a weak quivering in the air. 'Yes,' he laughed. 'You demons can't help but obey *me*.'

'Daddy, what are you doing?' His daughter's voice cried out; she sounded small, and very young. 'Let's go, Ben's ready.'

Matthew stared up into the high branches.

Quickly, he tore off his shoes and socks and tossed them aside. That was better, Matthew nodded; he needed to connect, and he needed to know. He breathed quickly, the warmth of the ground soaking into the soles of his feet even as his toes spread, gripping the earth.

Behind him, Matthew could feel Rosalind and Ben watching him. Their eyes hot on his back. They were confused, he knew, but if he succeeded, his daughter would never know the loneliness of her lover growing older, withering, while she barely changed.

Abomination.

Where was the witch?

The trees towered tall, straight, and white, with great strips of bark hanging free, exposing the flesh beneath.

Matthew placed his hand on a trunk and closed his eyes. He didn't have to search, he didn't have to particularly change his breathing, he just let his senses roam, feeling for the life force. Unmistakable, it was there. He could hear the sap creep, oozing through the veins carrying nutrients. He could feel the quiver of the leaves as they absorbed the energy of the sun. But it was faint, the life force was faint. This tree, as all the others in this forest, stood weak and soon it would die. Matthew smiled. Toppling, it would take a clutch more with it as it fell.

First the forests, then the seas, and then the earth will be scorched.

'And then', he whispered, 'then we will be taken up into heaven, whole and pure in the fullness of our flesh.' Longing coursed through Matthew's being, so strong it caused him to almost stumble.

Movement whipped through the clearing, silent, and barely perceptible. The air quivered. The tree seemed to absorb it, innocent, standing tall and still overhead. Matthew tensed and then abruptly whirled around.

'Come to me!' he raged. The clearing dulled to an unnatural stillness, but a leaf, falling to the earth, betrayed their presence. 'Come to me!'

Five beings materialised. Thin strips of bark fell from the crowns of their heads and their skin was pale and flecked. They stood tall, their narrow heads at an angle, their bodies arched away as though each one longed to flee.

'Where is she?' he demanded.

Twitching and trembling, the faeries fought to resist his command. One clamped its jaws shut; one collapsed its elongated body to ground. Another strove to merge itself back to safety within branch, leaf, wood…

'Enough!' Matthew roared, tightening his will around them like a rope. He lashed them tight. *You cannot escape.*

Rose ran up beside him.

'Hey, Dad? Is everything okay?' Her smile was tight, though she held out her hand as if unconcerned. 'I've got a thermos of iced tea,' she was speaking quickly, the words tumbling in a rush. 'Ben's been carrying it, I know how much you like it, and it's so hot here, and we have to go-'

'Quiet.' Matthew grabbed her hand tightly. 'We don't have time for this. But,' Matthew's heart thudded, 'look, Rosalind, look at them. You can see, I know you can.'

Rising to their true height, the faeries turned towards his daughter, their dark eyes glowing as they studied her.

Matthew waited, hoping that after all these years his talent, his gift, might be shared.

Rose dropped her hand with the thermos and turned her gaze pointedly upwards, her eyes wide. She didn't move. Matthew could see she was breathing rapidly. The beings leaned closer. Abruptly Rose laughed. 'Nope,' she shook her head. 'Nothing.'

Matthew turned away. Enough. Let his daughter close her mind if that was what she chose. There were more important matters to hand.

'Ben,' he signalled, and turned his attention back to the five faery beings.

'Where is Ba Set?' he demanded.

At once, with tight, awkward movements, each of the tree creatures gathered themselves and, in unison, turned and began to walk towards the entrance.

In the centre, Ben emptied the can first over the clumps of twigs and grasses at the foot of the trees. Working quickly, he circled the clearing, dousing the entire area in kerosene. The sharp stench of fuel cut the air. Ben stopped where he had started. Above him, a dozen nests spiralled down from the branches.

'In the name of the Lord!' cried Matthew.

325

Bowing his head, Ben struck a match to the woven mass of grasses, in an instant each one burst alight. Heat whipped up the slender trunk, so loud and scorching, it sounded as though the tree itself was roaring in pain.

Rose shrieked, whether in joy or terror, Matthew didn't know. He grabbed her hand and ran. Ben followed close on their heels. Squeezing his shoulder through the gap in the rock wall, Matthew caught a glimpse of the ash-grey face of a faery as it disappeared with its fellows into the trees. Behind in the clearing, a shriek erupted as a bolt of super heated air shot out of a giant, its crown ablaze, embers shooting metres in all directions.

The heat was already intense. Gripping his daughter's hand tighter, he pulled her faster through the tightly spaced grove, and together they burst out into the open forest.

'Wait!' Matthew bellowed. At once, the faeries bound to his will froze.

He looked up. Through breaks in the canopy, he could see the sky above the clearing remained a perfect, cloudless blue. Matthew allowed himself a smile of satisfaction. 'Praise God,' he whispered. Bone dry, there was no hint of moisture left in the trees to give them away, no telltale signs of smoke.

The witch will never know.

In an instant, the air churned and a torrent of flame engulfed the clearing.

THIRTY-ONE

New Forest, England, 1944

Miss Dorothy's nose was pressed close to the glass. 'It's hard to believe France is just over there, isn't it? And that beastly man is so close. Well, not literally, but you know what I mean.'

The sea raged, driven by the onslaught of a howling wind, its dark green crests slashed with foam. The panes of the window rattled, and above the noise, bells were tolling, calling worshippers for the evening service. Ellie watched as a group hurried along the footpath, clutching their hats, their shoulders hunched, their umbrellas braced against the downpour.

'And no matter what the weather, the churches are full,' continued Miss Dorothy. 'Everybody is doing their bit for England. And the vicar is a lovely man, though a bit stuffy for my personal liking.'

'You go to church?' Ellie was surprised.

'Of course I do, and why wouldn't I?' answered Miss Dorothy huffily.

Ellie turned from the window. At the other end of the room, Miss Gladys sat on a spindly, high back chair. She was leaning forward, deep in consultation with the tall, black-faced mirror. In the reflection, Ellie could see her face was ashen, her thin lips pressed and her face was drawn with tension.

'We're all the same,' Miss Dorothy was saying airily, 'and the Vicar knows it, we're all on the side of good. It's the ones who don't believe anything at all, I'd be suspicious of, especially nowadays. But then if you have a good heart who am I to doubt. You can't judge a book from the outside –'

With an impatient frown, Ellie hushed the old lady quiet. Miss Gladys smoothed down her grey woollen skirt and straightened her grey blouse. Gravely, she turned her attention back to the room.

'The mirror does not reject the idea,' she rose slowly, giving Ellie a sharp look. 'It must work. If it doesn't the success of the entire war could be at stake.' She shook her head. 'But I do not like it.'

'But Gladys, we no longer have any choice.' Miss Dorothy took the other woman by the hand and led her towards the sofa. 'The weather is not clearing, and the moon is nearing full. It's in Scorpio tonight, so you know there will be a treacherous flick in its tail.'

Gladys grimaced, and laid her face in her hands. 'Dorothy we cannot fail, if we do, the mirror shows the people of England will suffer endless hardship under the yoke of that man. And so will we. We will suffer, those like us and everyone else who runs foul of them.'

Dorothy patted her shoulder. 'My dear,' she murmured gently, 'that all may be so. However, you and I both know what we are doing is no longer strong enough.'

Miss Gladys looked back toward the mirror, then her pale grey eyes swept around the room before finally settling on Ellie. 'It's you,' she said bitterly, giving her a long hard stare. 'Before you came to us, the circle was working. Under my direction, we each did what we knew to do and the spirits obeyed us. But now it is all for nothing,' she said bleakly. The windows shook. 'The sky is not clear. The storms have come. We have failed, we are lost.'

'No, we are not.' Miss Dorothy reached into the pocket of her dress and took out her dark, smooth hag stone. She laid it on the sofa in front of her friend. 'This will help us.'

'That?' Miss Gladys sniffed derisively. 'We all have them in our families. The power left them when the Empire exceeded the covenant John Dee made with the sea god Mannanon. You know that.'

Ellie didn't know what the woman was talking about, but she too took her hag stone out of her pocket and laid it on the sofa in front of Miss Gladys. 'Yes,' the older woman almost sneered, 'am I to be impressed because you have one too?'

Dorothy sighed. 'Gladys, stop it. Stop being such a woolly headed, obstinate Scotch woman. The mirror has not rejected young Ellie here; in fact it welcomed her. We both saw it. That we are in grave danger, we both know. You're not the only one who can feel it, we all can. Please, it's imperative.'

Miss Gladys said nothing. She closed her eyes and Ellie could feel a tremendous fight going on within the older woman, though she sat still, scarcely breathing. 'Dorothy Clutterbuck,' she murmured at last. 'If you are wrong, I will hound you and your descendants for a hundred lifetimes.'

'Oh, that's all right,' Miss Dorothy sniffed. 'You'd never be able to catch us.'

'Hmmm, so you fervently hope,' said Miss Gladys, arching an eyebrow. 'What do we do?' She turned crisply and faced Ellie with a pursed, expectant expression.

Gripping her own hag stone in her hand, Ellie gazed up at the two witches. 'W-w-well...' she began. Searching for the right words.

'We need a different kind of magic,' interrupted Miss Dorothy.

Ellie blinked in surprise, but the old lady ignored her.

'It is quite simple, but very effective.' Closing her eyes, Dorothy sang out a wavering, mid tone hum. It wobbled in the air. 'Like that, my dear,' she explained in a businesslike manner. 'Form an intention of what you want, imagine it in your mind, and make a sound. It's all in the connection.'

With a determined set to her shoulders, Miss Gladys opened her mouth, her brow furrowed with concentration.

They complemented each other, Ellie realised, watching them. The small, round, red-cheeked figure of Miss Dorothy and the taller, thinner Gladys trying as hard as she could. In only a few moments, their voices harmonised, forging a strong apex of power above their heads.

Quickly, Ellie placed her hag stone on the rug, and sent a note of her own towards the floor. At once, like flicking a light switch, the air crackled, and a pulse of light flared from its centre.

Miss Gladys didn't miss a beat; she stared at it, her eyes bulging in surprise.

Ellie reached for Miss Dorothy's stone and glanced up, waiting for a nod of permission or something from the old lady, but Dorothy's eyes were closed, her head was lowered.

Concentrating, Ellie held the old lady's stone. It felt different - darker, smaller, and yet denser. It quivered almost like Miss Dorothy herself, the magic leaping bright and eager as though it held an impatient, quicksilver soul. Gripping it tightly, Ellie sang out a stream of sound. Her hand warmed and Miss Dorothy's hag stone began to shine with a bright, intense heat.

It wasn't uncomfortable and it didn't burn - it was more like the idea of heat, or the hot passion of excitement. Ellie held onto it firmly, testing its strength, feeling how ready it was to be gone. Then, spinning the time ring into the palm of her hand, Ellie closed her eyes.

THIRTY-TWO

Blue Mountains, Australia, present day

She woke up with a jerk, hot and hungry in Ba Set's cottage. Ellie jumped up from the sofa, her hair crackling wildly around her face as though surging with static electricity.

'Ba Set,' she cried, her teeth were almost chattering, 'I need to leave this here.' Holding Miss Dorothy's stone, Ellie felt huge, towering over the tiny, oldest woman in the world. Ba Set didn't respond. She remained still, sitting, with her eyes closed, at the end of the sofa.

Come on, Ellie pleaded silently. The muscles in her legs felt jumpy, as though she needed to run and not stop. She wrung her hands, desperate to get out, desperate to go.

Through the window, the setting sun was radiating long, golden slices of light that burned across the tips of the trees like fire. Ellie danced impatiently on her toes. Should she shake Ba Set awake, or something? Would that be too rude? Stifling an impatient sigh, Ellie dropped Miss Dorothy's hag stone onto the sofa.

Colours flared, radiating vividly from the centre - reds, blues, greens.

'I need to leave this here,' Ellie spoke loudly, as the stone burst a beam of brightness up into the room. It hit the ceiling and flashed out through the window outside. Ellie stared at it in shock. Miss Dorothy's hag stone behaved differently than her own, and suddenly, her impatient, eagerness to be gone contracted into a spasm of fright.

What if I can't get back? All at once, her courage shrank and Ellie felt very small, and very young. She groaned. *Oh my God, what am I doing?*

Ba Set stirred, and in a small, neat action, rubbed her hands down her neck, flexing her narrow shoulders as she did so. She shook them to the floor. 'Do not waste your time with fear, Soul Flyer,' she said. 'The time for that has past. Fear is an indulgence, use your skills, do what you must.' She opened her eyes and looked directly at Ellie. 'We both need to eat, one never thinks clearly when one is depleted.'

Ba Set stood, her hands trembling a little as she steadied herself. Ellie could see the burn on the side of her face still looked angry and sore.

'Are you all right?' Ellie felt a jolt of fear. What if something happened to Ba Set? 'Is there anything I can do?'

'Thank you for your concern.' The old woman waved her away. 'But it is not necessary. Decide what is important, and then act. But food first, Soul Flyer.'

'I can't, I don't know how long I have.' Ellie jumped to her feet. 'The moon will be full in a day or so, and Miss Dorothy said that will be the most powerful time. I need to be there.' Quickly, she grasped for her teacher's hand. 'Ba Set please listen, if you are okay, take this hag stone, it's Miss Dorothy's. It's been in her family for generations, it's powerful, it has got something to do with some Manannan guy –' Ellie shook her head;

why was she rabbiting on like Miss Dorothy? 'We hope this will form a gateway that is linked to mine … please, it has to be kept safe.'

Nodding, Ba Set took the stone and held it, breathing, balancing its weight in her hand.

'We need to make a huge circle.' Ellie continued, excitement rising in her voice, 'Ba Set, the rain is coming. I think it's going to work.'

'I will call the others. But first, child,' Ba Set was implacable, 'you must sustain your body, or there will be no vessel for your soul to return to.'

Ba Set handed back the stone and left for the kitchen.

A few moments later, Ellie gobbled a couple of sandwiches as fast as she could and, she had to admit, after taking a swig of water, she felt better, calmer and the edge of desperation had eased.

Ellie hugged Ba Set and lay back down on the sofa. 'I hope this works,' she said. 'I really hope it does.' Taking a deep breath, Ellie twisted the ring, and then all was black.

Wrapping her cloak closer around her shoulders, Ba Set gazed down at the young body lying empty on the sofa. With her hair spread out around her, Ellie looked so vulnerable, so trusting, so like a child, and yet so much rested on her young shoulders.

Reverently, and taking care not to brush her hand against Ellie's form, Ba Set placed the hag stone on the table beside the Soul Flyer's head. She gestured to the black faeries. They stepped closer, the powerful beings flanking the young woman as she lay deeply entranced.

Stretching her arms out straight, Ba Set shook them, flexing the muscles in her hands and up into her forearms. She stepped outside. With her arms still extended, Ba Set rolled back her shoulders and, with her senses opening, she turned her gaze back to the cottage. She listened.

Silence.

The Soul Flyer lay safe, protected from prying eyes, and protected by the Watchers from even the most innocent of disturbances. Still Ba Set hesitated; no one - no human, no spirit, no creature must touch the Soul Flyer as she lay - for to do so could send vast ripples through the magic. And there was more. Ba Set remembered an ancient warning, scrawled on a tablet left deep within the desert. While the Soul Flyer lay empty, she must not be touched - for whosoever was unfortunate or foolish enough to lay a hand on an entranced Soul Flyer, their souls would be also wrenched free.

Ba Set shook her head. That would not happen. She was being fanciful to even consider it a possibility. *Fear is an indulgence.* Turning back she sent a piercing whistle out over the stricken forest and, crying a single, powerful word, the shapeshifter leapt into the air.

Far below, the fire was burning out of control.

Hurrying over ground dotted with chips of stone and torn, broken sticks, Matthew's bare feet were bleeding from a multitude of cuts. He didn't stop, the pain only spurred him on. The end was close, his mother was near; he could feel her presence like a taut trill of energy.

'Dad, my God, can you wait?' Rosalind's voice sounded fainter, and further away than he had hoped.

'Hurry,' he shouted, 'we have to hurry.'

Soon the fire would consume all the fuel in the clearing, and be reaching out, ravenous for more. He could feel it in the panic trembling through the trees and in the fevered heat in the air.

'Faster!'

And the faery beings ran on.

The sun dropped and the great eagle banked high, catching the tide of slightly cooler air sweeping over the canopy. Her eyes flickered, focusing on the streaks of brightness soaring below, a multitude of incandescent faeries rising to meet her.

Ba Set dropped, her wingspan barely moving as she joined the mass of multifaceted beings. The air was convulsing, riven with heat, as another blaze of orange burst up out of the shadowed trees.

Her pinion feathers dipped, and she shrieked out a cry of anguish.

Matthew froze, his eyes locked on the winged darkness rushing towards the setting sun. The call sounded again, a wretched, piercing note that faded away to silence. His heart constricted. That hateful sound; how it filled him with loathing.

Matthew checked back through the trees. Rosalind and Ben were a short distance behind. He could see them resting with their arms around the other, drinking in turns from the thermos of tea. Rosalind's eyes were closed and she was leaning into her lover's shoulder.

Before him, towered a cliff wall, an immense shadow, huge against the dusk streaked sky. Roots fringed its face, trailing from trees clinging foolishly to life.

Matthew bowed his head once more, praying for guidance. He looked up.

'Onwards,' he ordered.

His destination was near, and he could no longer wait.

The bound faeries recoiled, their eyes rolling in anguish, straining on the invisible leash to get away.

'No.' Matthew snapped it tight. 'Go on, take me to her.'

Placing his foot on the first stone, Matthew began his ascent. The faeries climbed swiftly, not heeding the fallen branches or stones that lay scattered like marbles across their way. The steps themselves were carved directly out of the rock face. Each one was covered by a treacherous matting of lichen, and so roughly made the forces of nature could have sculpted them.

'Climb slower,' he spat the words at his unwilling guides. 'Do not deviate, do not harm me, take me directly to *her*.'

The path ascended, criss-crossing up the steepest gradients, until Matthew was reduced to crouching on all fours like a beast.

It took an age, but just as a doubt began to bite into his heart, and the first stars brightened, Matthew saw, built high above the shadowed outline of the cliff, a small structure, leaning precariously out over the edge.

He allowed himself a small, satisfied smile.

At last.

Never again would he be that boy in the woods, lost and abandoned by a heartless mother.

The moon shone through the window. Night had descended and Ba Set knelt to the floor. Gently, she hovered her hand over Ellie's brow. The girl felt damp and hot. She lay on the sofa deeply entranced, her limbs still and breathing so slowly it seemed as though she was barely breathing at all.

Ba Set reached for an electric fan from one of the lower shelves and turned it on. Keeping the Soul Flyer cool and safe, that was her most important task. No matter what or *who* was approaching

Settling back on her heels, she wrapped her cloak around her shoulders and closed her eyes. Ba Set, the ancient shapeshifter, waited with Dorothy Clutterbuck's hag stone quivering in her hand. Bands of colour splashed against the shadowed ceiling. Energy was shifting. With a breath, Ba Set connected to the earth below.

The gateway was opening.

And the Watchers were outside, waiting.

Matthew studied the cottage squatting in the gloom. Its weathered walls were partly obscured by a tangle of decrepit vines and a brace of ghost-grey trees. Branches hung low, scraping the ground and the faeries yearned towards them. Their elongated bodies arched, as though with a single reflexive movement they could spring clear of their captor.

'No!' Matthew roared. He slung them onwards with a curt snap. Take me to her.

A shadow lunged at him. A dog howled, its voice pitched high in terror. Before him, Matthew could see wide loops of energy, sharp, like blue-white smoke, circling the cottage. Matthew laughed. *How pitiful.* 'Your puny attempts at distraction, Mother, are powerless against me!'

Stones dropped against wood as he stormed the stairs. On the landing, a web of hanging objects whistled and leapt for his eyes. He tore them aside without a thought. At the door stood the two Watchers, coal black, their great eyes gleaming red like embers, their bodies twisting into two tortuous shapes. They barred the entrance.

Matthew hesitated as light spilled through a crack beneath. The air sizzled with power. He shivered; he could feel it like a thousand pinpricks darting over his skin.

She was here.

With a roar, Matthew confronted the faeries. 'Incorporeal beings, as black as the pit from whence you came,' he cried. 'You will serve me, and mine!'

They struggled - their sinuous bodies curling in on themselves, as a force like icy-white smoke settled over their charcoal forms, drawing them tight. Desperately they battled, their long hands contorting as they fought to escape from the intensity of Matthew's will. But it was hopeless. The noose closed, and with a final defiant cry, the faeries vitality dimmed and shadow claimed them. They vanished.

Matthew kicked open the door.

In the centre of the room, a figure knelt, cloaked in darkness. Long, greying hair hung loose down her back.

Matthew couldn't move, his senses assaulted, overwhelmed by a powerful, familiar scent spiralling from a burning brazier. He stared, transfixed by the bitter memory of his mother pounding spices in the morning air. But, Matthew shook himself, no, the scent was not the same, and it wasn't strong enough to mask the fetid reek of decay. The room stank from every surface littered with rubbish, hoarded from the forest.

'Tey!'

The cry hit him like a slap, and Matthew flinched. An ancient woman reached for him. Her face, still burnished bronzed, was parched, wrinkled, her arms were skeletally thin, and her hands shook in the shadowed light.

No...

'Tey.' she struggled to her feet.

Matthew couldn't turn away. She was old ... *old*.

Dear Lord, he prayed silently. *What is Your will?*

As if in answer, the old woman's eyes flared bright and golden, and as piercingly intense as he remembered. *Harpy*.

Matthew clenched his fist.

His mother may appear frail and harmless, and as weak as a sparrow. She may emulate the cries of heartbreak. But no matter what decay befell her cursed form, he wasn't fooled. This witch sucked on the teat of Satan and she had survived for thousands of years - she remained strong, and as wedded to the dark as always.

Matthew snapped a command.

The forest faeries writhed in agony, their hands flailing towards her, their dark eyes desperate, begging to be set free.

'What are you doing?' Ba Set rose to her feet. 'They love you, Tey, why do you command them in such hatred?'

'Do not call me that!' Advancing towards her, he thrust the faeries out in front like a shield. 'I am Matthew,' he cried, 'the faithful servant of the one true God. I am not your son!'

With a shocked murmur, Ba Set reached out for the tree spirits. Matthew could feel her concern. It sang to the air, filling his being, flooding his heart with fury.

'Leave my mind, witch!' He raised his fist. 'Or I will kill you, and you will burn in hell and damnation for all eternity.'

'Foolish boy.' Ba Set shook her head. 'Our kind does not perish so easily.'

'I have found a way to kill *our kind*, Mother.' Matthew laughed bitterly. 'We burn, witches like us burn. That is how we die. How do you think I spent my many years away from you? You were wrong. I too live a long, cursed life! And I have found the way, if we wish to end the blight of our existence, we must burn in pain and horror.'

'Tey, you are talking madness.'

'Oh no, *Mother*,' he spat the word out. 'I am talking truth. When witches burn, the flames burn bright and hot, and the fat of our skin sizzles, just like the others. That has been my calling these past hundreds of years. Seek out the witches, like you, and destroy them. I am the Witchfinder!'

Ba Set turned from him in horror. Roughly, Matthew grabbed her arm, and as he did so a wind whipped in through the cracks in the door, hot and stinking of fire.

Ba Set gasped. 'Tey, you must go.'

He ignored her. Through the picture window, Matthew saw a wave of flame cutting through the night. Orange and red, it convulsed with heat. In darker areas of the forest, away from the firefront itself, brightness erupted as single trees burst into flame. Matthew froze, as a low, urgent moan shook the cottage and a hail of burning debris scattered against the glass.

Rosalind ... his sweet Rosalind was out, in that...

Twisting, Ba Set fought to free herself. 'You must go, it's not safe - ' She cried again.

But as she struggled, Matthew beheld a figure lying prone on the sofa beside her. Its face was young and pale, and surrounded by a mass of red-gold hair.

Ellie. Here.

Abruptly all thoughts of the fire vanished.

He stopped as a fresh wave of loathing rose, like bile in his throat. 'You treacherous, manipulative liar. You are using one of my flock to destroy me!'

'No, you don't understand,' Ba Set shook her head. 'You must go!'

'*Mother,*' he bit out the word and stood over Ellie, his form huge in the tiny room. The candle flared, throwing his shadow streaming against the wall. 'I understand well enough. I am no longer a frightened, ignorant child. In your desperation, in your aloneness, you are training her in the evil arts, because she is *a girl, a young woman?*' His eyes flashed with hatred. 'You sicken me. You are revealing the ancient ways. Something you never did for me.'

He stepped towards her, pain and fury twisting his face. 'You never came for me! I was a crying child, and I waited for you for years.'

'Please Tey forgive me.' Ba Set reached for him. 'I was out of my mind with grief. By the time I came to my senses, I returned and tracked the abbot's progress through the forest and every day, every night I stood outside the dead walls of that dead building, and called for you, over and over.' She closed her eyes, 'but I was too late.'

'Liar,' he hissed. 'You left me. You flew in your monstrous form and left me to rot! Heartless, unnatural devil, the abbot was right. But, that is not all. You were right in one thing. I did not inherit your gift of flight. I do not fly. But yet I carry the blood-curse - the abomination of the ancients flow in my veins.

'You did not prepare me for this horror. You did not share any of your precious secrets with me. I am as long-lived as the rest of our kind, *Mother*. And for eight hundred years, I have watched as all those I loved have died.' Matthew's heart ached so painfully, it felt his chest would surely burst.

'You abandoned me to this wretched life!'

He shoved Ba Set to the wall. She hit it hard and as she did so, a stone dropped from the sofa, landing with a sharp crack onto the floor.

Moaning, Ba Set twisted, reaching for it, but Matthew kicked her away.

Colours flashed from its centre, searing across his vision.

What devilment was this? Matthew grabbed the stone, and at once, a stabbing heat seared into his hand. Yet he didn't let it go, this thing was strangely alluring. A low sound jolted up from its centre, like a rasp of song, it lifted, hovering, and stopped at Matthew's eye height.

His grip trembled. The colours were flaring hotter now, brighter, dazzling his eyes. But still he held it and the sound became louder, increasing in intensity as a bolt of light shot towards the heavens.

The tree spirits crooned in response; they lifted from the floor, and streamed high over the stone, whirling, their forms splitting into multifaceted beings.

Matthew fought for control. The stone was writhing, increasing with power as the sound burst through the room. Desperate now, he fought to release his hand from the thing's grip; his body shook, burning with heat, his blood felt on fire.

Ba Set's face wavered beneath him, her eyes wide, piercing gold. She was mouthing something, but Matthew couldn't hear. A rising wave of power and song was coursing up through his being, inhabiting him, possessing him. Trembling, he clamped his jaws shut, but the song rose higher into his throat, building in strength, intent on forcing them apart.

Not this! Panicked he searched for the door. He was suffocating. Through the candlelight Ba Set reached for him, her shadow immense.

'No!' Matthew found his voice at last and, raising his fist, he smashed her away and reached for Ellie.

At that moment, the door burst open and heated air roiled into the room, carrying the stink of the forest and a rain of blazing embers.

'Dad!' cried Rose.

She was too late, as Matthew's hand connected with Ellie, the hag stone rippled, pulsed, and exploded with an incandescent burst of light.

THIRTY-THREE

New Forest, England, 1944

Matthew woke to silence. A vast dark silence. Darkness saturated his senses. He closed his eyes, but that didn't help. Darkness remained.

 Had he died? In a burst of terror, Matthew lashed out with his arms and feet, but hit nothing. Matthew shook his body hard, like a dog, shaking from his crown right down to his toes. But nothing. He was suspended in a void of darkness.

Later, he didn't know how long, he became aware of an eerie, rhythmic sound that had begun softly and was now, gradually, increasing in volume.

A line of light was traversing the night in a single file. Moving, without hurrying, the line split in the centre and formed the shape of a circle. When it joined, power crackled like a charge of electricity, splitting a radiant blue-white light into the blackness.

Matthew shook himself. Away in the distance, lightning forked and an icy wind sliced over his skin. He shivered; the thin shirt he wore was no protection from this cold. He slapped his face hard, seeking the assault of pain. *Wake up!*

The sound rose in intensity.

People. He realised after awhile; they were people, figures in dark cloaks holding lanterns aloft. Those at the rear were beating on circular hand-held drums. It was strange, looking down from the height he was, as though he were looking through the eyes of God.

The full moon peeked over the edge of darkness.

His fear ebbed, and Matthew, more fascinated now than frightened, watched as loops of energy, like tendrils of bright coloured smoke, rose up from the ground beneath the figures. As they walked, it eased up and over their feet, spreading out over the land like roots made from insubstantial but powerful matter.

As this was happening, four figures had separated from the circle and were positioning themselves on the outer edges. With elaborate flowing gestures, they thrust long wooden staffs into the ground in turn and lit them. At the quadrant of the circle, each flaming torch marked the quarters.

At the centre, a hooded figure cried out a warbling, eerie note. The air seemed to thrill in response. Matthew stiffened as a great yearning of emotion rose up from the surrounding darkness and coalesced into a stream of white, crystalline shards. Piercing straight towards the circle, their brightness split the blackness like a knife.

It was so unexpected, Matthew gasped out loud. What demonic creatures were these?

White feathered beings with black faces. Black feathered beings with white faces. Amongst them were enormous, angular entities wrought of wind, cold and frost. En masse, the creatures whirled high above the circle, shrieking with a laughter that held the sound of cutting glass.

The central figure spoke a word and the creatures fell, carelessly collapsing into a single torrent of freezing air that whipped around the circle.

The central figure changed. Firmly pulling her fluttering cloak around her stout form, this new one turned to a different direction and uttered a long, scorching tone; it strengthened and soared, red hot, up into the freezing darkness.

Out of the sky, a twisting heat appeared. Undulating like a mammoth serpent, it spiralled above the upturned faces and then, molten hot, it poured into the centre of the circle, layering the chilling wind with a bright, searing flame.

What power is this? Matthew stared in disbelief. This was no dream. He took in a deep breath and stopped, as warmed air bathed his senses.

Stunned, Matthew could only watch as another figure called to the sky and a stream of rain coiled over the waiting gathering.

A fourth cried out with a high commanding gesture, layering the circle in a blanket of calm and silence.

Stillness held, and in the quiet the black clad figures lifted their heads back. A shot of sound streamed up past Matthew, into the midst of the storm cloud massing high above.

Matthew felt a jolt, like an electric current. It had been a long time since he felt such power. But it was here. These were not meddling women and men, dabbling with forces they didn't understand. No. They were individuals who understood the true balance of power and nature. Knew the balance and knew how to play each one ... like an orchestra.

Witches.

Matthew hissed as hatred rose like a poison. His eyes were glued to the circle below and he could not turn his gaze. These truly were witches and he yearned to howl his abhorrence to the heavens.

Another figure moved into the centre, smaller in stature than the others. She raised her hands, as layers of cold and heat, rain and calm soared around the circle. In the increasing tumult, her hood fell back to reveal a pale face surrounded by a tangle of swirling, red-gold hair.

Matthew choked, it can't be, what was *she* doing here? Ellie tipped her head back and her voice rang out. In response, the woven current of wind, heat and rain swirled faster, tugging on fabric. Hoods billowed and they whipped off to reveal a circle of women and men - some old, some young, all standing firm singing out a rich layer of harmonies.

Neatly coiling, the vortex dropped lower and Ellie redoubled her song, sending it high up into the cloud. At once the spirits responded. Their luminous forms resolved into a flash of images that pulsed through the night, of flowing streams, moisture-soaked leaves, and spreading forest.

Watching, Matthew understood at last.

Ellie's hand held a tiny dot of brightness, growing wider with each moment. At the outer edge of the circle, the witches joined hands and held firm, as the brightness began to open. Above them all, a massive column of rain spun in a tight whirlwind above the circle.

No.

Molten with rage, Matthew raised both his arms and opened his mouth. A sound choked out - a smouldering, ferocious hiss of fury, of power denied. His face contorted as he took in another ragged breath, deeper this time, and cried out a dark mass of sound into the night.

No!

348

Matthew clenched his fist.

He was the spirit master; he could not fly like an eagle, or bow low to the earth, but the spirits must obey him.

Come to me!

With her feet locked to the ground and her knees bent, Ellie stood balanced, ready for the moment when the hag stone opened. Her heart was bursting with pride and hope as she watched the faces of the witches linked with her in this circle - Billy, his eyes wide with wonder; his twin brother, Raymond next to him singing out in the rain; and Miss Gladys, her cold exterior gone and her face shining as she sang out a strong clear stream of power.

Miss Dorothy caught her eye and, smiling, sent another tone, her cloak buffeting in the rising wind.

Ellie raised her hand. Her hag stone jolted and a crushing, thunderous roar erupted from the heavens.

The earth shook as a bolt of lightning smashed into the hill behind, sending the acrid stench of ozone bursting over the circle.

The massive storm cloud roiled, its dark belly convulsing.

Clutching the hag stone, Ellie fought to realign the harmony. It was no use. Mouthing a great scream, the wind beings were sucked from the circle, their forms flashing black and white, their feathered wings torn against the sky.

Blue Mountains, Australia, present day

'What have you done to him?' Rose ran to her father. He lay collapsed on the floor, his body contorted, his hands raised in front of his face.

There was no answer. Ba Set was lying unconscious, and blood seeped from a cut in the side of her face. Outside the cottage, came a ferocious howl as a glow of orange heat pulsed up from the valley.

Rose clasped her hands, her body shaking in terror.

A sharp crack hit the window, and another. The wind, fuelled by the heat of the fire, was gathering pace, hurling rocks and stray flaming embers with machine gun ferocity.

'We've got to get out of here!' shouted Ben, pulling at her arm.

'What about them?' Rose was panicked. Her father having some sort of fit, and Ellie... She stared at the sofa in disbelief. Ellie was lying ramrod straight, her face twisted in anguish, her hands gripping the side of the sofa.

'Ben, what do we do?'

'We have to pray.' Your father is right, we have to have faith-'

'No! We're going to die, Ben. Oh my God,' she spun to the window as with a demonic roar a ball of fire erupted into the surrounding trees.

Rose sank to the floor. 'We're going to die!'

'Get up!' Ben battled to drag her to her feet.

Rose tore at him, her hands were like claws, and as she fought to free herself of his grasp, her necklace broke and the obsidian stone clattered to the floor.

'Help us,' she cried, sobbing. 'Please God, anyone, help us!'

At once, a spray of debris lashed against the side of the cottage, and through the broken door came a lethal, searing heat. The candles flared, and a vision of twisted, contorted faces streamed against the ceiling. They coiled down the walls, their features blurring and melting into the other.

Crying in terror, Rose shrank back as a desperate agony swept into the room.

Delicate bones smashed to the floor. Stones and fragments burst from the shelves. The tempest twisted, knocking books flying. On the middle shelf a carved statue of wood, quivered, and moved abruptly as though it had been shoved. At once, the pressure in the room seemed to drop and the wind paused. And then a carved statue shot straight up off the shelf.

It was only a split second.

Without thinking, Rose dived and pushed Ellie clear as the carved wood smashed into the sofa, just inches from her friend's face. As Rose's hand connected with Ellie, the hag stone flared and Rose fell to the floor.

THIRTY-FOUR

New Forest, England, 1944

The thunderhead convulsed, spewing rain and murderous flashes of fire.

Gladys screamed as water whipped through the circle, driven by a chaotic, biting wind. Beside her, Billy lay on the ground, his body jerking, his eyes staring in horror to the sky.

'Stop this!' She pulled on Ellie's arm so hard the woman's nails cut into Ellie's skin. Thunder cracked and it felt the sky would split in two.

Billy's brother, Raymond, dropped to his knees and, in a cracked and heartbroken voice, beseeched the family spirits to heed his call.

Standing stock still in the centre, Ellie could only stare at the apparition possessing the heart of the storm.

The Reverend Matthew Hopkins. What was he doing here?

Rose's father was suspended in the middle of the mightiest cloud, his arms outstretched like some kind of deranged demi-god. Rain drove into her eyes, filling her nose and mouth. She didn't understand, but she couldn't look away. Matthew looked to be dancing with the spirits, cavorting, as he pulled them close.

A hand grasped her shoulder. 'What is *that*?' whispered Miss Dorothy.

Ellie shook her head. 'That is the minister from our church.'

'Doesn't look like any minister I've ever known.' Dorothy sniffed. She pulled her sodden cloak around her.

'What do we do?' A silver-haired man pushed Dorothy aside. He grabbed for Ellie, his face a mask of anguish. Raymond had risen to his feet. 'This was your idea!' He shouted bitterly. 'Do something!'

'Make it stop!' The voices cried and the circle of black-cloaked witches rushed towards her, hands outstretched.

'Do something.'

'Fire! Come to me!'

'Why isn't it working?'

'What are we going to do?'

The question cut through the ravaging wind, and Ellie shrank back as the brace of agonised faces bore down out of the darkness.

Oh my God. *I don't know!*

Chaos.

Lifting his fist, Matthew roared his victory. From all points of the compass, spirits of earth, air, and fire streamed towards him, their eyes wild, their insubstantial forms streaking long across the night.

Countless, they raged up through the ground, up from the water, and shrieking, they materialised out of the very fabric of the air. Matthew, dazzled by the power at his command, stretched forth his arms and cried

353

louder, calling all to heed him, and defeat the witches. Grind them out of all existence.

Out of the blackness, an ancient enmity stirred.

From the bowels of the earth, from the cracks in the sky and hidden beneath the vast continent across the sea, an ancient enmity answered.

Demons.

They roared towards him, dragging bleakness, blackness, horror...

They came shrieking, dragging a veil of infinite storms and chaos. An all-consuming terror.

What was he doing? Matthew faltered. He was nothing but a small, puny boy insignificant against this massed, heaving malevolence.

'*Stop.*' Matthew whispered, his voice a pathetic scratch above the raging nightmare.

At once, the darkness heeded his will.

They halted, churning the sky in the form of a gigantic cloud, an anvil of sky-bruising thunderstorm, so huge it would dwarf heaven itself.

Cold, sweet triumph raced though Matthew's veins.

I am stronger.

Yes. Even entities such as these must obey him. Of course they must. *All spirits must.* Faery, angel, and demon alike - *he* was the spirit master and all would obey his will. That was *his* very special talent.

Lifting his jaw, Matthew pointed his finger to the circle of puny witches. *There.*

The dark spirits did not have to be told how to fulfil their nature. Howling with a sound as menacing and as destructive as a hurricane, they swept low, smashing huge clumps of ice to the ground.

Matthew raised his fist higher.

Ellie and her friends would not last long. They hadn't moved, their cloaks were whipping around their bodies, billowing in the tumult, while their faces stared upward in horror. Somehow, they had managed to form a shield of some kind. It arced over them, a protective, transparent dome interlaced with fine lines of blue-white light. Like the thinnest of membranes, its surface swirled with shadow and colour as subtly as the sheen of oil on water.

A note soared upward.

Ellie, her red-gold hair crackling with energy and brightness, sang a note. It flared up from the centre of the circle like a beacon. *Hope...* They were holding the shield of protection up with that most fragile of human emotions.

Matthew laughed. *Hope...* It will never last. He knew from personal experience, it was the first one to go.

Colours blazed and Rose woke to chaos on the ground. Footsteps crashed around her. Without thinking, she rolled herself away. Mud and ice splattered into her face. She closed her eyes. 'This isn't happening,' she whispered.

It was like a knifing pain. Each time Ellie lifted her voice, it felt as though she was shredding something physical, like her voice itself was a thing that could be harmed. It hurt, her throat hurt, though she still forced a sound through.

Standing right beside her, Miss Dorothy sang with operatic fervour.

Billy Buckland, still lying prone, had his hands up, feeding her a current of power. Dorothy's eyes locked with his.

Above them, colours arced up into the protective dome. Ellie watched it flare in amazement, a force field that had sprung into being, powered by magic.

Dorothy grinned.

The other witches were crouched low behind her, shaking with terror, while more were shouting entreaties to the storm, pleading for respite.

The dome shook.

To Ellie, it seemed as if the black shards of fear and terror from the inside were weakening the force field above, tearing it apart.

The song had fragmented. If it wasn't for Dorothy...

'We have to get out of here, now.' Gladys's command pierced the gloom.

A cloak whirled and Ellie felt rough hands grabbing at her.

The heavens had turned an ominous, sulphurous yellow and directly overhead, high up in the maelstrom, a huge finger of cloud pointed right towards them.

Suspended within the heart of the thunderhead, Matthew laughed at the thin, coiling brightness rising up within the dome, powering the lines of energy running across its surface.

Pathetic. What could those scared old men, old women, and a girl - this a circle of insipid, singing witches, do stop to *him*? Their pitiful protection was weakening with each airborne assault.

Matthew laughed again, his hair crackling with the snap of lightning sizzling through the super-saturated air.

He held the massed power of the spirits; *he* controlled the storm shades, the wind dancers, the rainmakers, the driving, obliterating energy.

With their power, he would bring searing winds to burn the face of the earth; he would bring drought, despair; he would cause the seas to rise upon the land.

Nothing could stop him; the prophecies would come to fruition. He was the avenging sword. He would strike, cut, blast, and wipe out all that was in his path. And the earth would be scorched as the Good Book foretold and then he would rise, ascending to heaven with his rightful inheritance, as one of the blessed.

Matthew clenched his fist. He was the Instrument, and these puny inconsequential witches, who dared to think they had any hope of stopping him, would be the first to feel of his wrath.

There was a single burst of lightning and Matthew sent a smash of thunderous power, as focused as a missile, straight into the circle's heart.

'If you stay, you are on your own!' Gladys cried. 'This is madness. Madness what this girl, this *stranger,* has leashed on us! Where is she from? She is not even British! Who is she, Dorothy?'

'Who is she?'

'Who is she?' The voices echoed. In an ugly shriek, their fear and suspicion convulsed upwards and tore a single, gaping hole into the centre of the protective dome.

It was enough.

Powered by shade, by hate, by destruction, the bolt ripped into the heart of the circle with a deafening roar.

Dorothy and Billy fell to the ground.

'No!' Ellie screamed as the circle collapsed around her, falling in graceful folds, the scent of forest, warmth, life, hope...

From his vantage point, Matthew cried his triumph. The dome was down. The witches were exposed. The shades were poised.

The heavens heaved with fury.

More came. From out of the darkness, from further across the wind whipped sea, a focused presence came rushing towards him - fetid, heavy, singed with horror...

And the might of the storm began to spin.

Knocked to the ground, Ellie could only watch as the Reverend Matthew Hopkins thrust his arms out from his body, cross-like, and the multitude responded - a vast, murderous storm front gathering across the heavens. She felt numb, like her body was encased in a quiet, blanketing coverlet. She couldn't feel a thing. Ellie was vaguely aware of Miss Dorothy lying still beside her, the old lady's cloak heaped and sodden beneath the baleful sky. Lightning forked.

'I'm sorry,' she whispered.

Ellie closed her eyes, her cheek pressed into the cold, muddy earth. If she died now, what would happen to her body? A rich scent filled her nostrils. It made Ellie think of mushrooms, and tiny growing mosses. She breathed in deep. *Sorry Ba Set, I failed you. You were right, we must mourn Her passing, what can we do to stop death?* Briefly, Ellie thought of her mother and father, and bit back a sob. *Annie and Tom, I'll miss them, will we meet in heaven? Probably not... Sorry to the trees, sorry to the beautiful forest, I love you.*

An image of Rose came into view, and her shoulder spasmed with a sudden knife of pain. *Oh God, Rose, I was an idiot. I thought I could help heal the world...*

Her shoulder hurt again, and the vision sharpened into a mass of dark curly hair, a dress fluttering in the chaos of the storm, and words mouthed against the sky.

'Wake up, Ellie, hurry!'

'Yeh,' Ellie whispered sadly. 'I'm also slow.'

'Wake up!' A bolt of pain whacked into the side of Ellie's head, and the image of Rose snapped into a loud, angry focus.

The ground shook as the air quaked with renewed violence. *I'm dead,* Ellie smiled. *I'm dead and Rose is here to take me to heaven.*

Ice bit into Matthew's skin as the temperature dropped. The weather shades gathered tighter still, and out from the twisting cloud there came the sound of a ruthless, guttural roaring.

'God, show me if this is your way.' Matthew's body shook with the fervour of his prayer. 'Show me!'

He'd never felt so alive.

Thunder snapped as the agents of destruction surged for release, each one bound inexorably to his will.

Brightness scored the night. Below, a pair of figures moved in a stop-start awkward fashion.

Why don't they ever give up? Matthew studied the witches for the briefest of moments. One had lost her cloak, her arms were uncovered, and her long, dark hair whipped around her crown like a thing alive.

A growl, and the storm coiled tighter still, contracting into a viscious cone of rain, hail, fury...

Curious, Matthew flexed his will, forcing the architects of destruction to wait a heartbeat longer. This one seemed so insubstantial, and young. Her slender form was clad in only the thinnest of summer dresses, and she struggled to pull her prone companion to her feet. Abruptly, the young woman halted, and in frustration, she smacked her hair out of her eyes and dropped her charge to the ground.

'Wake up!' Rose screamed.

Ellie smiled, she liked this version of Rose. She looked like her friend of old, back when they were kids, muddy and sort of wild; she only wished she'd just stop pulling at her.

Ellie clenched the hag stone tighter.

Below, the young woman stamped her foot on the ground.

The wind moaned as the storm, held in check, began to heave and buck.

Matthew's skin prickled in the super-charged atmosphere. *Why doesn't she just give up?*

The young woman was standing alone, her pale form surrounded by the black-cloaked bodies of her fallen companions. *Like a pyre of blackened embers,* Matthew mused, like embers surrounding the burnt husks of witches. His hatred flared.

'It's over,' he bellowed, his voice strengthened by the roaring of the wind. 'You, and all your kind have failed.'

Stretching forth his arms to release the storm, Matthew unclenched his fists, just as the lone, remaining witch lifted her head and met his gaze. *Golden-eyes…*

A thunderous howl rent the sky and Ellie snapped awake. Pain pummelled across her back. She rolled away, struggling in the sodden mess of her cloak and wrenched it off.

Rose stood before her, golden eyes flashing, with her fist raised to strike.

Ellie shook her head. Her face hurt, her body ached all over.

Chunks of hail were pelting out of the heavens, as hard and as large as stones.

She lurched to her feet.

'Hurry!' Rose was shouting; she looked on the edge on hysteria. 'God, you're always so slow!'

Mutely, Ellie gazed at the wreck of the circle and then back to her friend. 'Rose? What are you doing here?'

'I don't know!' Suddenly Rose tipped back her head and laughed, the sound a clear, bright bell lifting above the deadening roar of the storm. 'It's crazy, Ellie. I don't know what the hell is going on, but look my Dad is up there, in the middle of that!'

Ellie followed her friend's gesture. The sky hung, blackened and bruised. The thunderhead had swelled double in size and now spanned the heavens like a vast, malignant disease. It was circling, moving in on itself and shot through with streaks of deepest red. At its centre lightning pulsed, and, as if revelling in their attention, thunder cracked, like an echoing, mocking laugh.

Below it, illuminated on the muddy ground, were the witches - Miss Dorothy, Billy, Gladys, and all the others. The flaming torches had long been extinguished, and the circle lay broken and silent, devoid of any hint of magic. Ellie dropped her face in her hands. It was over, Gladys was right; her meddling had destroyed them all.

'Wake up.' A slap hit Ellie's shoulder. Rose raised her voice. 'If that storm breaks it will kill us all. Come on, Ellie. Think! What have you been learning all these months?'

'Nothing you would understand.' Exhausted, Ellie closed her eyes. Her shoulder ached.

'Well try me.'

Ellie shook her head.

Rose laughed, but she didn't sound amused. 'For God's sake, Ellie, stop being so stupid. You're not the only one who's been caught up in this craziness. God, you are always so self-obsessed.'

Ellie stared at her friend in disbelief. 'Me?'

'Yes, you,' Rose snapped back. 'Look, I believe you. Does that change anything? No, it doesn't. Just tell me what that hideous creature has been teaching you.' She paused, flashing a grin. 'Besides, it can't be that hard, if you and all these badly dressed witches can do it.'

Ellie didn't reply. *Rose, it didn't make sense, how come she was even here?*

The ground lurched, and Ellie felt she was falling deeper into a world that she would never, ever, understand.

She closed her eyes. Paradox. Is that what Ba Set had called it? A state of being or a thing that was so absurd it couldn't possibly be true, and yet somehow, it turned out to be real, even if it didn't make sense.

Like magic...

Ellie shivered.

'What does she say, Ellie?' cried Rose, stamping her foot. 'Hurry!'

'She says you have to feel the magic in here.' Ellie pointed to her heart, 'like it's a part of you. And sing.' Ellie tensed, ready for her friend's peel of teasing laughter.

'That doesn't sound so bad,' Rose was gazing up into the storm, 'and I've got the best voice in church. What do we sing?'

'Not words ... exactly,' Ellie said slowly, acutely aware of how crazy it sounded. 'We use our voices and connect to power - in the earth.'

'What? Is that all?' Rose snorted in disbelief. 'Where's the magic in that?

Overhead, an eerie sound shrieked through the sky.

'Okay, hurry.' Rose ordered.

'What?'

'Do it!'

The sky convulsed and the great roiling cloud tightened still.

Within the heart of the thunderhead, Matthew shook in agony, howling in bitterness, over and over, until at last he hung suspended in the midst of the storm, doubled over, and retching in horror.

His sweet girl, they have taken her.

The curse had been fulfilled.

Her blood is tainted. Her accursed heritage has come to claim her.

Pulsing with malevolent light, the spirits heard him. Massing closer, tighter, they lent their combined energy to feed his own.

Bile, blackness, hatred.

Destruction, death, chaos.

Shade, fury.

Obliteration.

'Hurry!' Rose shrieked.

Ellie held the hag stone to her cheek. Around them, chips of ice bit into their exposed skin, but it was weird; the wind had dropped almost completely, and it felt hard to breathe as though all the oxygen in the air had fled.

Her hag stone, how she loved it, and it had chosen her.

Closing her eyes, she breathed a deep tone towards the earth, more a vibrating rumble than any kind of real song. Barely audible, it hummed low and close to the ground. But it was enough to send minute particles of soil shivering, like dust vibrating on the surface of a set of speakers.

'Bass, tone, earth,' Ellie sang again into the stone, and a thin, coiling brightness erupted from its centre.

Matthew unleashed his despair. Darkness fell completely.

Across the New Forest, windows smashed, and debris, sticks and branches cartwheeled across the sky, torn free by a mindless, demonic wind.

The air whipped into a frenzy and with a lost and desolate howl, the storm swell raked the coast, lashing a spray of wild foam across the shoreline. Seawater smashed over roads and the wind tore on, felling posts, electricity poles, and blacking out the sky.

In the towns, dogs barked in a frenzy of baying panic. Metal shrieked on metal, weather vanes spun, and any untied object was flung in a cacophony of sound over the anguished groaning of the surrounding forest. In the following breath, from the heavens came a deafening, guttural roar. The centre of the storm darkened, and a giant funnel of cloud stretched towards the ground.

Ellie and Rose's voices were barely audible as they sang in a field in the centre of the ancient forest. Ellie sang for the trees, for these ones lashed by the wind around her, and for the giants at home poised to die. Her throat hurt, ice bit into her skin, but she didn't stop.

A sound came, so faint that at first Ellie didn't notice it. Yet it strengthened with each passing moment. Ellie opened her eyes. Miss Dorothy. Her voice pitched higher than the relentless howling.

The rest of the circle were struggling to their feet. They gathered close, shoulder-to-shoulder, weaving their voices into a renewed circle of power. With them was Rose, with her dark hair plastered to her head, her dress muddied and torn, singing with her arms raised to the sky and with her gaze locked to her father.

Lightning cut across the heavens.

Unflinching, Matthew beheld the vision of his daughter. So beautiful, so pale, so perfect, with a face so like her mother's ... except for those accursed golden eyes.

A single bolt, aimed and powered by clear, cool intention, was all it would take. Rain coiled, a vast reservoir held aloft by the rotational forces of the wind. Matthew sensed its strength. His life was poised at this moment. Everything he had ever accomplished in his long, long life came to this.

The witches had risen, and they challenged the very will of God - heretics, witches, they were all the same and they all must die.

This was the price, he realised. The blood price. If he was ever to be rid of the taint of his family, he must cleanse the final drops. Unto the fifth generation, isn't that what the Good Book said?

Below him Rose was singing, and her face, as beautiful as always, held sweetness and an openness he'd rarely seen. Loneliness knifed his soul, but...

This was the price of love.

Matthew quietly flexed his will, and the shades that came to his call were bright, searing hot, and forked with flame.

He felt their incendiary power like a slap.

How apt. He smiled at the perfect symmetry. His daughter would burn, burn like all the others of her kind.

He was the Instrument.

The warning prickled along her skin, but Ellie didn't notice. She'd stopped singing and stood concentrating on the hag stone. It was leaping like a live thing, sending erratic jolts of electricity shuddering up her arm.

She gripped it tightly, terrified it would fling itself from her grasp. Light swirled, and from within its centre came a glimpse of a void as vast as a spiralling galaxy, and as tiny as the spinning dance of atoms. Ellie shook her head. Above her, thunder rumbled and Rose's voice soared even higher, so high and clear and free it seemed it could crack the very air itself.

The wind slackened, and at that moment, the heavens exploded, and a burst of lightning forked, unimaginably wide and blue, and so riven with colour that Ellie could only stare. Burned against her retina was the image of Matthew, his head back, and his body balanced within the centre of the vast cyclonic storm.

Ellie stumbled. Sound hit her head, her ears, like pain, a sonic wave ripping through her body. There was nothing she could do, sound possessed her being, it pounded through her consciousness reverberating out and on into the darkness.

Crying out, the witches fell to their knees as the spirits returned - ice, flood, fire - expelled from the heavens by wanton forces of destruction. Wind spirits, black-faced feathered ones, their wings ripped and useless, smashed into the earth. Clear, liquid ones, their strange forms refracting colour and brightness, fell, driven by a demonic, spinning wind. The ground quaked, and out of the sky burst a brutal ear-piercing shriek. Fire spirits appeared, molten and twisting with rage.

Ellie stared in momentary fascination; forked tongued and bright of eye, they moved with incendiary speed. Then she coughed, choking, as heat tore at her throat and dry, scorching air filled the centre of the circle. Laughter crackled loud and close, and the torches staked in the ground burst alight. At that moment, Rose fell to her knees screaming, her light summer dress erupting into flames.

It happened so fast.

Horrified, Ellie ran to help her friend.

Rose screamed again, writhing, enveloped in fire. Ellie tore her gaze away, her eyes streamed, burning in the heat. She blinked them as rapidly as she could, desperately trying to find relief. Again Rose screamed, an agonised, tortured sound, and when Ellie turned back, her friend's body was shuddering, her pale form becoming darker, shifting, changing … her arms lengthening, her dark hair fanning outwards. Flames surged, red, yellow, twisting shades of darkness, and her form seemed to flicker from long-haired girl to winged creature and back … all the while her eyes, burning gold, stayed the same.

Panicked, Ellie threw the hag stone to the ground. 'What's happening,' she cried, 'I don't understand!'

Lightning cracked, and the great finger of cloud bored down from the heavens reminding them, reminding her, Ellie, of how puny, insignificant and worthless she was.

Ellie dropped to her knees. 'Help me, help me, I don't know what to do.'

Around her, she could hear Dorothy and Gladys, still singing, their voices shooting up into the heavens like bursts of hope.

Now Soul Flyer, a voice seemed to whisper across the ages. *Now. You don't need to understand it all. Remember, breathe and trust.*

Discarded where she'd thrown it, the hag stone flashed, reflecting the red and yellow of the flames. Without taking her eyes off its its central core, Ellie tilted back her head and poured out a single defiant note. It was all she could do; it was all she had left.

Then she launched herself through the fire at her friend. They hit the ground and rolled across the muddy earth as a brilliant, piercing light shot into the night.

Iridescent, and as true as an arrow, it soared beyond the circle of witches, and up through the darkness above.

Lightning scattered, and beneath the peak of the massive thunderhead, deep gashes of angry purple radiated outwards through the storm. The cloud pulsed, roiled, its underside darkening as the concentrated beam of light pierced its central point.

Resolute and without pause, brightness enveloped the funnel, following it down to earth, draining its fury, pulling the massive storm down into the centre of the stone.

THIRTY-FIVE

Blue Mountains, Australia, present day

'Rose, get up!' Ben gasped. The heat was suffocating, and his eyes burned. A thunderous crack erupted overhead, shaking the cottage as though the roof was about to be split open. Embers pelted the window. Oxygen tore from the room. 'Come on!' Choking and crying with terror he ran out into the night.

The forest was ablaze.

Ben stumbled down the stairs and fell gasping to the ground. They were going to die. *Help us. Lord Help us.*

A roar of fury erupted, so hot Ben convulsed as his breath was sucked out of his lungs. He turned, horrified, expecting to see Rose fleeing the chaos, sure that flames were engulfing the cottage.

He stared. A column of incandescent light blazed. Blue-white and interwoven with sheets of red and gold, it soared up through the roof and into the heavens above, obliterating the surrounding shadows.

As if in response, thunder boomed and a searing brightness flashed so acute Ben fell backwards to the ground, his arm up shielding his eyes. Wind roared.

Ben curled into a tiny ball to protect his body from the assault.

Overhead thunder cracked again, and cold, hard drops of rain poured out of the sky. Hitting his skin, they pummelled the earth, quenching the fire, and fell in great streaming torrents over the cottage.

Dazed, Ben struggled to sit up, as branches fell hissing to the ground around him. The wind intensified and he saw, spreading out over the forest, a vast curtain of falling water. Flames flared and sparked as they were extinguished, and the earth around him turned to mud.

Ben ran inside. His clothes were sodden. On the floor, Rose was moaning, her eyelids fluttering. Her dress was torn, and burn marks and lacerations were seared across her face.

'Help me,' Rose cried. 'Help me.'

She fell sobbing on to the floor. 'He tried to kill me.'

Ben dropped to his knees. 'Thank God, you're alright,' he crooned. 'Look outside. Rose, look. Our prayers were answered.'

'No.' She shook him off. 'My father has gone mad.'

Ben grasped her hand. 'No, Rose, we're safe. Your father is a man of the Lord-'

'No!' Wrenching herself free, Rose staggered to her feet and leant against the wall with her eyes closed. 'I just have to get out.' She whispered weakly. 'Now.'

'Wait!'

Ignoring him, Rose stumbled out into the storm.

Quickly Ben surveyed the room. His sister lay on the sofa. Her hands by her side, she looked peaceful. At her feet, Matthew was stirring. He moaned and clutched his head. Then he sat up. Ben couldn't see if Rose's father needed help; he hesitated, unsure. In the corner, an old woman lay motionless with a great red gash open along her face.

'Ben!' Rose cried.

At that moment Matthew rushed past him and without a word lurched out into the torrential rain. Ben jumped to his feet, and as he turned he saw a dark shape glinting on the floor, no bigger than his thumb. The obsidian stone - Rose wore it everyday hanging on a silver chain. Ben grabbed it. He smiled in relief. *This will make her feel safe.* She never let it out of her sight.

Whispering a quick prayer of gratitude, Ben ran out into the miraculous storm.

THIRTY- SIX

New Forest, England, 1944

Stars shone in a clear sky. Ellie sat on a bench overlooking the sea. Miss Dorothy and Miss Gladys had gone indoors for a chat and a cup of tea, but Ellie hadn't wanted to follow; she needed to sit on the edge of the cliff in silence and think of nothing at all.

Waves washed in, and Ellie watched as fluffy remnants of sea foam ebbed and flowed along the shingled beach. Yawning suddenly, the salty freshness stung her skin. Ellie felt awake and shivery with excitement, but she wasn't ready for the long cycle back to the village.

There was a slap of footsteps and Miss Dorothy appeared, clutching a silver thermos. Ellie smiled hello, her stomach rumbled. After a mutter of, 'my old, poor knees,' Miss Dorothy eased herself down. She produced a small set of cups from her pocket and poured out a stream of hot sweet tea.

'The best kind,' she murmured. 'Why, if we had some toast that would be simply heavenly…'

Ellie let her friend extol the virtues of tea, toast and butter, the holy trinity of life, but she wasn't really listening. Taking another unhurried sip, she looked out. Dawn was beginning to break. In the grey light, the serrated streaks of last night's storm wisped high above and in the last hour Ellie had watched as it slowly dispersed. Stars glittered, and low in the west she could see the shape of the setting moon.

'I didn't know it was full?' She turned in surprise.

'Oh yes.' Miss Dorothy took a comfortable sip of tea and licked her lips. 'Ah that's good. Yes, the full moon before the summer solstice, Tuesday, 6th June 1944, just before dawn and therefore in Sagittarius. Always my favourite, you know. It heralds freedom, adventure, and risks...' She glanced at Ellie. 'Maybe that's why you are here, my dear, you bring us adventures.'

'Maybe...' replied Ellie slowly. 'But Miss Dorothy,' she gestured back out to sea, 'what's all that about?'

In the silence of the predawn, Ellie had been watching black shapes leaving the mouth of the bay. They seemed to be ships, hundreds of them, steaming out, their hulls glinting as they bore through the water. Each one was packed so close together, it seemed she would be able to run across them all and never wet her feet.

As Ellie and Miss Dorothy studied them, other shapes appeared in tight formation over the top of the ships. As dark as shadows, they were hard to see in the gloomy light. Yet as they flew closer, the sound grew and Ellie felt a rippling shockwave in her chest. Bombers, hundreds of bombers roared overhead, heading over the wide tranquil sea.

'Oh my God,' she whispered, unable to believe what she was seeing. 'This is the English Channel, isn't it?'

Miss Dorothy nodded.

'And today is the 6th of June 1944? Oh my God, it's World War Two, D-Day. We were studying it in history at school. I can't believe it.' Ellie shook her head in wonder. 'This is crazy. We saw a documentary about D-Day in class. I remember it, people were talking about the storm – "the worst storm in forty years", an old guy said. And he'd been there. "The Germans weren't expecting anything, and we snuck in and clobbered the lot of them."'

As Ellie spoke, another mass of planes buzzed low over the ships. These ones were much smaller - hundreds of them, flying in a tight V formation close to the waves. A moment later, they lifted higher and screamed overhead, like angry hornets blackening the sky, heading for the beaches of France.

'Dorothy? Do you know what this means?' Ellie jumped to her feet. She felt like running, jumping around with excitement. 'We did it. It was us. The guy in the film said the break in the weather had been a miracle.'

'A miracle and I think it was,' whispered Dorothy. As she watched the planes disappear into the horizon, her eyes glistened with tears. 'Tell me,' she said, after wiping her nose delicately on her handkerchief. 'Tell me, Ellie, do we win? Do we get rid of that nasty Adolf Hitler?'

'Oh yes', smiled Ellie broadly. 'Yes we do.'

Ellie woke with a feeling of warmth drifting gently across her face. She stirred, too sleepy and too comfortable to move much more. From the window, came the twitter of tiny birds as they skitted through the leaves.

Her stomach rumbled and a few seconds later, the door opened after a quick knock.

'Good morning, dear,' Miss Dorothy bustled in, a red scarf covering her curls and a large wooden tray balanced in her grasp.

'Oh, I should get up -' Guiltily, Ellie pushed back the bed covers.

'No no,' the old lady smiled. 'This is your last morning with us, and I've made you something extra nice. Besides, you have slept virtually a whole day and night and you must be starving.'

'Really?' Sitting up, Ellie glanced out the window. The light sparkled, glinting with the special quality that came after a good saturating rain. With a chirrup of welcome, Queenie jumped up onto the bed and settled heavily, his purr made a loud vibrating rumble over her legs.

'They are strange beings, aren't they,' began the old lady, eyeing the trees outside.

'What are?'

'Well, spirits, faeries, those type of beings. I never really spent much time with them before…' she gestured towards Ellie. 'And I don't know anything about them really, except of course what I read in the old tales.'

'But I thought you worked with them all the time?'

'Yes, with our family weather spirits, they come as a matter of course. But those ones, the ones you work with, the faeries that come out of the trees, the grass —' she turned back to the window. 'They're all new to me.'

'Me too,' mumbled Ellie. 'They just sort of appear all by themselves.'

The old lady nodded and handed Ellie a steaming cup of tea. 'Now, I've made you a special tea cake, it took a few eggs and a bit of flour which was hard to get with the war on, and I know it's early but we're worth it.'

Queenie watched them both silently through his big orange eyes as they finished the rest of the cake. Miss Dorothy brushed down her skirt and stood up, 'I expect you'll be impatient to go?' she said, picking up the tray.

Ellie looked up at her in surprise.

'Home,' said the old lady, 'isn't it time to know what's going on in your world?'

For a brief blissful moment of peace and cake, Ellie had completely forgotten.

'Oh,' she stared up at Miss Dorothy. 'I'll miss you-' and to her horror, a tear ran down her cheek.

Miss Dorothy laughed. 'Oh be off with you, it's not that bad,' her blue eyes twinkled. 'You can always come back here for a visit, you know, you just need to leave something behind,' she pursed her lips wistfully.

Ellie laughed. 'And I'll bring you back your hag stone.'

'Oh don't worry about that. I had a feeling it was going to leave me soon anyway, off to greener pastures as they say. Objects of power do that, you know, we can never keep them for good, they have their own journeys.'

'Miss Dorothy?' Ellie was quiet for a moment.

'What is it, dear?'

'Last night ... my friend, Rose, she was here. I'm sure of it. But...' Her voice trailed off. 'I don't understand. How did she get here? Do you know? It doesn't make sense...' Ellie frowned.

'Well I expect a lot doesn't make sense, just yet. My advice is not to fret over it too much, my dear - important things have a habit of making themselves clear, just when you least expect it.

Miss Dorothy nodded, 'I'll just sort this lot out,' and taking the tray she hurried off down the hallway. 'Oh!' she shouted, her voice echoing off the confined walls, 'speaking of objects of power, I have something here for you.' With that her small busy footsteps pattered away into silence.

Ellie sat in the bed, watching the play of light dance across the ceiling. It wasn't over she knew, remembering with a jolt of fear the sight of the Reverend Matthew Hopkins as he commanded the weather spirits to bend to his will. What had happened?

She shook her head, parts of that night felt fuzzy, reduced to sensations, colours, sounds; it was like trying to remember a dream in the clear light of day. There were whole patches she could barely recall.

Pulling on her normal everyday clothes - jeans, t-shirt and comfortable running shoes, Ellie took a last look around the little pink room. The red raincoat still hung, neat and tidy, over the back of the bedroom chair where Miss Dorothy had left it. Smiling, Ellie turned and walked away; it never suited her anyway.

The old lady was in her living room, writing at her scroll top desk. It was covered with discarded papers, and the fountain pen scratching sharply was the only sound in the quiet. Queenie lay sprawled over on a cushion at Dorothy's feet, sleeping in a pool of sunshine.

'Listen to this,' Miss Dorothy looked up. 'I have a poem in honour of you, my dear.' She coughed. 'It's new,' she added a little sheepishly, 'so it might not have the polish of the best of my work, but I wanted to give you a flavour before you went.' Squinting at the paper in her hand, Miss Dorothy placed her glasses on her nose and proceeded to read.

'*O'er the sea, o'er the sea,* she began softly
I saw her free
The heart of spirits flying

378

The friend of spirits sighing
'O-er the sea, o'er the sea.

Miss Dorothy grimaced, she stopped. 'That's not quite right, is it? *The friend of spirits sighing…*

She looked thoughtfully down at the word.

'Well,' Ellie began, not sure what she should say 'I really like the start.'

'It's the last line', Miss Dorothy huffed. 'I never can get the last line right, straight off, can I Queenie? Everything else flows.'

The sleeping cat didn't deign to answer, but his long tail swished in the warm summer air.

'Oh,' cried Miss Dorothy, dropping her glasses. 'I almost forgot. I have something for you have to take. How silly of me.' The old lady's head vanished as she bent down to the bottom drawer of her writing bureau. It was deep, and Ellie heard a few muttered curses before Miss Dorothy heaved a heavy object onto the wooden surface of the writing desk. About the size and shape of a child's head, it was hidden from view by a dark green covering.

Without warning, the old lady pulled the cloth free. Ellie gasped, a soundless bottomless vibration resonated through the room. It tugged at her mind, demanding her attention, seeking her name, compelling her to look in closer, with a decisive, sharp insistence.

Turning quickly, she searched for someplace to rest her gaze, anywhere except its deep, impenetrable structure.

'I don't like it,' Ellie whispered. 'I really don't like it.'

'Yes,' Miss Dorothy nodded. 'Strange, I feel like that too when I'm around it, but,' she placed the green cloth back over its surface. 'I don't believe it is dangerous as such. Just make sure you keep the scarf on. It's perfectly safe when it is covered. It must be silk mind you, natural silk keeps the energy vibration silenced.'

'But why are you giving it to me?' Ellie was appalled.

'Do not panic, child. It is obvious you have the strength to resist whatever power may be locked inside, and besides, feel it, the vibrations have ceased.'

She was right. As Miss Dorothy tied the scarf securely around the crystal, the room felt clearer, gone was the suffocating sense of pitiless, implacable will. Ellie felt almost euphoric, she'd just overreacted, us usual. She shook her head, *stupid...*

'It has been in my family for hundreds of years.'

Ellie snapped her gaze up, wondering for a split moment if Miss Dorothy had been talking for a long while.

'My father never spoke of it, nor his mother, nor has it been mentioned in any of the family grimoires. It is not for me, for that I am certain. My family have merely been the custodians. However,' she continued briskly, 'I dreamt of it clearly this morning, for the first time since I was a child. The quartz made it clear it wishes to move on, and wishes to travel with you, my dear.'

Ellie's eyes widened.

'Keep it covered, and well hidden. Keep it away from prying eyes. This crystal is not for you, so it keep it safe until the time comes to past it on.' She smiled reassuringly. 'Are you all right, my dear?'

Ellie felt woozy and she didn't answer straight away. *It didn't really matter,* she told herself. If she took the thing, she could keep it safe and hidden somewhere far away and never ever look at it. *Ba Set,* Ellie

380

brightened. *Of course.* The strange smoky quartz was so powerful it probably wanted to get to Ba Set.

Ellie sighed in relief and looked up at Miss Dorothy. 'I'll be fine.'

The old lady beamed. 'Of course you will, and next time you come back, stay for longer.' She held out her hand, 'I'll miss you, you know.'

Taking it, Ellie enveloped the older lady in an impulsive hug. 'I'll be back before you know it.'

Ellie reached down. 'Look after your person,' she whispered, patting Queenie's thick white fur. The cat purred, his large orange eyes watching her every move.

Ellie lay down on the sofa, the cloth covered quartz touching her feet and her hag stone held tight in her hand. Ellie yawned. The sun glinted in through the open window like a shaft of radiance. Colours danced, split and banded in the light. *Time to go home,* Ellie thought.

'Promise you'll come back and see me sometime,' called the old lady.

'Okay, as long you make more of that amazing apple teacake.'

'I'll teach you to make it yourself.' She retorted primly. 'No student of mine would be given something without learning how it was accomplished.'

Ellie laughed and closed her eyes.

'Oh, my dear, one more thing.' Miss Dorothy continued, but her voice was already sounding softer. 'Tell me, what was the name of the minister, you know your minister in the storm?'

Ellie felt her weight settling down onto the sofa. 'Reverend Matthew,' she mumbled, not really paying much attention.

'Matthew - and his surname, my dear? Asked Miss Dorothy.

'Um, Hopkins,' she mumbled, 'the Reverend Matthew Hopkins.'

'What?' exclaimed the old lady, and her chair crashed loudly to the floor. 'The Witch Finder General? It can't be!'

But Ellie was no longer paying attention. She gave the time ring a single twist and a moment later she was gone.

THIRTY- SEVEN

Blue Mountains, Australia, present day

The sound was strange, like a sibilant, streaming hiss, though it wasn't quite in the room…

Ellie blinked her eyes then closed them tight; she didn't feel ready to wake. And besides, the sound wasn't unpleasant. It wasn't quite a steady hiss, it had gaps and depths and was more like a constant, crinkly whispering that dropped and splattered. Crinkled splattering … what a crazy idea. Ellie laughed and opened her eyes.

There was an expanse of grey light and she blinked rapidly, trying to focus. She was lying on a narrow red sofa, pushed up against a clear expanse of streaking, glittering light. Plunging, plummeting off the roof, it ran in rushing rivulets down the long transparent pane. Suddenly awake, Ellie pressed her forehead against the glass of the picture window, eyes wide with wonder, trying to take in the full magnitude of what was before her.

Rain.

Magical, shining rain sweeping down from the sky as far as the eye could see. Dropping heavily on leaves, it bounced and poured in a vast torrent over the forest below.

Ellie watched for a long moment. 'It worked Ba Set,' she whispered, 'it really actually worked.'

Turning, squinting a little to give her eyes time to adjust to the change of brightness, Ellie peered into the living room behind her.

'Ba Set?' she called softly, imagining the old woman sitting somewhere half hidden in the quiet.

'Where are you?' Ellie stood up and her foot landed on a hard brittle shape. It collapsed at once with a sharp snap. Cursing herself for being so clumsy, Ellie reached down and picked up a slender, porcelain limb; an arm of one the dancing statues that Ba Set displayed with such care. It had snapped in two.

But that wasn't all. The rug was covered in debris. Ba Set's treasures lay scattered - multi-coloured rocks, coiled twigs, feathers - all the magic the old woman had collected from the forest lay strewn across the room. In the corners beneath the shelves, were the heaped remains of Ba Set's statues - the dancers, the laughing deities, all of them smashed and broken.

Rising to her feet, Ellie stood and listened for a long moment, scarcely breathing. Outside the rain rushed in noisy streams, but inside not a thing moved. No teacher, no sense of faery, nothing. The cottage felt as abandoned as a grave.

Working quickly, Ellie gathered up fallen pieces of statues, candles, twigs and stones, and piled them back onto the shelves. She leaned some of the treasures together to make them stand, adjusting them, setting the room to right, trying to ease her own rising sense of disquiet.

At last, the room no longer looked as though it had been hit by a tornado. Ellie turned to leave, then stopped as a taut ripple of warning flickered through her being. Ignoring it, and eager to be outside in the clean, fresh coolness, Ellie took a step forward, but the feeling came again - a hard, tight calling, pulling with increasing urgency.

Ellie sighed and looked out longingly at the clear, wet day outside. She shook her head. Oh no... The crystal, the weird smoky crystal, she'd forgotten all about it. Biting back a curse, Ellie lifted the heavy weight off the floor and carried it through the silent cottage and into the kitchen.

On the side bench, a jar of peanut butter was still standing, open. Ellie stared at it for a long moment, and then, trying not to think about too much, she shoved them both away in the pantry and closed the door tight. The quartz was safe enough, Ellie decided, safe until Ba Set came back and claimed it.

Hurrying back into the living room, Ellie retrieved her hag stone from the sofa and quickly scouted around for the other, but Miss Dorothy's was nowhere to be found.

Well they say magical objects always come and go, she thought, and then, anxious to be gone, Ellie shoved her own holed stone deep into her pocket and ran out into the fresh, rainy day.

Glorious, at last she could breathe. Water pelted onto her head, hitting her hair, dripping into her eyes. Opening her mouth, Ellie stretched out her arms, tilted her head back, and spun around slowly under the sky as the miraculous, cool liquid splashed down from the sky and onto her face.

Then she turned and dashed down the cliff steps and on into the forest. Old man tree ferns stood, hunched in a gully, their blackened husks dripping in the pale light. Ellie tilted back her head, so her eyes rested on the remains of their great hairy trunks. 'Life will return to them,' Ellie whispered. 'Life will emerge, soft and green in the spring.'

Beneath them all, the ground ran with water. It spilled across the soil, pouring in rivulets across the forest floor.

Laughing, Ellie spun around and around, faster and faster.

'I love you,' she cried to the trees, dripping loudly all around her. 'I love you!'

We've won!

Something was wrong. Ellie knew it the moment she rounded the final corner and saw her house set back from the road. Rain poured off its wide, wraparound porch, turning the front garden to mud with a torrent of stormwater sweeping off onto the road. But that wasn't it. Ellie slowed to a walk. Ben's truck was parked in the driveway. Pamphlets covered the front seat. Ellie peered in through the water smearing the glass. She couldn't quite make out the words, but the print was large and black, against a red background.

Warily, she headed towards the front stairs. The rain hammered down onto the tin roof with a loud, rhythmic precision. Inside, every light was off. Ellie swallowed; it all felt wrong, very, very wrong.

A quiver flicked beside her ear and a shape materialised out of the downpour - a silvery being wavered in the pearl-grey light. Agitated, it moved around Ellie, holding its elongated arms out wide, long fingers stretched raking through the air.

'What is it?' Ellie whispered.

As if in answer, the being looped away from her towards the house.

Be careful. The words were unsaid, but the meaning emanating from the faery was clear. It came closer, its face hovering, before abruptly it vanished. *Be careful.*

Ellie swallowed and dug her hand into her pocket, gripping the hag stone tightly. She opened the front door. 'Ben?' she called, her voice sounding thin and anxious in the darkened hallway. 'Dad, I'm back.'

She reached for the light switch and flicked it on. Nothing, Ellie snapped it once more, but it clicked uselessly in the silence. Struggling against an instinct urging her to run to safety in the forest, she crept through the hallway and peered around the living room door.

I have the ring, she told herself, trying to calm. *I have the ring and the stone, nothing bad can happen.* In the dim light, she could see the telephone, lounge chairs, television, and that was all.

Moving slowly, Ellie crept down to the back of the house, wincing at every creak of the floor. The bedroom doors on each side were shut tight. The twin's bedroom had been empty for a over a week, and Ben's dark blue door was still plastered with the stickers and photos he'd collected as a teen. She hesitated, her mouth dry with anxiety.

'Ben?' she called softly. 'Are you in there?' Reaching for the handle, Ellie stood on the threshold and peered in. Nothing, and there was no sound save for the ragged quality of her breath.

Her heart thudding, Ellie almost ran to the end of the hallway, her footsteps echoing, not caring now if she was quiet; all she wanted was somewhere safe and familiar. She wanted to be home.

She flung open her door to her bedroom and gasped.

Water flooded her room, pouring in through the wet flapping curtains of her window. Ellie slammed it shut. Who was the idiot who left it open?

She closed her eyes. Then with a loud sigh she opened them again, ready to confront the damage wreaked by her own stupidity.

But no storm, wind, or rain was capable of *this*, Ellie almost gagged. It was as if a maddened looter had ripped through everything she held dear. Her cupboard door had been wrenched off its hinges and her clothes, shoes - all the contents of her life, had been flung callously over the floor. Her books, their spines trampled, lay torn in a sodden heap. Who would do such a thing, and with such vehemence? Heart thudding, Ellie ran out of her room and burst into the kitchen.

'Ben?' she called. 'Dad?' But it was empty, only the leftover remains of a meal, eaten at the bench, showed that anyone had been there at all.

Where were they? Ellie sagged to the floor. Her heart thudding, maybe it had actually happened ... *Ascension.*

Wrenching open the back door, Ellie ran out into the rainstorm. The grass was unable to soak up the torrential downpour after years of dry and neglect. A lake had formed in the yard, lapping almost to the fence. Normally the sight would have filled Ellie's heart with wonder, but now, she spun around, her feet slipping in the mud beneath.

'Dad! Ben!' she cried. 'Where are you?'

There was no warning. A swoop of darkness lunged for her, its fingers grasping for her, its eyes wild and blue.

'You!' The cry was like a whipsnap of fury. Hands, slippery with rain and as brittle as bone, yanked her close.

Ellie screamed in terror.

She fought back as desperately as she could, but Matthew's grip was already around her throat, burning; he was strong. She could feel her Adam's apple pressing back, crushing her windpipe; her knees buckling as pain, intense like she had never felt before, overwhelmed her senses. It cut sharp and suffocating, trapping air, denying breath, refusing any avenue of escape. Flailing weakly, she tried to hit, to pummel, to make him stop.

Help, she pleaded mutely, as weak and as helpless as a trapped bird. *Please someone help.* Desperately, she struggled as waves of oblivion lapped at the edges of her mind.

'No!' A voice cried out and footsteps ran closer.

'Reverend, there's no need for this. Stop!'

Released, Ellie fell to the ground. She heaved, writhing in the mud, sucking in as much breath as her lungs could hold. She wanted to vomit, her stomach heaved again, and she was only dimly aware of Matthew standing with his arms up, and face shining towards the heavens. Thunder boomed.

Ellie's father looked over her, his body towering against the sky like some kind of protective shield.

The rain fell like heavy bullets piercing the earth.

'The Lord heard us!' Matthew cried, his voice a bright peal of triumph.

'Bring it on!' Ben laughed. He was standing alongside Matthew with his arms extended, ignoring the sharp drops pelting onto his upturned face.

Weakly, Ellie turned away from the onslaught. A figure stood watching her from beneath the eaves. The rain streaked, but Ellie could feel the intensity of her gaze. It seemed to burn in the hard-grey light.

Ellie shook her head.

Desperately she tried to make sense of what she was seeing. 'It can't be true,' she whispered.

Golden eyes … here…

Ellie struggled to her knees, her grip slipping on the sodden earth.

Rose flinched, but she didn't look away, her chin was high, and around her neck, dark against her skin, hung a black stone shaped like a tear. Rose was as beautiful and as proud as always, and yet Ellie could see she was holding herself carefully, in a strange awkward position with her arms angled away from her body. As if she were afraid to move.

No... Ellie breathed. She scrambled to her feet. Seared along the length of her friend's arms was a line of savage burns. Forked and red, they looked like deep whip marks, or... Ellie gasped. *Not whip marks.*

A pattern was seared into Rose's pale skin. Edging out from over her shoulders, it travelled down her arms, over her hands, and ended at the tips of her fingers.

Elle stared, stunned into a horrified silence. *Wings...*

The whole of Rose's upper body had been claimed by a pattern of cruelly scorched feathers, branded in pain.

'Oh my God!' Ellie rushed toward her. 'What happened?'

'Stop.' Rose backed away, her face contorted. 'Please. I can't speak with you, Ellie.'

'But you were there!' Ellie cried, her voice rising in tone, as the enormity of what she was seeing, sharpened with painful clarity.

Rose dropped her face in her hands.

'Leave her alone.' Ben shoved past and placed his body protectively in front of Rose. 'Just let her be, Ellie.' He snarled. 'Can't you see how much pain she's in? You need to get a grip for once.'

Softening his voice to a protective murmur, Ben placed an arm around Rose's shoulders. 'Leave her be,' he repeated. 'We're doing the work of the Lord.'

Ellie watched in silence as Rose allowed herself to be drawn away.

'You have to leave.' Her father spoke the words behind her as Ben put the truck into gear, and it roared away. Abruptly the wind began to strengthen.

'I don't know what you are getting yourself into, but Ellie, you must understand, you're not welcome here anymore.'

'No Dad, please.' Ellie cried, in her panic the words tumbled out. 'It's all going to go back to normal. Look, the rains have come. I can go back to school. Mum and the twins can come home. Everything is going to be fine.' She tried to smile. 'It's a miracle.'

'Don't say that.' He snapped. 'This is a one in a hundred year storm - it will never be normal.' He pulled his coat tight. 'You will go up north to your mother -'

'But Dad, please-'

'Enough.'

Ellie closed her eyes, hugging herself tight. 'Dad...' she begged. She began to shake as around her the rain hardened, whipped into relentless drops. Her father didn't answer.

'You are a fool. And you will not be so protected.'

Ellie's heart thudded as Matthew eyes locked onto hers. Desperately she looked to her father, but he stood away from her now with his hands clasped in prayer. Behind him, the shed door banged mindlessly in the rising gale.

'You cannot win,' he hissed. 'I am Matthew Hopkins. I am the Witch Finder General. Know this, Ellie Malone. In the Name of the Lord, I mark you as my enemy. We shall be free, my daughter and I. You, and that foul creature that is my mother, cannot stop us. The earth shall suffer and die. The Lord has answered us. We are more powerful than ever before, and this, this is just the beginning. My prayers have been answered.'

He laughed, and above them the great storm began to churn.

The shapeshifter flew.

Wings labouring, she flew high, so high above the earth that it fell away as a soft blue curve beneath her. Stars glittered against black. But there was a place within the darkness, blacker still.

A void.

A hole.

A bruised crack in reality.

From this great-nothingness poured creatures of mindless destruction and despair.

She could see them coiling and massing, drawing closer, following the storm cloud down

They fell to earth, a great writhing mass.

Storm clouds bucked and roil. Gathered.

A demon screamed straight at her.

Pinion feathers dipped and she banked, soaring higher still.

Far below, the seas fought.

And rising waves flooded the earth.

Water Weaver, Book 2 in The Dancing Stones trilogy

Coming soon.

Printed in Great Britain
by Amazon